WHENEVER
You Call

VICKI JAMES

WHENEVER YOU CALL
Copyright ©2022 Vicki James

Whenever You Call is a work of fiction. While certain cities, towns, and villages are real, the author has chosen to make several of the establishments, buildings, and places as fictional as the characters. The names, characters, events, places, and incidents are a work of the author's imagination only. Any resemblance to actual persons, living or deceased, events or any other point of the story are entirely coincidental.

COVER DESIGN: Lou Stock of L.J. Designs
FORMATTING: Lou Stock of L.J. Designs
EDITED BY: Claire Allmendinger of BNW Editing.
PROMOTIONS: Wordsmith Publicity
www.wordsmithpublicity.com

DEDICATION

*For my fellow panic attack sufferers, and
for those of you who continue to blame
yourselves for things you never really had
any control over.
It's time to let go and breathe again.*

Grief is the price
we pay for love.

QUEEN ELIZABETH II

PROLOGUE

Hannah

The lure of the drugs had won again.

Now, everything inside me was numb. My love for him, dead. His last chance, over.

Standing in the doorway of his music room, I stared at my husband slumped in the oversized chair. He didn't take his eyes from the wall of accolades in front of him—his achievements gave him something to focus on, despite the fact he probably couldn't even pick his wife and child out of a lineup if his life depended on it.

It shouldn't have surprised me that we were here again. He was never going to change, and I'd been a fool for far too long; the ever-doting wife welcoming him back from his latest stint in rehab. I'd forgiven his many public affairs when he'd been away from home for months on end. I'd let him walk all over me for years, always falling for his false promises of change and a happier future if I gave him just one… more… chance.

I had no more left to give. He'd taken everything and ruined it.

"Mommy?" our six-year-old daughter cried from another room, her voice growing closer. "Where are you guys?"

"Stay where you are, honey. I'll be there in a minute," I called, not taking my eyes from Cole.

"Is Daddy there?" she asked. "Can I see him?"

"Not right now, he's…" *out of his mind. Lost to drugs again. Choosing the high of chemicals over the high of us.* "Working on his music," I said instead, sparing her the agony of knowing the man she worshiped was, in fact, a tragedy wrapped up in a charming face that got him out of trouble more than he deserved. "Why don't you head downstairs and put your shoes on so you're ready to go out, Bella?"

"Where are we going?"

"It's time for a trip to Cupcake ATM, don't you think?"

"*Yes!*" she cried before her little feet scurried down the marble staircase, away from the one person she wanted to be with more than anything: her father.

The famous rock star daddy America adored, yet I had grown to despise.

This life had become a circus where he performed to the crowd and set the world on fire publicly before he slipped behind the curtain and made sure the flames only scorched the hearts of the ones he was supposed to love.

He was slouched in his chair now with his legs parted, a fist pressing against one side of his head, causing his black hair to ruffle. His eyes were droopy, lost to whatever sensations currently tore through his veins. It hurt to look at him, and I was convinced there was no greater burden on Earth than to love and hate someone at the same time.

Walking across the thick, black carpet, I went to him, dropping to my haunches in front of his parted legs and resting a hand on his thigh. A final plea for the sake of my daughter to such a handsome man, carved out like a god of rock 'n' roll. His skin had turned ashen, his trademark black hair a greasy mess that hung over his striking blue eyes, which eventually rose to meet mine. There wasn't even a hint of a spark in them now.

"Go away, Hannah," he croaked.

"You promised, Cole. You swore to me this time you'd stay clean. Not for me, but for Bella."

"Go. Away."

"I hate you for doing this."

"Are you finished?"

"What?" I scowled.

"I came in here for peace. You're ruining it." He sighed, his cracked lips forcing him to run his tongue along the bottom one.

"Is that what you want? Peace?"

"Am I not being blunt enough for you?"

"What the hell have you taken?"

His head slumped back as he closed his eyes and groaned in annoyance. "Just go already."

"Why are you *doing* this?" I whispered.

He didn't respond, and I didn't need his lies to know the truth. The high never got quite high enough for Cole, no matter what he put in his body, what he achieved with his music, or how much money he dropped into his account. He'd always wanted more, and that would never change, especially when it came to my patience and forgiveness.

I was all out of both, drained and depleted, broken from a toxic love instead of healed from a marriage I'd desperately wanted to be real.

"Fine," I said, pushing up to standing and hovering over his limp body. "I'll give you your peace."

"Praise fucking Jesus."

"Take an entire life of it because I can't do this anymore. I won't let you continue to hurt me, and I won't let you break that little girl's heart the way you keep breaking mine. It's over. All of it."

He didn't respond verbally, but his head fell to one side, and he pushed two fingers to his brow before he offered me a half-hearted salute, inserting the dagger of his indifference straight to my heart without a care in the world about how much it made me bleed.

What is wrong with you? I wanted to scream. *When did you stop caring? Why can't you see the wonderful life you have and how amazing it could be if you'd just stop for a minute to think about somebody but yourself?*

"I'll never forgive you for forcing me to do this when you promised me you'd never let it happen," I said instead. "I deserve better. Go to Hell, Cole."

Despite my shaking limbs and the new hole in my heart, I turned and walked away without looking back. There was nothing there for me now. Nothing but a man made up of broken promises, endless lies, and poisoned blood—blood I refused to have on my hands.

"Enjoy your divorce," I told him. "You've earned it."

one

Logan

Los Angeles

He was going to die by my hands.

The unmistakable noise of the paparazzi helicopter above us became the soundtrack to a movie scene I didn't want to be a part of. We tore through the streets of Beverly Hills, the distinctive sirens of the LAFD ambulance doing nothing to get us to Cedars-Sinai any faster. The entire unit rocked, making shit fall off the shelves whenever my partner turned a corner and the vehicle swung out wide.

"Fuck this traffic!" Jerry shouted up front. "Get out of the way, asshole! *Move!*"

The patient lay on the gurney in front of me with clammy

skin, his pallor turning a frightening shade of blue I never liked to see. Beneath the bag on his face sat dry, cracked, purple lips he now refused to move. There'd been no response to pain stimulus. Narcan hadn't done shit to bring him round. The chest compressions didn't seem to be doing a damn thing anymore other than testing my strength and rhythm.

Come on, you asshole. Come on!

"I can't hear you talking, Logan! Why can't I hear you?" Jerry called over his shoulder as he drove us through the streets of Los Angeles to get our patient to the ER as fast as humanly possible.

Not just any patient, either. This one was known the world over.

Cole *Fucking* Newman.

Rock royalty, the man of the moment, and the face on every billboard within a hundred-mile radius of the West Coast of the United States.

Yet all I could see when I looked down on him were the memories of my best friend. The one who'd died of an overdose in my arms all those years ago, when I hadn't known what the hell to do to save him because I'd been a naive, foolish kid who'd panicked when forced to choose between life or death.

Like this, with fatality knocking on his door, Cole looked just like Dale. Even their names sounded similar, making an icy chill creep down my spine until my arms turned numb, my actions useless.

Dale's death-soaked face haunted me as I stared at Cole on the gurney.

Why did you have to look like him, man?

"Logan, we're two minutes out from Cedars. They're ready and waiting. What the hell is going on back there?" Jerry called. "Speak to me!"

I'd devoted the last decade of my life to ensuring this never happened again. Pulling off miracles was what I did. *Lucky Logan*, they called me. A goddamn magician who could drag a live rabbit out of a hat of death. I could keep anyone alive in the back of this ambulance for at least fifteen minutes, but now all of that had gone to hell. I'd frozen on the job for the first time in my life, caught up in long distant memories that had mixed with a reality that felt like a Hollywood horror show I couldn't escape.

Cole's lids were closed, littered with tiny spider veins that held a famous gaze behind them. I imagined him never singing another song. Never using the voice that had forced America into submission. I imagined the little girl he'd be leaving behind— the one who, when Cole was sober, he showed off every chance he got. I imagined his bandmates finding out we'd lost him. I imagined the fans, the reporters, and the horror that would tear through the music industry. I imagined his wife and how much rarer her already rare smiles would become.

Snap out of it, Logan! I thought I heard Dale cry. *He's not me!*

"He's not you," I whispered, my lips barely moving. "Fuck, he's not you."

Cole's body jerked in front of me, and the blood rushed back to my brain at once, forcing me to blink back into reality and stare down at a dying man who needed my help, not my fucking sob stories.

"*Logan?*" Jerry called again.

"I-I'm working on him, Jerry!" I cried over the noise of the sirens and helicopter. I kicked some stray medical kit away from my feet, hating how there was barely room to move back here, never mind save a life. "I've got you, man. I've got you," I whispered to Cole before I pushed his already torn shirt out of the way.

I hadn't lost anyone in the back of my unit to an overdose yet.

Today wasn't going to be my first time. The most famous man on the planet wasn't going to die because of me and the demons I'd carried for far too long.

"You're going to see your family again, Cole," I told him. "I'll make damn sure of it."

BREAKING NEWS!

Lead singer of Envy-98, Cole Newman, has died at the age of thirty-two after overdosing on what has been described as a 'lethal cocktail' of drugs while alone at his home in Beverly Hills.

Fans around the world have been left shocked and devastated by the tragic news of the nation's favorite frontman. Reports claim that a call was made to 911 in the early hours of the morning of January 24th by Newman himself after experiencing chest pains he could no longer control on his own. Paramedics arrived on the scene of Newman's Beverly Hills home to find him unresponsive, where he was immediately rushed to Cedars-Sinai Medical Center in Los Angeles and confirmed dead on arrival.

Envy-98 has indeed become the envy and the heart of America in recent years, and this untimely news has sent shockwaves throughout their almost cult-like following, with vigils being held in Newman's name around the country. The band were due to arrive in England next month to start their four-date residency in one of their favorite venues, Wembley Stadium. All shows since the announcement of his death have been canceled.

Newman leaves behind his twenty-nine-year-old wife, Hannah Moore, as well as his six-year-old daughter Bella Newman-Moore. The family has asked for the band's fans to respect their privacy at this distressing time.

two

Logan

One Month Later

"**L**ogan!"

I kept walking, hoping to avoid another therapy session from Jerry after a grueling nightshift where I'd already had my fill of trauma.

"Logan, wait up!"

I begrudgingly came to a stop in the parking lot on dead feet, blowing out a breath before I turned to see Jerry jogging toward me in his navy-blue uniform.

"Why do you always make me run, bro?" he asked when he came to a stop, winded.

"I don't *make* you do anything. I walk—you insist on chasing me. You just can't seem to take a hint."

Jerry raised his brow at me and sighed, clearly exasperated. "Are we really going to do this?"

"After the shift we've just had, yeah. I'm tired. Let me go home."

"Today wasn't that bad."

"I've had better."

"We've had worse."

Of course, I knew which night he meant, and my brows pinched together from the sting of it.

It turned out that I hadn't been a magician after all. I'd just been a fool that had gotten lucky enough times for him to think he knew what he was doing until something came along to remind him that he didn't have a clue about anything.

Jerry's blue eyes studied mine. He was a few inches shorter than me but as strong as an ox with his broad shoulders and pumped-up biceps from all his time spent at the gym at the station. Even though he was at least ten years my senior, Jerry had a body most men were envious of, not to mention that signature peppery hair the women went mad for. Jerry Dakin put the work in for every part of his life... even his friendships—*especially* his friendships—which didn't bode well for me at that moment.

He reached up to place a hand on my shoulder, his mouth setting into a sympathetic line, which meant 'the talk' was coming. I should have run when I heard him calling my name.

"Not this shit again." I sighed.

"Come on, man. Would it kill you to speak to someone?"

"It's not happening, Jerry."

"But—"

"Discussion over. See you Wednesday."

I shrugged his hand away and turned to leave, not willing to have that conversation for the hundredth time in the last five weeks.

Cole Newman had died, and there wasn't a damn thing I, Jerry, or any therapist could do about it. He'd died on our watch. In my care. He'd died when he had so much to live for, and nothing would change that. I couldn't bring him back to his mother, his father, his wife, or his goddamn six-year-old kid. I couldn't figure out a way to go back in time and do things differently so that when we pulled up outside Cedars, Newman hadn't already taken his last breath. I couldn't turn back the clock and stop myself from freezing—from the agonizing memories of my childhood best friend dying in my arms taking over and ruining everything.

All I needed to do now was carry on with life, just like I did the last time, and hope that enough time passed for me to get the damn thing out of my head once and for all. To not take it so personally.

Because right now, my failure felt personal.

The drive back to my one-bedroom condo in Van Nuys would take around forty-five minutes on my usual route, thanks to the standstill morning traffic that seemed to be a permanent fixture on the roads of LA. With my window down, I rested my elbow on the ledge, pressing my index knuckle against my lips as I stared up at the usual sight of bright blue sky and green trees while I waited at yet another stop light. Fifty minutes, and I could be home in bed, stripped down and ready to sleep. I could forget about the graveyard shift I'd broken my back for. I could forget about the guys at the station constantly giving me shit for being a miserable fuck. I could forget about Jerry and his endless need for talks and walks and fucking therapy.

But there was also an alternative. A different option that made me wince inside to think of, but one I did every now and again, anyway. An attempt to purge the dark feeling inside my soul that told me I could have done more.

Driving past Cole Newman's house in Beverly Hills—the place where the nightmare began—and studying it from afar weren't the actions of a sane man. I knew that, but something kept dragging me back there. Something constantly whispered in my ear that if I watched over that house, everything would be okay. For what and who, I had no idea, but that shit didn't seem to matter at this point because nothing made sense anymore. Especially not my thoughts or actions. All I knew for certain was that from time to time I needed to see Newman's home standing tall in the sunlight without the misery of drugs and death hanging over it. Without the ambulance and fire trucks parked outside, wailing into the night.

"This is a real bad idea, Logan," I said to myself.

But thirty minutes later, his house sat in front of me on a tree-lined street I'd become way too familiar with, anyway.

The cream building had a classical charm you wouldn't have expected from a rock star—at least I hadn't—and it sat on at least half an acre of land, surrounded by greenery that gave them privacy from the passersby, apart from a large, black electronic gate halfway up a thick driveway. From where I sat, only one top-floor window and the roof were visible, but still, I took it all in, committing it to memory, relieved when I saw that nothing was overgrown or unkempt. The window I could see gleamed. The plants lining the pathways bloomed. The driveway remained tidy.

Everything seemed... alive, and something about all that made me feel a little bit more alive again, too.

The world still turned without Cole in it, the same way it had done all those years ago for Dale's family and me. The people once around him kept on breathing. All existences didn't end because of one death, and I didn't know whether that was a relief or a fucking tragedy, thinking about how we were expected to keep on living after losing someone who was supposed to have meant the world to us.

"*Fuck!*" I growled, slamming my hands on the steering wheel. "Get a *grip* of yourself, you pussy. You can't go on like this!"

I exhaled heavily and shook my head in annoyance before I leaned forward to start the engine, only to glance up just in time to see a white SUV rolling to the edge of Newman's driveway. The front windows were rolled down enough so that, when the driver turned left, I could see her behind the wheel clearly.

Hannah Moore.

The widow.

She was real, and she was there, not just a headline on the front cover of a magazine. Not a distraught wife plastered across the news, carrying her child on her hip who had buried her face in her mother's neck to hide her grief. Hannah was there in front of me for the first time, wearing dark shades and driving up the same road I needed to take to get myself home.

I should have held back and waited for her to disappear out of sight. I should have driven back to my condo, locked the door on the world, and let every thought of Cole, Hannah, and anything to do with this sorry mess die once and for all.

And I almost did.

I almost waited until I lost sight of her...

But then that familiar itch to check on everything Cole had left behind grew stronger, and before I even realized what I was doing, I pulled up behind her at the next stop light in the Subaru Outback I'd inherited when my pa died a year earlier, looking out of place among the gleaming supercars of The Flats.

My heart hammered in my chest, and a cold sweat formed on my spine.

Things were going too far.

I should have turned around, taken another route home,

leaving her well alone.

This was fucking toxic. I shouldn't have held any guilt over Cole's death, but it was there, as I followed a woman who didn't even know I existed, to a destination I had no place going, that I realized I was screwed...

Because I did have guilt.

I was drowning in the stuff, and I didn't know how the hell to come up for air.

three

Hannah

Bella sang to herself in the backseat of the brand-new Range Rover Cole had insisted on buying only weeks before he… left us.

Before he *died*.

He'd been gone over a month now, and I still tripped over that word when thinking of him, even though I thought it often. All the time, in fact. Most nights, I lay on the bathroom floor, staring up at the ceiling while the bathtub filled beside me, trying to wrap my mind around the truth of just two tiny words:

He's dead.

My husband no longer existed—a man who shone so brightly that the idea of him having faded away to nothing seemed almost impossible somehow. Like death shouldn't ever have touched him. He'd been too much of a star to turn to nothing like that.

He's dead, Hannah. Gone.

I was navigating waters I didn't know how to swim, and I'd been struggling to stay afloat for the past five weeks—the last words I ever spoke to him stuck on an endless loop in my mind; the guilt, a noose around my neck, twenty-four hours a day, seven days a week.

Go to Hell, Cole.

If only I'd given him just *one* more chance, he'd still be here—my daughter would still have a father—and I despised him even more for that. For making me suffer the consequences of his decisions for the rest of my life because a grieving wife was only supposed to mourn her famous husband's death in one way for it to be deemed acceptable:

With absolute, unfixable, wailing to the skies heartbreak.

For me, it was a little more complicated.

Grief was a cruel bitch at the best of times but throw in the agony of trying to mourn a man you'd taught yourself to despise over the years, and the torment became unbearable. A constant weight of mixed emotions chewing you up and spitting you out every goddamn day.

My body missed his touch.

My heart remembered the way it had felt to love him and have him love me in return.

But my mind? That couldn't forget the unforgivable amount of pain he'd caused over the years. It also couldn't figure out how the hell to help me cope with so many conflicting emotions, forcing me to break down and cry one minute, only to get annoyed for being so weak the next. No part worked properly now, not knowing what to do or how to react anymore. Even my memories had become confusing, never knowing which were real and which were nothing but a fantasy I'd tried to create along the way. Because despite the way things had ended with us that night, no one had wanted our marriage to work more than I had.

And now I wanted him back more than anything, to give us the ending we surely deserved, even if that ending had to be a proper goodbye. One without so much hate and disappointment fueling it from both of us.

Cole had been the only love of my life, but we'd been over for a long time. I knew what he'd done behind my back throughout the years. The whole world knew… except for the little girl currently curling the pigtail of her doll around her finger while singing along to some Disney classic I couldn't even remember the name of.

Songs, music, lyrics… none of them mattered. Movies no longer made sense. The words in books blurred together. Each color managed to look the same as the next. Even my little girl's voice failed to bring me back to life the way it once would have. All I heard when she sang now was the way she sounded so much like her daddy. I wondered if he ever knew he'd passed that on to her while he'd been busy with the band, out living his life to the fullest without a care for what we were doing or how we'd cope when he'd gone.

That's the problem with losing someone to drugs.

You couldn't just be sad. You had to be angry, too.

I'd been angry at him for far too long, but nothing could compare to the state of total numbness I'd been in when Bella had looked up at me in the kitchen earlier and said, "Mommy, we never go out for our special car rides anymore. Is that because of Daddy? Can't you drive us for ice cream anymore because he's gone to live in Heaven?"

The way her bright blue eyes had shined with pure sadness had, for the first time in a month, made that cracked and beaten-up heart of mine throb at least one strong beat that changed everything.

She deserved a better, stronger mother. It was time to become that for her.

Not long after, I drove her into Culver City, and we pulled into the right lane of her favorite drive-thru, The Frozen Spoon.

It only took a split second—one glimpse of the illuminated menu board staring at us, inviting me forward to go to the kiosk where a server would be waiting to look me in the eyes and hand over our order—and the panic set in, twisting me up and spinning my whole world upside down.

My confidence waned, and my blood ran cold, the fear of speaking to absolute strangers for the first time in weeks setting in all too quickly.

What had I been thinking?

"I can't do this," I whispered to myself.

I couldn't be here ordering ice cream like this was an everyday occurrence. Since the funeral, the entire world had been waiting for that first candid shot of me looking like the grieving widow so they could make money from my agony. I'd unwillingly been on every magazine cover for the last four weeks. There'd been pictures of Cole and I together from the last decade. Images of the scandals we'd faced, the highs we'd reached, and the lows we'd tried to avoid. While the people of Los Angeles would hopefully forget about me within the next year, right now, my daughter and I were fresh in everyone's minds.

What the hell am I doing putting us both in danger like this?

Without thinking of anything else but my escape, I put the SUV in reverse without looking behind me, only for my bumper to immediately hit the front end of another vehicle. The crack and groan of metal on metal reverberated throughout the car, and I slammed on the brakes, hard.

"Shit!"

"Mommy…"

"Bella!" I cried, unbuckling my seatbelt. I reached behind me to check on my daughter. Her beautiful eyes were wide, her hands holding onto the edges of her car seat. "Oh, God, baby, I'm so sorry. Are you hurt?"

She shook her head and pointed down to the footwell. "But I lost Dolly."

Glancing down at her Barbie, I closed my eyes and blew out a breath, allowing myself a moment of relief before a tap on the driver's window made me jump and turn toward the person standing there, trying to get a look at me through the blacked-out windows.

I glanced in the rearview and saw the car I'd bumped into still behind me, which meant I was officially trapped in with nowhere to go unless I curbed it and drew even more attention to myself for running away from the scene of an accident I'd caused.

If this is you getting payback for what I said, Cole, I swear to God...

The man by the window knocked again and leaned closer. "Hey, it's okay. Don't panic. I'm not here to yell at you or anything. I'm a paramedic. I just want to check if you're okay."

A paramedic?

Memories of the hospital and the number of doctors, nurses, porters, and paramedics there flashed through my mind, and the memory of how mad I'd been at them for being unable to save Cole twisted at my gut. They hadn't been able to save him, which meant I would never now get the chance to change the last words he heard me say. I would always be the wife who told her husband to go to Hell hours before he died.

A paramedic was the last person I wanted to see, but since I had nowhere to go, I didn't have a choice but to sit up in my seat and roll down the window.

When our eyes met, he offered me a warm smile.

He had kind brown eyes that held a world within them. His dark hair was pushed back, away from his face like he'd run his hands through it enough times that it had got stuck there.

We seemed to study one another for a second too long before a small scowl creased his brows, and I immediately turned rigid again. Thank God I was wearing my oversized dark sunglasses because it was at that moment that I realized this guy was the first person outside of family and friends I'd seen in the flesh for over a month.

"I'm—" *sorry*, I was about to say, only to be cut off as he narrowed his eyes and searched my face.

"Everything okay? Are you a little shaken up?"

"I'm fine. I'm… I'm sorry about that. I'll pay for any damage. Just give me your details, and I'll sort it. Money isn't an issue."

"I'm not worried about the car. I'm worried about you."

My brows rose in surprise. "It was just a bump."

"Yeah, well, I see a lot of bumps turn into something a whole lot bigger within minutes, and you already look too pale for my liking. Mind if I see your eyes to check your pupils."

"My pupils are fine. This car is strong, and I was barely moving when I hit you."

"You were going faster than you realize. I hit the horn to try to warn you, but…"

"I… didn't hear you."

His sympathetic smile drew my eyes down to focus on the small dimples that formed in his cheeks, barely noticeable, but there all the same. Cole had had dimples. Big ones that his female fans obsessed over. Perfectly placed dots in his cheeks that Bella had always loved to stick her index finger into when she'd been a baby.

"I must have been a little spaced out," I admitted, even though somewhere in the back of my brain, Cole's voice warned me to shut up talking before I walked us—me—right into a lawsuit I couldn't get out of.

"Does that happen a lot?" the paramedic asked.

"No," I lied.

"You're always like that now, Mommy."

Bella's voice cut through me like a sharp blade, and I closed my eyes to let the regret wash over me. She'd spoken nothing but the truth, and the reality of that made my stomach churn even more than it already was. Heat rose in the back of my neck, blurring my vision. My breaths suddenly felt short, and I gripped the steering wheel in front of me, not missing the damp warmth on my forehead. A familiar sense of nausea rose quickly, not giving me a chance to get everything under control until hot bile singed my throat, and despite my empty stomach, I knew I was going to puke.

I needed air, and I needed it quickly.

Pushing the car door open, and no doubt hitting the paramedic on my way, I leaned forward just in time to vomit in the middle of the drive-thru, where a small queue had already started to form behind us. My body wretched again, my back tight with the pain of trying to eject the anxiety inside of me like that was even possible.

The sting of the last month stabbed at every nerve ending I had within my skin.

The unexpected loss and complicated grief.

The worry of parental failure.

The gut-wrenching loneliness.

The never-ending regrets and the anger.

That *motherfucking* anger.

My armor had cracked, and there I sat, bleeding out in front of the very people I'd wanted to hide from... until the paramedic I'd almost forgotten about came to stand in front of me, blocking me from view of those behind us in the queue, while I struggled to catch a full breath.

Bella's worried voice echoed somewhere in the background, but I could barely hear her over the sound of my own heartbeat rising like the swell of an unstoppable tide. Her conversation soon turned toward the paramedic, who now had a hand pressed against my back, and I faintly heard him reassure her while somehow reassuring me, too. He shouted at the cars behind us to back up so he could get both vehicles out of the way, and when his hand eventually slipped away from my spine, I thought he'd finally left us on our own for good. But soon enough, he returned, somehow sliding me over to the passenger seat so that he could take my place behind the wheel, and all I could think when he did that was:

What kind of mother falls apart like this, allowing a stranger into a car with her daughter without even bothering to put up a fight?

Sometime not long after that thought, my eyes closed without my permission, and everything around me faded to black.

***

The comforting hand on my forehead had me reaching up to hold it against me. It felt nice, that familiar touch. A man's touch.

"Cole," I whispered, but when I opened my eyes and turned to look at him, another man sat in his place.

The paramedic guy.

Watching my reactions, he carefully raised his hands in surrender. "I'm no one to worry about. You blacked out. Only for a few seconds, but I couldn't leave you until I was sure you were okay."

"Bella?" I croaked, barely recognizing my own voice.

"I'm here, Mommy. Logan rescued Dolly for me," my daughter chirped up from the backseat.

"Logan?"

His eyes searched mine for a moment, and he nodded once. "Hey."

"Logan," I sighed, forcing myself to sit upright in my seat.

"You should rest. Panic attacks are serious business, especially severe ones. It can take your body a while to recover."

I winced. "I feel that."

"You should probably get checked out."

"I thought that's what you were doing. Checking me out."

Logan cleared his throat and scratched at his brow. "A doctor would be able to give you a more thorough examination."

I shifted more, trying to stretch my aching limbs out, only to wince again when my chest tightened. "I'm fine," I pushed out, both of us knowing that another lie had slipped free.

"Easy. Just… give yourself a minute to come around."

"I don't have a minute. I need to get my daughter home where she's safe, not sitting in a car in a parking lot with a man she doesn't even know," I said, immediately regretting my tone, until Logan's lips pressed together in sympathy, of all things, instead of annoyance.

I'd rather have seen his anger. I could have dealt with that. But pity?

I wanted to smack the look off his face. I was sick of seeing it on everyone who made eye contact with me lately. It made me feel like I had a plastic bag over my head and couldn't breathe. Nobody knew how it felt to grieve a man you'd taught yourself to hate so that it would be easier to walk away from him—to break a family apart because you couldn't survive another day of the mental torture, even though the daughter you shared together idolized her father endlessly.

And people could never understand how I could be so confused about needing him back now when all I'd ever wanted to do was to run away and never see his face again before he died.

"Sorry," I said. "I shouldn't have snapped at you like that. I know you're trying to help—"

"Do me a favor. Try to move your toes," he said, cutting me off.

"Excuse me?"

"Your toes. Can you move them?"

"I… yes, I can feel my toes." I tried to wiggle them in my sneakers, quickly recognizing that while I could in fact move them, they felt strangely tingly, as did my legs, arms, and fingertips.

"Yeah, you're not driving anywhere," Logan said. Shifting in his seat, he started the engine, pulling his seatbelt over his chest.

"Hey," I cried, reaching over to touch his forearm, unable to miss the warmth that radiated from his skin as my palm pressed against it. It was only then that I registered that he wore full uniform, the navy blue, short-sleeved shirt hugging his biceps in a way I used to admire on Cole when his T-shirt cut into his muscles. A gold-trimmed, American flag badge had been sewn into the right sleeve of his shirt, and it made my gaze drift over all his uniform, noting an LAFD badge on the opposite side, proving that he was who he said he was, and he hadn't been lying.

I swallowed again, catching Logan's concerned gaze as I looked back up at him.

"What the hell do you think you're doing?" I eventually asked with a broken voice.

"Driving you home."

"The hell you are."

"It's either that, or we're calling an ambulance. I'm happy to do either. Your call."

An ambulance…

More people, more scandal, more unwanted attention.

He waited for me to get my thoughts in order, and I couldn't take my eyes off of him as my mind raced at a thousand miles an hour, unable to find the words to say that this felt too weird.

"You have no right to believe me when I say this, but you *can* trust me," he said, as though reading my thoughts. "It's my job to take care of people. I'd never do anything to purposely hurt anyone."

***

I wouldn't admit it out loud but as soon as we hit the road again, I knew Logan was right. I'd been in no fit state to drive myself, let alone Bella, anywhere. My entire body was wrung out from the panic attack that had left me feeling like a limp noodle. All I wanted to do was collapse into my bed and recover. I'd given Logan my address, wondering if he would put two and two together to figure out who my husband had been, but all he'd done was put the car in motion, making sure Bella had her seatbelt in place and her doll on her lap again before we set off.

Whoever sent him to me, thank you.

When I thought how different the consequences could have been, it only made my stomach twist harder. What if someone had been hurt? What if I'd blacked out and Bella had panicked? What if the authorities had gotten involved and decided to take Bella from me in that state? Who would she have gone to stay with?

I had no family, and Cole's biological parents were across the country—not that I'd have let them anywhere near her. They'd abandoned Cole much the same way my parents had abandoned me at an early age. It had been one of the things that pulled us together: the shit we'd been through as kids. The shit no child should ever have to go through alone.

I wouldn't allow that for my daughter. Not today, not tomorrow, not ever.

It didn't take long for Logan to turn us into the driveway of my home, sliding us through the big, black electric gates that I'd opened in advance, into the safety and privacy of our land.

Turning the engine off, Logan sat back in the driver's seat, looking up at the home my husband bought without even showing it to me beforehand. Typical Cole. Always asking for my forgiveness rather than my permission.

"It's ridiculous, isn't it?" I said as I turned to my six-bedroom, six-bathroom home, knowing in my heart that it was far too big for just the two of us now.

We didn't need so much space. We didn't need an indoor cinema, the oversized pool, or the gym neither one of us would ever use, let alone the music room filled with Cole's accolades that I'd locked the door to ever since that night, unable to be in it again, knowing it was the last place we were together in any capacity. The last place we'd shared so much hate.

"It's what my husband wanted," I added, explaining myself even though Logan hadn't passed comment. "He tended to always get that—what he wanted."

Logan's hand twitched on the steering wheel, but when I glanced his way, his face remained neutral, as though he was purposefully trying to act indifferent about being here, which usually meant one thing…

"You knew him, didn't you?"

His jaw tensed, the muscles there working hard before he turned to me with even more sympathy in his gaze.

"I'll take that as a yes," I whispered.

"You said his name when you first woke up in the parking lot. *Cole*. Then Bella told me your full name when you were having your panic attack."

"So, you put two and two together?"

"Something like that."

I nodded. Of course, he knew him. Everyone in this city did.

"What happened today stays between us," Logan said. "I won't tell a soul about any of it. You have my word."

"That's what they all say, but somehow people still slip up, and soon the dollar signs are being waved around, opening their mouths for them."

"That's not really my style."

"They all say that, too." I smirked.

I searched his eyes, seeking out a motive, but all that shone back was the gentle, kind face of a handsome man that I'd first seen when he'd come to my aid.

"We should go," I said quietly.

He nodded once and quickly slid out of his side of the SUV before walking around to open my door and holding out a hand to help me down.

I stared at him, dumbfounded. "You didn't have to do that."

"I know."

Carefully, I slid my hand into his and jumped down onto the pathway with a thud, my tired body falling to one side until Logan caught me in his arms and righted me. I looked up at him, unable to deny the pleasurable feel of a strong man's arms around my body. It felt like a goddamn lifetime without it, and I so desperately wanted Logan's face to be Cole's so I could slap it in outrage before I reached up to kiss him with such intensity, he'd never forget the feel of my lips against his again.

He'd remember who we were before fame found and destroyed him.

He'd have looked at me and seen enough.

Logan must have seen something in my expression that made him uncomfortable because he cleared his throat and moved his hands to the tops of my arms to create some distance. He was taller than Cole, at least six-foot-two—maybe three—which meant he had to bend at the knees to look me in the eyes properly.

"You're going to feel a little out of it for a while today. Do you have anyone at home who can keep an eye on you and Bella?"

"Erm. Yes. I… We have a… maid. Housekeeper," I said, embarrassed by how that sounded to a paramedic hero who must spend all day, every day, chasing his own ass. "She's more like family now, though. I don't—"

"Hannah?"

"Yeah?"

"I don't need you to explain your life to me. Just make sure you tell your housekeeper exactly what happened earlier. You're going to need to keep your sugar levels up and stay hydrated, even when you don't feel like eating or drinking. If you're tired, rest."

"Okay."

"The important thing here is to listen to your body."

I nodded along.

"If another attack starts, monitor it. Any sharp pains in your chest or down your left arm, you need to call 911. They can have an ambulance here in less than two minutes."

"Right," I said, knowing he meant it. Beverly Hills had the fastest response times in the whole of America when it came to the emergency services, hence the hefty price tag to live here. It had been one of the reasons Cole had chosen it as our new home. "Okay," I added.

"Panic attacks can feel a lot similar to the symptoms you get with a heart attack, so don't wait until it gets too bad. Don't risk it."

"Okay."

"There are breathing techniques you can look up online to help that will—"

"I got it. I got it. I'll be responsible."

He looked like he didn't believe me, but he exhaled anyway

and said nothing more about it. "I'm going to help Bella out of her car seat. You okay to stand without me holding on?"

No, I wanted to cry. *I don't want to stand on my own anymore. It's only been a month, and I'm so lonely and tired and scared and broken from standing on my own. I want someone to hold me up like this forever. Someone who towers over me and shields me from the outside world. Someone who won't let my knees give out beneath me or allow me to fall.*

"I'm good," I said instead.

"Promise me you'll take care of yourself from now on?"

"I promise, Logan."

"Okay," he sighed, holding my gaze. "I'll let you go now."

Eventually, he lifted Bella out of the car; her doll held tightly in her grip. As soon as I saw her looking up at me with a worried expression, I bent down until our faces were at the same level, and I scooped her up into my arms.

"I'm so sorry I scared you, bug," I whispered, closing my eyes. "I'll try not to do that again."

"Are you okay?" she asked quietly.

"I am now, thanks to you."

The feel of her, the smell, the fact I could hear her breaths and feel her heartbeats had *my* breaths evening out, and when I opened my eyes again, Logan had already started to walk away. I watched his retreating form slip out of the open black gates; his hands tucked into his pockets as though he'd done all there was to do, so he had no reason to hang around a moment longer. He'd fulfilled his duty. He didn't need a reward. No claps on the back or to see his name in lights for having done his job.

"Thank you," I whispered anyway, knowing he'd never hear it but hoping he somehow felt it as he walked from our messy lives, leaving us a little bit better than we would have been without him.

four

Logan

"**W**as it Jerry who made you do this?" I stared at my supervisor sitting on the opposite side of the table, annoyed that he'd demanded my presence at his favorite diner after our last shift together. "Because honestly, Buck, I'm getting real tired of these constant interrogations."

Buck stirred his coffee as he studied me. In his fifties, he'd been a part of the LAFD for almost thirty years. There wasn't anything he hadn't seen a million times over, which was why I was struggling to hold my shit together and not shrink under his scrutinizing gaze. The way he said everything without saying a damn word unnerved me.

"I don't have to have a talk with you to see you're not

yourself," he said in his trademark, deep, unwavering voice. "You're not the same man you were a few months ago, and that's the kind of thing I have to act upon."

"I don't know how many times I need to keep saying it to you both. I'm fine."

"That's what we all say. Doesn't mean we mean it."

"Some of us do."

"Some of us *lie*." His brows rose.

My nostrils flared. It had been three weeks since the incident with Hannah and Bella, and despite me promising myself that they weren't my problem anymore, an annoying itch gnawed at my skin, urging me to check on them one last time. To somehow find a way to make sure Hannah was doing well after her panic attack and to ensure Bella always kept her Barbie in her hand. But I couldn't risk going back there again. Not now Hannah knew my face, my name, and my job. It wouldn't take her long to figure out who I was and what part I'd played in her life already, should she ever become suspicious.

Although, that hadn't stopped Hannah's face from plaguing my every thought since walking away from her. Her porcelain skin and those sad, curious, yet passionate green eyes had kept me awake at night. The grief she wore like makeup and the way she tucked her short blonde hair behind her ear every time she had to take a moment to think haunted me, but still, the media hadn't done her justice.

She'd left me speechless without trying, even when hidden beneath baggy jeans and a sweatshirt that was too big for her lithe body. I'd had to force myself to look away so she didn't catch me staring. My adoration hadn't been what she needed back then, only my help.

"Listen," Buck said, resting his arms on the table, breaking me from my thoughts of Hannah, and making me look back up at him. "It was a high-profile patient we lost that day—"

"We?"

"Yes, *we*. I may not have been there, but *we* are a team. You don't get to carry the burden of this on your shoulders without my support."

"Maybe I deserve to."

"The only thing you deserve is a harsh wake-up call, kid."

"I don't need to hear this."

"Well, I need to say it, so shut your mouth," he said, bringing me into submission the way only he could. "We all have that one incident. The one we can't let go of no matter how much time passes. The one that changes who we are as professionals as well as human beings. Ain't nothing you can say to me to make me believe that you aren't suffering the aftereffects of that *one* right now, is there?"

He had the decency to wait a beat and let my silence answer for me.

"That's what I thought," he said, reading me like a damn book. "Mine happened when I was twenty-eight years old with a young woman who we'd come across four times already. Pretty little thing, but boy, was that girl broken in the head after everything her husband put her through."

I scowled at him, watching as he let out a heavy sigh and leaned back in his seat, his eyes drifting down to his coffee.

"She reminded me of my younger sister. Not just in looks but in the way she tried to convince the world around her she was doing okay, even when everyone knew that poor woman was crumbling inside." His eyes rose back up to meet mine. "Suicide," he said. "Both my sister *and* the woman who would become my *one*."

"What happened?"

Buck shrugged. "Sister passed away the year before. Too

many demons she couldn't get a hold of. Back then, mental health wasn't talked about so much. Not like it is today. Everything about the subject was considered taboo. I guess she thought that made her taboo, too. Nothing could be done. She knew what she wanted." He filled his cheeks with air and blew it all out in one long breath. "Fortunately, I didn't attend the scene of my sister's death, but a year or so later, we got a call to a house in Culver City. Possible suicide attempt. As soon as we saw the address, we knew who it was." He shook his head. "That poor girl's sorry excuse for a husband had beat her up a few times before. We'd taken her in with multiple injuries; you know how it goes. Broken ribs, cracked femur, contusions to the cheeks, head, jaw. You name it, she had it. That bastard refused to take her to the ER every time. Of course, she always denied it was him. She'd either *fallen* or been too *clumsy* or *not been paying attention to where she was going.* Man, that side of the job sucks, doesn't it?"

I nodded, having seen my fair share of unreported domestic violence over the last six years. The number of times I'd had to walk away from a patient, knowing full well they were going to go back to the very asshole who'd split their face open, killed me. It was a side of the job I struggled with, having to stay quiet and respect their wishes when all I ever wanted to do was push them to safety behind me before I gave their sadistic abusers a taste of their own medicine.

Buck cleared his throat. "When we found out it was a possible suicide, and we'd got her in the back of the ambulance, my partner drove like crazy to the hospital. I stayed in the back with her. That's when it happened." His face turned stern. "I froze. For the first time in the back of that unit, I froze. All I could see were the rope marks around her neck and the life literally bleeding out of her eyes, just like my sister. She didn't make it, and I should have saved her. I should have saved both of them."

"Buck…"

"What? You gonna tell me it wasn't my fault?" He raised a brow. "You gonna tell me I probably did everything I could?"

"I know you'd have done everything."

"Just like I know you did everything you could for Cole Newman."

I closed my eyes for just a second before I looked up at him again.

"Like I said… we all have that one that never leaves us. The one we blame ourselves for. Yours just happens to be a famous guy." Buck took a sip of his coffee before dropping it back to the table and leaning forward again. "The sooner you accept that, the sooner we can get you the help you need."

"I don't need any help. I need time."

"Then take your damn time but use that time to forgive yourself for things you don't even need to forgive yourself for. Take a vacation, a road trip. Hell, I don't care. Just don't come to work for a while," he said, bringing my attention back to him. "We can arrange that within a week."

"And what would I do with that time off, huh? My job *is* my life."

"You just answered your own question. It's time to go out there and get a life."

I rolled my head back on the booth, staring up at the ceiling.

"You know I can put you on forced leave any time I want for however long I want, don't you?" he said.

Bringing my head back up, I laid a confused look on him. "Buck, c'mon…"

"I'm not messing around, Logan. This job requires mental fitness as well as physical, and you're letting yourself down. Times have changed, and we *do* talk about mental health these days, but even if we didn't, after my sister, I'd still be sitting here putting this out there. There's no shame in struggling. There's no need to hide it. Nothing is taboo. Even if it makes you uncomfortable, as your superior, it's my job to fix whatever's broken."

"So, you've already decided what's happening."

"Correct."

"Care to fill me in?"

"I'm not an unreasonable man. I'll let you have some time to wrap your head around this. I'll give you two weeks more on the job if you take two weeks off after that to get your shit in order."

"And then you'll leave me alone? Get Jerry to leave me the fuck alone, too?"

Buck sat back in his seat and shrugged. "Guess it depends on how much of a life you find while you're out there."

five

Hannah

"**B**ella!" I slid her lunch into her small backpack and pulled it off the kitchen island. "Bella!"

I'd already called her ten times, and she'd yet to show. When it came to timekeeping, my daughter unfortunately took after her father. It had always been a point of contention in our relationship. I lived on the edge of my nerves, always wondering what other people thought of me. I panicked when we'd show up late somewhere out of fear of others whispering behind our backs. Cole had always told me to stop being ridiculous, which more often than not led to an argument minutes before we got in the car to leave for wherever we were headed.

I'd give anything to shout at him just one more time.

A sad smile rose on my face, and I stared at the kitchen island Cole had sat me upon a thousand times before he'd temporarily kissed all my troubles away.

The anxiety queen and the overconfident rock star.

We shouldn't have worked, but we did for a while… before everything got messed up.

"*Bella!*" I cried louder, snapping myself out of another daydream.

Her little footsteps echoed down from the foyer before she came into view, wearing her dark green and navy uniform that made her seem so much older than I was ready for her to be. Her hair was its usual scraggly mess, but I didn't have enough energy to argue with her over it this morning. I knew how to pick my battles.

"I'm here, Mommy, sheesh," she said with a dramatic flair as she brushed the hair out of her eyes with the flat of her hand. "You ready?"

"I've been ready for a while, lazy bug. The question is, are *you* ready?"

"I'd rather be in bed."

I couldn't help the small laugh that escaped me. *Just like her father.*

Bella turned to make her way to the garage, and I followed, watching her every step as though I still couldn't believe she was real or mine. She'd been the best thing to come out of my marriage. Actually, my life. I wouldn't regret a single day that led me to her.

Before long, we'd loaded ourselves into the Range Rover, opened the electric gates, and were making our way to her school, only a ten-minute drive away. It was the one place I felt comfortable going, given the amount of security and privacy surrounding it. No press was ever allowed anywhere near the building, its reputation relying on the children's safety. Their no tolerance policy had been one of the added bonuses that drew me to it knowing that Bella would, without question, be safe there and among like-minded children who also had parents in the public eye.

While Cole may have gotten to make the decisions on most things, I gave him no choice when it came to where our daughter went to school, and he backed down easily, seeing he couldn't get the last word in on that particular argument. I had no plans to be a pushy mom, but I wanted her to have every opportunity Cole and I never had growing up, especially when it came to her protection.

After finally dropping Bella off and making sure she was okay, her teacher gave me a sympathetic smile and wave from the classroom door—the same smile she gave every morning, even though she could barely see me through the slight crack of my car window—and I gave her a half-assed wave back, hating that I couldn't muster up enough strength to just get out of the car to go and say hello.

There's a constant fatigue you carry around with you when you lose someone. It's a weighted vest strapped around your chest, pulling you down to the ground, and I had to learn how to grow extra muscles to carry that around with me every day because the only other option was dropping to my knees and wailing.

I loved my daughter too much for that.

I closed my eyes, and a sharp stab of grief hit me out of nowhere.

"I'm trying so hard here, Cole," I whispered. "Even when I was mad at you, just knowing I could call you and hear your voice always made me feel better. Now you're gone, and I... *fuck*. I don't know if I can do this alone anymore. How do I know I'm enough for Bella now without you?"

Heat rose up the back of my neck until it cupped itself around my head like Cole's hands were there, pressing me to him.

"I just want you to hold me again. To annoy me again. To look at me like I'm your everything, even when we both knew it was a lie." I sucked in a breath that stuttered on its way back out. "I miss you, you selfish fucking bastard, and I hate that I miss you because I'm still so mad at you for *everything*. All of it."

The silence lingered around me, much to my despair. I wanted to press all of his buttons, even in death, just so he'd *have* to come back and argue with me because Cole always had the last word in any fight, whether he'd been in the right or the wrong. Most of the time, I swore he'd done it just to see me angry. He'd always said I was at my most attractive when mad at him.

The shitty games we played…

A pitiful laugh bubbled in my chest, and I was about to set it free when I heard an almighty bang somewhere up ahead that had me sitting bolt upright and looking out of the windscreen.

"Oh my God," I whispered.

Two vehicles had collided. A dark green Jaguar had taken the brunt of the impact on the driver's side, where a black Ferrari sat, the front end of it crushed up with white smoke pouring out of the hood. It took me a second to register what I was seeing, and it took even longer to realize that I was the last parent still parked outside the school after everyone else had driven away.

"*Shit!*"

Without thinking, I scrambled out of the Range Rover and jogged over to the wreckage. The closer I got, the more I saw. An elderly couple were still in the Jag, their heads hanging forward, unresponsive. The Ferrari held two passengers, too, but I could only see the top of the head of the guy on the non-driving side, which rested against the cracked window, limp.

My skin turned cold, goosebumps scattering over every inch.

I pulled the phone out of my back pocket and dialed 911

before bringing it to my ear.

"I-I need an ambulance. There's been an accident. Hurry!"

***

A few teachers from the school had gathered around me since the fire department arrived, which had EMTs working on the injured parties as much as they could. Mrs. Seymour had her arm wrapped around my shoulders, and it wasn't until she began to rub my skin that I realized I'd been shivering, despite the heat of the LA sunshine beating down on us.

Soon, more sirens filled the air, and a red paramedic truck sped toward us before coming to a stop in front of the collision. A man in a navy-blue uniform jumped out of the unit with a heavy bag slung over his shoulder, springing into action, instantly making my heart skip a beat.

I'd recognize his face anywhere.

Logan…

The stranger who saved me not so long ago.

As if he'd somehow sensed me, his head snapped up, and his eyes found mine. He paused in his steps, his lips parting as he stared for a second too long before he snapped himself out of whatever thoughts he was having, and he ran to those in need.

It's my job to take care of people.

"See, sweetheart," Mrs. Seymour said, pulling me closer. "They'll make sure those poor people get the help they need. Everything's going to be okay."

Logan got to work quickly, confident in his every action, with not a moment of self-doubt on display. He moved without instruction, shouting orders to the men behind him who could help, making sure the cars were cut in the right places to get the immobile patients out of there safely. I watched on in utter rapture.

His body was strong and lean, the muscles in his arms working overtime whenever he had to lift or pull or drag something across to the scene that would help keep the people involved alive and well. I had no idea of his position or whether he was in charge of the other man working beside him, but on duty, Logan had a commanding presence about him that everyone bowed to. He knew just what to do and how to keep everyone calm and where they were supposed to be.

I couldn't take my eyes off him.

It took a lot of effort to get all four people out, and by the time they'd loaded them up onto gurneys, more emergency services had arrived to help out. The way the paramedics worked was hypnotic to watch, their movements a subtle yet well-choreographed dance they performed around each other, each of them knowing exactly where to go, what to do, and when to do it.

But when I saw the first gurney with an injured party being wheeled over to the ambulance, I imagined that being Cole's body. That it was him being whisked away by people he didn't know, with no one familiar around him. No loved ones to beg him to stay.

I left him. I walked away, and he had to suffer through his last moments alone.

The hands of guilt snaked up my spine before they tightened their grip around my throat and began to squeeze, making it harder to breathe.

The world around me started to shrink, the dizziness stealing all of my control. My breaths came short, and my limbs began to tingle until they turned numb. The stabbing pain in my chest had me sucking in a sharp breath that didn't quite reach my lungs, and that was when my knees began to buckle.

· "Mrs. Newman? Are you all right?"

I barely recognized my married name from her lips.

Newman.

I *had* been Mrs. Newman, even though I'd insisted on staying Mrs. Moore.

Was that why Cole was taken from me? Had I not been devoted enough to him to deserve him for a moment longer? Had I given up on him from the very start?

That thought faded away when Mrs. Seymour cried out to the paramedics in front of us, but the noise around me grew foggier until I was blinking rapidly to try and bring everything back into focus.

Breathe in, breathe out.
Breathe in, breathe out.
In... out.
In...
Out...
In...

My head rolled forward, but then a strong pair of arms curled around me until I was hoisted up as though I weighed nothing. I curled into the unknown body, resting my head against a strong and fast heartbeat as my hand clung onto a damp shirt.

Da dum... da dum... da dum.

"Take control of your breathing, Hannah," the man said above me, his breath falling softly against my hair. "You're in charge now; the panic isn't."

By the time I was carefully laid down onto something soft and padded, the sensation began to return to my fingers and toes. My heart slowed. The cool sweat at the back of my neck warmed. The heat of the sun settled on my face as someone lifted my arm and began to press their thumb against the pulse in my wrist.

"Her pulse is slowing," he said, though it sounded as though he was talking to someone else. "No, we don't need to bag her. She's already coming around. You guys take off. I won't be far behind. I've got everything I need here."

Another voice said something in response, but I couldn't quite make it out.

My head rolled on the gurney while my chest rose and fell heavily.

"Hannah?"

His voice had me opening my eyes and staring up at the cloudless sky.

"Take a deep breath in, and then let it out slowly," he said. "That's it. Just like that."

I did as I was told, one breath after the other until my body slowly began to calm, and then Logan leaned over me, his face blocking out the sun until his dark shaggy hair and his concerned brown eyes were all I could see. Framed against the bright blue sky, he looked like a work of art—one you'd find hanging in a museum for millions of tourists to stare at, each of them dumbfounded that someone like him could ever have been painted, let alone existed. His strong, stubbled jaw created a flawless structure that housed a perfectly angular nose and those warm, deep, soul-searching eyes that somehow sucked a person in, refusing to ever let go.

"You," I whispered.

"Hey," he said with a half-smile.

"You're here. Again…"

"Some women get all the luck." The way he looked at me should have knocked the wind out of me had it not already deserted my entire being.

I willed myself to picture Cole. Only Cole. I closed my eyes for just a second before I opened them again, but there Logan stayed. I hadn't been dreaming. He was really here, seeing me having yet another breakdown.

Embarrassment tore through me, and I tried to sit up too quickly, only for my head to spin out of control again and for

Logan to gently push me back down, his hand on my chest.

"Easy now. We've got a few checks to run on you yet."

"No. Those people… in the crash…"

"They're all taken care of and on their way to the hospital as we speak."

"But—"

"And that's where I'm taking you right now."

"Oh, no." I tried to sit up again, but his hand on my chest wouldn't allow it, and I flopped back onto the gurney in defeat, my breaths pouring out of me.

I couldn't go to the hospital. Not yet. Not so soon after Cole…

"I know," Logan said softly, his voice full of understanding, and I looked at him in confusion. "I know it's hard for you to think about going back there after everything you've been through."

"Then, don't take me. I'll get over this in a minute. It's just another one of those panic attacks you told me about. I can handle it. I *will* handle it. I just need to get used to looking for the signs or… something. I don't know."

"Don't know isn't good enough. You need help with these, Hannah. Shock is a response to trauma, and after seeing what you've just seen—"

"Logan, if you take me to the hospital, the press will find out, and I'll be splashed across every website and newspaper you can imagine, probably with a headline declaring how unfit I am to be a mother now Cole's…" I swallowed hard, not needing to finish.

Logan looked at me with an intensity that made me believe he was looking for something he had no hope of finding. My resilience had deserted me in my greatest hour of need again like the traitorous bastard it had become.

"Please," I begged quietly. "Don't insist on saving someone who doesn't want to be saved."

He eyed me skeptically. "How many have you had since that

day in the parking lot?"

"None."

He raised a brow and waited.

"Fine, a couple, but only really mild ones. Usually, when I'm in bed alone at night, and they've never been anything like this." The admission of being lonely at night slipped free like a slimy eel, and I hated that he'd heard it. "But I don't need the hospital. I don't need to waste anyone else's time. I just need to go home."

"What you need is to find a way to deal with them at the root before they're allowed to grow each time."

"No shit," I said with a huff of humorless laughter. "Any ideas how I can do that, Mr. Lifesaver?"

He seemed to flinch at the name I gave him, and I opened my mouth to apologize for making him feel uncomfortable, but he cut me off before I could speak a word of it.

"You have to start by allowing people to help you," he said.

"No, thanks. It's embarrassing enough knowing that you, a total stranger, know about this."

"Your mental health isn't an embarrassment, Hannah. Especially not when it's affecting you physically."

I shook my head. "I can't do it, Logan. I can't talk to anyone else about it. I can't let any more people in."

"It'll only get worse if you don't."

"It won't. I'll find a way."

"How?"

"I don't know," I said, out of ideas before even one had come to life. "I don't suppose you offer therapy on the side, do you? You have a trustworthy face," I asked teasingly. "Scrap that idea, though. I think your job is hard enough as it is without having to deal with someone as neurotic as me."

"You should stop talking about yourself like that," he said carefully, making my pale cheeks blush for the first time. "And if you needed someone to talk to, then yeah, I'd do it."

The two of us stared into each other's eyes for a moment, neither of us knowing if the other was bluffing or telling the truth, and suddenly the idea of having this man in my life as someone I could reach out to lit a tiny spark of something deep inside of me that lifted me up instead of dragging me down. Something I hadn't felt in so long.

"Although it would be easier if you let me put you in touch with someone who can help professionally," he said, breaking me from my thoughts. "A doctor, counselor, someone more qualified—"

"You," I said with conviction, cutting him off. "Only you. No one else can know about this."

"Right." He nodded, swallowing down his own thoughts. "Then, it's done. Just say the word, and I'm yours."

***

Once home, exhausted and ready to fall asleep on my feet, Livia instantly knew what was wrong. She was so much more than a housekeeper to Bella and me. She'd become our best friend. Our family, actually. It was because of that family instinct that she'd insisted on taking Bella out to catch a movie straight after school to give me more alone time to rest.

I didn't tell her that I couldn't. Not when I had someone on their way to see me. A stranger I knew nothing about that I'd stupidly invited into my home like a prized idiot after telling him that I did, in fact, need his help...

And I needed it today.

I couldn't go on like this.

Now, though, part of me hoped he'd get called out to another emergency so he couldn't make it here in time, but then I had to scold myself for wishing that on innocent people just so I didn't have to sit awkwardly in my own house with a man I'd invited here myself.

My thoughts were all over the place when the doorbell finally rang.

"Please don't be a serial killer. Please don't be a serial killer," I whispered as I made my way to the door, very aware of how ridiculous I sounded, even to myself.

Logan's face appeared on the security screen next to the door. He scratched at his jaw and shifted from foot to foot, seeming equally, if not more nervous than me.

Put him out of his misery, Hannah. He never asked for this; you did.

I opened the door, and there Logan stood in his navy uniform, his hands now tucked into the pockets of his pants as he looked at me and waited.

"Aren't you meant to take your uniform off after you finish your shift?" I asked, wishing he'd shown up in more casual clothes because I was a grieving woman, starved of affection, and a handsome man in uniform was the last thing I needed to see.

He shrugged his shoulders. "I was in a rush to leave the station."

"For me?"

Pulling his hand out of his pocket, he rubbed the back of his hair and cleared his throat. "I figured you'd want to get this over with as quickly as possible."

He wasn't wrong, but I couldn't work out how he'd known that. I reached up to worry the silver chain around my neck between my fingers, realizing what a bad idea this had been. The ghost of my husband no doubt watched over me now, shaking his head and calling me a fool for having thought this could ever have been anything other than stupid.

Logan waited as silence took over again, and it felt like he was studying me, figuring out everything going on in my head.

"You've changed your mind," he eventually said.

"I don't know," I answered, tucking my hair behind my ear.

"You know, Hannah, and it's okay. We can pretend this never happened."

"Can we?"

"Whatever you want. Your life, your rules."

"What I want is to feel like my old self again."

Logan's weak laughter barely made a sound before he pressed his lips together and toed the pathway beneath his feet. "Yeah, I know how that feels."

"I'm sorry you do. I wouldn't wish this on my worst enemy."

Something about that made his eyes narrow on me. "Listen, I know privacy is important to you, and I understand that what you're going through is personal and you don't know how to ask for help right now, but don't try to handle all of this alone, either. It's shit. Everything is shit. You can say that—you should say that and not feel any guilt about it. But if you keep trying to carry all the weight by yourself, you're gonna break."

"Sounds like you're speaking from experience."

"I've seen my fair share of it over the years. Everyone is becoming an island these days, thinking it guards them from noise, discomfort, and pain. But the truth is, it just makes us all lonely, and then we spend our days trying to pretend that the loneliness doesn't hurt. It's why the whole world is in agony right now."

"Including you?"

"I have my moments."

"What if I have no one around who I trust enough to help me?"

"Maybe it's time you find someone."

"Like you?"

"You could do a hell of a lot better than me, but if that's what you want, sure. I've already told you I'd listen when you needed me to."

"You don't even know me. Why are you doing this?"

"Because I know what it's like to feel lost."

There was something about him I couldn't put my finger on. Whether it was his job, his caring nature, his ability to read my mind, or simply those kind eyes, I didn't know, but I wanted to trust him—to believe good people really did exist out there.

"I'd like that," I admitted quietly.

"Yeah?"

I nodded, trusting my gut for once.

Reaching around to his back pocket, Logan pulled his cell out. "I'll give you my number, but don't give me yours, and always block it from me should you ever decide you need to call. That way, no one can find you through me. You'll have your privacy, and this will be on your terms. If we never speak again, that's your decision, but should you ever feel like there's no one else around... I'll be there." He paused, staring into my eyes. "Whenever you call, Hannah."

six

Hannah

The moment I shut the door I knew I'd never use his number.

One glance at his name in my cell had the sting of betrayal tearing through my veins, burning like poison until I almost deleted it there and then.

Logan - Paramedic.

It looked foreign.

He didn't belong there.

But when my finger hovered over the delete button next to his name, another emotion took over.

Hope. Finally.

Logan's name gave me hope.

It's my job to take care of people.

I believed him, too.

"Hannah? We're back!" Livia called out only moments before Bella's footsteps came charging toward me out into the backyard, where I sat under the outdoor canopy, overlooking the pool.

I dropped my coffee cup onto the slate table just in time to catch my daughter in my arms when she threw herself at me, her tangled, long hair suffocating my face in the process.

"Hey, bug." I smiled, squeezing her back. "You missed me?"

Bella nodded and tightened her hold around my neck, which immediately had me tensing beneath her. It didn't take long to realize my girl was sad. I pulled her back so I could look into her eyes. She tried to fight it before eventually giving up, her arms hanging limp as she sniffed up and tried her best not to let her tears fall.

I brushed her hair out of her face. "Bad day?"

She nodded sadly.

"Wanna talk about it?"

She shook her head in defeat.

"Okay." I gave her a soft smile, letting my hands rest on her shoulders and brushing my thumbs over her delicate little neck. "But can you tell me if I should be worried or not? You know how Mommy always wants to make sure everything is okay in Bella's world, don't you?"

Glancing to the side, she brought her thumb up to her mouth to chew on it before she said, "There's a Daddy-Daughter dance at kindergarten. They said it doesn't have to be a daddy who goes. Some kids only have mommies, anyway, but it's stupid because I *want* Daddy to go, but he can't because he's dead now, which means I don't have a daddy anymore, so I can't do the dance. Not properly, anyway."

The agony that tore through my chest was crippling.

"Then two of the other girls laughed at me about it," she added.

"People who hurt other people to make themselves feel better are the ones we should really feel sorry for, Bella. It means they don't have a lot of love in their lives like we do."

"I don't care."

"Yes, you do, and that's okay, too."

Her eyes drifted back to mine, and a tear finally fell down her cheek like a small bomb that had the ability to destroy me. "I don't care what the girls say. They're stupid."

"Bella…"

"But I miss Daddy, and I want him back. I want him back, and it's not fair that he's gone away and won't ever be here again because he should be here so I can dance with him. He told me he'd *always* give me everything I wanted, and I want this more than anything. I want him, Mommy, and he lied. He can't give me anything anymore."

Livia marched outside the open glass doors, stopping in her tracks when she saw the two of us together; me sitting on the edge of the gray patio furniture while Bella stood helplessly in front of me. My girl was having to grow up and deal with things she shouldn't have to. I hadn't wanted this life for her. *We* hadn't. We'd always strived to spare her as much pain as possible, but here she was, suffering the most.

Livia's gaze met mine, and the look on her face said everything. She had loved and lost Cole as much as we had. She lived the life she lived, working here for us, taking care of our family and home because he'd seen something good in her once when she'd been down and out with nothing left to lose. That little spark had gained his trust in a split second, and then he'd invited her into our lives even before Bella had been conceived, promising Livia that she would never want for anything again so long as she promised to love and protect me like I was one of her own.

She'd never let any of us down since.

I pulled Bella closer, wrapping my arms around her waist and dropping my forehead to hers. "I want him back, too, bug," I whispered, watching as another tear fell down her rosy-red cheek. "I don't think we'll ever stop wanting him back because you and I—we loved him so much. So much that sometimes we forget the love we had for him didn't go away just because he did. That love will always be there. It sucks that it makes us cry sometimes, but it also means we were so, *so* lucky to have Daddy in our lives. It means we had something good that we'll never forget. We just have to find a new place for our love to go now every time we feel it overwhelming us this way."

"Like… to a new person?"

I shook my head against hers. "There'll never be anybody who can take your dad's love from you. But we can find somewhere special to take it when it becomes too much for us to carry by ourselves. Somewhere only Daddy can hold on tight to it, and it can be anywhere we want it to be. Wherever makes you think of him the most."

"His grave?"

"If that's where you think is best," I said, hating the thought of having to visit Cole's grave. The moment his body had been lowered into the ground, I'd closed my eyes and tried to erase the memory from my mind forever. Spending an eternity in the dirt wasn't what I wanted to imagine for any of us. "Or we could make a special place of our own in his memory."

I glanced around the yard at the expansive green lawn that had been the main reason Cole had bought this place, saying it had been the dream he'd wished for as a child. A dream he'd wanted to give to all the kids he'd have in the future.

My attention drifted to several tall trees that allowed us total privacy in a city where privacy seemed impossible. I listened to the gentle breeze blowing over the pool, and I imagined Bella having a place to go without needing my permission. Somewhere she could speak to her father without having to tell me about it.

"See that spot over there?" I pointed to the far corner where Cole's favorite tree sat, some of its branches low enough for Bella to reach. "How about we make that his special place? Somewhere you can go any time of the day, morning, noon, or night, without having to ask Mommy if it's okay."

"What would we do to make it special for him?"

"Anything you want."

"Anything?"

"*Any*thing." I looked back into her eyes, our foreheads pressed together again.

"Will he hear me if I stand at his tree and talk to him?"

"We'll make sure he does."

"How?"

"Let's see. Well… Daddy loved his microphones. How about we tie one to one of the branches and use it whenever we have something to say to him? Something we think he'd like to hear."

"You think that'll really work? You think Daddy will hear me from Heaven?"

"He never missed a show of his own, did he, bug? There's no way in Heaven he'd miss one of yours."

seven

Logan

Whenever you call, Hannah.

Christ, I'd sounded like some z-list actor in a bad TV movie.

Fortunately, after ten days, she still hadn't reached out to me, and I was grateful for her silence. I hated feeling lame when I'd built my reputation on being alienated, aloof, and unaffected by anything or anyone. I needed to get back to that, to how I was after Dale died when I decided that loving people carried too many risks, and I could still serve my life's purpose by trying to prevent anyone else from suffering the effects of that.

*Un*fortunately, two weeks had passed since my chat with Buck, and it was officially time to begin my forced leave. Project Find-a-Life-to-Shut-Everyone-The-Fuck-Up was about to begin whether I wanted it to or not.

I'd finished my last shift in the early hours of the morning, which left me with nothing to do but hang about in my condo. I could only see the very tops of the trees that surrounded the building I lived in, and as I laid on top of my comforter, wearing nothing but a pair of black boxers, my feet crossed at the ankles, I wondered if I could get away with nothing but this: just me in the comfort of my own home, not wearing pants for two weeks unless I needed to go to the store to grab beers or food.

I closed my eyes and tried to force myself to relax, only for my cell to vibrate on the bed next to me, flashing with a number I didn't recognize.

"Hello?" I answered with a scowl.

"Hello?" a young voice greeted me. "Is this... is this Mr. Logan?"

"Erm... yeah?"

"Are you the man who saves people?"

"Who—?"

"—Because I need your help, and your number is in my mommy's cell, and I remember you helping Mommy when she had a headache at the ice cream parlor, and now I need you again because—"

I sat upright instantly. "Bella?"

"It *is* you!" she cried. "I was right!"

"How did you... I mean... are you okay? Is your mom okay?" I glanced around my room for the first clothes I could find, grabbing the dark sweatpants and gray T-shirt in a hurry.

"Mommy? She's the best," Bella said. "Are you okay? You sound wheezy. Have you been running too much?"

"I, erm, I'm just surprised by your call, that's all." I balanced the cell between my ear and shoulder while I climbed into my sweatpants. "Is your mommy there? You said you needed my help. Has something happened?"

She sighed dramatically. "There's a stupid cat stuck in my daddy's tree, and I don't know how to get it out, and so I took Mommy's cell from the kitchen because I was going to play the cat some music. Daddy always said the only way he could get me out of bed in a morning was by playing music. He told me that AC/DC made me run down the stairs, even when I didn't want to, so I thought maybe if I played the same songs to the cat, the cat would run down the tree the same way."

"I see." I slowed my movements, tossing my T-shirt onto the bed and letting my shoulders fall. "How did that work out for you?"

"I don't think the cat likes music so much."

"Ah."

"I stuck my tongue out at it to see if that would annoy it, but it didn't, and now it's just staring at me."

"Cats have thick skin." I rubbed the back of my neck, feeling awkward and out of place talking to this kid I barely knew. "I'm not sure why you're calling me about it, though?"

"Because you're a real-life superhero. You save people."

I squeezed my eyes shut, the sting of that lie gripping my heart too tightly.

"I was going to call Livia from Mommy's cell, but then I saw your name next to Livia's. It said Logan - Pama... Para... It's a tough word, and I'm not very good at reading yet, but I thought maybe you'd know how to save the cat's life more than Livia would... because you rescue people, just like you rescued Mommy. That means you can save animals, too, right?"

Shit, she sounded adorable, but this was exactly the wrong thing to be happening, and my thoughts went straight to Hannah and how she'd feel about it. I was surprised she'd even kept my number after closing the door on me ten days ago, and now I had hers, too. Bella hadn't known to block it from me.

Dropping to the edge of the bed, I ran my free hand across my forehead. "Okay, Bella. Walk me through this. Is the cat distressed?"

"No, it's just lying on a branch. Shall I stick my tongue out at it again?"

"I'm not sure that's going to work."

"Huh."

"Is it crying out?"

"No."

"Does it look… stuck?"

"I don't know. It hasn't moved much since I came out here. It turned its back on me and showed me his butt when I played the music, though."

"Not an AC/DC fan?"

"This cat is stupid."

"He's probably just a little uneducated."

"So, can you help me get it down?"

"I don't think you need my help, kiddo. Sounds to me like the cat's happy enough where it is. Maybe just give it some time to move on. They're stubborn creatures, and if they think they're annoying you, they'll do it even more."

"But I don't want it in my tree. Any other tree but this one, *please*. It's my special place to sit and talk to Daddy, and I don't want this stupid cat to hear everything I have to say to him because it's private, and I—"

"Bella?" sang a voice in the background—one I recognized instantly. "Who are you talking to? Is that my phone?"

"Uh oh," Bella whispered.

"Bug, what are you doing?" Hannah asked, drawing closer.

"Don't worry, Mommy. I'm not buying anything," Bella answered, her voice aimed away from the cell for a moment before she came back to me. "Stay there, Mr. Logan. Mommy's here, and she's probably going to get mad at me for taking her—"

"Who are you talking to?" Hannah asked. I listened while the two of them had a little back and forth until Hannah gasped in horror, and then the cell changed hands, and Hannah said, "Logan? Is that you?"

"Hey, yeah. Hi," I said, sounding like a complete moron.

"Oh, my goodness. I'm so sorry. I had no idea she had my phone."

"It's fine. No worries."

"Don't shout, Mommy," Bella said. "Not near Daddy's tree. The microphone is right there. He'll hear you in Heaven, and I don't want him to think you're mad at me."

"I'm not mad, honey," Hannah told her, and I felt like I was the one intruding on a private moment that had absolutely fuck all to do with me. "But could you do me a favor and go find Livia for me? I think she's in the laundry room."

"But Mom—"

"Bella, *please*."

I closed my eyes, trying to shrink away from the situation until Hannah had me opening them again with just four words. "Logan, I'm so sorry."

I cleared my throat, not knowing what to say.

"I had no idea she was calling you; I swear."

"Don't worry about it."

"She's going through… a lot… lately."

"I understand," I lied. I didn't understand because I couldn't. I hadn't ever been a sweet, innocent little girl who'd lost her father at such a young age.

Neither of us said anything for a moment, and I opened my mouth to wrap things up, but then Hannah's voice hit me again.

"How are you?" she asked, as though she cared.

"I'm good. You?"

"Good," she repeated.

"Really?"

A soft laugh escaped her. "No, probably not, but it's what we all say, isn't it? When people ask us how we are, we hit default and say we're good because the alternative of saying that we're falling apart piece by piece makes us sound pathetic, and no one really wants to hear that. Or worse, *be* that."

"They probably shouldn't ask how you are if they don't want to know. That's on them."

"Very true. Why do we do that?"

"I don't know. Why did you ask me?"

"I was genuinely interested."

I ran my free hand through my hair. "I'm…"

"Good, yeah. You said." I heard the smile in her voice, and for some reason, I liked it. Imagining her with a smile on her face rather than the constant sadness I'd always seen there made *me* feel better.

"Not much of a talker, are you, Logan?"

"I wasn't expecting you to actually call."

"Oh."

Shit… wrong thing to say.

"That's not what I meant. I guess I just assumed you'd get rid of my number once you closed the door that day. I saw how uncomfortable it made you to have me there. Plus, it's been almost two weeks without hearing from you, so I kind of figured you, you know…"

"What?"

"That you didn't have a need for me. For what I offered."

"I didn't realize there was an expiry date on that offer."

"There isn't."

"So, it still stands?"

"I said whenever, Hannah. I meant it."

"Okay then." That smile of hers was there again. I could practically see it. "Maybe one day, I'll need to take you up on everything."

My lips twitched at the thought. "You do that."

"I'm sorry Bella called you, though. I hope she didn't wake you or anything. You must work some crazy hours."

"Actually, she couldn't have timed it better. I'm on leave."

"For a vacation?"

"More like a staycation. Forced time off from my boss. Apparently, I don't have much of a life outside of work," I admitted, making myself sound even lamer than I probably already did. "He thinks it's about time I went out there and got one."

"Let me know how that goes," she chuckled, just as Bella called out to her in the background. Hannah covered the cell up, and they had a conversation I wasn't privy to. When she eventually came back on the line, she blew out a small breath. "I'd better go."

"Is Bella okay?" I asked, remembering what Hannah had said only minutes earlier about how she'd been struggling lately.

"She will be. We're working on it. It's not easy but…"

"You'll get there. Give yourselves time," I said, acting like I'd known them my whole damn life, even though my sentiments were true. She would get there, with or without anyone else's help. There was a quiet strength in her eyes every time I looked into them. If I had to put money on it, I'd bet she'd spent a lifetime perfecting the art of that quiet strength, and then I began to wonder what the hell she'd been through to have to do that in the first place.

"Thanks, Logan. Maybe I'll speak to you again soon."

"I'll be waiting."

"Enjoy finding that life you're looking for," she said quietly before she ended the call, making me pull the phone down in front of me. Hannah's number sat there waiting for me to decide what to do with it, but I'd promised her privacy, and that's what I was going to give her.

My thumb swiped left across the number before hitting the red delete button.

Probably never to be seen again.

eight

Logan

The sound of men and women training filled the air when I stood at the entrance of the TKO MMA Gym, where I'd once spent the majority of my time before my career had taken over.

It sure had been a while.

"Can I help you?"

I turned to see a middle-aged, tall, bald guy beside me, running a sweat towel over both his hands. He wore a smile and a scowl that somehow seemed to work.

"Just admiring the view," I said with a flat smile.

"First time here?"

"Not exactly. Used to train here a few years ago."

"Back in the Viper days?"

"He isn't here anymore?"

Viper had opened TKO Gym and was the very first guy to give me a leg up into the world of MMA when I'd been an inexperienced twenty-something kid who didn't stand a chance. He'd seen potential that turned me into one of his best amateur fighters, and I'd always regretted losing contact with him once my paramedic training took over, consuming my life and making this place a thing of the past.

"He still comes in from time to time. He begrudgingly took early retirement at fifty-five. His wife had his balls in a vise over it, and while Viper may have been a hard bastard, no one ever goes up against Gloria and wins."

"I remember." I laughed, gesturing to one of the many cages at the back of the huge warehouse space. "Does he still own it?"

"He's a shareholder, but it's small now. He cashed out to take Gloria around the world, though rumor has it that he still hasn't made it out of the states. Viper likes what he knows." He raised his chin, tossed his towel over his shoulder, and held out his hand. "I'm the new owner. Real name's Mark Shaw, but this lot call me Creed."

"Creed?" I shook his hand.

"Viper was the peoples' champion. I'm the second—the guy who came in to replace his legacy, only I don't think I've ever quite matched up to it. People like me being here, but I'm no Viper." He smirked, crossing his arms under his solid chest, and I immediately liked him, despite it looking like he could eat me for breakfast with a spoon. "You're looking to get back into the game?"

"Something like that. I have a little free time over the next couple of weeks. Thought it was time to stop making excuses for not doing what I used to love."

"Love, huh? Were you any good?"

"I held my own."

"Any professional fights?"

"Unfortunately not."

He reached over to grip my right bicep in his hand, his fingers and thumb feeling the size of it before he offered me a downturned smile and nodded once. "Got some muscle on you still. Your job keep you fit?"

"It… keeps me on my toes."

He jerked his head to the right. "Well, lucky for you, I have a bit of free time. Let's see what you're about after some time out, shall we?"

Two hours later, I walked out of TKO dripping with sweat. My muscles ached, my knees and knuckles throbbed, and the soles of my feet burned. Creed hadn't lied when he'd warned me that he was going to put me through my paces after agreeing to sign on for a year's membership. He'd asked a lot of questions— more than Viper ever had—and despite not usually being much of a talker, something about being in the gym around men and women who wanted to forget about reality for a while had me answering every damn one of them.

It was easier to offload to a stranger. They didn't show as much judgment.

By the time I got home, I was ready to call it quits for the night, but my growling stomach soon reminded me that I wasn't going anywhere without eating first. I took a quick shower and climbed into a fresh pair of sweatpants before I made my way into the small kitchen area of my condo. The cupboards were never full. Doing what I did, I often ate on the go, if I got to eat at all. Convenience food had become my best friend, but no doubt about it, my body craved wholesome meals and healthy greens every once in a while.

"I need some damn groceries."

I searched for something that would fill me up after that

workout. In the end, I decided to make protein pancakes with a little syrup on top, vowing to get out of the condo tomorrow and buy some fresh, healthier food.

I was sitting at my tiny breakfast bar, watching the sun go down through the window, when there was a knock at the door.

Nobody ever knocked on my fucking door.

I stared at it with a mouthful of pancake in my mouth, wondering if someone had stumbled upon the wrong place, but then knuckles rapped on the door again, this time harder.

Swallowing down my food, I made my way over to it and peered through the peephole, only to see Buck staring back at me.

I opened the door and held it in place, pushing my free hand into my pocket. "Home visits a thing now?" I asked with a raised brow.

"Not usually, but here I am anyway."

"I see that," I said, unable to hide my small smirk. Buck may have been able to bust my balls more than most people, but that didn't mean I didn't respect the guy. When he cared, he cared. I admired that about him. Most people were all talk these days.

"Let's call it a welfare check, shall we?"

"Let's call it you being a nosey bastard."

"Mind how you speak to your boss."

"I'm off duty. It doesn't count."

"It always counts," he said, smirking back at me. His eyes trailed over my chest. "You waiting to impress someone, or don't you wear shirts off duty?"

"I'm in the comfort of my own home. Mind your damn business."

"I'll take that to mean you *are* expecting a friend. Thank God. The idea of you rotting away on your own for two weeks has kept this old man awake at night."

"I didn't know you cared so much."

"Don't you dare tell a soul."

"My lips are sealed."

"Don't keep them sealed all night. Your *friend* won't be happy." He winked and laughed roughly, and I didn't correct him. Let him think whatever he wanted to think if it made him feel any better. That had nothing to do with me.

"You want to come in?" I asked, holding the door open.

He waved a hand in front of me. "Nah, I'm outta here already. You were a pit stop on my way over to…" Buck laid a playful look on me. "Never you mind."

With a roll of my eyes and a small salute from Buck, I shut the door and turned back to my barren life, pushing both hands into the pockets of my sweatpants while I looked around the space.

White walls. Gray floor. White comforter against a wooden bed frame, a small gray couch, and a white kitchen that hardly got used. The place lacked some serious color and personality. I'd often thought about investing in a bigger home, but it had never happened. I didn't need the room, and it seemed like a waste of savings. I liked to keep my living space like my life: compact, easy to take care of, no fuss, and out of the way.

That's when my mind drifted back to Hannah and that huge house she now had to live in without her husband. All that space, and for what? For who? I doubted she cared how big her home was, only that she had one.

Maybe we had more in common than I thought.

Or maybe that was wishful thinking on my part. A wishful thought I quickly suffocated, refusing to give life.

I made my way over to the breakfast bar and picked up my fork to tuck into my sad little pancake dinner when my cell vibrated against the countertop.

Spinning it around to face me, I looked at the number, recognizing it instantly. Maybe I hadn't suffocated that thought quite enough. Maybe I'd manifested it instead because my heart started beating faster as I watched my phone ring over and over again.

I swiped right to accept it without much thought.

"You're meant to hide your number from me," I answered, my voice a little gruffer than I intended.

"How did you know it was me?"

"Bella didn't hide caller ID earlier."

"Shit, I never thought about that."

"I deleted the number straight after, don't worry."

"You must have one of those photographic memories then."

"Not usually," I said, clearing my throat, not wanting to sound like a total stalker. "Everything okay?"

She sighed, and I thought I heard her fall back against something soft. "Do me a favor, will you? Don't ask me how I am or if everything is okay when I call. It forces me to answer honestly, and then the conversation becomes depressing—about how we're finding things hard but trying not to let it show. How we're surrounded by this shitty thing called grief every day. And right now, all those things—the things that kill me slowly—are the very things I'm trying to avoid thinking about."

"What would you like me to say instead?" I asked, pushing my half-eaten food aside and making my way over to the bed. I laid back against the pillows, my feet crossed at the ankles.

"How about... talk to me, Hannah?"

"Okay. Talk to me, Hannah."

"I like that." I heard the smile in her voice before she drifted off into some thought that kept her quiet for a while. The two of us didn't fill the silence. While I couldn't be sure of her reason, I didn't feel the need to. She'd been the one to call me. This conversation was on her terms, despite hoping to hear her voice again soon. It was hard to believe it had come to this. That she was calling me of all people.

"Is there love in your life, Logan?"

The question caught me off guard, and I had to clear my throat. "Excuse me?"

"I mean, do you have a wife or a girlfriend?"

"No."

"A boyfriend or husband?"

"I'm straight."

"Good news for the women of LA," she said, aiming for humor that had my lips twitching on one side. "Ever had a relationship?"

"A few," I said, wondering why the hell she wanted to talk about my love life.

"Tell me about them."

I opened my mouth to protest, quickly thinking better of it and blowing all the air out of my lungs instead. "There isn't much to tell."

"Am I making you uncomfortable? I didn't mean to, I just…"

"Just what?"

"I guess I find you intriguing, and I want to know more. Talking about you keeps my mind busy, but if you don't want to go there, just tell me to shut up, and I'll go." Her embarrassment and awkwardness shouldn't have been as endearing as they were.

"My first serious relationship was over twelve years ago. I'd just turned eighteen," I answered, refusing to overthink things. I never talked about my fucking past, let alone to someone I barely knew. "Her name was Melody."

"Did you love her?"

"No," I answered tightly.

I've never loved anyone romantically was the real answer, but I didn't want to admit that out loud, knowing it made me sound like a cold-hearted asshole. Love always resulted in loss in some way or another. I saw it every day on the job, and I'd experienced the torture of it when Dale died. Since then, I'd taught myself to keep a distance from anything too good because I knew I wouldn't know how the fuck to handle it once it was gone. Just like last time.

"What happened?"

"We were too young, and I didn't give her enough romance or some shit like that. She ended it less than a year later."

"Were you upset?"

"No. Relieved."

"Oh," she whispered. "Poor Melody. And after her?"

"Same story, different woman."

"They ended things with you…"

"… Because I'm emotionally unavailable, yeah."

"I find that so hard to believe," she whispered as if lost in her own thoughts. "I know I've only met you a couple of times, but I didn't get that impression about you. I mean… look how you helped me… twice."

"That's what I do, Hannah. It's easier with strangers."

"Do you really believe that, or are you just trying to hide something from the world? From yourself?"

"Like what?"

"That underneath the surface, you're possibly the most naturally caring man a woman could wish to meet. You're probably full of love, Logan. Maybe you've just never found the right way to show it."

I didn't know what the hell to say to that. Not with this giant secret sitting between us. Hannah didn't have a clue who I really was, and truth be told, neither did I.

"Of all the women you dated," she said, breaking me from my thoughts. "Did you ever think you could love any of them if you just let yourself go a little? Leaned into it instead of away from it?"

I didn't have to think about it. "No, not even close."

"Damn." She sighed. "That's rough."

Running a hand along my forehead, I couldn't disagree.

"Lucky you, though, huh?" she added.

"Lucky?" I scowled, my skin prickling at the mention of that word in any capacity. Lucky Logan died weeks ago, right alongside Cole Newman.

"Mmhmm," she said softly. "I'd give anything to never have been in love. It's the one thing we have no control over, but the one thing that has the ability to break us like nothing else. It's dangerous. It's worse than a drug, more painful than any weapon, and you've made it so far into life without being tainted by it." She paused before adding softly, "I knew there was something different about you. You haven't let another fuck up your heart so badly that you now look at everyone with suspicion, wondering if they're going to be the next person to walk into your life and screw it over. So, yeah. Lucky Logan."

nine

Hannah

I tried to avoid calling him.

I'd occupied myself around the house, annoying Livia with the need to keep my hands and mind busy, but there was something about Logan that made me want to talk openly for the first time in months. I didn't know what that something was, but I did know I liked it.

I liked the way he listened without thinking he had to fill me with false promises of time being a healer or how I had the strength to get through this. The usual cliché bullshit everyone else around me seemed to repeat over and over again, as though saying the same thing a thousand times would somehow 'fix me'. Grief was unfixable. It didn't evaporate or even dilute over time. People like me just had to learn to live with it and adjust to a new way of life under a slightly darker cloud than before.

I stared out at the backyard from mine and Cole's bedroom, the balcony doors open so I could watch the trees do… nothing. Absolutely nothing.

"There are many forms of heartbreak, Hannah," Logan finally said on the other end of the line, his voice tight, almost angered. "It's impossible to avoid them all."

"I didn't mean to say you've never suffered. Just that…" I blew out a breath. "We make a choice to fall in love, don't we? There's a moment. A distinct point in time where the person you're staring up at is smiling down on you, and something inside your entire existence just… changes. You suddenly *know*. You know the answer to a question you hadn't even asked yourself. It's just there, and when it is, your chest doesn't feel big enough for your heart, and you lose control of everything. It feels like you're actually falling. I think that's why it's called falling in love. That moment is scary as hell. It's when you decide to run with it and let it happen, no matter how risky it seems—or you run away. Save yourself the trouble of being vulnerable, even if the stuff you experience in between makes you feel more alive than you ever thought possible. While I was living the good times, I never regretted falling in love. I praised myself every day for taking that chance."

"And now?"

"If it weren't for Bella, I'd wish I'd never laid eyes on Cole."

I waited for him to tell me I didn't mean that—that my thoughts and emotions were an overreaction. That it was the grief talking.

"I understand," he said instead, making me close my eyes in relief before opening them again to look out at Cole's tree.

If Cole had something to say about me thinking that then he'd find a way to show it.

Nothing happened, though, and the annoyance that twisted at

my gut confused me.

Did I want Cole's anger, even now? Would it make me feel better somehow to know I'd pissed him off as much as he had me in the years we'd spent together?

"It's a difficult thing to love someone with your whole heart but to resent them at the same time," I whispered without thought. "Perhaps I shouldn't have said that."

"Say whatever you need to say. Forget what other people think."

"That's what Cole always told me," I said with a sad smile. "That I worried too much about what other people thought. I'd argue that it wasn't a bad thing, being conscious of others' feelings, but he always told me that I should be conscious of my own before anyone else's."

"Looking after yourself should always be a priority."

"Until it hurts those around you. I think everyone should be part selfish and part empathic. Everything should be balanced."

"Easier said than done sometimes."

"I suppose it is." I sighed, running my free hand through my hair and resting it at the back of my neck. "Damn. Would you listen to me? You're meant to be out there looking for a life of your own right now, not listening to what's wrong with mine."

"You're fine, Hannah."

Something about the way he said it made my skin prickle with a feeling so foreign, I didn't recognize it. Whatever it was, it felt treacherous and forbidden. A knot in my stomach that warned me against letting someone get too close, too soon.

"I should go," I said. "Sorry for getting deep for a moment there."

Whatever it was that Logan possessed that made me want to spill my guts to him, it was dangerous, and I didn't need any more danger in my life right now. I needed assurance, stability, zero drama.

"Goodbye, Logan."

He didn't say anything for a few seconds, but then his voice, softer than ever, simply said, "Bye, Hannah," and I hung up, unsure how to feel about the way goosebumps broke out at the nape of my neck.

I dropped my cell onto the small coffee table in front of me and tugged on my ankles, pulling them even farther under my ass on the couch as a mixture of emotions slid over me. Guilt for talking to a stranger so negatively about the love of my life. More guilt for feeling such resentment toward my husband who could no longer argue his case like he always had done. Fear that Logan would tell the world everything I'd said to him. Abandonment that everyone I'd ever loved apart from Bella had left me. Loneliness because of the above.

But among all that sat that little flicker of relief, burning like a barely-lit candle, showing me a slither of light in an otherwise dark world. To unburden myself for just a minute had been a greater pleasure than I could have ever expected.

I closed my eyes and focused on that positive emotion, basking in it, tugging it to the forefront so it could grow brighter than the negatives.

It worked, too, until my cell buzzed on the coffee table, forcing me to open my eyes and reach for it before pulling it into my lap to read the message that had just come through.

LOGAN-PARAMEDIC

I have two new rules if you ever decide to reach out to me again. One: hide your number. Once I delete it from the call log, along with this message, I don't want anyone having a way to get to you through me. Two: don't ever apologize for anything you have to say. If it's what you're thinking and feeling, it's valid, and I don't need to hear you asking

LOGAN-PARAMEDIC

me for forgiveness because I won't
give it.

I read over it a dozen times, trying to control the mixture of
feelings I had about what he'd said. I got up and walked away
from my cell and tried to busy myself with more jobs that didn't
need doing before I found myself with my cell back in hand and
my thumbs typing out the only thing I could think to say to him.
The only thing that mattered.

ME

Thank you, Logan.

I meant every word.

ten

Logan

Creed kicked my ass the next morning.

After tossing and turning all night long, I'd woken up impatient and exhausted. I didn't know what I'd needed, only that I couldn't and wouldn't find it waiting for me in an empty, lifeless condo.

One look at me after walking into the gym had given Creed all the information I'd hoped to hide. I needed whipping into shape, and I was damn fucking grateful for the radio silence that the workout he put me through offered up.

It had been an hour of torture that had quietened my soul.

After running a towel over my face and packing up my kit, I threw my bag over my shoulder and headed out of the gym, but not before Creed got one last gentle jab into my ribs by the exit.

"Good work today. I can see why Viper championed you.

There's a fire in that belly of yours." He grinned.

"Thanks," I said awkwardly. "You were brutal, though."

"You handled it." He planted his feet apart as he crossed his arms over his chest. "What have you got planned for the rest of the day?"

"Nothing much. Heading home. Maybe stare up at the ceiling for a bit before watching a movie." I smirked.

"That's it?" He looked appalled. "You're telling me that a good-looking guy like you hasn't got a little black book full of women he can call up for a good time? Because if that's what you're saying, I'm not buying it, Romeo."

"I'm sensing there isn't a right answer here."

"Hell yes, there is. You said you have two weeks to get your life in shape, right?"

"Yeah..." I said wearily.

"Well, I happen to know a hell of a lot of people in this city. There's never a night in LA without a party, and fuck it, I'm taking you to one. You can't sit around all day doing sweet FA with so much fire in your belly, my man. Meet me back here at nine tonight. You don't show, I'm canceling your membership with immediate effect."

I opened my mouth to argue, only to be silenced by his pointed finger and stern glare.

"FYI: You don't ever get to win against me, so don't even try. May as well throw in the towel and admit defeat now."

***

I waited outside the gym's entrance later that night, just as Creed had instructed, wondering what the hell I'd gotten myself into. Fighters walked out of the warehouse at closing, each of them glancing up and down at my blue jeans, black T-shirt combo as if to tell me I looked too clean for their sweaty, dirty lifestyles. As though being clean somehow made me weaker than them. If only they knew I had enough anger and resentment in me to knock every fucker out if my heart desired.

Creed hadn't been lying. A sleeping beast had been lying dormant inside me for over ten years. A black, worn out, tired creature that had the ability to rise slowly, erupt wildly, and destroy whatever stood in its way. I had no fear of getting hurt physically. That part never worried me because most things were fixable, and it allowed that beast to grow. I'd always been aware of its lingering presence on the very edge of my being. I'd just made a conscious effort to keep it at bay from the moment it was born.

Like I told Hannah, I helped people. I didn't break them.

But sometimes, I wanted to tear the entire world to pieces with nothing but my bare hands.

The shutters started to roll down on the gym, snapping me from my thoughts. I pushed off the brick wall and turned to see Creed locking up, a different man to the one I'd been with only a couple of times before. In regular clothes, he looked bigger somehow. Like the material wrapped around his muscles was suffocating pressed against them.

"Hey, has anyone ever told you that you look like—?"

"If you say Dwayne Johnson, I'll come over there and kick your ass more than I already have," Creed said, turning to me with a sly smirk.

"Sensitive to doppelgänger references. Noted."

Creed tossed his keys in the air before catching them and shoving them in his pocket. "Nope. Just fucking sick of it." He walked closer, landing a strong hand to my back as he scanned me from head to toe. "Looking sharp. You'll fit right in."

I thought about asking him where I'd fit in specifically, but I knew he had zero intention of telling me a damn thing no matter how hard I probed, so I didn't bother. Whatever I'd signed up for, I couldn't get out of it now.

Twenty minutes later, in West Hollywood, Creed's black Dodge Ram pulled up outside a bar I'd visited a handful of times while on duty.

The white neon sign hanging above a heavy, gray, open door read: *Alter Egos.*

It was the big city place to be, where A-listers slipped in with ease, and Z-listers got thrown out, crying. It had become notorious in recent months for the parties it held and the people who wanted to be seen inside it.

I turned to Creed from the front seat. "You think they're going to let an average Joe like me in there tonight?"

"I don't think. I know."

"Bullshit."

He leaned closer and said, "Do I look like a bullshitter to you?"

It turned out he didn't, and he wasn't. Creed had trained some of the best and most well-known actors and stuntmen in Hollywood over the years, and I was starting to think his connections ran deeper than that of the mafia. For all I knew, the guy could run a mafia of his own. I sure as hell wouldn't mess with him.

As soon as he approached the four doormen flanking the entryway, it became obvious that Creed had a natural presence no one could resist. With a few handshakes, and a few curious looks my way, we were allowed entry. We headed upstairs to the rooftop bar where the lights were low, the music loud, and the people as plastic as the artificial paradise palms that stood guard in every corner.

It was, quite literally, Hell on Earth.

Regardless, I followed Creed, keeping a strained smile on my face and my body tight while I gripped a bottle of beer with white-knuckle force as we walked through the packed-out rooftop bar. I was a fish out of water. A hermit thrown into a dirty festival of one-upmanship. The air smelled like money, and the people were vomiting it left, right, and center, not a care in the world of what was happening on the streets below them as they lived out their dreams in the night sky.

It wasn't exactly a rarity for me to recognize people in showbusiness in LA, but it was another thing to find myself partying with them. Going to the same fucking urinals as them. Even passing awkward smiles in dark corridors with them. And it was even stranger to find myself standing next to Creed as he shook hands with the vast majority of people on that rooftop, never once failing to introduce me as though we'd been lifelong buddies who'd known each other through every one of our successes or tragedies. That was his ability.

Creed made you feel like you belonged.

The only problem with that? I didn't want to fucking belong. Especially not in circles where I knew the drink in their hand was for show, while the excess powder around their noses and the pinball eyeballs were the things to show me the truth behind the masks they'd so carefully constructed for themselves.

After a couple of hours and a few beers, I was ready to leave…

But then Creed slapped me on the back and began to introduce me to the thirty-fourth person of the night, and I recognized him instantly.

Jasper Jacobson.

Lead guitarist of Envy-98.

Fuck!

The two of them hugged it out, and then Creed quickly turned Jasper toward me, putting me as the sole focus of the famous guitarist's attention. I may as well have had *I didn't save your lead singer* tattooed across my damn forehead—I felt that exposed.

Jasper stepped forward with a curious smile on his face, his free hand stretched out while his other hugged a bottle of beer. His long blond hair hung down on one side, while the other had been pushed back behind his too-big ear, and his dark eyes studied me a little too closely—the sign of a man who'd had too much to drink as he swayed slightly on his feet and leaned in, waiting for me to shake his hand. I forced myself to take it.

He gripped it hard, squeezing for effect, and for a split second, I wondered if he knew who I was and what I'd done. But then his face lit up like consciousness had flooded back into his brain, and his eyes brightened.

"Nice to meet you, man," he said in his Canadian accent. "A friend of Mark's is a friend of everyone's."

"Thanks," I offered, keeping it simple as I pulled my hand away and tucked it into the pocket of my jeans.

"So, you're a fighter. Must be a damn good one if this guy brought you along tonight."

"He's put me through my paces a couple of times, but I'm no pro."

Jasper's eyes searched mine, and they narrowed again, making me nervous. The guy was wasted, and I didn't know how to play it the fuck cool around these people.

"You don't have to be a pro to be able to handle your own business," Jasper said. "And you..." He raised his beer bottle closer to my face. "You've got that look about you. The one that tells me you've got a lot of shit hidden behind that calm exterior you've got going on. You're a monster beneath those good looks, aren't you?"

I was about to ask him what the hell he meant when Creed's arm came around my shoulder, and he jerked me into him. "I've only sparred with him twice, but I know a warrior when I see one."

"That you fucking do!" Jasper cried, throwing his beer up in the air before he brought it down to his mouth and drained the contents in one. His head came back up sharply, making him sway on his feet a little before a young blonde woman slid under his arm, allowing him to use her as a means to prop himself up. She eyed Creed and me with a sly smile that spoke of victory. I didn't think Jasper had a fucking clue who he was holding onto anymore. Nor did he care.

"You said the same thing about Cole when we were shooting that video in Japan," he said, jerking his empty bottle at Creed. "Remember? You called him a natural-born killer."

The mention of Cole's name turned my skin cold, and I immediately shrugged myself out of Creed's friendly man hug and cleared my throat, my eyes cast down. I listened to them talking about how Creed had been on hand to help the band with some martial arts training for a music video they filmed on the other side of the world, and how Cole had shown a natural ability for it, even though he'd never trained in anything like that before.

I was about to make my excuses and head for a piss when someone behind Jasper stumbled backward on high heels, eventually crashing into him, forcing him to fall forward until he landed on the floor with an almighty thud. He went down like a newborn lamb, his beer bottle falling before him, his arms splayed out in front as the rest of us jumped back, trying to avoid the collision.

"Jesus. You okay, Jasp?" Creed bent down to help him up, but Jasper didn't care, shrugging him off instead.

His laughter grew manic until he rolled over onto his back with his arms above his head, and he looked up at the dark night sky with nothing but humor in his eyes.

"Hell, man, that was you, wasn't it? Reminding me how you

kicked my ass in Japan, huh?" he cried out. "You're still giving me shit even though you're dead, you fucker!"

I followed his eyes up to the inky sky above, my skin prickling with a chill I knew I needed to escape. My attention quickly fell back down to Jasper, but I wasn't a hero on duty tonight. I was the frozen guy again, caught in a world where Cole still existed, and I didn't know what the hell to do.

Jasper's arms flew up in the air, and he shook them violently before he cried, "I was saying good things about you this time, asshole. *Good things!* Leave me the fuck alone! You don't get to make the decisions anymore. You took that with you when you left us all the fuck behind, you arrogant prick."

The entire area around us turned silent, and Jasper pointed to the heavens above.

"Fuck you for dying on us, Cole Newman. Fuck you for existing at all!"

eleven

Hannah

The news report played out on the screen in front of me.

"Intoxicated Jasper Jacobson, the lead guitarist of Envy-98, was escorted out of Hollywood's exclusive Alter Ego last night after breaking down over the death of his bandmate and friend, Cole Newman. Jasper is the first of the band's members to be seen out in public since the singer's overdose, and eyewitnesses report that his uncontrollable behavior included him rolling around on the floor as he wailed openly about the loss of his bandmate. In exclusive footage obtained by us, Jacobson can be seen being escorted out of the bar by two men who, reports say, are close friends. One we know to be renowned trainer to the stars, Mark Shaw, while the other has yet to be identified. The band's management has so far

declined to comment."

I stared at the TV, numb. I'd been watching the same report for the last hour on repeat. Stills of Logan carrying that fucking asshole Jasper out of a bar, wasted, flashed across the screen. He had one arm slung around Logan's shoulder while the other clung to a much bigger, balder man who walked by his side, practically carrying him as his feet dragged on the floor.

But there was only one person I could focus on, and that was Logan.

He knew Jasper, and that changed everything. *Everything.*

He'd lied to me.

I'd let yet another untrustworthy soul into my life, and out of all the band members he could have chosen to know, it had to have been Jasper. He and I had never seen eye to eye. I saw him as the man who led Cole astray one too many times, and he saw me as the woman who tied Cole down with a baby, taking his wingman away when all they wanted to do was travel the world and party together.

Like that had ever stopped either of them.

Jasper was as much to blame for Cole's death as Cole, and seeing him beside Logan stung like hell.

I stared at Logan's face as the video footage of them leaving Alter Egos played on a loop. Bright camera flashes went off in his face, and he tried to shield his identity from them as much as possible, which seemed like a pointless act given how many men had gathered outside, waiting for them to leave. Someone inside had obviously tipped the press off and was now better off for it.

Fucking famous people and their golden opportunities. They made me sick.

Maybe it was a coincidence that Logan was there the same time as Jasper, I thought for a brief moment before I closed my eyes and pushed it aside, knowing it to be a lie.

Nothing in Los Angeles happened by chance. People were here to become somebody, and I was the woman who'd just lost her someone, leaving a space open for an opportunist to sweep in.

I knew he seemed too good to be true.

Opening my eyes again, I took one last look at Logan on my screen, picked up the remote, and I turned it off...

I didn't need to see anything else. Especially not his face.

twelve

Hannah

Livia stood at the kitchen sink, peeling back the lettuce leaves for the salad she insisted on preparing for the two of us while Bella was at school. I'd lost a lot of weight in the last six months. Some from before Cole left us and the stress he put us through. The rest after that fatal night. I hadn't had ten pounds to lose in the first place, but that's what happens when the shit hits the fan sometimes. We take it out on our bodies.

If it hadn't been for Livia, who knew what state I'd be in now?

She'd been the one to tiptoe into my bedroom, sliding plates of French toast and strawberries under the sheets. Leaving hot coffees on the side for me to drink or leave to go cold. It had become pointless arguing with her now when she told me that she was preparing lunch. My rumbling stomach would argue back against my whimpering mind, anyway.

She had a smile on her face as she shook out the lettuce leaves and turned to drop them into a bowl that sat on the kitchen island between us, while I sat on one of the spinning stools my daughter loved to use as her very own mini carousel.

"You should have seen Kelsey Benson this morning when I dropped Bella off," Livia said, her attention on the task in front of her as she reached for some plum tomatoes along with the already diced cucumber. "She's really going for this school governor thing. She had posters printed out as well as a little placard. She was trying to convince anyone who walked by her that she was the best person for the job. That it was all for her little Lucy's school and not her own ego."

"Ugh, it's like high school with everyone vying to be prom queen," I said with a smile. "That experience was bad enough back then. Why would anyone want to put themselves through that again?"

Livia's eyes lifted to meet mine. "Maybe she never got to be prom queen... unlike some."

"That was not something I went after, trust me."

"Must have been that natural charm of yours."

"Right," I chuckled. "Either that or people felt sorry for me back then."

Liv raised a brow. "High school kids? Come on. Empathy isn't a common trait of theirs."

"You make a very good point."

The security system pinged, alerting us to someone at the front gate, making my head rise in suspicion while Livia simply dusted her hands off over her little apron and went to investigate. I opened my mouth to try to stop her—I didn't want any visitors today, and a part of me worried it might be Logan—but I didn't get a chance to do so. From down the long corridor, Livia soon welcomed someone inside, and it didn't take long for them to appear in the entryway of the kitchen, their mouth pressed into a flat line and their eyebrows raised as they looked at me for the first time in months.

"*Chase*," I said on a breath, staring at Cole's bass guitarist standing in my home, his hands hanging listlessly by his side. "What are you... what are you doing here?"

He wore a brown, beat-up leather jacket, and his long black hair was tucked behind his ears. Chase had always been a looker with the ladies, although he did nothing for me. The kohl he wore around his eyes often smudged in the LA heat, making him look like he needed a good wash compared to Cole's rough yet somehow pristine appearance.

Chase blew out a breath and slapped his hands against his thighs. "It's been months, Han. I thought it was about time I put an end to all this. Ignoring our calls. Our texts. Refusing to see us. Refusing to talk with management or anything to do with the band. Cutting us off."

Livia came up behind him and gave me a look that said she'd make herself scarce, and she did so without much effort, disappearing into the background as Chase took a tentative step closer.

I studied him, so many emotions and memories taking over at once. All the time we'd spent together over the years. All the nights we'd partied before Bella came along and the deep conversations the two of us had had while Cole had been playing the fool with Jasper and their drummer Frankie. Chase had always been the man I'd trusted Cole with the most. He'd been the one to reach out to me about his funeral, the one to constantly try to regain some kind of contact. The one to ask about Bella.

And I'd been the one to push him away.

"I've missed you, Banana," he said quietly.

"Don't call me that, you idiot," I whispered. An unexpected tear fell, and so many unspoken things passed between us until Chase came close enough to take me in his arms and pull my head to his chest.

"I'm sorry, babe. For everything," he whispered against my hair, and for the first time in a long time, I allowed a rock star to hold me without trying to tear myself away from their arms.

"It's not you who should be apologizing."

"I know… but he'd want me to do it for him."

We stayed that way together for a while until twenty minutes later, we sat side by side on the patio furniture under the canopy. Chase glanced around the garden as though it was the first peaceful thing he'd seen in years.

"I forgot how beautiful it is out here," he said. "No wonder you've been hiding when this is where you get to hide."

He'd discarded his leather jacket over the couch's arm, now wearing a thin, overworn black T-shirt that was practically transparent in places. He held a bottle of beer in his hand while I had a bottle of water, not knowing what to say after crying in his arms.

When he turned to look at me again, he rested his elbow on the back of the couch, his fist on his cheek, while his other hand clung to the beer that sat in his twisted lap.

"You've lost too much weight," he said matter-of-factly.

"You stink of too many cigarettes," I countered.

His half-smile made one of my own come to life.

"Sorry," I whispered. "Bad habit of giving tit for tat."

"That was the way you and Cole operated. No need to apologize for it."

I nodded and looked down into my lap, realizing how long it had been since Cole and I had gone at each other like that.

Some people loved to watch our back and forth, while others felt ridiculously uncomfortable around it. I couldn't blame any of them for feeling the way they did. My husband and I were either deliriously happy and hilarious together, or we were toxic, too burnt out from our individual childhoods to be healed before we were thirty.

"I miss him," I admitted. "And I hate that I do."

"You guys were complicated."

"That's one word for it."

"It's okay to miss what wasn't good for you. It's okay to love what ruined you, too. You know that, right? Those feelings we have... those emotions that rise... they aren't there to make sense. They're there to make us feel alive."

"Is that what I'm supposed to feel right now? Alive?"

"You've just lost your fucking husband, Han. You know there's no manual on how to handle that."

I offered him a small smile and copied his pose.

"Why are you really here?" I asked, studying his warm rock 'n' roll exterior.

"I can't just be concerned about an old friend?"

"You can, but I think the timing's a little suspicious considering what I saw on the news about Jasper yesterday."

"Ah," he said, immediately looking guilty. "Caught red-handed. Wasn't sure if you'd be watching the news again yet. Not after—"

"After they tore my husband to shreds when he overdosed, telling the world what a sordid life he'd lived away from me, and sharing stories from any credible or non-credible source they could find as long as it had his name in?" I shrugged. "Sometimes I wake up in a self-destructive mood, and the news calls to me. What can I say?"

"You really did live with Cole for too long. You've turned

into him along the way." Chase wedged his beer bottle between his legs and reached over to rest his hand on my knee. "Well, just in case you're interested, what they're saying about Jasper isn't the whole truth. Yeah, he got drunk, and yeah, he mentioned Cole's name at some point and had a little cry about it, but it wasn't as bad as they made out. You know what those outlets are like, and we both know that Jasp has done a hell of a job keeping out of them since Cole's death."

I winced without intention, and Chase squeezed my knee in comfort, leaning closer.

"He lost his best friend, Han. We all did. This was always going to happen to one of us."

I nodded again, desperate to let him know with words that I understood what Jasper had done, but it had been the man standing beside him, helping him out of the bar, who had got to me the most.

"I saw he had two guys looking out for him that night. At least they got Jasper out of there safely. I mean… unless they were the ones who called the photographers to be there when he left. Has anyone looked into that?"

Way to go, Hannah. Smooth.

Chase frowned, taking a moment for himself before he shook his head. "No way. The big bald guy worked with us on a music video over in Japan a few years ago. Apparently runs some kind of MMA gym now in the city. Mark Shaw's as genuine as they come. He was also pretty protective of us out there when filming. He wouldn't do that to Jasp."

"What about the other guy I saw carrying him out?"

Chase shrugged. "Some friend of Shaw's, and he always makes sure he only mixes in the right circles. I doubt it was either of them."

My heart beat wildly, a dangerous dance of relief and

excitement building as I waited for the confirmation I needed from someone who would know the truth, no matter what.

"So, neither were friends of Jasper, then?"

"I don't think so." He studied my face, waiting for a response, but I managed to conceal whatever reaction was growing inside of me. "I'm glad Shaw was there, though. Who knows what Jasp would have done if he hadn't been carried out before he truly got himself fucked up?"

Who knows? I thought. *Logan seems to have a talent for being in the right place at the wrong time, and I don't know what to do with any of that information anymore.*

"Anyway," Chase said, gently shaking his hand on my knee. "Tell me something good. Something in your life that's made you smile in the last few months. Something besides me." He winked.

My thoughts went straight back to Logan.

To the open talks we'd had.

The lack of judgment he'd passed.

Instead of saying his name, though, my smile grew, and I pointed to the tree behind Chase. "See that microphone hanging down over there? Bella came up with an amazing idea. One I think Cole would have loved."

thirteen

Logan

Jerry and Buck were on my ass constantly after seeing me on the news with a stumbling Jasper Fucking Jacobson the other night. Not only had I had several calls from them, but there'd also been a couple of official emails from the people who actually hired me, questioning whether I was ready to return to work after just two weeks. Apparently, my recent shift in behavior had become a concern for all parties involved.

Brilliant.

As if it wasn't bad enough that I thought I'd become a total loser, every fucker out there now thought I'd become obsessed with Cole Newman's former life and was trying to integrate myself into it to make up for feelings of guilt that ate me alive at night.

Part of me wondered if they were right.

Everything was getting real weird, real fast.

On top of all that, Hannah hadn't called.

She had to have seen the news. She had to have seen me standing there next to Jasper, even though I tried to shield my face from the cameras. She had to have heard about it from someone…

And she still hadn't called, making me think that it was the end of everything.

The gym hadn't done a damn thing for me over the past two days. Long hikes, trips to the diner, and even an early preview of the latest blockbuster movie had done nothing to take my mind off of Hannah, and that right there had become the fucking problem.

More guilt. More shame. More fucking issues than GQ.

Was this some fucked up, misplaced sense of attachment I felt to the widow of a man who died at my hands? Or was it because of her sweet voice, her damaged heart, her sad yet gorgeous smile, or the fact that when her eyes stared back at mine, breathing felt easy for the first time in forever?

I shook my head to try and remove those ridiculous thoughts once and for all, but her face was a picture my mind didn't want to erase, and all I could do at four o'clock in the afternoon on a regular weekday was throw myself back onto my bed, stare up at the ceiling, and wait for a sign that now was the right time to let it all go and move on.

Ten minutes passed by.

Then another twenty.

By the time an hour had been wasted, I began to drift to sleep. A sleep I welcomed.

I was about thirty seconds away from diving headfirst into that black hole when my phone buzzed on the comforter beside me, making my tired eyes blink open. I turned my head on the pillow to look at my cell, seeing 'No Caller ID' staring back at me on the screen.

Hannah.

I sat upright and pulled the phone to my ear. "Hello?"

Nothing but silence lingered down the line, yet despite everything my mind told me *not* to do, my heart had other ideas.

"Hannah?"

"I thought about not calling," she said softly.

The sound of her voice made me close my eyes and fall back onto the pillow, my free hand coming up to worry my forehead. "I know," I said carefully.

"A big part of me wanted to ignore you and make you go away for good."

"I'm that bad, huh?"

"Apparently not. I'm here, aren't I?" She sounded confused as fuck about why she'd called me at all.

"I know, but I'm sorry you sound messed up over it."

"Are you? Are you sorry, Logan?"

"No."

"Then why lie?"

My eyes scrunched together, the knot of dread tightening in my stomach at the thought of me having to tell her who I was and why we'd first made contact.

"I'll try not to do that again." Another fucking lie. "Of course, I'm glad you called. You probably have questions, and I want to be the one to answer them."

"Let's get straight into it then. Why were you with Jasper Jacobson the other night?"

"I'm still trying to wrap my head around that myself."

"The truth, Logan. That's all it takes."

It was the very least I could give her, so that's what I did. I told her about my recent sign up to Creed's MMA gym, and about how I'd met my new trainer, and we'd struck up an instant friendship that made little sense to me. I told her the truth about how I didn't think they'd let me into Alter Egos, never mind let me stay there, and how Creed seems to know every name and face from any trashy celebrity magazine to exist, and that's how we came to be in Jasper's company.

"Once Jasper was put in his car, Creed drove me home. He said that was enough drama for the year for him, and I agreed." I ran my hand through my hair and fisted it. "I know what you must have thought when you saw me, Hannah. That I was another fame-hungry wannabe who'd somehow found a way to get close to you when you felt weak."

"I'm not weak, Logan. I'm tired. I'm tired of being confused. I'm tired of overthinking. I'm tired of having such contradictory feelings. I'm tired of wondering when the next panic attack is going to hit. I'm tired of wondering if I'm good enough for Bella now. But do you know what I'm tired of more than anything? I'm tired of being stuck in this house, too afraid to go out in case someone sees me and judges what I've become, how I act, or what I look like. I just want someone to knock on my door and tell me they're breaking me out of this fancy prison I've become stuck in. I need…"

"What? You need what?" *Tell me, and I'll give it to you.*

"I need to escape."

My heart hammered in my chest, heavy and hard, fighting to be heard over every other thought in my mind that told me not to do or say what I was about to do or say.

"Do you know what I hated the most about seeing you out with Jasper?" she asked. "I was jealous. I was jealous of your freedom. Of his, too. He can fuck up and be forgiven by the media in the morning. Me? I'm supposed to be a grieving widow, dressed in black, staring out of her bedroom window through a black veil until *they* tell me I can live again."

"It doesn't have to be that way. Just give me the word, and I'll help you break free," I said without thought.

She took her time to respond before she quietly asked, "You'd do that for me?"

"In a heartbeat."

"How do I know that I can trust you?"

"You can't know. Not yet. You just have to take a few risks first."

"Is that what you are, Logan? A risk?"

My mind raced with cheesy lines, clichés, and a thousand other things that didn't feel right until all I had left to offer her was the truth. All I could offer her was the very thing she seemed to offer me whenever we spoke.

"Everyone you meet is a risk, but maybe I'm the guy who accidentally came into your life to help you breathe easier for a while. It doesn't have to be forever, Hannah. It just has to be now."

A few seconds passed, the words I'd spoken lingering between us until she exhaled heavily and whispered. "Get me out of this place, Logan. Please."

fourteen

Logan

S he climbed into my car later that night wearing a black cap with her short blonde hair tucked behind her ears. Her jeans hugged her thighs and ass in a way that made me look the other way so that I didn't have to try and control my expressions. The big, black hoodie she wore hung off her slender frame as though it had belonged to Cole. When she shut the passenger door and turned to face me, a breath caught in my throat, and I had to clear it away quickly.

The woman didn't know just how insanely beautiful she was.

She fastened her seatbelt and sat back in the seat with a heavy sigh, her delicate hands landing on her thighs. "Am I stupid for doing this?" she asked, staring straight ahead at the garage that looked eleven times bigger than my condo. "No, wait. Don't answer that. I don't want to know. Let's just go."

I studied her profile, seeing every bit of nerves she so desperately tried to hide.

"It's just a drive. Nothing else," I told her, careful not to spark a reaction.

She turned my way, and her eyes searched mine, seeking out the lie before she gave me a small nod. I reversed out of the electric gates, back out onto the street, and Hannah glanced around to search for any vehicles or press that may have been waiting. A clear sign that she'd never really gotten to grips with this lifestyle, no matter how much her husband may have wanted her to. Despite living in a neighborhood that prided itself on privacy for the rich and famous, Hannah still lived on the edge of her nerves, her life a special dance of when to step forward and when to step back to keep her and her daughter safe.

"There's no one around," I assured her, facing the road. I figured the less I looked at her, the more she'd relax, even if turning away killed me because Hannah Moore was fucking gorgeous, and my thoughts were starting to head in a direction I needed them to stay away from. "It's just us now."

"Just us," she said in a soft sigh.

The rest of the journey remained quiet. The two of us were practically strangers, and the fact we were, for the very first time, locked together in such close proximity, and not on the other end of a call, seemed to hit us like a ton of bricks. Neither of us knew what to say, so we let silence do the talking for us.

And I heard every fucking word.

This is weird.

This is awkward.

We don't belong together like this.

We should probably go home.

But despite the growing tension, I kept on driving until she told me to stop. I kept on going as her head twisted to look out of the window with every street we turned upon, as though she was seeing the outside world for the very first time. I caught her watching the streetlights when we drove under them. I caught her taking in the other millionaires' homes before we left Beverly Hills and headed toward Van Nuys. I took the long route to our destination, giving her a chance to bail out any time she felt the need to. But when we reached the lookout point that I'd hoped and prayed would be quiet, and I parked my Outback next to the railings that overlooked Los Angeles, Hannah's shoulders finally sagged, and her back curled into her seat.

"Isn't this the kind of place teenagers bring each other to make out?" she asked.

The thought of making out with Hannah made the muscles in my jaw tighten and my nostrils flare. "Thank God we're not teenagers anymore."

"Couldn't think of anything worse."

I turned to look at her profile, trying like hell not to get lost in how beautiful she was, which seemed impossible. "I get the feeling life hasn't always been easy on you."

"I live in Beverly Hills, in a house big enough for three families. I have no reason to feel sorry for myself."

"Money doesn't equal happiness or take away the stuff going on in your head."

"No," she said, turning to face me. "But it can buy you a hell of a lot of distractions." And as soon as she set those words free, I could tell she didn't mean them. That wasn't who Hannah Moore was.

Her eyes searched mine only briefly before she tugged on the sleeves of her hoodie, pulling them down over her knuckles, and she studied LA's skyline again. "Why here?"

"Well, when the world feels too big and overwhelming sometimes, I drive out to places like this and see how small we really are. It's like flying on a plane. You can be carrying a thousand worries on your back, but the minute that plane takes off and you look out of that tiny window and see the world below you for what it really is, a lot of those worries drift away. We're just dolls in a big fucking dollhouse. The shit we let destroy us is more often than not far more insignificant than we realize."

"You're deeper than you let people believe, aren't you, Logan?"

"Not usually."

"I don't believe you," she said with a soft smile. "But thank you... for bringing me here."

"Anytime, Hannah."

And even though I meant it, I also knew being at her beck and call wouldn't end well. Neither would being this close to her when she smelled so good and looked so vulnerable.

I was placing myself in the middle of a fucking car crash, but I couldn't do anything to take my foot off the gas and slow the hell down. Maybe I deserved to crash hard at the end of all this.

I just had to make sure I didn't take her down with me when it happened.

fifteen

Hannah

We stayed at Logan's lookout point for over an hour before he drove me home.

I didn't feel the need for unnecessary words. Our silences were comfortable—at least to me—and with every minute that passed, it became obvious that Logan had been right. I *was* able to breathe easier beside him.

He made me feel safe. Like I didn't have to be anything other than who I was with him. We may as well have been in the clouds together, and I'd have stayed there forever had it not been for the little girl back home asleep in her bed. As much as I'd enjoyed the great escape, I also couldn't wait to sneak into her room and wrap her up in my arms to say goodnight.

First, I had to say goodbye to Logan.

The car came to a stop in my driveway, and I turned to take

another glance at him with the outdoor lights illuminating his dark stubbled jawline, allowing me to appreciate just how ruggedly handsome he was.

Logan had it all: the looks, temperament, that unassuming charm, the ability to listen, the strength, and the body. Only one thing seemed to be missing, and that was his confidence. Even now, with one hand on the steering wheel and his eyes forward as though too afraid to look at me, he was unsure of himself.

There were a lot of things I could have said to build him up, and a big part of me wanted to give him that gift. To say thank you and tell him how much I appreciated him giving up his time and his energy for someone like me—someone he barely knew.

Instead, I leaned over the console and placed a hand on his face. Despite him flinching beneath my unexpected touch, I whispered, "Thank you, Logan. You truly are a gift."

Then, I placed a soft kiss against his warm skin, and I turned to leave.

He never said anything when I climbed out of his car, and he never came after me as I made my way inside. I couldn't ignore the knot of disappointment that twisted in my stomach as I made my way up the stairs to give my daughter a kiss goodnight, feeling lighter than I had done in months.

Lighter and somehow more alive.

All because of one man, his time, and his patience.

Maybe that's all a woman in distress ever really needs from anybody.

Not things. Just moments.

***

The weekend arrived, and Bella played in our backyard with one of her school friends, jumping in and out of the pool with their floaties. Seeing my daughter with a huge smile on her face filled my heart. Hearing her laughter was a tonic to my soul. It had been a long time since I'd felt so light, and I basked in the heat of the morning sunshine.

After kicking back on a sun lounger, I picked up my cell, not thinking about what I was doing until I heard his familiar voice.

"Hey," I said, feeling oddly shy.

"Hey," Logan answered, his voice slightly raised over a lot of background noise that I couldn't make out. "Hannah? You there?"

"Er, yeah, sorry. Just... you know... checking in," I said, pressing a palm down on the confusing sensation of butterflies springing to life in my stomach. "I wanted to thank you for the other night."

"You already did," he said, and memories of that kiss on his cheek flared to life. It felt like the right thing to do at the time, but I'd spent hours lying in bed, agonizing over what I'd done, and wondering what he must have thought.

"It doesn't hurt to say it twice."

He huffed out a laugh that made my stomach clench again. I didn't know what the hell was going on, but I wanted to end the call immediately and get a grip on my body.

"As long as it helped, that's all that matters," he said smoothly.

"It did."

"Good."

"So... found yourself a life yet?" I asked with a wry smile, aiming to keep things light between us, just as Bella's friend Ivory jumped into the crystal blue water, creating a splash that touched the bottom of my bare legs.

Logan laughed properly that time, as though he didn't have a care in the world. "Not unless being down at the Farmer's Market counts as me finding a life, no."

"Sounds like you're looking in the wrong places. I'm not sure they stock those on the shelves."

"Good point. Got any suggestions?"

"How about more of that Hollywood scene you tried the other night? Lots of single men seeking out new pals and hot ladies looking for the very thing you're looking for."

"And what am I looking for, exactly?"

"Companionship? Excitement? The thrill of the chase."

"You mean sex?"

The thought made my cheeks flame.

Memories of Cole above me, taking his time to play with my body, flashed through my mind, only for his face to slowly change into Logan's, making me frown again. What the hell?

"Like I told you before, Hannah, my track record with women and relationships isn't something to shout about. I doubt any of my exes would even give me a reference if I asked for one."

"Ah, see. That's where you're going wrong. You never ask for references. You just embellish your resume a little and hope the new ladies don't stumble across the old ones anytime soon."

"Is that right?" he asked, a certain rasp to his voice before I heard him bump into someone and apologize.

I pulled my knees up closer to my body, my focus on the two girls having the time of their lives in front of me instead of the weird reactions I was having, speaking to Logan. None of it made any sense, and I didn't like the uncertainty that tore through me.

More noise around him had him apologizing to somebody else, and I couldn't help the soft smile that rose at just how nice he seemed to be in all walks of life. Perhaps it was his nature, or perhaps his job had nurtured it out of him, but Logan was a good guy.

Good, reliable, manly, strong, hot, and…

Woah, no, enough already, I thought, quickly losing my smile and dropping my legs back down on the lounger. *No, no, no.*

There will be no more of those thoughts, Hannah Moore. He's just a friend. Someone to confide in. Someone to be there whenever you need to speak without being judged.

"Sorry, Logan. It sounds busy where you are," I said, running my free hand across the sudden dampness of my forehead. "I should let you go."

"It's fine." I heard him rustle a paper bag in the background before the ringing of a cash register floated through the line, and Logan said thank you to who I assumed was the server. "I'm just leaving the market now. Thought it was time I ate something other than pop tarts, pancakes, or ramen noodles."

"What's wrong with ramen noodles?"

"Believe it or not, you can have too much of a good thing, and apparently my palate is now demanding something that will make my stomach last a lifetime rather than something that will rot it from the inside out. It's no use me preaching to my patients about self-preservation and then ignoring my own advice. Nobody likes a hypocrite."

"Just don't take it too far, okay. You'll be going vegan on me next."

"I've considered it. A woman at the station is vegan, and she's shown me some amazing options. Brought some meals to work for me a few times, too."

"Ah, when a woman brings you food, she's trying to sleep with you."

"She's fifty-seven with a husband she's been with since she was fourteen." He paused. "Banging body, though."

I barked out a laugh I hadn't heard from myself in such a long time. It made me clamp a hand over my mouth just as Bella looked over at me with another beaming smile on her face. I gave her a soft wave, and she waved back with such enthusiasm, I wondered if her hearing my laughter had the same effect on her as hers had on me.

"That's gross, Logan," I said, trying to sound appalled, even though I knew he'd been joking.

"Sorry," he laughed again.

"You sound… different today. Happier than usual. It sounds good on you."

He exhaled heavily but didn't respond, and I began to panic, wondering if he could sense the shift in my thoughts toward him.

"Did you like them?" I asked, changing the subject. "The meals she cooked for you."

"I like anything that's good for me."

Me, too, I thought. "You'll have to send me the recipes."

"Ah, see, that's the problem. I know it tastes good, but I don't know the first thing about actually making the stuff."

"That's a shame. I'd love to be able to cook."

"Me, too."

"We could always figure it out together. I have a big kitchen I don't know what to do with most of the time, and we both know how to use Google, right?"

He paused again, a man who always processed his thoughts before he spoke. "Did you just invite me over?"

"I… I think so, yeah."

"What about Bella?"

I looked at my daughter from across the pool, her eyes alight with the joy of sun, water, and friendship, and all I could think about was needing to keep that spark there. She needed to see some life in this huge house we now lived in. She needed to keep jumping around, laughing, and singing, not afraid to tread on eggshells or worry about her mom crying or finding herself without energy from one moment to the next.

"I think it's about time Bella had a mom who could do something other than mope around, don't you?"

sixteen

Logan

Hannah opened the door to me standing there holding two brown paper bags filled with groceries. I shot her a smile, and she shone one right back before tucking her hair behind her ear and gesturing for me to step inside.

That little hair tuck was starting to kill me.

I followed her to the kitchen, trying hard not to pay attention to the foyer area where I'd first seen Cole when we'd barged through the open doors and slid to our knees to try and save him. But no matter how hard I tried, my skin prickled to life anyway.

You shouldn't fucking be here, you asshole. You're taking this too far.

I had no idea if that was Cole's voice or mine, but either way, I sucked in a deep breath and followed Hannah into the kitchen, trying desperately to leave the memories of that night behind.

Clean, white marble flooring set off the tone of the space we walked into, the interiors a mixture of white and gold, with glossy counter space and matching tiles, finished off with obviously expensive finishes that made the place look like something straight out of a showroom catalog. Funny how the white décor in my home made it look barren while this felt like the perfect place to raise a family. Despite its size, it was warm and welcoming, and I could see why Cole had chosen it for the women in his life.

Hannah moved around to the opposite side of the kitchen island while I dropped the bags to the center of it. Her eyes caught mine, and something shot into my chest that made me want to fucking vomit. A pain I found I liked, leaving a lingering ache that somehow settled and grew at the same time.

"Where's Bella?" I asked, just for something to say.

"She had a friend here earlier for a playdate. That friend's mom came to collect her, and Bella whined enough to get an invite round to theirs for the afternoon. Luckily, she's one of the moms I trust endlessly, and my daughter knows it. She also gets what she wants more often than not," she said with a small smile, tilting her head and narrowing her eyes at me. "You don't have to be so nervous, Logan. I invited you here."

"Who said I'm nervous?"

Her brow arched as she reached for one of the brown paper bags and began to unload some of the groceries.

"Fine, maybe a little," I admitted, smiling back at her. "This is just a big-ass house."

"Takes your breath away, doesn't it?"

Not as much as you do, I wanted to say, but I wasn't an asshole about to hit on a dead man's wife. I chose instead to hold onto that stray thought while I dragged the other bag closer to me to unpack with her.

"I still can't believe it's ours. Well... Cole's, I mean, but..." Hannah trailed off, the happiness slipping off her face like an oily mask she had no control of.

My hand stilled around a can of coconut milk in the bag, and Hannah's eyes pinched at the corners as though she'd only just remembered that her husband no longer existed and this house was, in fact, hers now. She stared into the distance for only a few seconds before she shook her head and got back to unpacking the bag.

"Sorry," she muttered. "I still can't get used to those moments. The ones where it hits me that he's gone, and the pain comes back for a second, as though I'd allowed myself to forget at some point." Her eyes met mine again. "Stupid, isn't it?"

"No."

"How do you do it, Logan? How do you see so much death and move on from it?"

My throat closed up. I pulled the last few items out of the bag I was working on. "I try to avoid that part of the job as much as possible."

"Does that work out for you?"

"It has its good days and bad."

Her eyes filled with sympathy. "It's you guys who should own homes like this, you know. Not us. Not people who sing and dance and perform for a living, but those who fight what you have to fight and then head home knowing they lose sometimes."

I wanted to curl up in a ball and fucking die at her feet. The guilt of everything ate away at me, starting at the tips of my toes and rising up like a slow, soul-eating poison that turned everything black in its wake. But I couldn't react—not with her looking at me like I was some kind of fucking god she admired when the reality was that she'd eventually come to hate me one day.

"Everything's the way it is for a reason," I said, picking up the empty paper bag to fold it over on the countertop. "People like me might be there for the life-or-death situations, but I think a lot of us forget that it's the stuff in between that the artists are there for. Music, books, film, television… it's those things we turn to when we're stuck in between living and dying. It's those things we rely on to get us through. And you know what they say…"

"What?"

"The journey is always harder than the destination. The arts get us through the journey. The destination, well, it's shorter."

I chanced a glance up at her to see her smiling, her arms folded across her chest.

She was beautiful, and I couldn't deny it for a moment longer—not that I ever had. Especially not when she looked at me as though I was the one who lit up the room instead of her. I'd screwed many women, and I had a lot of tales to tell of one-night stands that I'd fucked over by being so indifferent, but in Hannah's company, I became a damn child. A lost boy who didn't know how to function. One filled with lust and guilt and longing and self-loathing.

A total contradiction of everything I *should* have been for her.

She shook her head, her smile growing wider. "You really do know how to make me smile."

Despite my desperate need to tell her the truth about everything, the only thing I could do was smile right back.

If I could be the guy to give her a moment of peace during her mourning, I'd let her take it. Even if it ruined me in the end.

***

We cooked together side by side, making small talk as we figured out how to make something good with both of us being so bad, but once we had the main ingredients laid out, and with the help of Google, we soon found our rhythm, working together as a team. Too many times, we'd reached for the same ingredient or the same utensil, and our fingers brushed past each other's, making me pull back and look away as I tried to control my reactions to her.

I had to keep this platonic.

I couldn't go there in my head—couldn't allow myself to feel any more attracted than I already was. Not with everything she didn't know hanging between us. I was there to be a friend, not stare into her eyes and imagine things I wasn't supposed to imagine.

An hour later, we sat in the backyard under a thick canopy that overlooked the pool. The patio furniture was probably more expensive than my entire condo, and the same went for the low, slate table with an inbuilt fire pit in the middle.

Hannah saw me glancing around in some kind of muted awe, and she pulled her bowl into her lap, dipping her fork into the naked vegan burrito bowl we'd made together. She smirked before lifting her fork to her mouth and wrapping her lips around her food. Her eyes closed, and a small moan of appreciation rumbled in the back of her throat, making the hairs on the back of my neck rise.

Jesus.

I quickly copied her to distract myself, taking a fork-full from my own bowl and pushing it into my mouth.

Damn. It really did taste good.

"This is unbel*ievable*," Hannah muttered. "Did we really make this ourselves?"

"We did."

"Holy shit!"

"Although, I can't take too much credit. You did do the majority of the work, after all."

"Only because you read the instructions so eloquently," she said, lifting her eyes to meet mine, forcing me to look away again.

We ate in silence for a while, neither one of us uncomfortable, which was weird in itself, like we'd known each other a lifetime already. When Hannah finished eating, she pushed her almost-empty bowl away and fell back in her seat, her eyes drifting toward the pool. I studied her profile for a second too long, causing her to look my way and hold my gaze.

I wanted to look away again, but I couldn't.

"Everything okay?" she asked.

"Yep." I nodded and pushed my empty bowl away before sitting back in my seat, an elbow resting on the chair arm and hands resting over my stomach. "You?"

"I'm thinking…"

"About?"

"How that, when you're here, I don't panic about panicking."

"It's the paramedic in me. Makes you feel safe."

"No, Logan, it's the you in you. You're just a good person to have around, but you don't like hearing that, do you? Compliments make you feel awkward."

"Talking about myself is boring. I live with me every day."

"Ah, I'm not used to being around people who think like that. Cole's favorite topic was always Cole." A small laugh escaped her, but something told me she didn't find it funny.

"He achieved a lot," I said. "In a short amount of time, too. Can't blame the guy for being proud of that."

"Oh, I can blame him for a *lot*," she said, any happiness falling from her face quickly, making me feel like a fucking idiot the moment the words fell from her mouth. "I can, and I will."

"That wasn't—"

"That's the problem though, isn't it? I'm meant to think of him fondly in these early stages. I'm not meant to be angry, disappointed, or even a little relieved that I don't have to deal with his bullshit anymore."

"I didn't mean you couldn't blame him. It came out wrong."

"No, it came out right." She moved to the edge of her seat before picking up the bowls and standing.

I stood with her, my hands falling by my side as I watched her move around the table and head back inside, into the kitchen. I followed, watching as she dumped the plates into the sink with a little too much force, the sound of them hitting together ringing out around the room until she pressed her hands to the top of her head and looked up at me with wide, helpless eyes.

"Sorry," she muttered weakly.

"Don't be."

"I just hate how mad he still makes me."

I took a step closer. "Nothing you feel is wrong, Hannah."

"Then why does it feel wrong? Why do I feel guilty talking to you about him like that?"

I took another step. "Because you're letting other people get inside your head. You're worried about their needs over your own."

"He had a lot of people love him."

"But he loved you the most."

She puffed out a sarcastic laugh and dropped her hands to her chest. "He loved himself the most."

I wanted to tell her everything right there and then. To confess how he'd looked up at me through eyes that knew they were dying. To tell her the last word to fall from his dying lips. But I couldn't confess any of that shit. Not while her emotions were bouncing all over the place from one minute to the next. All I could try to do was help her feel better about this fucked-up situation she'd become stuck in the middle of.

I took another step closer, and then another, until she was

only an arm's length away from me, staring up into my eyes as though I held all the answers that could heal whatever Cole had broken inside of her.

I didn't have any answers.

But I did have a story.

"I know the pain you feel inside. I know the confusion. The anger. The bitterness. The regret."

"How?" she whispered.

"I lost my best friend when I was eighteen. Drug overdose. Just like Cole."

"Logan, I'm so sorry—"

"And I was with him," I added, cutting her off.

A look of disappointment washed over her. "Did you... take them too?"

"Sometimes," I admitted. "But never like Dale. Never like—"

"Cole," she finished for me, clearing her throat, and carefully folding her arms beneath her chest. "What happened?"

"Dale took one ecstasy pill too many. He wasn't hydrated enough, and he had a bad reaction to the trip." I never relived that night for anyone, and I was desperate to give the bare minimum when it came to the details, but my mouth wouldn't stop talking. "We were by the lake. Some stupid college party at a mutual friend's house. Dale never knew when to just enjoy a beer or keep it lowkey. I don't think any of us really understood how deep into the whole scene he'd fallen, and that night, he disappeared for a while. I'd tried to keep my eyes on him all evening, knowing something was... *off*. But he was good at slipping away. Good at making people think they had nothing to worry about, and I stupidly got sidetracked by some girl in a tight dress." I swallowed harshly. "Once we realized Dale had been gone too long, a few of us went looking for him down by the lake and... you know."

"He'd... gone?"

"Almost," I croaked, feeling the walls of my throat closing up. I never talked about this shit with anyone. Never spoke about the reason I'd left Michigan and come to Los Angeles to start a new life—one where I could try to right the wrongs of the people who hadn't saved Dale that day, no matter how hard they'd all tried. And, fuck, did they try.

Hannah took a step closer to me, leaving nothing between us. Her delicate hands landed on my chest, just over my rapidly beating heart.

"The paramedics couldn't save him," I said, holding her gaze like she was the anchor to my emotions, tying them down, keeping them steady, unwilling to set them free. I was desperate to touch her, too. To hold her somehow and bleed all my regret and guilt out so I never had to look at her and feel either of those emotions again, but deep down, I'd changed as a man. I'd become a fucking coward who couldn't own up to his own feelings. One who couldn't handle seeing this woman angry at him for a single moment because she was already broken, and I got off too much on trying to fix her.

Hannah pressed her palm down against my racing heart. "You feel guilty, I see that, but it wasn't your fault, Logan."

"I should have saved him." *I should have saved them both.*

"Some people can't be saved."

She couldn't have said anything worse.

*Every*body could be saved. It was the very code I lived by.

My face must have shown it, too, because her confused expression returned, and her hands drifted down my chest until I stepped away completely, putting some much-needed distance between us so I could get some clarity.

What the fuck am I doing here? This isn't normal. This isn't healthy. This...

"This is fucked up," I whispered to myself without thought.

"What?"

I looked up to see a sadness in her eyes that didn't belong there. But my thoughts weren't aligning with my need to make sure she was okay, and the memories of Dale's face mixed with Cole's were at the forefront of my mind, making everything turn red and hazy as the grief and disappointment crept in at a pace I couldn't control.

Running my hand through the back of my hair gave me a moment's pause, and I shook my head before glancing around the kitchen, trying to find anything to focus on that wasn't this woman who was stealing all of my rational thought and morals.

But they only drifted out to the foyer in the distance, reminding me of the first time I stepped inside this house—of Cole's dying face and the panic in his eyes.

"I… I should go," I said in a rush.

"Logan, wait—"

"I can't. I…

"Logan…"

"I'll see you around, Hannah."

Before I could be drawn into her again, and before she could even get my name out of her mouth again and tempt me to stay, I walked out of her place with nothing but the weight of two deaths on my back and her sad eyes forever burned into my mind.

seventeen

Hannah

I'll see you around, Hannah.

Logically, I shouldn't have wanted to check up on Logan.

I definitely shouldn't have been bothered by the way he'd practically run from my home, desperate to get away from me and my touch. I barely knew the guy. He didn't owe me a damn thing, and there I'd been, pressing myself against him like we were lovers. I'd been an idiot, and I should have cut my losses and moved on from the entire incident once and for all.

But as the night went on, and after Bella returned from her playdate, ate her dinner, showered, and went to bed, I still couldn't get Logan off my mind. There'd been something in that look he'd given me before he left—I'd seen it. A vulnerability and rawness I recognized in myself. A pain he'd yet to recover from over a decade later.

Was that how long it would be for me to be able to live again? To get over the frustration and shame I carried around with me every day since Cole died.

Or hadn't I loved Cole as much as Logan had loved his best friend? I'd had another man in my home, cooking, laughing, and teasing me, for Christ's sake. Had I been wrong in asking Logan here to keep me company?

And if so, why had it felt so right him being here?

Nothing made sense, and a never-ending stream of questions whizzed through my mind while I stared at the blank television screen in our living room, nursing my third glass of wine.

Logan made it quite clear that he didn't want to carry the burden of having my cell number, and Cole's voice in the back of my mind warned me about bringing my guard down so quickly... but Logan had only ever given me a reason to trust him, and Cole was no longer around to lecture me about the dos and don'ts of my own life.

Replacing my glass of wine with my cell, I sat back into the thick cushions of my couch and pulled up Logan's number, not giving a damn about any of it until I'd typed out a message and hit send.

ME

I've had enough people trigger me over the last few months to know that I said something wrong. I'm sorry. The last thing I would want to do is hurt you after you've been so good to me.

He deserved my apology. I'd pressed on a wound he'd opened especially for me.

I waited and prayed for a response, suddenly needing it like I needed the air in my lungs.

Twenty minutes went by, but nothing came back.

ME

I don't want you to get rid of my number this time, either. I know you said you didn't want the responsibility of it, and on top of this sudden responsibility you seem to have for me, I understand that it's a lot… but I can't be in any more one-way relationships, Logan. I need this to be a two-way street.

LOGAN

Relationship?

My brows rose at his quick response and the one word he'd chosen to home in on.

Shit! That's not what I'd meant.

ME

Friendships, obviously. But any relationship I have of any kind with anyone going forward has to be based on mutual trust. This is me letting you know that I trust you.

LOGAN

You trust too easily.

ME

Not true. It takes a special someone to earn my trust as quickly as you have. Consider yourself lucky.

LOGAN

That's the second time you've told me I'm lucky since you met me.

ME

You don't think you are?

LOGAN

Only sometimes.

ME

Tell me when.

LOGAN
Earlier, when I was sitting opposite you, watching you smile. I felt pretty lucky then.

I blew out a breath. An unexpected giddiness tore through my veins that I quickly pushed back down. My dead husband's ghost lingered behind me, its brow raised and judgment on display, like his nails were scratching down my back in warning.

Still…

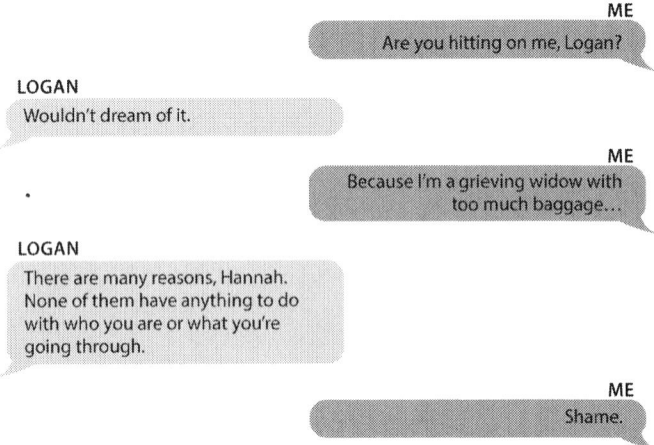

ME
Are you hitting on me, Logan?

LOGAN
Wouldn't dream of it.

ME
Because I'm a grieving widow with too much baggage…

LOGAN
There are many reasons, Hannah. None of them have anything to do with who you are or what you're going through.

ME
Shame.

I hit the send button and watched in utter horror as the message delivered.

Shame?

Why the hell had I sent that?

My toes curled, and my skin prickled at the embarrassment. I tried to think of a suitable add-on I could send—something that would let him know I'd been playing around. I didn't want *that* from him. This was all happening too soon, and I had no control. My emotions were tethered threads, too strung out and messy to make sense anymore, even to me.

Instead, I stared at my cell, willing Logan to respond.

Shame.

I reached for my wineglass and drained it, enjoying the temporary burn in my throat that distracted me from the stupid mistake I'd just made. It only lasted a second before my phone alerted me to another message.

LOGAN
There isn't a man on the planet who wouldn't want you... but I'm not the right guy for you or that.

I wanted the entire world to swallow me whole right there and then.

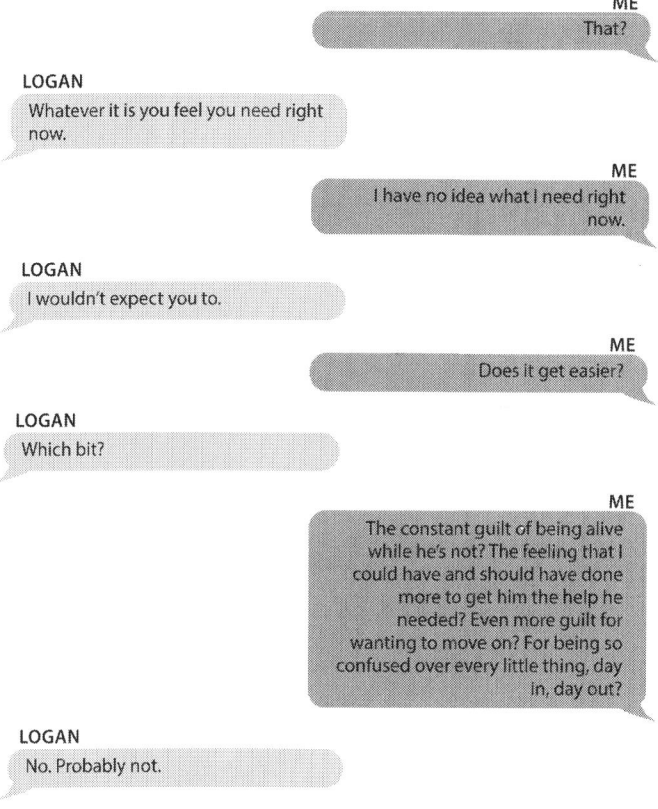

ME
That?

LOGAN
Whatever it is you feel you need right now.

ME
I have no idea what I need right now.

LOGAN
I wouldn't expect you to.

ME
Does it get easier?

LOGAN
Which bit?

ME
The constant guilt of being alive while he's not? The feeling that I could have and should have done more to get him the help he needed? Even more guilt for wanting to move on? For being so confused over every little thing, day in, day out?

LOGAN
No. Probably not.

LOGAN

But you will learn to live with it, and one day, you'll have your answers to those questions. You don't need mine or anyone else's. Everyone does it differently. There's no right or wrong, Hannah. There's just what makes you feel better.

ME

Right now, that's you.

I closed my eyes to imagine Logan's reactions to my messages. I could call him to explain that it was probably the wine giving me the courage to speak to him this way, and perhaps I'd wake tomorrow full of regret, but at that moment, I meant everything I sent. Whether that stayed the same in the morning, who knew?

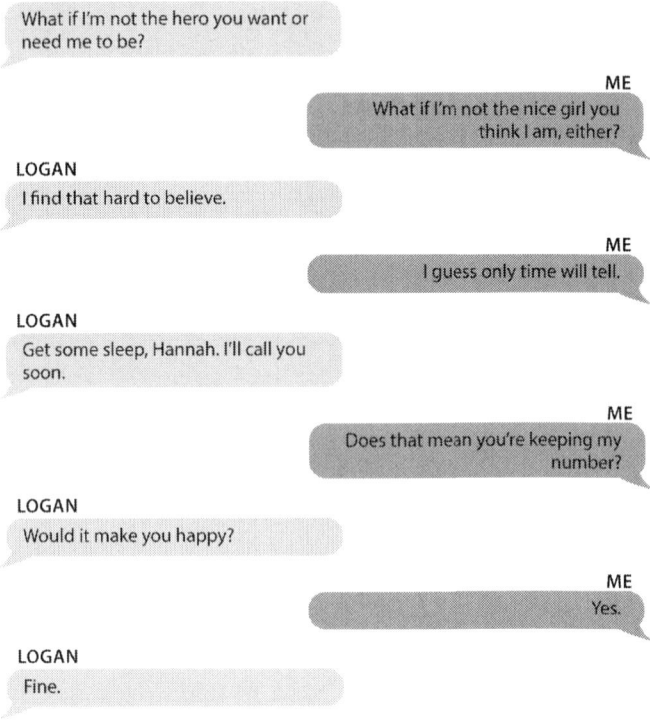

LOGAN

What if I'm not the hero you want or need me to be?

ME

What if I'm not the nice girl you think I am, either?

LOGAN

I find that hard to believe.

ME

I guess only time will tell.

LOGAN

Get some sleep, Hannah. I'll call you soon.

ME

Does that mean you're keeping my number?

LOGAN

Would it make you happy?

ME

Yes.

LOGAN

Fine.

I smiled to myself and let my head fall back against the cushions, dropping my cell into my lap.

Fine.

That would do.

eighteen

Hannah

Two days passed, and Logan made no contact.

I went back and forth, grateful for his silence one minute, only to be agitated by it the next. In such little time, I'd come to look forward to hearing his voice—a calm anchor in a loud, stormy sea. I thought back to the night at the lookout point and how he'd been nothing but patient with me, letting me sit back and just… *think* as I looked out over the vast city, trying to figure out my place in it after so much change.

I wanted more of that.

More moments of serenity.

More guilt-free time.

More company with someone who made me feel good.

I was using him as a crutch, and I couldn't stop myself.

The number of times I'd picked up my cell to call him was borderline ridiculous. Thankfully, that voice in the back of my mind—whether it was Cole's or not, I wasn't so sure—told me not to do it. Logan wasn't the kind of guy to do anything he didn't want to. If he wanted to speak to me, he would.

The ball was in his court.

That didn't stop me feeling like a wound-up ball of string, which led me to step into the underground gym of our home, pushing open the door to reveal the pristine, barely touched equipment inside it for the first time in months.

My eyes roamed up to take in the reflection staring back at me in the floor-to-ceiling mirrors that lined every wall. Even though I'd seen myself a hundred or more times in the last few months, seeing my body in gym leggings and a sports bra with my hair scraped back by a hairband was like seeing myself for the very first time.

And it wasn't good.

I'd lost too much weight; the size of my waist and the way the bones of my hips poked out through the black waistband were proof of that.

I walked toward the mirror, taking in every inch until I couldn't look at it anymore, and I pulled out the barely-used yoga mat. It curved up at the edges when I laid it down, taking its time to flatten after being rolled up for far too long. I could practically hear Cole's sarcastic whispers in my ear.

That thing cost me four hundred dollars, Han, and you've used it twice.

"I never asked for you to buy me it," I responded. "I never asked you for anything."

I wanted you to have the best of the best.

"You wanted me to have things."

My wife wasn't going to be the only wife in Beverly Hills not to have one of these mats. Everyone went on and on about them.

"Not me."

It wouldn't hurt you to show a little gratitude.

"Right," I muttered, my eyes filling with moisture. "Do you even know what it's for?"

I imagined him placing his hands on my bare arms, his chin resting on my shoulder. *Stretching that beautiful body of yours out in ways I can only dream of.*

"You could have had me any time you wanted me, Cole."

I did have you.

I shook my head. "I'm not sure you did."

The sound of my cell ringing pulled me from my daydream, and I quickly swiped the back of my hands over my eyes before I pulled it from the back pocket of my leggings.

I didn't even look at the caller ID. "Hello?"

"Hannah?"

The familiar British accent made my eyes widen. "*Kate*? Is that you?"

"The one and only, beautiful." Her husky yet soft voice swept over me like a comfort blanket I hadn't known I'd needed.

Kate, one of the only true friends I'd made while married to Cole, because of Cole. I barely heard from her throughout the year, but every time we spoke, she lifted me up like no one else could. A fashion designer to the stars, she lived in London and flew around the world on a whim, always here, there, and everywhere, but never in one place for too long. For one of Cole's first events as a global star, he'd flown Kate in to dress me, and the rest had been history.

I fell to the yoga mat in a heap, my legs crossing as I pressed my free hand to my mouth. "God, I've missed you."

"I've missed you, too. So much. How are you? How's Bells?"

"She's… amazing," I said, my smile brightening at the

thought of my daughter who was currently upstairs with her guitar teacher—something her father had insisted on, and I hadn't thought to quit, even though Bella didn't seem all that enthusiastic about it. At least not yet. "She's growing every day, and she's so incredibly strong, Kate. Her resilience is something else."

"Just like her mama." I heard the grin in her voice.

"Yeah," I said instead of bursting out laughing and telling her that only thirty seconds ago, I'd been having a full-blown bickering session with my dead husband.

"That was a pathetic *yeah*," she said, mimicking my voice. "You are strong, Hannah Moore. You might not feel it right now, and that's understandable, but even strong people are allowed to feel weak when their world has been torn apart."

"So soon into the conversation? Really?"

"You know how I love my pep talks."

I chuckled, looking down into my lap before picking at some invisible lint on my leggings. "I've missed them."

"I'm sorry. Time just flies by, and I don't know my boob from my butt most days. Life has been so bloody manic."

"That's a good thing though, right? I mean, the label is doing phenomenally. You're achieving everything you set out to achieve from the start. You're the queen of the catwalk at every fashion show."

"I'm also a micromanaging asshole who can't delegate or let anyone make a decision about her company in case they get it wrong, which means I constantly have to do everything, despite there being literally twenty people around me who could do it perfectly well, and I'm absolutely knackered with no one to blame but myself."

"Knackered?" I asked, sometimes needing help with her British ways.

"Tired, baby. Exhausted. Sodding knackered."

"Ah. Sounds like you need to give yourself one of those pep talks you're good at." I smirked.

"I would never listen to me. Like I said, I'm an asshole."

I laughed lightly.

The conversation went on with the two of us catching up on the little tidbits of each other's lives. Kate, despite being desperate to be here for me, hadn't been able to fly over for Cole's funeral, and apparently, she still felt horrendous about it. I didn't tell her that, at the time, I'd been grateful. She would have fought for me to get up out of my slump too quickly. I'd needed that time to wallow. To drown in the misery a little without having to entertain other people or their ideas of what I should have been doing.

Kate was still in London now, about to collaborate with an A-list celebrity on a one-off winter collection, and from what she was telling me, her and said celebrity were not gelling together too well. I listened to her moan about her life for twenty minutes as I sat on that yoga mat. It was nice to hear someone else's problems and realize I was still perfectly capable of giving advice of my own.

At that thought, my mind drifted to Logan and the look on his face when I'd told him not everyone could be saved.

That had been the moment he'd pulled back, and I felt like an idiot for not having the words to make him feel better, the way he always seemed to do with me.

It was only when Kate said my name that I blinked back into the moment.

"Sorry, what?" I asked, clearing my throat.

"Am I really that boring? Ugh. I am, aren't I? It's happened. I've turned into my mother. I'm sorry, Hannah. I called you to see how *you* were doing, and here I am going on and on about myself."

"Stop it. You've been the perfect distraction. You always

seem to know when I need your call the most."

She didn't speak for a few seconds, the silence lingering until she said, "What's going on? Besides the obvious."

"What makes you think there's something else?"

"Because I know you, Hannah, and I may be across the ocean right now, but I can practically see you drifting in and out of our conversation. That usually means one of two things. Either you're tired and about to fall asleep where you are, or... you're worrying over something you have no control over. Is it Cole? Has something else come out in the press?"

"Actually... no," I said with a long exhale. "It's..." I bit down on my lip and scowled, not knowing how the hell to say what I so desperately wanted to say to someone. *Anyone* at this point. Not even Livia knew about Logan's position in my life. Here he was, this incredible guy, and I couldn't tell anyone about him. I didn't dare for fear of what they'd think of me.

Maybe with Kate being so far away, I could finally confide in someone about him.

"Hannah..." she said, a clear and obvious warning etched into my name.

"I met someone." The words came out freely.

"A man?"

"He's a friend."

"Oh..."

I closed my eyes and pictured Logan's ruggedly handsome face and then I told Kate everything. How he'd been there for my first panic attack and then again for the second. How he always seemed to be in the right place at the right time, and how he'd been adamant he didn't want my cell number or the responsibility of it. I told her how he calmed me, easing my soul, making me feel safe in a world where I suddenly felt exposed to the sharks of clickbait. I must have been going on and on more than I intended to because when I finally came up for air after explaining how Bella had brought us together with her phone call to him, Kate blew out a long breath.

"Shit, Han," she whispered, and something about the tone she used had me scowling and looking up at my reflection again. "You sure he's just a friend?"

I searched my own eyes, feeling the direct hit of that very question—the one I'd tried to avoid asking myself at every turn.

"What else could he possibly be?" I asked instead, my cheeks suddenly warm.

"I don't know, but the way you talk about him." She sucked in a breath, making a funny noise in the back of her throat when she sighed again. "That's some reverential shit right there."

"Hey, I speak about you the exact same way."

"Bullshit."

"He's *just* a friend, Kate. One that's good to me."

"Okay, fine, but I'm going to be the pain in the ass who states the obvious here. Be careful with those kind-faced, big-hearted boys. They're the ones that turn from friends to heartbreakers in a minute, and your heart has already taken a pounding. I'd hate to see you have to survive another."

"It's not like that. Can't I have a friend who's a guy? One who looks after me and makes me feel…" I trailed off just as a hammer of betrayal hit me square in the gut.

"Makes you feel what?"

"Like I could actually learn to be happy again. Go back to the old me. Live a little."

"Well, when you put it like that."

"I promise this isn't anything more," I said, pushing down on that twisted gut again. "It's just nice to have someone in my life close by. Someone out of the spotlight. Someone—"

"I get it, Han. I do, and I'm sorry. I was being a judgmental prick even questioning you about it."

"You were being a friend. A good one. In fact, there's only one thing you could do to be a better friend than you already are."

"Oh, yeah? What's that?"

"Move to LA. I'm tired of not seeing you."

Kate laughed, breaking any awkwardness between us, and as the conversation bled into something else, I didn't take my eyes away from my reflection.

I almost expected Cole to appear beside me, shaking his head, his face filled with disappointment because everyone in this room could see it clearly…

Kate had been right.

I spoke about Logan with far too much reverence, and I didn't know how to stop.

nineteen

Logan

Nothing had worked.

The fighting. The running. The skipping. The sparring. The sweating. None of it.

No matter how much I tried to clear my head, all I could see were Hannah's eyes staring up at me like I was some kind of fucking hero while she told me I couldn't possibly save everyone.

For two days, it haunted me in my dreams. It plagued my every waking thought. No matter how many times I considered calling her to have a conversation and get the awkwardness out of the way, I couldn't do it.

The texts she'd sent had been the final nail in the coffin, reminding me everything I'd been doing was wrong. I'd made her trust me. Made her think I could be *that* guy to lend a shoulder for her to cry on, hoping it would absolve my own fucked-up guilt for even a minute, only for it to have the opposite effect.

I was ruining her...

And I couldn't stop.

I'd never understood people with addictions. Not until now. Every time I got a call to attend an overdose of any kind, I'd look into the eyes of the patient and think to myself, *why can't you just say no? This is your life you're playing with. Is it really worth it? Don't you care what you're doing to those around you?* Now, I understood all too well how someone, or something, could make you feel so damn fucking high just by looking at you, you never wanted to come back down.

That's why I'd found myself in the gym for the last two days. I'd been trying to go cold turkey, hoping that it was that easy to go through. It wasn't. Nothing worked. The urge to go to her just grew stronger.

Creed gave me the eye as I packed up my kit bag and threw it over my shoulder, brushing my free hand through my hair and feeling the sweat covering me from head to toe. Everything was soaked. I could barely pull in a sufficient breath, I'd run myself into the ground that much, desperately digging for answers.

If I didn't have answers for myself, I sure as hell didn't have them for him.

I looked away and made my way to the exit, trying to make a swift escape before anything came out of his mouth, but Creed always seemed to be one or two steps ahead, and he was blocking my path before I could find a way around it.

"I've seen many a man walk through those doors to try and exorcize their demons," he said, standing in front of me with his arms folded beneath his chest.

I looked up at him, not saying a word, my breaths still coming short and sharp.

"Most trainers wouldn't give a shit who walked in carrying baggage and who walked out with that baggage still on their shoulders, so long as they got their money at the end of it. Unfortunately for you, I'm not that guy."

When I didn't respond, he reached out and put a hand on my shoulder.

"All I'll say is this: you can fight like hell in here and give it all you've got, but as soon as you walk out of those doors, the noise will come flooding back. Trust me, kid. Take it from someone who knows." I opened my mouth to speak, only for him to cut me off. "And before you try to tell me you're fine or even tell me what's got you trying to kill yourself off, I don't want to hear it. Just know that it's okay to not be okay, but it's not okay to try and ignore it and hope it goes away. Whatever's eating away at you... deal with it. This place is good therapy, sure, but it's no magic cure."

With a tap to my shoulder, Creed winked and walked away.

Of course, my thoughts went straight to her.

I pulled out my cell from the pocket of my shorts, and Hannah's name soon stared back at me. Before I could overthink it, I hit the call button, and she answered at the same time as the cool air of the outdoors hit my warm skin, a welcome reprieve to my overworked senses.

"Logan?" she said, my name sounding like a question.

"Hey."

"You're alive then."

I climbed into the driver's seat, throwing my bag into the passenger footwell before I leaned back and exhaled. "Just about."

"I was starting to worry."

"Why?"

"I thought you might have called sooner."

"You don't have to worry about me, Hannah. I can take care

of myself."

"I don't doubt that for a second." And the way she said it, all soft and tender, made it impossible not to kick myself for not calling sooner. "It's not my business anyway. You've probably been out there trying to find that life you're searching for."

A half-hearted huff of laughter escaped me. "Nah, just spent far too much time in the gym trying to get my thoughts in order. My head got kind of noisy. I tried to shut it down for a while."

"Oh." She paused. "How did that work out for you?"

"It didn't. That's why I'm calling you."

An awkward silence lingered between the two of us before I heard her suck in a breath. "Logan, listen, I really am sorry about what I said to you that day in the kitchen. I've thought about it even more over the last couple of days, and I can't believe what a stupid thing it was to come out of my mouth. It wasn't my place to make you feel—"

"Stop," I said calmly, cutting her off. "That's not why I've been quiet."

"It's not?"

"No."

Another heavy breath escaped me, and I ran my free hand over my damp forehead, knowing that one day soon, she'd need to know the truth, but not wanting to hurt the shit out of her today.

"I guess I've been questioning my intentions with you," I told her.

"What do you mean?"

"I mean you're an incredible woman, and you're living through one of the worst periods of your life. As much as I want to be there for you, there has to be boundaries."

"Like?"

"I think that's pretty obvious."

"Not to me."

"It would be easy for anyone to become addicted to your company, Hannah. I don't want to be the guy that blurs the lines. You need a friend. Someone to be there for you. I get that, and I'm more than willing to be that. But I don't want to take advantage of your beat-up heart when you're at your most vulnerable. I don't want to make you think my company is the only company that matters. I could become too used to that, and that's not fair on you or me."

"Are you saying you want me to back off?"

Hell no, my heart screamed as I closed my eyes, while the rest of me realized that this could be the perfect opportunity to part ways and leave her to rebuild her life without me…the man who'd already failed her in an unforgivable way.

"I'm saying I want what's best for you, and sometimes I'm not sure that I'm it."

"You know, Logan. Sometimes the best people for us in one particular moment aren't always the best people in general. I get you have stuff going on in that head of yours. I see it every time you look at me like you're torn between who you are and who you want to be… and that's okay. I get it. I get it because I'm the same. I always have been. I want good things for those around me, but sometimes I wonder how I'm going to give them those things when I don't even know how to give them to myself. Have you ever thought that maybe you came into my life for a reason, and maybe I came into yours for one, too. Maybe that day in the drive-thru happened because we *both* needed someone. Not just me."

I ran a hand down my face, exhaling into it before I let my head fall back against the seat. "I just don't want to put a step wrong with you, Hannah."

"Why? Because you think I'm made of glass?"

"Because I think you deserve the best and nothing less."

"And I happen to think you're the best thing for me right

now," she said, matter-of-factly. "In fact, I'm so certain of it, I've got some groceries here with your name on them. If you're free tomorrow, you're welcome to come over. I figure with enough practice, the two of us will learn not to be so awkward going forward," she said with an obvious smile. "Who knows? We may even have some fun while we're cooking, too."

There'd be no going back if I saw her again.

I wouldn't be able to stay away.

And as much as I knew I should have made an excuse, I found my own stupid smile growing at the thought of spending time with her, and I dropped my forehead to the steering wheel in defeat. "What time shall I be there?"

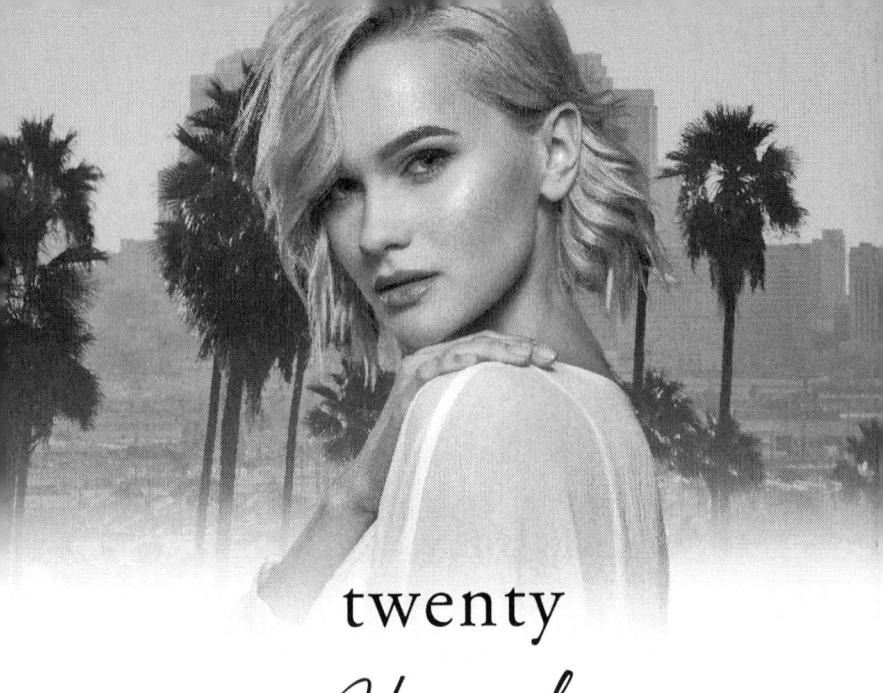

twenty

Hannah

He showed up at my door the next morning, tall, handsome, with eyes that seemed to penetrate my skin and an awkward smile that showed me he felt about as comfortable around other people as I did. He wore dark jeans and a short-sleeved white Henley shirt that highlighted every muscle he'd put under strain for the last two days.

He was gorgeous, and he didn't even know it.

"See," I said, blinking up at him. "This isn't so hard, is it?"

With a soft smirk, Logan rolled his eyes and followed me as I led him into the kitchen. Whatever cologne he wore enveloped me until I imagined laying against his chest, soaking it in. But then Cole's face appeared in my mind, reminding me that mere months after his death was far too soon to be thinking of another man that way.

I pushed those dark thoughts away and strapped on a smile when I turned back to Logan.

"Do you want anything to drink? Coffee, water...?"

He shook his head, looking around the place like he hadn't already seen it before. "I'm good, thanks. Is Bella here?"

"She's upstairs. Liv's watching over her while she cleans her bedroom." I chuckled, the memory of my daughter looking aghast when Livia and I had told her she had to take pride in her own space, and just because Livia and I could clean it, didn't mean we had to. "I'm trying not to raise a Beverly Hills brat. Starting with the small things and all."

"I doubt that's just a Beverly Hills thing. No kid wants to clean their room at six years old." He grinned, and that smile on his face almost took my breath away. I had to busy myself by turning around to open the refrigerator and start pulling things out.

"True, but in this environment, it would be easy for her to get lazy. Hell, it's easy for me. I have to argue with Liv daily about helping her out. She insists she enjoys her job."

"Does she live here with you?"

"She has her own place, and she has a room here." I grabbed some bits for a salad and turned to drop them on the kitchen island. "The last few months, since... you know... she's stayed here more than before."

"That's good. The thought of you and Bella being alone in this big house doesn't sit well with me."

I chanced a glance up at him. "I'm a big girl."

"Yeah?"

"Yeah."

"Okay, big girl, how about we do something different today, then?"

My hands stilled, not moving from a pack of fresh spinach and a red pepper. My heartbeat raced. "Different?" I asked, arching a brow.

Logan rested his hands on the island, pressing his weight down on them, making the muscles in his arms pop as he studied me. "You may have been onto something yesterday when you said we could help each other."

I searched his eyes, not sure where this was going.

"I thought about what you needed from me the most, and I think it should start with you getting out of this house."

"Today?"

"Today." He nodded.

"Logan, I—"

"—will make a million excuses as to why you can't, I know. I understand the fear, too, but you can't live like this, stuck indoors, waiting for my phone calls to be your only connection to life."

I scowled at him, hating the way my heart was racing. Was that really how he saw me?

"We can take your car—Livia and Bella, too. You need to do something besides the school drop-off and pick-up. You need to do something for yourself."

"And you think inducing panic is the way to go?"

"Just because it gets your heart racing doesn't make it a bad thing."

"Bad and dangerous are two very different things, Logan."

"You won't be in any danger. I'll be right there beside you."

"I'm afraid your argument isn't strong enough."

"Okay. How about this then." He leaned closer. "Cole would want you to get out there."

"You're an expert on Cole now?"

"No. I just know what I'd want if I left you and Bella behind, and I'd want you to find your happiness again, no matter who or what it took to get you there." His eyes searched mine. "You can do this, Hannah. I know you can. You're strong. Time to remind yourself just how strong, that's all."

His faith in me shouldn't have held so much weight, yet the way he said it left me with little to no argument, and somehow, only thirty minutes later, I sat behind the wheel of my car with Livia in the passenger seat beside me.

I'd had to speak to her privately about his idea. She'd looked at me with concern she couldn't hide, and I knew she probably questioned his intentions—I would have done the same—but after a brief explanation to her about who Logan was, how Bella already knew him, and about how he made me feel, she relented, agreeing to go along with whatever I thought was best.

That's what I loved about her. She knew when to step in and when to back off.

Bella and Logan sat in the backseat—a move he suggested, with them having the stronger blacked-out windows. As soon as Bella realized what was happening, she ran downstairs from her room and straight to the feet of Logan, thanking him for getting her out of cleaning her room.

He'd rubbed the top of her head and smiled down at her before pushing his hands into the pockets of his jeans, waiting patiently for us to get ready, like this was no big deal to any of us.

Now, with my hands curling around the steering wheel, I cast a quick glance in the rear-view to see Logan offering a small nod of encouragement—a gesture that told me I could do this. He believed in me. I had nothing to fear, but if I did fall victim to a panic attack, he'd be right there to help walk me through it.

It had been all I needed to take Bella to the one place I'd failed to take her before.

We drove into the drive-thru of The Frozen Spoon, and I glanced at Logan again for reassurance, only to see him deep in conversation with Bella in the backseat. Bella held his attention as she went on and on and on about her friends at school, telling him which friends were her ride or dies and which were actually frenemies. It scared me how grown-up she sounded at just six years old, but I couldn't help noticing the huge smile on her face as she looked up at Logan in wonder while he hung off her every word as though they were the most important ones he'd ever heard.

When it came time to order, I did so with only a slight quiver in my voice. Bella tried her luck by ordering the supersized portion of praline ice cream, and I didn't have the heart to deny or fail her a second time. I barely looked at the server as I pressed my card to her machine, and she didn't bother to look up at me, either. I was just another customer on her long-ass shift. No one special.

I could do this.

Cole had been the famous one. I'd just been his wife.

With a milkshake for me and ice creams for everyone else, I pulled out of the parking lot, releasing a huge exhale when I took a right turn, *away* from home. Logan's eyes lifted to mine in the rear-view, and he gave me a small smile that said everything he didn't want to say out loud.

Well done. I'm proud of you. Keep going.

It had been such a long time since someone else's approval had mattered to me, but his obvious pride made my heart race again, and I had to remind myself of his words only a little while earlier: *Just because it gets your heart racing doesn't make it a bad thing.*

Logan was good. A bright, unexpected light in my darkened world that I couldn't help but drift toward now. He continued to bring sides out of me that I hadn't seen in so long, and he did it with such little effort, it almost felt like some kind of twisted magic. A spell he'd cast over me that I hadn't noticed he'd made until it was too late.

With a smile on my face, I shot him a look back that said, *Thank you. I'm proud of me, too.*

"Hey, Bella," I said, shifting slightly to catch her eye.

She looked up at me with ice cream around her lips, which she tried to lick off. "Yeah?"

"Do you want to go and see the whole world?"

Her eyes lit up like I'd just lassoed the moon for her, and I knew then that Logan had been right to make me do this. For myself, sure... but mainly for my daughter.

Definitely not because it was what Cole would have wanted, though. This...

Now...

It was for us.

twenty-one

Logan

She'd surprised me.

Not when she demanded I tell her the way to the lookout point I'd driven her to not so many nights ago, but by the way her eyes sparkled when she looked back at me. I'd pushed my luck asking her to get out of the house, and then she'd pushed back, daring me to test her again with something else.

I didn't need to now. I knew she'd pass everything else. All she'd needed was a little nudge to remind herself of what she was capable of.

Bella talked and talked and talked the whole way to the lookout point, and I soaked up her happiness, unable to stop myself from smiling at seeing her acting so... *normal*. When we finally reached our destination and Hannah parked the car, it didn't take long for Bella to begin to climb out.

"You coming to see the view, Mr. Logan?" she said as she struggled to push herself out of the high seat.

"Like I'd miss it."

"Race ya!" She beamed.

Of course, I let her win. The kid needed all the wins she could get right now.

The sun had been diluted by the smog that left a constant haze over LA, and even though I preferred it up here at night, there was no denying the beauty of it in that moment when I walked to the edge of the cliff, grateful for the small barrier that stopped us from worrying too much about Bella's safety.

"It's so beautiful," she cooed, her eyes wide as she looked out at the city. "It really is the whole world, isn't it?"

"Sure looks like it, doesn't it?" I said, watching how she tracked every building, every street, every palm tree, and streetlight in sight. "You've never seen anything like this before?"

"Nope. Daddy took us to a lot of places with his band when I was smaller, but he liked to keep me in a *lot* of hotel rooms, too. Sometimes we'd travel, and it felt like I was still at home."

"I'm sorry, kid."

"For what?"

"I... don't know."

"Then, don't be sorry, Mr. Logan."

I looked down at her, dressed in a pretty coral summer dress, her long hair braided, dangling down her small back. For such a young girl, she had a weirdly grown-up attitude to everything thrown her way—a price she no doubt paid for having to grieve the love of her life at such a young age.

I fucking hated it for her.

"Just call me Logan, Bella," I said. "Calling me Mr. makes me sound old."

A small laugh bubbled from her chest. "You *are* old."

"Hey!" I shot back, feigning offense.

"Bella," Hannah chided, coming up behind us slowly and standing next to Bella. "That's no way to talk about our senior citizens."

My brows rose. "Oh, really?" I narrowed my eyes at her, unable to stop the smirk tugging at my mouth. "Remind me, Miss Youth, how old exactly are you?"

"She's twenty-nine. Mommy turns thirty just before Christmas. Daddy made fun of her for it on her last birthday, even though he was thirty-two," Bella chipped in, her arms resting on the railing in front of her as she propped her chin on the back of her hands.

• "Thank you for *that,* daughter." Hannah shook her head but couldn't stop the smile that rose to life, despite the mention of Cole, as she looked out at the city in front of her and blew out a breath. "What about you, Logan? Seems only fair that you tell us your age since you know ours."

"How old do you think I am?"

She glanced at me, studying my face in its entirety until she said, "Forty-two."

"Wow. Our friendship is over."

She laughed, a real look of happiness taking over. It was only a second or two. A pure moment in time where I caught a glimpse of who she could be and who she probably was before she had her world ripped out from beneath her feet.

It made her impossibly more beautiful.

"I know how old he is," Bella said, her focus still on the skyline.

"You do?" Hannah said.

"Yeah, he's thirty."

I glanced down at her, nudging her with my thigh. "Good

guess, short stuff."

"How did you know that, bug?" her mom asked.

"It was obvious. You and Logan are the same. The only difference is one's a boy, and one's a girl."

"What do you mean?" Hannah smiled with curiosity.

Bella shrugged like she didn't really care about the words that were about to fall out of her mouth. "You're both warm people. You smile at the same things. Frown at the same things. Listen to me the same way. It made sense you'd be the same age." Her nose wrinkled, and she scratched at it. "And the boy always has to be older than the girl in stories, so that means he's thirty."

"Stories?" Hannah asked.

"Yeah. Like the princess and her prince stories."

At that, Hannah's smile dropped, and a look of pain mixed with confusion creased her brow as she turned back to the city, lost in her own head.

I opened my mouth to say something—make light of it and break Hannah from whatever thoughts had taken away that spark in her eyes—but quickly closed it again when another voice interrupted the conversation.

"Hey," Livia said, slightly out of breath, as she came up behind Bella and placed her hands on her shoulders. "Sorry about that. Had to take a call." Livia glanced at me, and I saw the apprehension on her face. "Didn't miss anything, did I?"

I shook my head and turned away from her, taking in the view like everybody else. "Not a thing."

But I could feel the weight of her stare upon me.

The air of judgment, too.

Livia didn't trust me, and I had to be okay with that. I didn't trust myself, either. At least with her around, I could be certain that Hannah had someone looking out for her. Someone who cared and would always do what was best because I couldn't be that person anymore.

The best thing would be for me to walk away and never come back, and I couldn't fucking do it no matter how hard I tried. And that made me a selfish bastard.

It only took one last look at Hannah to know I was right.

Wisps of her short blonde hair blew across her face. She pushed them back behind her ear, and the faintest blush-pink rose on her cheeks before she turned my way and our eyes met again as though she hadn't been expecting to catch me staring so openly.

The pull I felt toward her grew stronger—a tangible force I couldn't ignore even if I wanted to.

Maybe Bella was onto something.

Maybe her mom and I were the same.

***

By the time we made it back to Hannah's place, she seemed like a different person.

She didn't look all around her when she opened up the electric gates from the comfort of her car. The frown lines between her brows had softened, and she smiled freely, as though the air outside her home had given her new life.

Bella had fallen asleep in the back—her head lolled to one side while the seatbelt kept her body upright. When Hannah went to lift her out, I offered to do it instead. Carefully carrying people from one place to the next was practically a part of my job description.

Hannah had looked up at me with those bright eyes of hers, and for the first time in a few hours, the caution had returned until she must have found whatever she'd been looking for, and she gave me a nod of approval.

As carefully as I could, I picked Bella out of her seat and

began to carry her inside. Her head fell against my chest, right next to my racing heart, and she curled her body into me before she wrapped her arms around my neck. The way she'd no doubt done with Cole a thousand times and never would again.

Yet another stab of betrayal hit me square in the gut, all too aware that he should be the one doing this, not me.

I'm just trying to do the right thing here, man. I know this is fucked up.

The ghost of him lingered again once we were inside. The urge to hand Bella over to her mom and get the hell out of there was strong, but then Livia's eyes caught mine as I walked to the wide, spiral staircase, and a need to prove myself took over.

"Where am I taking her?" I asked either of them.

Livia stood in front of me by the entrance to the open-plan kitchen while Hannah traipsed somewhere behind. I wasn't sure of her proximity until her gentle hand on the small of my back had me looking to my left, where she came around, a motherly vision, pointing up the staircase.

"There's a reason I call her lazy bug. She adores her naps. Her bedroom is the last one on the left. Want me to show you?"

"Please," I said, doing everything I could to ignore the looks Livia no doubt sent my way.

Bella didn't flinch as we climbed the stairs and walked down the long, white corridor that led to a huge floor-to-ceiling arched window at the very end. Her room sat to the left, and Hannah turned to me with a small smile before she pushed through into it, with Bella and me following closely behind.

There were no pink walls like I'd expected. Everything had been decorated in whites, beiges, and creams, with hints of pastel colors strategically placed here and there. In the center of the room, against the far wall, was a bed far too big for a little girl, filled with teddies and cushions she'd surely get lost in. A white princess domed canopy draped down from the ceiling, which Hannah quickly pushed back, opening the bed up and allowing me to lay Bella down from one side of the mattress while Hannah tucked her in from the other.

It was impossible to miss the way Bella tried to cling to me that little bit longer when I first tried to let her go.

"Easy, Bella. Shh," I whispered, soothing her when her arms eventually released me, and she curled into herself on the mattress, beneath the comforter. "You're okay."

Hannah caught it, too, and her brows furrowed as though the sight of it had caused her physical pain.

That's the thing about dying. It's not the fact that your existence fades away to nothing that hurts the most. It's knowing the ones you're leaving behind have to deal with a thousand different moments like this, where small, insignificant things suddenly become the greatest heartaches to exist, causing a slicing pain no one can ever truly prepare for.

I hated to see her suffer, and I hated even more that there was nothing I could do about it now.

Once we'd tucked Bella in, Hannah and I stood over her bed, and our eyes connected. We stayed there looking at each other for far too long, neither of us knowing what the hell to say. The moment felt far more intimate than I was comfortable with, and all my thoughts came crashing together until my mouth moved without my permission.

"I'm not trying to replace him, Hannah," I whispered. "I swear."

"I know," she said on a heavy exhale.

We both looked at Bella again, who had curled her hands around the first teddy she'd been able to find—a lemon-colored bear as big as her torso. She nuzzled into it, and as I watched her, I found I had something else to say to Cole, too:

What the fuck could possibly have been wrong with you to need to chase a high higher than this, you fucking fool?

***

Livia made herself scarce, telling Hannah she'd chosen to stay at her own place that night... much to my relief. I didn't dislike the woman, but I didn't particularly enjoy the way I felt more exposed around her, either. Like any minute now, she'd walk up to me slowly, point a finger my way, and say, *You're the reason he didn't make it, aren't you? What are you trying to achieve here? Why are you doing this?*

I lingered in the entryway of the kitchen, not knowing whether to go or stay as Hannah walked around the island to grab herself a glass of water. Neither of us said anything until three or four minutes had passed, and she turned to me, an almost-empty glass in hand.

"You don't need to feel guilty for doing things he can no longer do," she said, her voice quiet yet somehow strong. "He made his choice, and we weren't it."

"I know."

"You don't, Logan, but that's okay." She smiled sadly. "I understand this is weird for you."

"It's not."

"Stop lying," she whispered, and those two words shouldn't have pinched at my conscience as much as they did.

The tension between us grew, and I was about to make my excuses to leave, only for Hannah to take a step closer toward me.

"Don't go," she said.

"What?" I frowned.

"I want you to stay. Even if you think you shouldn't, which I can tell you do, I want you here. Just for a little while longer. I don't want to be alone tonight, Logan."

I inhaled through flared nostrils, releasing it slowly. "You want me to stay?"

"Is that a problem?"

"You tell me. This is your home, Hannah."

"Which is why I'm asking you to enjoy it with me for a while."

"Do you think that's a good idea?"

"You tell me," she countered, a small smirk growing right alongside the spark in her eyes.

I knew this was a mistake after what had happened in Bella's bedroom, but I was no longer able to deny Hannah anything she needed if I had the power to deliver it. How could I possibly leave her after she told me she didn't want to be alone tonight?

I couldn't.

I was a slave at her mercy, willing to serve and provide whatever she demanded from me, and that shit should have scared me far more than it did.

"Okay," I said, my own smile growing. "I can stay a while… if you insist."

"Good, because I do." She turned around and walked across the kitchen, bending down to another small glass-fronted fridge I hadn't noticed before.

She pulled out a bottle of white wine and held it up to me.

"Glasses are in the big cupboard to your right. Grab two, will you?" Then she sauntered away, pushing back the glass patio doors until they opened up the kitchen to the outdoors fully, and she took a right to where the seating area waited underneath the canopy, keeping her—us—tucked away from the world.

I closed my eyes for ten seconds, giving myself some time to try and think of more reasons why I shouldn't get too comfortable here or in her life, but two minutes later, I walked outside to meet her, anyway.

Two wineglasses in hand and not a single reason in mind strong enough to make me leave her life that night.

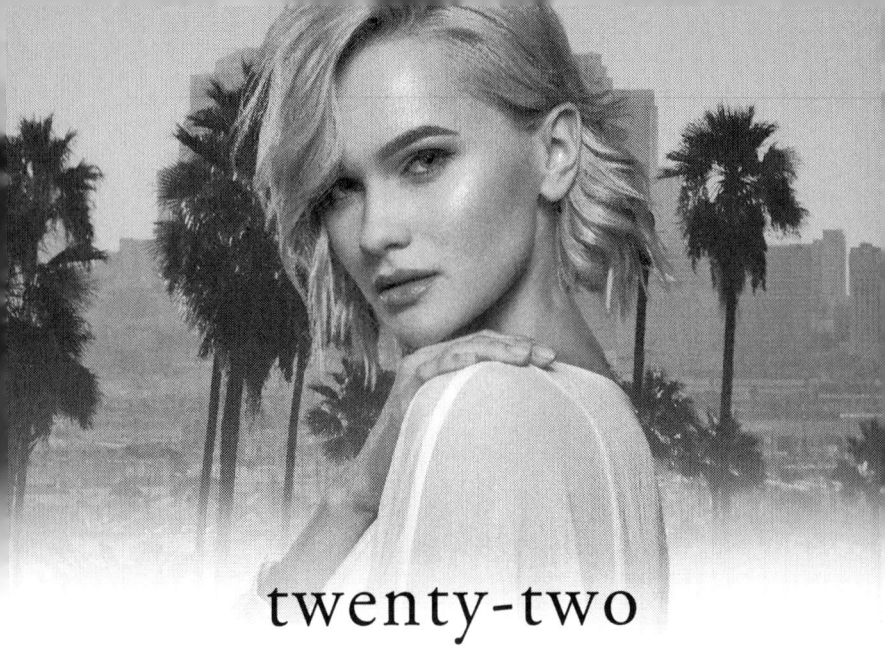

twenty-two

Hannah

I'm not trying to replace him.

I couldn't get those few words out of my head. I didn't want him to replace Cole in Bella's life, but I couldn't help the way my heart had stuttered seeing him take care of my daughter and imagining having someone like Logan to do the small things with—the things that mattered the most.

Watching a strong, capable, sober man laying my daughter down with such tenderness and care had opened something in me I thought would never see the light of day again: the desire to have another guy in my home. One like Logan, who happened to be everything Cole hadn't been. I didn't have to spend years in his company to figure that out. Cole had been an unstoppable force from day one, tearing through life, taking what he wanted, when he wanted it, and everyone else obediently fell in line because that was the kind of power he held over them all... including me.

Especially me.

Logan, however, wasn't an unstoppable force. He was the calm air a person soaked up in a stormy sea. He was the rock-solid hand needed when traversing the edge of a rocky cliff. He was the gentle truth not many of us wanted to hear... that people like him—good, strong, selfless people—were who we should focus on. Ones who stared into your soul, desperate to find what we tried so hard to hide from the rest of the world just so they could understand you better. So that when you spoke, they were sure to hear every word.

Logan heard every one of mine, even the ones I didn't say aloud.

That didn't stop him from acting a little awkwardly when he sat down opposite me. I poured him a glass of wine, which he barely touched, while I drained the first glass far too quickly, only to pour myself another.

"You're not going to sit there and make me drink this all alone, are you?" I asked, looking up at him through eyes I hoped didn't betray me by showing their attraction.

"Wouldn't dream of it," he said, reaching for his glass and taking a long sip, his eyes never leaving mine until he saw my satisfied smile come to life.

Eventually, once he began to relax in my company again, we talked about mundane things for a while before we moved on to more serious stuff, like his parents, and where he grew up. Originally from Nevada, his family moved to Michigan when he was ten years old to escape the men his father had run up a huge amount of gambling debt with. Logan told me how that gambling had affected his dad's entire life until he'd passed away just a year before, leaving his mother back home with a sibling he had very little in common with. A younger sister who he said acted as though she knew everything, had seen everything, and quite enjoyed being the favorite of the family.

I was fascinated—enraptured, hanging off his every word, and only more determined to find out every single thing about him as long as he kept talking so openly this way. I wanted to dig deep. To find out if Logan had any bad inside of him at all, or if he really was made up of nothing but goodness and warmth, which were all he'd ever shown me so far.

"How often do you go back to visit them in Michigan?" I asked, my legs tucked up under my ass, and my cheek against my fist as my elbow rested on a thick, gray cushion beside me.

Logan looked at me, glass of wine in hand. "I don't."

"Never?"

"Not if I can help it. I find it hard to go back there after everything that happened."

"Twelve years is a long time to be away from home, Logan."

"Home isn't a state for me."

"Where is then?"

"Wherever I feel like I can be myself, I suppose."

"And that's here in LA?"

"For now," he said simply. "I figured I could hide away in this overpopulated city while still doing some good. There are enough people here to keep me busy, and when I help others, I feel better about everything else."

"You really do, don't you?"

Instead of answering, he took a sip of his wine, draining the glass only to lean over to reach for the bottle and hold it up to me, asking for my permission to take more.

"Go for it. What's mine is yours." Realizing how strong that sounded, and noticing his raised brow, I added with a smile, "While you're my guest, at least."

"Damn. I was about to stake claim on the Range Rover."

"You can have it. It's not really my thing."

"Score."

"Stop deflecting," I said when he sat back again, resting an ankle across his opposing knee and letting his wineglass sit upon that.

He looked good.

Really good.

Too good.

"What am I deflecting from?" he asked, bringing my thoughts back on track.

"Telling me why you never go back to Michigan."

He looked off to the side, exhaling heavily before he brought his eyes back to mine. "People say death is inevitable. Like we should all be there, ready and waiting for it, holding a placard, and welcoming its arrival, no matter how much we dread it along the way. They put a timestamp on grief once it's been and gone, too. *Time's a great healer. You'll learn to live again.* All those cliché, bullshit remarks we're all guilty of using. Especially me with what I do…" He trailed off, glancing down at his glass and running a finger around the rim of it slowly. "But some deaths… we're not meant to move on from them, and I got so sick and tired of people telling me that losing my best friend wasn't my fault. That Dale made the choice. That there wasn't anything I could have done. So, I decided to prove them all wrong and do something instead. Because there *was* something that could be done. I believed that then. I still believe it now."

His eyes drifted back up to mine, and he let his hand fall from the rim of his glass back down into his lap.

"My family and old friends back home aren't do-ers, Hannah. They're 'don't do-ers'. They meet a problem with complications—with all the things that will get in the way. They linger around in misery and their strict, unwavering views on *everything*. Spend enough time with that, and it really drags a person down. When Dale died, I realized how short life was, so I decided to be the change. To be the person who said that yeah, death can affect me, but I can also fight against it. I can pick up a sword, swing it around, and at least scare the bastard off for a while. I couldn't bring Dale back. I couldn't do any of the stuff to protect him the way I should have all those years ago… but I can sure as shit do it for him now. But every time I went home, I'd get dragged back down again. My family didn't want me to be a paramedic. That was no good to them, and they reminded me of it every time I visited. The best thing to do? Stop visiting."

I frowned. "What did they want you to be instead?"

Logan licked his bottom lip, dragging his teeth over it. "I had everything I needed to be a pro-football player."

My mouth parted, and I stared at him, blinking only once. "Are you serious?"

"Apparently, I made a pretty good quarterback."

"Logan…"

"Don't," he said, his eyes piercing mine. "I didn't want it. They did, Mom and Dad. It wasn't my dream. If I got dropped, I didn't care. I liked football, but I didn't *live* it. Dad did, though. Any game he could bet on, he would. He planned to make a fortune out of me until I could set him up for life."

"Was it going that far? Could you really have gone pro?"

"In a heartbeat."

I searched his eyes, looking for regret or nostalgia, only to find a brick wall closed off by the truth in his heart. He hadn't wanted the fame and fortune he could have so easily gotten through sport. Instead, he'd wanted to drive around in the city, saving the lives of strangers, and somehow his family didn't *respect* that?

"They sound like assholes," was all I could think to say.

"At my father's funeral, Mom turned to me and said, *'if only he hadn't had so much pressure in his life. If only he'd have had the money he could have had if you'd played football... maybe his heart would have been stronger'.*"

"She *blamed* you?"

"Still does."

"Do you blame yourself?"

His eyes held mine, a small scowl forming. "Not about his death, no."

"You shouldn't about anyone's. You aren't responsible for the choices other people make."

Logan scratched at his eyebrow. "Since we're doing family stories... Your turn."

"What do you want to know?"

"About you? Everything."

I chuckled to myself. "Be careful there, Logan. Everyone thinks they want to know my story until they hear it. It isn't pretty."

"Why would it need to be?"

"Because not everyone actually wants to listen to bad truths, do they? They ask you about your life, then look at you like you're stupid when you start telling them how shit it was. It's like these people ask you to tell them everything then silently beg you to shut up and give them nothing but fake pleasantries and a wholesome, happy upbringing they can cling to that will make them feel better."

"Do you think I'm one of those people?"

"No," I said quickly, not needing a second to think about it. "I don't."

"Then tell me everything, and if you think I'm not listening, tell me that, too."

So, I did.

I told him about the life I'd had before Cole, and how I'd been moved from home to home, trailer park to trailer park, as my parents fought constantly, breaking up one week only to get back together the next. I told him how their love reigned supreme above all else, especially their daughter, and how I'd been neglected by the two of them until one day, at the age of fourteen, they disappeared out together and never came home. Logan listened, focused, as I told him how they'd had enough of carting around their excess baggage, and child protective services had found me not long after with nothing but the clothes on my back and empty kitchen cupboards to show for it.

After that, I got passed around from foster family to foster family in Seattle. Some of them kind and comforting, others vicious and cold. At the last high school I attended while staying with one of those families, I met Cole, and that's when my life changed completely.

"Cole had been given up for adoption the moment he was born. His adoptive parents weren't the best for him, but they weren't the worst, either, and it suited him not having the blood bonds because he thought he'd have no problem leaving them behind once he tore off to find fame with the band. Not long after we left Seattle together, those adoptive parents died in a car crash on the freeway, and in Cole's eyes, that made life even easier. We were now free to go wherever we wanted, whenever we wanted."

"That's cold."

"He could be like that." I scowled, remembering the fights we'd had and how I'd warned him not to be so thoughtless. But Cole had somehow found a way around it, like always, and he convinced me that he didn't mean to sound heartless but the only love he cared about now was the one he had for me. Like a lovesick fool, I'd ignored every red flag flashed before me, and I'd believed him.

"And your parents never tried to track you down again?" Logan asked with a frown.

"No."

"Cole's biological parents?"

"They only wanted to know him once his name was in lights with Envy-98."

"Jesus." Logan ran his free hand over his mouth before dropping it back into his lap and leaning forward. He held the stem of the wineglass in both hands, twirling it around as he looked right into my eyes. "So, you really have done these last few months completely alone?"

"It's what I wanted."

"That's not what I asked."

"I've had Liv—"

"Apart from Livia," he cut me off. "There really isn't anybody else you trust?"

"Nope. Although I suppose there's you now."

Logan searched my eyes a moment longer before he stared down at his feet. "Damn, Hannah," he whispered. "You live like an island out here, stranded with no one to keep *you* afloat because you're the one doing all the work."

"Don't you dare feel sorry for me."

His head snapped up again. "Sorry for you? I'm admiring the shit out of you right now, and I'm goddamn angry that there are far too many people having kids just to hate them, pressure them, use them, fuck them up, and then abandon them."

"Not me," I said with a sad smile. "I had my daughter to love and raise for the rest of my life. Even if I have to do that alone now, I'll do it. Just watch me. She'll be the most cared for girl in the history of daughters. She'll have so much love, she won't know what to do with it."

"You're an incredible woman, Hannah Moore."

"I happen to think you're pretty incredible, too, Mr. Logan."

"Hey, that's my name for him," Bella said behind him, her little body coming into view as she stepped out of the kitchen, rubbing a sleepy eye and yawning out the rest. "He's just your friend Logan, Mommy."

My friend Logan. She wasn't wrong.

The guy slowly saving my life without even realizing it.

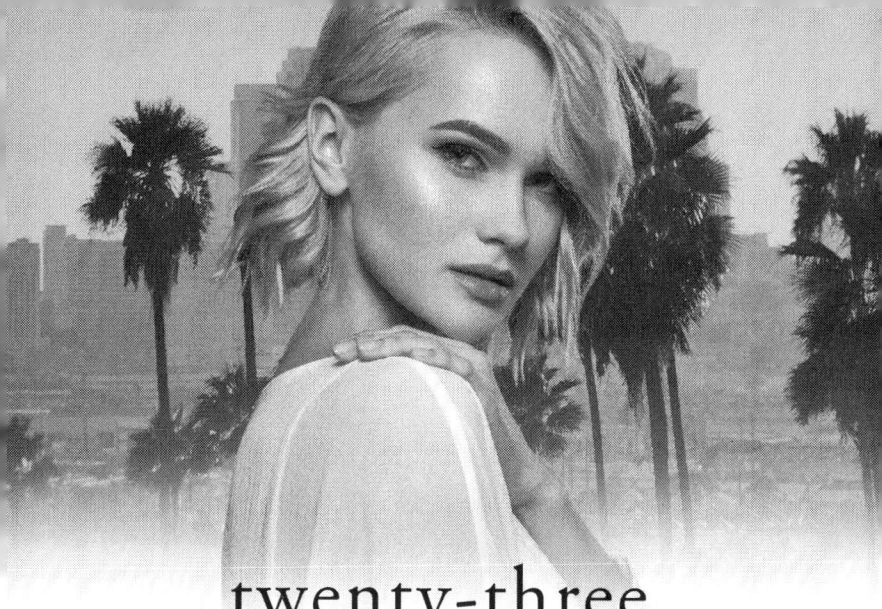

twenty-three

Hannah

"How do you feel about heading back to work tomorrow?" I asked Logan, my phone pressed to my ear while I lay on my side in bed. It had already turned midnight, yet we'd been speaking for the last hour.

Just like we'd done for three nights in a row since the night we'd drank wine and shared truths before he'd eventually left, even though I'd found myself wanting him to stay longer.

Logan made a noise in the back of his throat, and I imagined him running his hand through his hair while he lay in his bed and stared up at the ceiling. I tried to imagine what his bedroom looked like, but I quickly pushed it away because thinking of that made me think of the other things I was trying to avoid.

"Don't remind me about it," he grunted.

"I thought you'd be happy."

"Turns out *not* living to work isn't as bad as I thought it would be."

"Look at you, finding a life."

"I hardly call going to the Farmer's Market once or twice or spending my days in the gym, a life," he said with a gentle laugh.

"You don't know how lucky you are."

He let a heartbeat pass before saying, "You know you're going to have to let them get that first picture of you sooner or later, don't you? People only chase what tries to run. If you stop running, they'll have no need to chase."

"All of that sounds good in theory, but you're either made to be on the cover of a blog post or you're not. And I... am not. Whatever's printed, it'll be a lie. There's no profit in truth, and I'm sick of being the scandal that gets other people rich while turning me into a walking, talking ball of anxiety."

"What scandal could they possibly have on you?"

You, I thought. They'd twist that up into something juicy and make a three-course meal out of it, painting me as the heartless woman bringing a man into her life so soon after her husband's death because they didn't know the truth. How our marriage had been quietly falling apart before it even really started. They didn't understand how you could love someone with your whole heart, but also need to run as far away from them as you could possibly get for the sake of your own sanity.

"Who knows?" I said instead. "It's more about what scandal they have on Cole that will come back to bite me in the ass along the way."

"Did that happen a lot...?" The *'when he was alive'* went unsaid.

"All the time."

"I'm sorry."

"Me, too, really. Somewhere along the way, I got dragged into this lifestyle and was told it was a good idea. Now that person who dragged me here is gone, and without him, I don't know what I'm still doing here or where I belong anymore."

"The sooner you learn, the sooner life will be on your terms again."

"What are you suggesting?"

"That it's time to take back control of your life. All those things you think you got wrong, put them right. All those things you wanted to do but never did, do them. You're literally the captain of your own ship again. Steer that boat wherever the hell you want it to go."

I rolled onto my back, running my free hand through my hair. He'd planted too many thoughts in my head for me to choose one to focus on, leaving me with nothing to do but groan in frustration. "Boats, Logan? Really?"

"Oh shit. Did I just try giving you a motivational speech? I hate those." He laughed.

"A cheesy motivational speech, too. I may have to rethink our friendship."

"I wouldn't blame you. You don't need that kind of bullshit in your life."

With a soft sigh, I hugged the phone closer to me as I said, "Actually, Logan… I think I do."

***

The next morning, I stared at my reflection in the freestanding cast iron mirror that rested against the wall next to the bed.

My outfit was fairly simple: black yoga leggings, white cotton tank top, white sneakers, all finished off with a black cap, and my short hair tucked behind my ears. I pushed my shades over my eyes, aiming to be stealthy about the entire thing, even though I finally wanted someone—anyone—to get the shot. Logan's pep talks the night before had stayed with me all through the night, making me open my eyes with a renewed determination to take back control.

I could do this. The only thing standing in the way of me was me, and it was time to grow a spine and get out of my own path from this moment on. It was time to remember who I'd once been—the girl who'd already faced the worst thing she could have dreamed of when her parents walked away and left her. The rest, I could handle. I would handle them all again now, no matter the cost, and no matter what anxieties tried to trick me into believing they were the ones in control.

Livia had taken Bella to school for me that morning, and I kissed my daughter on the lips with full force, squishing her cheeks together as I held her in my hands. My voice may have told her to have a good day, but the thoughts in my mind told her that a newer version of our lives would have started by the time she came home.

A text alert came through on my cell, and I picked it up from the bed, seeing Logan's name waiting for me.

LOGAN
Remember. You're braver than you think you are.

ME
You're getting good at these.

LOGAN
Are they working?

With a smile on my face, I sent him a picture of my reflection, showing him my outfit and the fact that I already had my sneakers on, followed by a thumbs up emoji.

LOGAN

Good girl.

It was with those two words that my smile faded.

Cole used to say that to me whenever I did what he demanded, like it was a doggy treat I got for being good and learning to fall in line. For a moment, it made me wonder if I was making the same mistake again without realizing it, following another man's orders like some dumb little puppet who didn't have a mind of her own.

But then I remembered how our call had ended the night before, and how it hadn't been Logan who'd told me what to do. He'd simply given me a nudge to remember who I had the capability of becoming. Who I'd never really pushed myself to be yet in the last almost-thirty years of my life.

All of this had been my idea. *My* plan, which Logan had simply listened to and told me he supported if I thought I was doing the right thing.

Another text alert brought my attention back to the screen.

LOGAN

That smile looks good on you too.

How he had the power to tie my stomach up in knots without even trying, I didn't know, but I didn't have too much time to reflect on how he made me feel before another text came through.

LOGAN

Be safe. Any trouble, get out of there. Don't let anyone corner you.

ME

You're starting to sound like you really care, Logan Thomas.

LOGAN

No shit.

With a chuckle to myself, I tucked my cell into the waistband of my leggings, and I made my way downstairs to the garage. It wasn't long before I was driving through the streets of Beverly Hills, heading for the one place I sought solace but hadn't allowed myself to go to since losing my husband.

I went to Malibu Beach.

He'd always hated the ocean, and he despised any form of sand. It had been a dream of mine to wake up to both things every morning for the rest of my life, but because Cole had hated it, living on or even by the beach had never been an option. Even going for walks out there with Bella had been out of the question.

The thing that gave me joy, he denied so easily.

Now he didn't have that power anymore, and it was time for me to figure out what *I* wanted again.

My stomach twisted the moment I parked the car, trying to convince me to turn around and head back home. My gut didn't stop in its efforts to destroy any confidence I'd managed to muster, but all I had to do was read through Logan's text messages again, and imagine his smile and nod of encouragement, and I found myself climbing out of the car and slamming the door shut before I made my way to the beach, just like we'd planned.

The soothing sound of the waves crashing against the shore was an instant tonic to my soul. The moment I took off my sneakers and let my toes sink into the sand, I looked up to the sky, closed my eyes, and I inhaled a deep, healing breath.

And for the first time in years, I remembered what it felt like to be alive.

***

DISTRAUGHT WIDOW OF COLE NEWMAN SPOTTED OUT IN PUBLIC FOR THE FIRST TIME SINCE HER HUSBAND'S UNTIMELY DEATH EARLIER THIS YEAR.

I scrolled through the article, taking in the pictures they'd caught of me looking wistful as I stared out at the ocean, inhaling every breath as though each one was a hidden treasure I wanted to lock away and keep to myself for eternity.

It had been an amazing hour of calm energy, self-love, and freedom, yet they chose to see me as distraught.

It always amazed me how two very different things could be pulled from the same image and how two different audiences could take whatever message they needed from it, whether that message was accurate or not. But still, the deed had been done. My face was out there now, and I'd been in control of when and where it happened. A strange sense of empowerment ran through me, knowing I had all I needed to do that again if I wanted to, as many times as I felt necessary. I didn't need my husband to write the script for me. The pen had been transferred to my hand, along with the paper I was bound to write upon.

Scrolling back up to the article's title, I read over it one last time, and I whispered to myself, "I may always be widow of Cole Newman, now… but my name is Hannah Moore, and don't you fuckers ever forget that again."

twenty-four

Logan

"I'm starting to worry," Jerry said, glancing between the road and me as he drove the ambulance back from our last callout, where we'd been turned away when the patient refused to be taken to the hospital to get checked over.

I'd been back on the job a week already, which had dragged like hell. I never thought I'd miss being on vacation. I never thought I'd dread having to go to work—the thing that had given me purpose and kept me going for the last ten years of my life.

I glanced up at Jerry with my cell in my hands. "Worry about what?"

"You," he said, nodding to the phone. "You're on that thing at any given opportunity. Before your leave, you barely ever looked at it. Sometimes I wondered why you even had a phone. You never answered calls or texts. Now, though…"

"What?"

"Well, I'm starting to believe you actually went out there and got a life, LT."

"Pfft. I don't know what you're talking about."

"A defensive response is usually a sign of a truth you want to keep hidden, too."

"Oh, fuck off." I smirked.

He laughed. "At least I know I'm on the right track. Now, I've just got to find out who it is that's gotten under your skin so quickly."

The hair on the back of my neck rose, and a tingle of dread ran down my spine before I rolled my eyes at him, lifted my ass off the passenger seat, and pushed my cell back into my pants pocket before I sat down again.

"That better?" I asked with a brow raised.

He shrugged like he couldn't care less. "The next time you're smiling at your phone like a dumbass, though, don't expect me to keep quiet about it."

"You're an idiot," I said with a feigned huff of laughter, turning away from him in the hope he didn't see anything I didn't want or need him to see.

Hannah's smile flashed through my mind, and I had to push it away as I rested my elbow on the window and pressed a knuckle to my mouth. The streets of Los Angeles whizzed by, but I didn't take much of them in. Not the dark, murky poverty that sat on display for the rich to ignore or the way we quickly slipped into the bright, airy, palm-tree-lined streets of the Hollywood movies.

In such a short space of time, Hannah Moore had become my only focus. I wasn't sure how I'd let it happen, and I didn't know how the hell I was ever going to get out of it. Not without far too many people getting hurt. Especially her.

Every scenario possible played out in my mind, morning, noon, and night.

What if I confessed?

Maybe she'd forgive me. Maybe she'd understand.

Maybe she'd stare into my eyes for a second before she screamed and told me to get out of her life forever. Maybe she'd hate me for the rest of time.

I secretly hoped for both outcomes. I wanted her to listen and believe that I never intended to lie to her for so long, but I also needed her to punish me for doing what I'd done. Her forgiveness would almost hurt more than her hatred.

Jerry turned the wheel and took a right. "You think that last patient who refused our help will be our next callout or what?"

"No doubt about it. I give her thirty minutes, max."

You could almost set your watch by it with these people— the kind who ran their bodies into the ground, only for those same bodies to finally falter. Then they refused the care they so desperately needed, knowing they had no medical insurance or savings for medical bills when every spare cent they had went up their nose or got injected into their veins.

It was a vicious cycle far too many were caught up in, and the world had no solution other to keep making more of that toxic shit that destroyed good people so easily.

Sure enough, twenty-two minutes later, the call came through letting us know the woman had crashed again. Jerry turned on the sirens and spun the truck around in the middle of the street, making me cling onto the Oh Shit handle above my head until he straightened us out, and we flew down the boulevard to save someone's life again.

It was the worst possible time for my cell to vibrate in my pocket, and I side-eyed Jerry to see if he'd noticed before I pulled it out and tried to take a discreet look at the screen.

HANNAH

Thought-provoking quote incoming. Bear with me here.

HANNAH

I've realized it's possible to miss someone you barely know when they're not with you because that someone, somehow, brings a piece of you back to yourself that you'd never meant to let go.

A small smile tugged at my lips. Her face had been all over the Internet since she dared to step out into real life again, only five days ago. Most of the reports had been positive, too, showing respect for a young woman and mother who'd lost a husband and father to her daughter. I'd been drunk on pride the moment she'd called me to tell me where she'd been and how it had gone. She'd been giddy on her success for days after, while I'd been unable to stop looking at one picture of her in particular where she stood facing the ocean, her feet in the water, her baseball cap and sneakers in her hands, and her head tilted back slightly as though she'd closed her eyes and lost herself to the temporary calm she found herself in.

A moment like that had been all I'd ever wanted for her.

My only wish? That I could have been there standing beside her to see it for myself.

Another message came through before I had a chance to respond to the first two.

HANNAH

Thank you, Logan.

ME

Quit thanking me all the time. I've told you. I don't need it.

HANNAH

You're not the boss of me. 😊

"Get your head in the game, kid. We're almost there," Jerry said, making me push my cell back into my pants pocket, and stare straight ahead as I tried not to think of all the things that I'd do to her if she'd let me be the boss of her for just one night.

One hour.

One chance.

But I had to let those thoughts go the moment we jumped out of the ambulance, gathered our medical kits, and we ran back into the house we'd not long since left, hoping for a better reception than the first time. Hoping we'd be allowed to do our jobs.

Thankfully, knowing she was finally out of options, the woman and her boyfriend co-operated. We transported her to the nearest medical center without too much interference, and while Jerry drove us through the streets as quickly as he could, I pretended to be friends with the people in the back of the truck, keeping them on side until the time came to pass them over to be someone else's problem.

It had always been the best way to get them to comply; to act as though you were genuinely interested before you led them to a place they didn't really want to go. Reverse psychology worked, and it worked well in these types of situations. Making them think something was their idea all along meant they were more likely to go through with it in the end, doing what was best for them, even if they didn't realize it yet.

But when I climbed back into the front of the truck and we pulled away from the hospital, another thought entered my mind.

Had that been what I'd done with Hannah? Tricked her into thinking I was good for her until the time came for me to walk away and leave her in someone else's care.

The very thought made my stomach twist until I felt sick.

"That's your first week back done," Jerry said, bringing my attention back to him. "What have you got planned tonight?"

Oh, you know… just hoping to spend hours talking to the woman of the guy we let die. Remember him?

"Not a thing," I said instead. "You?"

"Not a thing," he repeated. "Want to grab a beer with an old man?"

We'd been on a grueling shift pattern together for days, and I wanted nothing more than to go home, shower, lie on my bed, and wait for Hannah to call… but a part of me knew that that was becoming a dangerous pattern to fall into, and right now, I couldn't be falling into anything.

Especially not her, even if hearing her voice had become the favorite part of my day.

"You paying?" I asked Jerry before I could talk myself out of it.

He laughed and shot me a quick look. "Don't I always?"

I sank back in the passenger seat and stared at the hills of Hollywood around us, trying to take my mind off the woman who had suddenly become the sole occupier of it. "You sure do, Jerry. That's why I keep you around."

"Bullshit. I keep you around."

"I'm glad you do, though."

"Someone's got to. Wouldn't want you living a lifetime of solitude now, would we? That *would* be a tragedy."

twenty-five

Logan

We were five beers down with no sign of stopping soon. Not that I wanted to. The buzz of the alcohol had quietened my mind, and I craved more of that silence. I craved more thoughts that didn't involve Hannah, because things were entering a dangerous territory, and I couldn't ever just fuck her out of my system like I'd done with other women before her.

But, damn, the thought of going there with Hannah, anyway…

Jerry and I had already played four rounds of pool. I found it amusing as hell that he'd become obsessed with dominating the jukebox, filling the bar with old eighties and nineties tunes, which the regulars definitely seemed to approve of. New Order's *Bizarre Love Triangle* blasted out around the place, and all I could think was:

You lot have no fucking idea.

An innocent widow, the ghost of a rock star, and a paramedic with too much emotional baggage. How's that for a bizarre love triangle?

After our shift, Jerry and I had changed into our civilian clothes back at the station. I'd tucked my cell into the back pocket of my jeans before I racked up the pool table and bent over to make the break for the fifth time.

Jerry sucked at breaking.

He also sucked at drinking, which did me a favor, because five beers now meant that Jerry's hand-eye coordination had already gone to shit, making my next win a sure thing. The twenty-dollar bet we'd placed was about to come my way. I never lost a game of pool, no matter my opponent. I'd grown up playing it at Dale's house with the boys, each of us taking it in turns to kick each other's asses every chance we got. I had no doubt about my ability to win tonight.

I just hadn't factored in Jerry's uncanny talent of reeling in those around him to help in whatever quest he had. Tonight's quest being beating me, no matter the cost.

Within ten minutes of our fifth round of pool, he'd roped in three scantily clad women to his team to distract me. The women were a matching trio of hot pants and crop tops, the bottom of their ass cheeks hanging out while the frayed denim edges tickled their skin.

Yeah, I'd noticed. It was hard not to when they kept jumping up to sit on the edge of the pool table, taking it in turns to twirl their hair around their finger while I concentrated on whichever pocket became my next target.

I couldn't help picturing Hannah in those shorts, and I quicky had to shake the mental image out of my head.

Jesus, this is getting ridiculous.

We were down to the last few balls on the table. I had one blue and white stripe to sink before I moved on to the black. Jerry still had a red and a yellow to get rid of. I lined my cue up and leaned over, ready to make the easy pot, just as the redhead with the curls jumped up onto the edge and let her ass cheeks hang just above the pocket that held my attention.

"Jerry, for fuck's sake," I grunted. "C'mon, man."

He laughed. "All's fair in love and war."

"There's no love at this table anymore," I said, aware that the girls watched on as intently as Jerry, who now stood opposite me, resting his cue between his hands. My eyes rose to meet his, a sly smile of my own rising before I looked back down at the ball in front of me. "Think it's about time I wiped that smirk off your face once and for all."

I took aim, and I shot, sinking the blue and white before I stood up taller and stretched my back.

"It's almost too easy."

"It isn't over until it's over," Jerry hit back.

"Bullshit. Get your money out."

I moved around the table, eyeing up the black ball, when my phone vibrated in my back pocket to tell me someone was calling. Considering the limited number of people I had in my life, there was only one person it could be:

Hannah.

Jerry's head tilted to the side. "What's the matter, hotshot? Performance anxiety kicked in?"

The women around him chuckled, and I wanted to roll my eyes, but my attention was mainly on the way my phone stopped buzzing, the call ringing out. I never missed one of her calls, but she wouldn't have to wait long. I'd sink the black, head outside, and call her back within ten minutes.

At least that had been the plan.

Seconds later, a flurry of texts came through, one after the other, forcing me to hold a finger up to silence Jerry and the women as I pulled the phone out of my pocket.

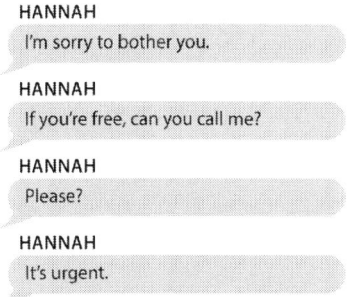

HANNAH
I'm sorry to bother you.

HANNAH
If you're free, can you call me?

HANNAH
Please?

HANNAH
It's urgent.

I dropped my cue to the side of the table, and without looking at anybody or even giving a fuck about who was there, I turned my back on all of them and called her back.

She answered instantly.

"Logan…" Her voice was breathless like she'd been running or crying.

"Talk to me, Hannah," I said, my voice raised over the music of the bar.

"I…" She paused. "Wait. Are you out?"

"Sort of. I'm just at a bar with Jerry, one of the guys from work."

She sniffed up, and it sounded like she ran a tissue under her nose as the sound around her muffled for a second until her little helpless breaths came out in fits and spurts. "I'm sorry, I didn't think you'd be busy."

That shouldn't have stung as much as it did, but I ignored my stupid butthurt pride that told me even she knew I didn't have a fucking life.

"I'll let you get back to it," she said.

"Not happening. Tell me what's going on."

"It's fine, really. It's… it's nothing."

"You said it was urgent."

"I…" she tried to speak, but she was breaking up.

I pushed my finger into my free ear and narrowed my eyes. "Hannah? I can hardly hear you."

"Go, enjoy your night, Logan. I'll call you later."

"Not a chance. Wait a minute."

The music seemed to grow louder with every beat of the song, so I stepped outside onto the porch surrounding the bar, letting the cool night air hit every sense I had when the door slammed closed behind me.

"What's happened? And don't say it's nothing, Hannah, because I know you wouldn't say it was urgent if it wasn't." I tried to hide the worry that had started to claw its way out of my throat, but I failed epically. I was fucking worried. Always when it came to her now.

"It's just…" She hitched in a sharp, shaky breath, releasing quickly. "I think I'm having another panic attack."

"You think, or you know?"

"I know."

"How bad is it?"

"The worst is probably over, but I'm pretty badly shaken."

"You know what to do, right? You remember the breathing patterns I told you to follow?"

"I've already done them but this one isn't going away so easily, and Livia isn't here, so I'm all alone with Bella, and I'm… scared. I feel ridiculous for saying that, but I am. For the first time in months, I'm scared that I'm alone, and I don't know what to do about it or if there even is anything I can do. That's why I called. You told me whenever, right? That's what you said."

"And I meant it. You can call me anytime, day or night."

"But I don't want to be a burden."

The sudden urge to call her *baby* bit at the tip of my tongue, and I quickly forced it back, shredding it to pieces before it came to life. I'd never called a woman *baby* in my damn life. I wasn't about to start now at thirty years old. Especially not a woman who wasn't mine.

"You're never a burden," I said instead. "I want to know when you're struggling so that I can help. I want to help. Do you want me to come over?"

"I can't ask that of you."

"You didn't."

She remained quiet, and another breath stuttered in and out of her before she took another too quickly. I could sense the panic rising inside her again.

"Hannah, you either want me to come and help you, or I'm going to have to phone an ambulance to get there and do my job for me because I'm not leaving you alone to—"

"No!" she said quickly, cutting me off. "No ambulance."

She didn't have to say another word before I turned back toward the door of the bar to grab my shit and say goodbye to the others. "I'm calling a cab now. I'll be there as soon as I can."

"Are you sure?"

"Hundred percent. Go lay down, close your eyes, and concentrate on those big, deep breaths. You hear me?"

"Yes, but Logan... Don't make a fuss. I'm okay. I'll be okay. I just need..." She didn't finish, and I imagined her telling me she needed *me*, even if the word never passed her lips.

"I'll be right there."

We ended the call, and I made my way into the bar, pulling up my Uber app to find the closest driver to the bar we were in.

"Everything okay, LT? You look shaken up," Jerry said from over my shoulder as I tapped away on the screen.

"Gotta go, Jerry."

"You forfeit the game?"

"It's all yours. Congratulations. You win."

"Christ. It must be something serious." He paused until his strained voice hit my ear again. "I didn't know you had friends in Beverly Hills."

I stopped what I was doing, not realizing just how close he'd gotten, or the fact that he hung over my shoulder, no doubt seeing what I'd typed into the Uber driver. Turning slowly, I caught Jerry's eye.

"Hannah, huh?" he said, brow raised.

"What?"

"That's what you called her on the phone before you walked out of here like someone had just shoved a rocket up your ass. *Hannah.* I'm assuming she's the emergency in Beverly Hills."

Shit.

Shit, shit, shit, shit, shit.

Of course, Jerry knew the name of Cole Newman's wife. Everybody did. He also knew how much I'd wrestled with all of this since that fateful night. It wouldn't take him long to put two and two together and get four, especially now he knew I was heading out to Beverly Hills late at night.

I could have stayed and fought my case.

I could have told him there were a million Hannahs in that part of the city, and the whole thing was just a coincidence. But I decided it was best to neither confirm nor deny a damn thing because either way, I would sure as shit fuck it up and make myself look guilty. Plus, Jerry was already drunk, and I had to hope that would delay him putting all the pieces of the puzzle together until I figured out what the hell to tell him should he ever ask me for the truth.

I ran a hand down my T-shirt, tucking my cell into my back pocket again. "I'll speak to you tomorrow, Jerry. Not tonight."

And before he could even open his mouth to respond, I turned and walked away, leaving behind a man with too many questions as I ran toward a woman who needed me more.

***

She opened the door wearing a long, thin, cream cardigan that she pulled around her body in a hug. Her hair had been pushed back with a black elastic band that exposed her beautiful face, even with the tear stains tracking down each red cheek. Her hollow, sad eyes rose up to take me in, and with just one look, a new wave of tears sprung to life, glistening against the diluted light of the foyer.

I wanted to hold her. I wanted to wrap my arms around her body the way she'd wrapped her arms around herself. I wanted to press my lips to the top of her head, sway her against me until the rhythm of us together lulled her into contentment.

Instead, I took a step closer, followed by another, until she began to step back, allowing me inside. Once the door fell shut behind us, Hannah hugged herself tightly again like her life depended on it. A woman so used to being alone even when she'd had somebody.

She stuttered in another breath and rubbed a sleeve-covered hand over her chest.

"It hurts," she said.

"Your chest?"

Her eyes rose to meet mine again. "Everything."

Fuck, now I *needed* to hold her. She looked like she needed it, too, and my arms were desperate to offer that up, but I didn't want to cross any boundaries, and I wasn't sure it wouldn't mess with her head even more. I didn't want to be the source of any more pain.

"What do you need from me?" I asked carefully.

Her eyes searched mine. "I don't know."

"You do, Hannah," I said, daring to take another step closer. "You're just too afraid to ask anyone for it because you haven't done that before. You don't need to be afraid of asking me. Whatever it is, you can have it."

"Why can't all men be like you, Logan?" she asked, inhaling another breath that sounded like it cut her in two on the way out. "Why can't all men be good?"

"Don't put me on a pedestal."

"Why not?"

"I don't deserve to be there."

"I think you do."

I lifted my hand to her face, brushing a falling tear away with my thumb before I rested my palm against her cheek. Hannah's eyes closed, and she leaned into it, her nostrils flaring as she pulled in her first real breath since I arrived.

"That's it," I whispered. "Keep breathing like that."

She nuzzled into my hand even more, and I heard a soft whimper before she swallowed it back down and licked her lips. Lips that were swollen because of her distress, tempting me more than ever before. I imagined pressing my mouth against hers and tasting her tears. I imagined kissing her back to life, my palms sliding over her shoulders until I had her neck cupped in my hands, her eyes fixed firmly on mine before I used my tongue to quieten every dark thought she'd ever had.

But I couldn't be that guy for her.

I had to be this one instead.

The one who never got to touch her as more than a friend.

"Does that help?" I asked quietly, too afraid of her answer being yes, too scared of it being no.

"You always help. You have this way about you. It's like you already know every part of me and know exactly what I need when I don't even know I need it myself."

I swallowed the lump in my throat, hating the way I was leaning into her, ready to catch her should she fall. I shouldn't be doing this. Things were going too far. We were getting too close.

Still, I couldn't have stopped if I'd wanted to.

And I really didn't want to anymore.

I didn't give a fuck if Cole's ghost lingered nearby. He'd been the one to win the lottery of wives and daughters only to throw it all away. He'd been the one to make this sensational woman cry, breaking her into tiny pieces until she no longer felt whole. Right there, with her face pressed against my palm, I didn't give a fuck about anyone or anything they had to say. The only thing that mattered was Hannah and figuring out a way to put all her broken pieces back together until she never remembered a time when she felt anything but whole.

Her lashes fluttered open to take me in.

We stared at each other for a minute, maybe more, as I watched her breaths steady into a pattern that didn't frighten me so much. Until I saw her slowly coming back to life.

The pink in her cheeks bloomed thanks to something other than the tears, but I didn't let her go. I wouldn't. Not until she demanded I do.

"Better?"

"Better." She smiled, even if that smile was filled with sadness.

"Good enough to make it to the kitchen so I can get you some water."

"Sure." She nodded feebly.

I wasn't sure of the precise moment I thought it would be a good idea to slip my hand into hers, but en route to the kitchen, it had happened anyway, and Hannah's fingers curled around mine, clinging onto me like I was the buoy keeping her afloat.

twenty-six

Hannah

The last attack had been slow to start. It rose in my chest like a fire growing life until the pain around my heart erupted and I could no longer ignore it. The only saving grace was that it happened after I'd managed to get Bella to bed. She'd crashed hard from spending the afternoon by the pool. It had been just the two of us. A time I'd treasured, my soul full to bursting as she laid on the lounger beside me, her eyes on the clouds in the sky while she talked about her daddy as though he'd never left us. Like he was about to walk through the door after a long tour, wrap her up in his arms, and tell her she was the best thing he could ever come home to.

I'd listened to her every word. I'd hung off them, desperate for her to turn *my* negative, angry emotions into something better.

I was starting to lose faith in my own memories—in my own judgment. It had been those few hours outside with Bella that had warned me that not everything had been how it seemed. There had been some good times, even if my daughter was the one to benefit from the majority of them. That was all that mattered in the end. Her happiness, and her memory of her father.

I wanted her to live with them for the rest of her forever.

Once I'd put her to bed, read her a story, and watched her fall asleep against my chest, the weight of everything had drifted over my body like a slow-erupting volcano, and that had led me to this moment in the kitchen, sitting next to Logan at the island, his hand resting over mine on the countertop.

"Is it right that another man's company makes me feel better about losing the company of my husband?" I asked him, watching his reactions carefully.

"Would it matter if it was a woman?"

"I don't suppose it would."

"Then, why should it be any different with me?"

"Because you're… you, and you're the kind of man who could get me in trouble."

"That's not what I'm trying to do here."

"That's the thing, Logan. You don't even have to try."

He pushed his free hand through the thickness of his dark hair before rubbing at the back of his neck awkwardly like he wasn't sure what that meant or how the hell to respond. He had no idea of the magnetism he held or the way I looked at him, and the way he made me feel.

"Sorry. I made that sound weird, didn't I?"

He dropped his hand from his neck to his lap. "You're free to say whatever you need to say around me."

"Even if I don't think you're ready to hear it?"

"Even then."

"Okay. I'm grateful for that day you ran into me at the drive-thru. I mean… the day *I* ran into *you*. Something good came out of something really shit, and I think that's kind of fascinating, don't you? How all that has led to this: you here when I needed you. This… friendship we have."

His hand squeezed mine before he leaned back, breaking the connection completely to bring his fist up to rest his cheek against it.

I wanted him to put his hand back on mine immediately, but I somehow schooled my face, desperate not to show the effect the loss of his touch had on me.

"Sorry," I said again. "Sometimes when my emotions are a wreck like this, I say too much."

"Stop apologizing. You don't say too much."

"Not true." I smirked. "Cole used to hate that about me."

"Sounds like he had a lot to say about everything." He raised a brow. "Did you ever tell him what you found irritating?"

"Sometimes." I rubbed my lips together in thought. "Not enough."

"Were you scared of him?"

I blanched. "Physically? Never. He wasn't like that. Emotionally, I wasn't scared, but I dreaded the way he could make me feel. Like I was a project he continued to work on. Someone that could and would eventually be molded into something perfect. The wife he really wanted."

"What about what you wanted?"

I huffed out a nervous laugh. "I forgot what that was along the way. I'm to blame as much as Cole. I wanted us to be happy. I wanted to be everything I could for him. For us as a family."

"And that dick doesn't sound like he deserved a *second* of it." Logan slowly closed his eyes and dragged a hand down his face before he let it drop against his thigh again. "My turn to apologize.

Sorry. I shouldn't have said that."

"No... Doesn't stop it being true."

"But, fuck, the more I hear about him, the worse it gets. You deserved someone who took you for you, no matter what got on his nerves or didn't. Not someone who tried to cherry-pick your best bits and erase the things he wasn't fond of."

"That's the trouble with abandoned kids. We become desperate adults. I took what he offered, and I didn't think to set my own boundaries. What kind of idiot did that make me?" I let my hands fall to rest on my thighs, twisting them together. "I grieve for him, yes. But I'm also grieving for the person I could have been. This woman he left behind isn't the woman I imagined being."

"You're young. You still have time."

"But just the thought of starting over..."

He leaned forward, placing his hand over mine. "The only thing you need to focus on is taking it one day at a time. Get through today first. Tomorrow is tomorrow's problem."

"One day at a time," I repeated in a whisper, my eyes dropping to his mouth for just a moment before another traitor tear of mine fell. I pulled my hands out from under his to wipe it away. "Sounds like a plan," I said, breaking eye contact with him because when Logan looked at me the way he currently was, it all became too much, but he soon had my chin trapped between his finger and thumb, and he carefully, oh so gently, brought my attention back to his face. He gifted me with a handsome smile before he let me go, making me smile in return.

We were so close; it should have felt invasive. Instead, I trusted him with me completely, knowing he'd never do anything that crossed the lines we'd drawn together. Even though I wasn't entirely convinced that *I* was capable of that for much longer.

We stayed that way for a while, each of us propped up

against the island, staring into the other's eyes as we talked, and I calmed, my breaths evening out little by little, thanks to Logan's distractions. He asked about my day, and I asked about his, feeling an odd sensation twisting in my gut when he told me the stories of his time in the bar with his friend Jerry and the three women trying to get his attention.

Logan didn't owe me anything, and I knew I couldn't be the sole owner of his attention forever, but knowing three beautiful females had been trying to distract him distracted me, and I didn't like the way it bit at my chest, as though I was now the only one who deserved to see those brown eyes staring back at her, as though I had become the only woman in Logan's life.

How fucking ridiculous, Hannah. What is wrong with you?

No matter how much time passed, though, or how much the conversation moved on, I couldn't shake that uncomfortable feeling away. It hit me that at some point, a woman would enter Logan's life and take him away. Whether that would be tomorrow, next week, next month, or next year, I didn't know, but I hated the very thought of it.

At some point in the evening, Logan glanced down at the watch on his left wrist, and he let out a tired sigh before pinching the bridge of his nose and suppressing a yawn.

"You're exhausted," I said, watching as he shook his head, scrunched his eyes together tightly before opening them and looking up at me with them narrowed, as though he was struggling to stay awake a moment longer.

"What makes you think that?" he asked with a half-smile.

I tapped the side of my head. "I have a sixth sense."

He rubbed at his eye again. "It's been a long week. I think I relaxed too much during my time off and it's been harder than I expected to get back into it." His eyes drifted to the nearest door before falling back to me. "I should go. Let you get some sleep, too."

"Okay."

I didn't want him to go anywhere. The thought of him leaving and not knowing when I'd see him again sent a shot of panic to the middle of my chest. When Logan was here, everything felt good. Protected. Without him, everything seemed emptier. Especially this house.

Especially *me*.

He made his way to the dishwasher, making sure to load the glasses and cups we'd used since he arrived because that was the kind of person Logan Thomas was: someone who not only cleaned up after himself but cleaned up after others, no matter when.

By the time he made his way to the door, I'd curled my cardigan around my body again and was hugging myself tightly, a reminder that it would just be me in charge in a moment. Me, in this big house, unable to sleep. Unable to switch off my thoughts.

Logan turned my way with his hands in his pockets, his brows raised as he looked down on me with a handsome face I was beginning to rely on far too much.

"You sure you're feeling better?" he asked.

Not even a little bit. "I'm sure," I said with a small nod.

"And you'll call me if you need me, right?"

"I'll be fine, Logan." But I couldn't meet his eyes when I said it.

A moment passed, and then he cupped my chin, giving me no choice but to stare up at him. His eyes searched mine. "You don't have to lie to me, remember?" he whispered. "I'm not cherry-picking your best bits and hoping you hold back the things you don't think I'll like. I'm not him, Hannah. If you're struggling, I need you to tell me. If you can't tell me, tell someone—anyone—so long as you don't try to do this alone."

Damn him.

Damn Logan to all Hell.

I wanted to stay strong. I *needed* to at this point. But the sincerity in his words and voice had a lump rising in my throat before more tears welled in my eyes.

"I hate it when you do that," I croaked.

"Do what?"

"Say things that make me want you to stay when I know you're desperate to go."

His brows pulled together, and his jaw ticked again, but he never released me. He just continued to stare into my eyes as though waiting for me to take it from here.

"But actually, I don't hate it at all," I whispered. "It makes me think there's at least some hope you might stay the night after all."

"You want me to stay?"

"More than anything."

"Do you think that's a good idea?"

"Probably not."

His lips twitched on one corner, but he never let a smile form. "It's definitely a bad idea, Hannah."

"Maybe, but I'm tired of always being sensible and cautious, aren't you?"

"Some things can't be taken back once they happen, and I don't want to cross any lines with you."

"You wouldn't have to. I have enough bedrooms. You can choose any you want. I just need you here. I need to know you're close, and I know it's selfish, and I know it doesn't make sense, and I know I shouldn't be asking this of you, but here I am doing it anyway. For some reason you're the one who calms me, Logan, and I'm desperate and hopeless enough to want to cling to that for as long as I possibly can."

He closed his eyes, like everything I'd just said had pained him.

"One night," he finally said, his voice quiet as he looked back at me again.

My chest deflated, and a weight I hadn't realized had been there lifted from my shoulders... until he released me from his grip and took a step back, his hand coming up to rub at the back of his neck again.

"That's all I can give you, Hannah."

"I understand," I said, hating the look he now wore.

"Do you?"

No, I didn't, but everything about Logan standing in front of me told me he was beyond exhausted, and now wasn't the time to ask him what everything meant.

"Yes," I said quietly, offering him a flat smile before I reached for his hand, grateful when he took it and allowed me to lead the way.

I turned off all the lights and locked every door. I set the alarm and then guided Logan up the stairs, where he'd already been before. I showed him the guest rooms he could choose from, hoping he'd take the one directly opposite my room.

He did, and after showing him where everything was, he stood on the threshold of the room while I stayed out in the hallway, trying to drag this out as long as possible.

"Get some sleep, Hannah," he finally said, towering over me, our bodies closer than they should have been.

"You, too, Logan."

I didn't linger at his door, waiting for him to say anything else. The pull I felt toward him scared me, so I turned on my heels and made my way inside my bedroom, closing the door behind me with a contentment in my heart I knew to be temporary, but grateful for it all the same.

He had a magic about him, Logan Thomas.

One I would find impossible to give up once the sun rose the next morning, but one I sensed I'd have to give up anyway.

My silent, unassuming, unexpected hero.

twenty-seven

Logan

I lay beneath the comforter in a foreign bed, staring up at the ceiling of a house I barely knew. No matter how exhausted I'd been, I couldn't switch off from the way Hannah had looked at me when she asked me to stay.

How could anyone be with her and not see perfection?

Why would anyone want to take someone as pure as her and break her down into little pieces so they could build her back up into a version that suited them?

It made me fucking angry to think about it. It was as crazy as buying a classic painting only to strip the canvas of the artwork so you could paint over it to make it something less worthy. Something anyone could make.

I thought I'd stay that way all night, asking myself impossible questions that could never be answered, but somehow my body and brain figured out a way to shut me down, regardless. I turned on my side, stuck my hands under the soft, white pillow, and let sleep claim me, dragging me down into a black void where Hannah's face was the only thing I could see.

In that world, I didn't need to feel any shame about the thoughts I had about her. In that world, everything was simple. She was a woman in need of me, and I was a man able to offer whatever she demanded. At some point, I rolled onto my back again, falling further into a peacefulness that was soon to be interrupted.

The sinking of the mattress was the first thing to make my eyes flutter open, half of me curious enough to *want* to wake up, the other half desperate to stay asleep and beat the tiredness that had taken over. The unexpected body heat that followed had me scowling, despite the darkness being the only thing that met me when I looked up at the ceiling again, disorientated about where I was and who could be there.

But then her hand rested on my bare chest, and she leaned down to whisper in my ear, "Logan," and my name had never sounded so fucking sweet in the last thirty years of my life.

I lifted my head instantly. "Hannah?" I croaked.

"Hey,"

"What are you doing?"

"I can't sleep."

I squinted harder, my sight adjusting just enough to see the outline of her flawless body as she knelt on the bed beside me. "Everything okay?"

"It will be… in a minute."

She pulled the comforter back and slid her bare legs beside mine, the heat of her skin making my breath stick in my throat as I willed my heart to stop racing. She lifted my arm above her head and slipped into place until she was curled up beside me, eventually placing my arm back down around her shoulder so she could settle her cheek against my chest and wrap her arm around my waist.

I froze in place, not knowing what the hell to do. My body turned rigid beneath her, knowing this was a step too far, as my hand hovered over her hip, too scared to let it fall against her in case she screamed at me to let her go.

Guilt and confusion consumed me, churning me up inside. There was no way Hannah couldn't feel it pouring out of me.

She wore some kind of nightdress that, thankfully, covered the most private parts of her body, but I could still feel her full breasts pressed against my skin. I felt her heart beating, and her warm, silky-smooth thighs tangled up next to mine.

I had to suppress a lethal groan that would have told her all too clearly how things were changing for me. How my thoughts were drifting into a territory I couldn't pull them back from.

I should have pushed her off and told her she'd gotten it all wrong, that this wasn't right, but then the memory of her tear-filled eyes came back to me, and I thought, *if this is the one thing that I can give her tonight to make tomorrow easier, she can have it. She can have anything she desires of me, even if it eats me alive and buries me in my own shame the next morning.*

My hand fell slowly toward her hip before resting there carefully, and she released a soft breath, her body relaxing beneath mine and her cheek nuzzling into my chest even more.

"I know I'm taking too much," she finally whispered. "It's something I've never really done before, but you make me feel like it isn't a bad thing to tell you what I need, and I need this tonight, Logan. I need you to hold me."

I'd become mute, too caught up in focusing on every point of contact where our bodies touched, desperate to stay in control and not grow hard or turned on beneath her.

Which seemed almost fucking impossible.

Hannah Moore was, without a doubt, the most gorgeous person I'd ever had the privilege of getting close to. I'd spent so long focused on respecting her, but now none of that seemed to matter when all the blood rushed to my groin, my every thought suddenly turning to a fantasy featuring her naked beneath me—my lips pressing promises of adoration against hers. Because if there was one thing I knew I was good at, it was worshiping a woman's body—of fucking them into oblivion until they forgot their own name, leaving them with only one thing to focus on as they climbed higher and higher beneath my touch: me.

I hadn't had sex in months, and that shit was starting to show.

I had to squeeze my eyes shut and force myself to breathe, which only sharpened my senses even more, making every place she touched me throb in delight.

"I figured holding me in the dark would be easier for you," she said, pulling me from my thoughts.

"Why would you think that?" I croaked.

"Because, for some reason, you look ashamed of yourself every time you get too close, and I've already seen too much of that in my life. At least this way, I figure I still get to be in your arms, and you don't have to hide yourself from me."

If words could cause literal agony, Hannah had just wielded that weapon over me, and now my chest had been split in two, torn between protecting her, and protecting myself.

She was always going to win.

"What do you want from me, Hannah?"

"Just this," she said, her arm tightening around my waist. "Human contact. Another thriving heartbeat next to mine. Another person's sleeping breaths filling the air. Someone I trust. A friend."

"A friend," I repeated, trying to convince myself that's what this was—that no other emotions were at play here because I had everything under control.

Like fuck you do, that inner voice of mine taunted.

This couldn't go on.

I couldn't keep drawing her closer, comforting her, and being the one she leaned on if she didn't know the truth about me. The truth about my connection to Cole.

The truth about how I hadn't stumbled into her life that very first day by accident, but I'd followed her until I stepped into it, whether she'd wanted me there or not.

I felt her breaths fall into a slow rhythm, while mine only grew wilder as the realization of what I finally had to do hit me.

I'd give her tonight. I'd let her take whatever she needed.

But tomorrow, I'd tell her the truth, and whatever she chose to do with that was up to her, even if it killed me to let her go.

Giving in, I curled my arm tighter around her, pulling her close to me before I moved my lips to the top of her head, inhaling the sweet smell of coconut shampoo and the irresistible freshness that had always been her.

"Sleep tight, Hannah Moore," I whispered. "Make it count."

I felt her smile grow against me. "I will."

***

When I woke the next morning, Hannah wasn't there. I rolled over, able to smell the scent of her lingering in the sheets and on my chest, causing my already hard dick to harden even more. I had to force myself out of the bed, only to find clean towels and a new toothbrush positioned on a lounge chair next to the bed, along with a small note that read:

Take as much time as you need.
And thank you for last night.

Her thank you poked at that ever-present guilt, reminding me I didn't deserve any thanks for anything. It was up to me to tell her the truth now. I refused to be someone who continued to let her down.

She wasn't in the kitchen, nor was she in the main living room when I went downstairs, and I hadn't ventured into any other of the rooms down there, so I made my way outside rather than investigating the rest of her home, already knowing I'd find her in her favorite spot under the canopy, out in the backyard.

When I stepped outside and saw her, that sharp stab of desire hit me in the chest all over again.

She was fucking beautiful.

Her eyes were closed, her face tilted toward the early morning sun as she nursed a cup of coffee in both hands, resting it against her chest. Eventually, Hannah's eyes fluttered open, and she turned to me as if she could feel my presence, a soft smile on her face that gutted me the moment I saw it. She was a total contrast to the swollen-eyed, heartbroken, panicked woman of the night before, and now I had to break her all over again.

"Hey," she said, her voice light.

"Hey." I cleared my throat and moved around the patio furniture toward the couch opposite her, my knees cracking when I tugged on the thighs of my pants and took a seat, resting my ass on the edge, my forearms dropping to my parted legs.

The knowledge of us having slept in the same bed hung between us, a secret I wasn't sure if she treasured or found dirty as she looked at me.

"Sleep well?" she asked.

"Like a log. You?"

"Better than I have in a while. Would you like some coffee? I just made some."

I shook my head, my gut too twisted to put anything in it until I'd said what I needed to say. "No, thanks, I'm good."

Her smile dropped, her brows rising. "You don't like coffee?"

"Love the stuff. Just don't want any now I've brushed my teeth. Mixing shit like that together makes me nauseous."

She laid a look on me. "I'm not sure I can trust anyone who doesn't need a coffee as soon as they wake up."

I forced a smile to my strained mouth, knowing now would be a good time to tell her exactly why she shouldn't trust me, even if she had been joking, but it tore me up to see her so relaxed, knowing what I had to say to her.

"There's something wrong," she said calmly. "You're upset about last night."

I opened my mouth to say something, only for Hannah to cut me off before I'd even begun.

"I'm sorry, Logan. I took it too far, didn't I? I abused your kindness. I didn't give you a choice."

"I had plenty of choice, Hannah."

"But you're too kind to say no even if you didn't want me there."

"And what if I did? What if I did want you there?"

"Did you?"

"More than I realized I would, yeah."

Her fingers twitched around her clutched cup, and I wasn't sure if she meant for me to see the surprise in her eyes before she forced it away.

I wanted to say more. To tell her how fucking good it felt to hold her delicate body and brush against her silky soft skin. I wanted to tell her how I'd listened to her steady heartbeats, counting them like some lovesick, fucked-up, whipped guy from one of those overly romantic movies everyone at the station moaned about their wives watching. I wanted to tell her all the things I enjoyed, but I couldn't because I had so much other shit going on in my head instead.

Twisting my dry hands together, I looked down at them, trying to put my thoughts in order, not knowing how the hell to finish this once and for all and get it out there. Not knowing how to even start.

"Listen, Hannah. What you do and don't do around me is up to you. I've made it pretty clear since we met that I'm here for you, no matter what you need, and I mean it." My hands stilled, and I finally raised my chin, looking up into her cautious eyes. "But before we carry on with this… *friendship* of ours. Before we continue to spend time together, calling and texting each other, and ingraining ourselves in each other's lives the way we've been doing this last couple of months, I think it's only right that you know everything you need to know about me… to make this fair."

Her eyes searched mine, the dread she'd been so used to rising to the surface. "What don't I know about you, Logan?"

"Too much."

"Like…?"

I closed my eyes, let my chin fall to my chest again, and I took a moment to blow out a breath, remembering her husband's face just moments before he took his last breath.

It was there.

Right there on the tip of my tongue.

And now was the time.

I was there with him the night he died. We didn't meet by accident. Our friendship wasn't written in the stars and left to fate. I made it happen, Hannah.

I was the guy who failed him.

And ever since then, I've failed you by lying to you, too.

But when I lifted my head to take her in, and I opened my mouth to speak, Hannah's attention drifted over my shoulder as something else caught her eyes, and a scowl furrowed her brow.

I followed her gaze, only to see a wrung-out, panting Livia there, with her brown bag slung over her shoulder, and her hand pushing her dark hair away from her face as she looked at Hannah and gasped, "Thank God you're here."

"Livia? What's wrong? What are you doing here so early?" Hannah asked.

"Oh, Hannah," she whimpered. "Have you... have you seen it?"

"Seen what?"

Livia's face paled. "I'm so sorry. It's everywhere this morning. I thought you'd already have heard."

"Heard what? What's going on?" I asked, the hairs on the back of my neck standing to attention as I glimpsed between the two of them.

But when I focused back on Hannah, she held herself poised before taking a long, deep breath. She uncurled her legs from beneath her, carefully dropping her cup to the coffee table and laying her hands on her knees. A quiet storm brewed inside her eyes as every ounce of lightness drifted away, only to be replaced by tension and darkness that actually fucking frightened me.

"Go on, Livia. Tell me," she said calmly. "Who else has Cole slept with now?"

twenty-eight

Logan

If Cole wasn't already dead, I'd have killed him myself. I'd have stormed into his life, wrapped my hands around his scrawny throat, and shown that cold-hearted prick what it felt like to go up against a real man. I'd show him physical pain. A favor returned for all the emotional trauma he'd put upon his innocent family. The only guilt I held over not being able to save him now lingered because of them; Hannah and Bella. Because, despite everything going on, it would have been easier for them to deal with it while he was still here rather than them having to go through this alone.

My fists curled, and my hands itched to be launched at something as I watched Hannah pacing around, dealing with her aching heart again, while fielding calls from the band's publicist, manager, and even some of the members themselves.

I hadn't heard the specific details, only that another report had come out from a model who claimed to have been having an affair with Cole Newman behind Hannah's back. Seeing Hannah's world collapse in front of her again had me turning away and forcing my own feelings of fury down.

To make it even worse, Bella had now woken from her lazy slumber, dragging her feet into the ridiculously large kitchen with her hair wild and tangled, and her eyes still sleepy enough for her to rub at them.

She didn't know what had happened, and we had to keep it that way.

Livia had originally gone to pull Bella away from Hannah, but I wasn't equipped for any of this. I didn't have a clue how to console Hannah without telling her what a waste of fucking oxygen her husband had been, and that definitely wasn't the right thing to say or do then. Instead, with a forced smile on my face, I beckoned Bella over to the other side of the backyard, far away from the drama indoors that Hannah and Livia could no longer avoid.

It fucking killed me for both of them.

Bella showed me every one of her inflatable toys as we strolled around the pool, her leading the way, walking backward in front of me as she looked up with excited eyes and a never-ending chatter that somehow made me smile, despite everything happening around us.

"Do you always have your hands in your pocket, Mr. Logan?" she asked as she skipped backward, pushing her bedhead away from her face with the palms of her hands.

"I've never really thought about it before. Why? Does it bother you?"

"I don't care. I'm just six, and six-year-olds have a lot of questions. Mom says not all of them have to make sense."

"Fair," I said in a huff of laughter, watching as she twirled around without a care in the world. "What's next then?"

"Do you want to see Daddy's tree?" she asked brightly, not giving me a chance to answer before she hooked her arm through my forearm and began to pull me toward it. "Come on. Let me show you. Here it is. Look at it, Mr. Logan. Look!"

There it stood, a beautiful green Californian Pepper Tree, a part of nature now decorated with a long, black wire hanging down from one of the low branches and a microphone attached to the end of it. Bella let me go to scoop the microphone into her hand, turning it the right way up.

She brought it to her lips. "Testing, testing. Daddy in Heaven. Do you receive me?" She turned to me with a bright white smile, as though this was an everyday occurrence, and a six-year-old girl having to talk to her dead father through an unplugged microphone wasn't enough to tear my heart in two.

Bella didn't deserve this.

Hannah didn't deserve this, either, but here we fucking were.

Bella continued to talk to Cole, and I glanced around everywhere to take it all in. The perfectly manicured and landscaped private backyard. The patio eating area with the expensive canopy. I looked over the white building that must have cost them millions, down to the open glass doors where the outlines of Hannah and Livia could be seen pacing, the cell glued to Hannah's ear as she ran a hand through her hair and held it at the back of her head.

"Look at everything you had, you selfish son of a bitch," I whispered to Cole, hoping that if this really was the way to speak to the dead, he heard me.

"What was that, Mr. Logan?"

Turning back to Bella, I strapped on a smile and dropped to my haunches, reaching up to place a hand on her arm. "I was just admiring your backyard. I couldn't think of a better place or a better tree for you to talk to your dad."

"You really like it? Even without the annoying but funny cat here."

"Especially without the cat."

Her whole face lit up as she studied me, but then a raised voice from inside the house caught Bella's attention, making her frown.

"Hey," I said. "What's that look for?"

Her innocent eyes turned back to me, holding me captive. "She cries a lot now."

"Who does?"

"Mommy."

Something sharp squeezed at my heart again. "She does, huh?"

"Yep. I hear her all the time."

"How does that make you feel?"

"I hate it. I just want her to be the old Mommy again. To be happy."

"She's trying, Bella. I promise."

"I know." Bella looked down at her bare feet, taking a moment before she looked back at me. "But I still don't like hearing her cry."

"Have you told her? That you hear her…"

"No, she'd be mad knowing I sneak over to her bedroom at night and listen. Sometimes I see her wiping her tears away in the kitchen before she turns around and smiles at me, but I can see the marks on her cheeks that made them go all puffy. I'm not as stupid as they think I am."

"You're definitely not stupid, Bella. Nobody thinks that."

She paused and took a quick glance at the back of the house again. "I bet that's what she's doing now. Crying."

I offered her a sad smile. "We don't always cry because of sadness. Sometimes it's frustration. Sometimes it's happiness. There are lots of reasons."

"Do you ever cry?"

Never. I trained myself not to many years ago, but I couldn't exactly tell a kid that. "Everybody feels like crying at some point. But you know what? Whenever I feel sad, I try to block that sadness out by focusing on something good instead."

"Like what?"

"Anything." I shrugged. "Humans are messy creatures. We like to focus on everything sad instead of everything good. Sometimes we forget we're in charge of our own brains, and if we really wanted to, we could turn things upside down until all the bad memories get replaced by the good."

"I'll try that next time. Maybe I could ask Mommy to try it, too." Bella's eyes drifted over my face, taking every inch of me in. "I like you, Mr. Logan."

"I like you, too, Miss Bella."

"Have you ever loved someone like that before? Like you're happy you loved them, even though they're gone now?"

I thought about my father and my best friend, both having left me with so much to say that I never got a chance to.

"Yeah." I nodded. "I have."

"A girlfriend?" She smiled.

"Oh. No." I shook my head. "Nothing like that."

Her eyes drifted back to Hannah. "I don't want Mom to be lonely forever." She looked back at me, and I saw what she was suggesting there. I heard the undelivered message in her tone, and I hated that the kid asked the one thing of me I could never give. It only made my need to tell Hannah the truth that much more urgent.

I never wanted to be an illusion for either of them.

"I can promise you one thing, Bella: your mom will never be lonely."

"Really?"

"How could she be? She's got you."

Her face lit up again like that had been the answer she'd needed to get through another day of seeing her mother upset.

"Bella?" Livia called from the back of the house, making us both turn to look at her. With a wave of her hand, she beckoned Bella to the house.

"Time to get that hair brushed, kid?" I asked her with a smile.

She huffed out an annoyed breath and rolled her eyes. "Not you as well. What's wrong with my hair?" She didn't give me time to answer before she turned and ran inside. When Livia's eyes locked on mine just before she turned away, I saw the unspoken request *she* asked of me, too.

Go to Hannah.

Of course, I went, walking through the open patio doors and into the kitchen, only for Hannah to place her cell on the island and turn to me, showing everything I'd been dreading seeing on her face. Utter loss, and devastating heartbreak.

Even dead, he continued to destroy her.

I came to a stop a few feet away, giving her space as I pushed my balled-up fists into the pockets of my pants. "How bad is it?"

She pressed her lips together and shook her head, fighting for her life. Refusing to let any more tears fall, but it was a pointless task, and I could see her at war with herself. She was a woman desperate to stay strong, too broken to hold on a second longer.

"Do you know what hurts the most?" she asked quietly. "He's turning me into a bad mom. The one thing I promised myself I'd never be. Above all else, I swore I'd never let my baby girl down."

"You haven't."

"Please... don't lie to me."

"Bella adores you. You're her whole world."

"But will she adore me when I have to tell her that her father slept with another woman and got her pregnant, leaving Bella with a half-brother or half-sister she can never know because I won't allow that shit into her life to hurt her the way it's already hurt me?"

I took the bullet she'd shot, letting it land straight in my chest.

The bastard had got someone else *pregnant...*

I didn't know what the hell to say. I turned into a live wire, ready to go off on her behalf. But instead of exploding with anger at *him*, I did the only thing I could think of. I marched over to Hannah and pulled her weary body into my arms, holding her tightly as her hands bunched up against my stomach, and her forehead fell to my chest.

I let her bleed out until she had nothing left to free, and I held her in silence, surrounded by nothing but her soft cries that sang a song of grief for more than just a lost love.

Eventually, I pressed my lips to the top of her head and spoke against her hair. "It kills me to see you like this, but Bella loves you, and she always will. You could never be a bad mom to her. I don't think you're capable of being a bad anything to anyone. Don't let his past mistakes destroy your self-respect, Hannah. *He* made every one of them. Not you. *He* failed you."

My body vibrated with a need to release so much anger, I wished for nothing more than to be in the gym with a punchbag in front of me to take my frustrations out on.

"Logan, you're shaking," she finally said between her ragged breaths, her forehead still to my chest.

"I'm fucking angry, Hannah," I whispered.

Slowly, she raised her head and looked up at me with narrowed, heartbroken eyes. "Me, too."

I brushed my hand down her hair until it fell to the exposed skin at the back of her neck and down her clothed back. She felt so delicate in my arms, and I wanted her to absorb my strength. To soak it into her bones and steal it from me until she became strong enough to stand up, tall and proud, to see her own worth.

She had some fight left inside. All I needed to do was pull it out of her.

"Take me away from here, Logan," she whispered. "I want out of this world for a minute. Take me to yours instead."

twenty-nine

Hannah

My mind had been ready to explode with the number of phone calls I'd had to take. Everyone had kept their distance in recent months at my request, but this scandal had proved too juicy for the majority to stay away. When the band's publicist and manager called, I'd told them, not so politely, to leave me the hell alone. They'd already failed me with no pre-warning about the article that was about to come out. I'd told Chase to leave me alone, too, although in a much calmer tone because, despite his connections to my husband, there was something about him that made it impossible to stay mad at. He genuinely cared.

Kate's text hadn't done anything to bring me around, either. *I'll see that guy in Hell, and I'll make him pay, baby. Don't you*

worry. Wish I was there to hug you.

Nothing had worked until I'd known for certain that we had a plan to get Bella away from the house to somewhere safe. Somewhere the paparazzi couldn't touch her... which meant she had to be somewhere away from me for the night. Cole cheating on me was hardly news anymore. But Cole cheating on me and getting someone else pregnant?

That would have the press desperate for some fodder to feed their rabid readers.

They wanted my distraught face on the cover of every magazine, and I refused to let them have it on their terms.

From now on, I was in charge.

Cole's legacy could go to Hell.

With a few cars already beginning to line up on the street, Livia and I had only one choice left to us. Bella would stay at Livia's tonight, and if I could, I'd try and persuade Logan to take me away from the house in one of our cars.

I was thankful he didn't take any persuading.

The three of us—Livia, Logan, and me—had bundled Bella off with nothing but smiles on our faces, promising her an exciting sleepover of ice cream, popcorn, movies galore, and all the sugar donuts she could suffer. Before she'd slipped out of the door, I'd pulled her into my arms and held onto her like my whole life depended on it.

And it did.

Without her, I had nothing to live for.

The very thought had my eyes drifting to the man beside me, who wore a black cap and dark shades as he sat in the driver's seat of another SUV we had stored in the back of one of the garages. It had impenetrable blacked-out windows, but Logan had the idea to put all the windows down and have me lying in the footwell behind the driver's seats, letting the photographers see he was a nobody they didn't even recognize, and the car held no precious cargo inside for them to try and chase when we pulled out of the driveway.

It worked.

As soon as we were clear, I climbed into the front seat and sat beside him, watching as the muscles along his jaw twitched and his forearm tensed at the wheel. Logan had always radiated nothing but kindness, but right then, he radiated quiet anger and a sturdy power that I couldn't look away from.

"Where are we going?" I asked.

"My place." He glanced my way, and I wished that he'd remove those dark shades so I could see his comforting eyes for just a moment, needing that connection with someone real. "That okay?" he asked.

"I don't care where we go as long as I'm with you," I told him, choosing nothing but honesty from now on. "Is that okay?"

"Whatever you need from me, it's yours."

He turned his attention back to the road, but every time I stole a quick glance at him, I saw the tension in his strong jawline. His muscles twitched, and his fingers constantly tightened around the wheel.

We eventually drove into the more urban area of Van Nuys, passing far too many coffee shops, as well as several parks along the way. I sank back into the passenger seat, grateful for a view that wasn't Beverly Hills. When he pulled the black SUV into a downturned driveway, it rolled under a white carport, disappearing into a dark enough space for us to climb out and not be seen. He didn't look at me before he got out of the driver's side, but he soon opened my door to help me out. I hopped down into his strong hands, sucking in a breath when he caught me by the waist.

Heat rose in places it shouldn't.

I wished I could have seen his eyes to see if he responded the same way, but those stupid shades and that black cap I'd convinced him to wear hid him and his reactions almost completely.

He took me by the hand and led me to a white door, where he pressed some numbers on the keypad. A moment later, we were buzzed in. We made our way up some stairs, until we came to another door at the end of a second corridor. Logan stopped to open it, holding it there for me to walk inside before him, removing his shades and hat as he did. I caught his eyes now, finally, and I saw the trepidation he tried to hide at having me in his home.

I stopped, just inches away from his face. "This is your private space. Why do I suddenly feel like I'm intruding?"

"Stop it, Hannah."

"But—"

"I want you here. That's where it begins, and that's where it ends."

Those words were enough to make me step into his room that held everything in one space, apart from the bathroom, including a small open plan kitchen to the right, with a double bed, small couch, and a television to the left.

"I hope you don't feel the need for too much privacy while you're here," he said, walking in behind me and letting the door shut behind us. "It's… compact."

"I like compact."

"Good job."

"And there's always the bathroom for me to hide if you become *that* annoying," I teased.

"To the left, through that door." He tossed his keys on the small kitchen island that you could walk all the way around without taking twenty steps. But the size didn't matter, not when I could smell nothing but Logan here. I wasn't very good with cologne ingredients. I couldn't tell you what sandalwood, rosewood, or patchouli smelled like on their own, but I could tell you when a man smelled clean—the kind of clean a woman wanted to bathe in, unable to get the scent deep enough inside her body. When it was more than just soap or shower gel. More than musk and spicy flavors.

Whatever Logan's scent was, I wanted to bottle it up and take some home to open up and smell when he wasn't there.

"There's not much to do here, but it's an escape. Somewhere you can lay your head, get some rest, maybe watch some TV." He studied me like he had something more to say. Maybe too much.

"It's perfect." *Just like you.* "Thank you."

"The next time you thank me, I'm going to do something to make you dislike me."

I looked away quickly, hoping he didn't see the blood that rushed to my cheeks or hear my racing heartbeat at the thought of being 'punished' by a man like him.

"I'm just going to change," he said, clearing his throat as though he'd only just realized how suggestive that had sounded. "I won't be a minute."

True to his word, he was quick, and when he returned, a wave of freshness followed him. I inhaled it into my chest, allowing it to calm me.

But then I realized he was shirtless, wearing nothing but shorts, and any hope of staying calm evaporated. My eyes raked down over the ridges and valleys of his abs before rising back up to take in his tanned chest, broad shoulders, and impressive biceps. His skin was clean, not a tattoo in sight, just a small smattering of hair across his chest that made me swallow the tight knot in my throat that had come out of nowhere.

Damn.

There was no way he missed my staring, either. The air had been sucked out of the room, and I had to break the spell he'd put me under, even if I wanted to spend the entire night just… *looking* at him.

I cleared my throat subtly. "Do you have anything I could change into?"

He looked down at my workout leggings that I hadn't put to use, and his eyes lingered on the profile of my ass for just a moment before he looked up at the cropped tank top I wore beneath a flowing, thin, blush cardigan.

"Nothing that would look better than you already do," he said, immediately scowling and turning away to find something in a small chest of drawers against the wall at the far end of the room.

"Logan?"

"Yeah."

"Never mind."

He pulled a T-shirt out, along with a loose pair of shorts, turning to face me with a straight face.

"What?" he asked, walking over and handing me the clothes, our fingers brushing each other's in the exchange.

"Am I... do you think I'm attractive?"

His brows rose. "Excuse me?"

"Am I attractive? Do you think I'm—"

"Jesus, Hannah, what kind of question is that?"

I wilted under his outraged expression for just a second, convinced I'd *definitely* crossed the line, only for him to huff out a breath of laughter.

"You're serious, aren't you?"

"Well..."

Before I could finish, he closed the gap between us, his eyes staring down into mine as he ran his knuckles over my warm, puffy cheek. "You're a ten and nothing less. Even with tear tracks down your cheeks, which I fucking hate to see, you're a ten. Whoever or whatever makes you feel less than that isn't worth a moment of your time. Not even a thought. So, yes, you're attractive, and that might be the craziest question anyone has ever had to ask me."

Goosebumps flared to life all over my body, making my nipples tighten, my toes tingle, and my head spin. Strange sensations flooded me, ones I hadn't felt in far too long.

That was the thing about Logan. He used such simple words, yet they landed powerfully every single time.

In a moment of stupidity, my eyes drifted down to his lips. He saw it, too, which meant he must have felt the desire I had to plant my mouth on his in a way I hadn't yet dared myself to.

Last night in bed with him had almost been too much. Doors had been opened that should have stayed closed. But still… I couldn't get those lips out of my mind.

Kissing him would be the end of us—this. Whatever this was. I wasn't ready for that. I needed him too much. I relied on him for moments like these that assured me it was possible to bring my body back to life after so long of feeling lost.

Clearing his throat, Logan took a step back, his hand rising to rub the back of his neck again. "I'll give you a minute. Go, change, and when you come back out, we'll order pizza and watch a movie." He allowed his eyes to find mine again. "If that's what you want to do, I mean."

"Sounds great," I said, grateful for the excuse to turn away and hide everything I was beginning to feel.

It didn't take me long to switch outfits in his tiny cream bathroom that had everything a human being needed and nothing more. After folding my clothes, I refused to look in the mirror, knowing I'd see a red, puffy face I'd already grown tired of seeing at just twenty-nine years old. Instead, I made my way out into the main studio, dropping my folded clothes onto the kitchen island before stopping to take in the scene in front of me.

Logan lay on one side of his bed, and for a moment, I froze, not knowing whether to join him on the other side or take the couch.

He caught me, lost in thought.

"It's up to you," he said, already knowing my dilemma, but in true Logan fashion, refusing to apply the pressure either way.

Part of me wished he would. At least then I'd know which way he leaned toward. A nod to the couch would tell me that he spotted my mouth-gazing earlier, and he thought it best we stay apart. A nod to the bed, however, would tell me to stop overthinking. He didn't care about any of that. He didn't see me that way.

Either one, I found I'd be disappointed with.

In the end, I found my courage and climbed into the opposite side of the bed, pushing my bare legs—which were only half covered by his baggy shorts—under the thin comforter while he laid on top of it, on his side.

"Are the clothes okay?" he asked, his attention on the television as he flicked through the channels, refusing to look at me.

I really wanted him to look at me.

"Great, thanks."

"I still say you looked better in the leggings." He smirked.

"Stop trying to make me blush, Logan Thomas."

"Never."

It was our second time in bed together in less than twenty-four hours, and even though my thoughts should have been on the way my life was falling apart around me, I found myself relaxing into the pillows anyway.

If Earth had a safe space for each of us, in bed next to Logan was mine, and I had no idea what that meant for either of us.

Or how we'd let it happen so quickly.

thirty

Logan

Hannah slept beside me—her peaceful face aimed my way, lit only by the shadows the moon cast through the thin curtains I hadn't pulled together properly.

She wore no makeup, and her face still had different shades of pink dotted around it, thanks to the tears that motherfucker had made her shed. Even with those, she looked perfect, and I couldn't take my eyes off her or the way her small hands were pressed together, wedged under her cheek.

The things she'd had to go through all because of a man who didn't love her enough to keep his ego in check. I couldn't fucking bear it.

I lay on my side, my arm above her head, and the very edges of my fingertips running through the stray strands of her hair.

Despite wanting to, I wouldn't wake her. She needed this sleep. She needed to rest, and it should have made me feel good to know that she felt safe here with me.

Instead, all I felt was more fucking guilt and more fucking shame.

I swear I wanted to confess today, I told her in my thoughts. *I wanted to get things out in the open and let you decide for yourself if you forgive me or not. But how could I do that this morning? How could I do that tonight when your feelings for him are all messed up? When your anger toward him could have allowed you to forgive me too easily?*

I wanted to purge myself of this rotten fucking feeling that was eating me alive, telling me I'd become no better than Cole with the way I chose what she should know and when she should know it.

My fingers continued to brush over her hair, and I wanted to bury my hand in it, fist it tight, make her eyes open, and bring her lips toward me more than I'd ever wanted any fucking thing in my entire life.

But I couldn't take what wasn't mine.

I couldn't ask for what I didn't deserve.

I couldn't last another day like this, wondering how everything would turn out once she finally knew the truth.

Exhaling heavily, I studied her face, bringing my forehead closer to hers for just a moment, and I whispered, "Tomorrow. I'm telling you everything tomorrow. I can't do this to you anymore. I can't do it to myself."

***

Hannah woke the next morning in a mood far darker than the day before. The sadness had disappeared, replaced by a soul-sucking rage that became a third presence in the room.

The first thing she'd done was phone Bella to make sure everything had been okay through the night, which it had, apparently, but since that phone call, Hannah had barely looked at me. There'd been no awkwardness between the two of us, but my chest pinched enough already knowing what I had to do, and Hannah stalked around like a small bear with a very sore head before she went to change after refusing to eat any of the breakfast I offered.

Then it hit me…

What if she'd heard what I'd whispered to her in the dark?

Fuck.

When she finally walked out of the bathroom, back in her workout clothes from the day before, all I could do was sit on the edge of my bed in nothing but my shorts and stare at her, silently pleading for her to talk to me.

Her eyes caught mine, and she did a double take before she came to a halt, and her shoulders sagged.

"I'm sorry," she said with obvious defeat in her voice.

"What for?"

"Waking up like this. Unable to strap on a smile and say thank you for everything you've done and continue to do."

"I don't want your thanks. I've already told you."

"But I don't want you to see me like this anymore." She gestured to herself. "It's frustrating to have all this anger inside me, Logan. I have nowhere to put it. I thought escaping and sleeping might help but…" She shook her head before walking over to the bed and dropping down beside me. I turned to look into her eyes, and of course, my heart began to race ahead of itself, the same way it always did when she was close. "What can I do? I'm so tired of trying to hold everything in. I'm drained. Emotionally ruined. Yet, I can feel all this energy flowing through me like I…

like I need to *punch* something."

I raised a brow as I leaned away from her.

She rolled her eyes and laughed softly. "Like I'd hit you when I need you the most."

More fucking guilt piled on top of more fucking guilt.

I brought my hands between my parted thighs, noticing the way Hannah's eyes had drifted to my naked torso before she blinked quickly and looked down at her feet, clearing her throat as subtly as possible.

Tell her. Tell her now. Put her out of her misery. Put yourself out of it, too.

"I may be able to help you unleash some rage," I said, bringing her eyes back to meet mine.

"Don't sacrifice yourself for me, Logan."

"Maybe I want to."

Her brows furrowed. "What are you talking about?"

"Get your sneakers on. I'm taking you somewhere. Somewhere you can unleash whatever the hell you need to on whoever offers themselves up, and when it's over, you'll either feel better, or you'll feel the same. What have you got to lose?"

***

We pulled into the parking lot of TKO Gym, and Hannah's sudden laughter had me grinning to myself when I brought the SUV to a stop.

"I see where this is going," she said with a smile I fucking loved to see. She turned to me. "Will there be a lot of people inside?"

"A few, but they won't care about us. They're not like that here. Just in case, though, I called ahead and spoke to the owner. Remember him? The guy with me that night at the club with

Jasper."

She nodded. "I remember."

"He's got a room in the back he rents out for all different reasons. Films, stunt work, one-on-one training. That sort of thing. I asked him if it was free and if I could call in a favor. He was happy to help."

She looked back at the gym again. "You did that for me?"

"It's no big deal."

She shook her head. "You never think anything you do is a big deal."

You have no idea.

We got out of the car and made our way inside; me leading, while she trailed not far behind, keeping herself close without holding my hand the way I wanted her to, even if that did make me a selfish bastard.

I waited for people to look up from their workouts—for their eyes to linger on Hannah for a second too long—but none of them bothered. They didn't register our arrival. Everyone in that gym was there to fight their own demons, which made me relax as I turned to put her in front, placing my hand on the small of Hannah's back, noticing the way she flinched a little before sinking into my touch.

I guided her to where Creed stood against a wall at the back of the gym, his arms folded as he studied the men and women in front of him. When he caught sight of us, he offered a small nod, a slight smile, and he tipped his head to the left, gesturing for me to take the door that led through to the private training room. I offered him a nod of my own, grateful when he never cast a glance Hannah's way.

Once inside the training room, I locked the door and turned to see her already peeling the cardigan off her arms before dropping it to the floor like it didn't matter.

"You ever done this before?" I walked over to the selection of boxing gloves and pads displayed on the wall, trying my damn best not to focus on the tanned sliver of skin that now sat exposed between Hannah's high-waisted leggings and her flowy cropped tank top. Any part of her I caught a glimpse of, I savored, but that damn strip of skin would make me lose my mind if I didn't keep my eyes off it.

"I've thrown a few punches," she said. "I've held my own on occasion."

I stopped in my tracks, turning to look at her with a raised brow. "Really?"

"Don't look so surprised."

"I didn't have you down as the fighting type."

"I was a lot of things before I became Cole's timid little wifey."

"I don't doubt that for a minute," I said, trying to hide the growl in my voice. Even the mention of his name now made my jaw tick. If I felt this angry, I could only imagine what was going on in her mind.

Reaching for some gloves, I eyed them up, eventually choosing the size I thought would fit best before I walked back over to her and held one up so she could slip her hand inside. She pushed her tiny hand in, but I focused solely on her, waiting for her to expand on that particular story.

"I had a rough childhood," she eventually said. "And with that comes a big attitude at various points throughout my teen years. Some girls once tried to make fun of me. I had to show them why that wasn't a good idea. Back then, before I had money in my life, it was eat or be eaten. I chose to eat."

"Damn, Hannah," I blew out in a breath. "That's kinda hot."

"I was hoping for smoking hot, actually."

"Goal achieved."

A mad blush ran to her cheeks. "I'm a woman of many talents. There's a lot you don't know about me yet."

"So, what you're saying is, I should be on my toes when you start throwing punches my way in a minute."

"I prefer not to hurt the people I like. You're safe." She slipped her hand into the next glove, and that tension was there between us again, unavoidable.

"Don't make promises you can't keep," I said quietly before I broke eye contact and walked back to the far wall to collect the pads for my hands.

Several punch bags hung down from rafters, but I didn't want her to have to use them. They were heavy and unresponsive. They wouldn't offer her the answers she needed. They wouldn't drive her to insanity, forcing every bad thought out of her mouth the way I could with the pads and nothing more than a few simple moves.

She needed to purge herself, but she also needed to let her agony out, too.

I only hoped that, however this went, I did right by her in the end.

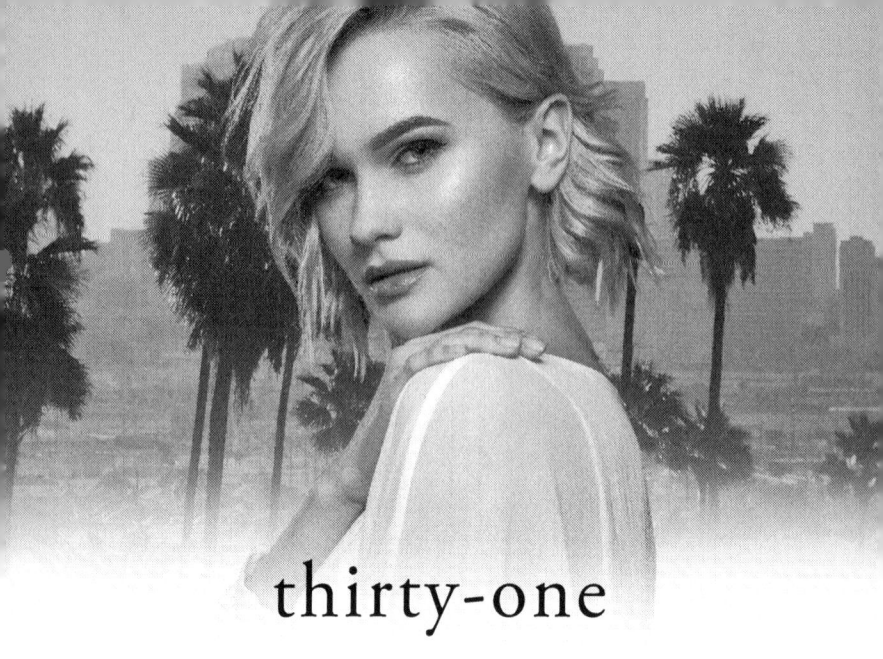

thirty-one

Hannah

"**S**on of a—" I gritted my teeth and pushed damp hair away from my forehead with my forearm.

Logan didn't take my stink eye to heart. He just smirked and challenged me to keep track of him—to hit the pad this time when he moved instead of missing it. I'd have called him an asshole, but we both knew I wouldn't have meant it.

Knowing *why* I was doing what I was doing made me feel like a performing monkey, but I performed anyway, willing everything bad and toxic inside me to pour out and free me from the tormented prison of confusion I'd found myself caught up in.

It wasn't easy, grieving a man you loathed.

It wasn't easy being around a man you'd grown to desire only to feel guilty about it.

That's why I pounded the boxing pads Logan held up in front of me, even though I was clumsy on my feet when he turned us in a different direction, trying to rile me up when I wasn't hitting him hard enough.

His movements were smooth. Coordinated.

Mine were a bundle of missteps, missed shots, and frustrated growls, but it made me work up a sweat. I was so out of practice and unfamiliar with this aggressive side of me that I hadn't realized how far down I'd buried it until Logan forced me to try and pull it back to the surface.

He didn't say a word during the movements. He didn't let me know which way he'd go, how high he'd place his pad-covered hands, or how low he'd drop them. He didn't tell me when he was about to bounce back suddenly or press forward and make me think about my steps. And because I had to think so much about what I was doing, my mind let go of all the shit that felt like unwanted guests in there.

"Goddammit," I said in a rush when my glove didn't connect properly.

"You're fine. Keep it up."

"I'm so out of shape."

"Like hell you are." His eyes drifted down to my waist for just a moment before he forced them back up to my gloves, his jaw tense again.

That little look of *something,* whatever it had been, made a fresh dose of adrenaline rush through my veins, making my nipples harden without any way to cover them up.

"Feeling good?" Logan asked, and I wondered if he'd noticed my obvious arousal before I realized he was looking everywhere *but* there. I raised my hands and threw several more punches.

"Is that what I'm meant to feel?" I asked through panting

breaths as a rivulet of sweat dropped from my forehead to my nose. I wiped it away with my forearm, looking up at Logan through hooded eyes, trying not to think about the fact that every time he braced himself to take the pressure of my punch, the muscles in his arms tensed, tightening the already-tight fabric around his biceps.

I smacked my glove into the middle of the left pad before moving to do the same to the right—my eyes focused on the targets.

"Because if it is, then yeah, I guess I feel good," I pushed out through gritted teeth before landing another punch.

"Time to turn it up a notch." He nodded to his left pad, then to his right. "We'll do a four-punch combination. Two uppercuts followed by two jabs on either side. We go until I say stop."

"So bossy."

"You haven't seen anything yet."

"You don't scare me," I wheezed, following him as he moved the pads, first aiming them down for me to hit upward, then quickly switching to placing them upright, so I could jab either side.

"Again," he ordered, making me frown, but I did what he asked of me anyway, repeating the combination, barely taking a breath in between. "Nice," he said as he watched me. "Again."

He repeated his instruction another ten times, draining me of life and slowing my movements down.

"Jesus, Logan," I huffed.

"One more."

"Let a girl breathe, will you?"

"You're breathing just fine. Stop whining."

I scowled harder, my face turning murderous as I eyed him while I threw all four punches to the pads and stepped back.

"Last one."

"You said that last time!"

"I lied."

"Logan…"

"Come on, slugger. You've got this." He winked, bracing himself for the attack. "Use that anger you woke up with this morning."

"This anger?" I challenged, throwing an uppercut to the pad opposite to the one he expected me to go to. His hand recoiled farther back than usual, and his eyes lit up with mischief.

"There she is."

"Yeah?" I smacked the pad again, my frustration rising up from the very depths of my belly. "What about that anger?" I said, smacking the second pad with even more effort than I thought I was capable of.

"Good." He nodded, his face turning serious as he studied me, readying his feet for my next move. "Give me more."

"What if I don't have more?" I grunted, throwing another punch that landed, followed by another. "What if I'm tired? What if I'm worn out?"

Smack, smack, smack. My hands flew everywhere, and I wasn't sure what was more impressive. The way Logan moved, taking it all in his slick stride, or the way I now followed him, the clumsy woman of moments ago long gone.

"What if it isn't about what you want, but what I want for a change?" I challenged.

"I wouldn't believe you," he said with a huff of air escaping him when my glove connected with him again.

"Why not?"

"Because there's too much fire in your eyes. There's too much rage in your voice. There's stuff in there you need to set free. You either do it now and leave it in this room, or you throw the gloves down and take it home with you. Spoiler alert: I'm not letting you leave here until you give it everything you've got."

"Who made you the boss?"

"I did."

"Well, screw you, Logan," I said. *Smack.* "And screw…"
Smack.

"Finish that sentence."

"Screw the whole world."

Smack, smack.

"Tell them, Hannah. Get it out."

"Screw the public. Screw the press," I raged on, my sole focus those pads on Logan's hands now as the venom I'd tried so hard to push down rose and rose and rose until it took over my veins, rushing through my body, turning everything black. "Screw the band, the management, the publicists."

"Keep going."

"Screw everybody who thinks my family is their business."

Heat rose into my face, and my breaths came heavy and hard, the sound of them echoing off the walls around us.

That was the problem when the anger rose.

So did the tears.

"Screw the family I never had," I lashed out. "Screw my lying, cheating, dead husband who left me." My fists flew, my arms growing weaker while my emotions grew wilder. "Screw him for saying those vows he never meant. Screw him for tricking me into loving him, then leaving me to hate him once he'd had enough."

Smack. Hard.

"Because I do hate him now. I hate him because he left me, and he took *all* my choices away when he went."

I pushed forward, wiping at a stray tear that fell down one cheek, and I sniffed up to swallow back the aching lump in my throat. I pictured Cole's face on either pad, and whether it made me a bad person or not, I launched my fists at them, over and over, words falling out of my mouth about what he'd done to me—what he'd done to our daughter. I lost track of every curse word I set free. I forgot Logan could hear them. I didn't care about the sweat now dripping down my forehead, my chest, my arms, or my back. I didn't care about anything but fighting and crying and shaming the man I'd once loved with nothing less than my whole heart.

"Everybody leaves," I croaked, my voice strangled. "Everybody makes the choices for me."

I drove on and on and on, every secret dark thought I'd ever had about my late husband and parents pouring free until I had no more secrets left to hide, and I pushed Logan back against the wall, leaving him with nowhere else to go and nothing else to do other than to stare at me with a blank expression.

No judgment.

No anger.

No shame.

He let me be, the way he always did.

"Screw him, Logan," I whispered, my voice barely recognizable as I looked up at a different kind of man. One who I could never imagine letting anybody down. "Screw him for turning me into this."

My heart pounded wildly as he dropped his arms and pads down by his side, his chest rising and falling as heavy as mine now. His wild eyes searched my even wilder ones as though he was seeing them for the very first time. Really seeing them. The way no one ever had dared to look for them before. Vulnerable and cold. Hardened yet fragile. A clusterfuck of emotions that continued to contradict one another over and over again.

"Why couldn't he be like you, huh?" I whispered, my brows creasing together.

"Hannah, don't—"

"You're everything he's not and more."

I took a step closer to him, not afraid of anything now and somehow feeling freer than I had in months as my body bled without bleeding.

At that moment, I saw Logan clearly, too.

I saw a selfless man in front of me that any woman would be lucky to have in her life.

Somehow, I'd become one of the lucky ones. He was here… with me. My savior. My friend.

Closing the distance between us, I pressed my fists against his chest, able to feel the pounding of his heart even through the thickness of the gloves as I rose to my toes, watching as Logan's attention fell to my lips.

That clean, fresh, intoxicating smell of his mixed with his masculine sweat made my head dizzy, and his warm breaths falling over my face made my stomach tighten.

I stared up at him, waiting for his eyes to meet mine again, not caring if this was okay, only knowing that finally taking what I'd denied myself for a while somehow felt right now.

Another tear fell down my cheek, a remnant of anger leaking out without my permission, catching Logan's gaze.

"What are you doing?" he whispered.

"I haven't decided yet," I panted "But it *is* my choice, isn't it?"

A heartbeat passed us by before he said, "It's always your choice, Hannah," and the sound of my name on his lips became my undoing.

"That's what I thought." Pushing up to close the distance, I closed my eyes, pressed my mouth against his, and I kissed him.

I kissed Logan.

The man I'd come to rely on to get me through each day, and the man who now released a low moan in the back of his throat that made my nipples tighten in want and send a jolt of desire straight between my legs.

I'd missed that feeling, and I wanted more.

He couldn't touch me with the pads still on his hands, so I led the kiss, my tongue meeting his as though it was always meant to, the gentle sweep of them together making my body melt until I couldn't stand the thought of pulling away and never kissing him again.

He didn't stop me. He didn't push me away, and my heart fluttered with contentment at just how *right* this felt, the two of us coming together as one this way.

Fuck, he could kiss.

The pads on his hands came up to brush against my thighs, pulling me closer, and his hips pressed to my body while I only pressed into his chest even more.

More… I wanted more.

I wanted to climb inside him and drown in his affection. I didn't care about anything outside of this room. It didn't feel like I would again.

But then Logan suddenly froze, his lips still against mine, and his hands falling away from my thighs. I tried to urge him to carry on. To make this last forever because it had been the first time I'd felt so calm in years, and it was all because of him… but it was too late.

He'd grown cold beneath me.

His hips fell away, making my eyes flutter open to take him in before I broke the kiss and stared up at him.

He looked in physical pain as his eyes searched mine.

I opened my mouth to ask him what was wrong—had I crossed a line he hadn't wanted me to cross? Had I ruined *everything?* — but I didn't get the chance.

"I was there that night," he said, his voice low and sorrowful as he stared at me, his breathing growing heavier. "It was me, Hannah. I was on duty."

"What?"

Logan closed his eyes, hiding his regret before he unleashed them on me again. "I swear to you. I did everything to save him. I gave it my all. I did everything I could, but none of it worked. It wasn't enough. *I* wasn't enough, Hannah. He's dead because of me."

"What are you talking abo—"

But then it felt like my heart stopped as Logan's words fell into place, and one name whispered its presence all around us.

Cole.

He was talking about Cole.

No.

No, no, no.

This isn't happening.

My body turned to ice in an instant.

I fell back onto flat feet, putting distance between us as I took a step away, and then another, my confusion growing as I narrowed my eyes on him.

"Logan, no…"

"I'm so sorry, Hannah."

"Please…" I whimpered. "Please tell me you aren't saying what I think you're saying."

"I wish I could but—"

"Cole? You were *there*? The night he…"

Logan swallowed again, tossing the pads off his hands in two swift movements. "Let me explain. Please." He tried to take a step toward me, but I quickly held up my hand, needing space. Needing distance.

I'd just kissed him.

I'd thrown myself against his body, and I'd enjoyed it.

Wanted more. But now…

Now…

I felt sick.

Logan stopped in his tracks while my eyes fell to the floor as I tried to piece everything together, but nothing made sense, the only truth I could cling to being that Logan wasn't who I thought he was. I'd created a version of him in my mind that I'd *wanted* to be real, and that version no longer existed.

"You didn't tell me," I said quietly.

"I wanted to. It's eaten me up inside, Hannah. I've tried so many times."

"You lied."

"And I've hated myself for it. Every day."

"All that time together…"

I looked up to take him in, hating the way my heart skipped a beat at the sight of him, and how his eyes held every regret he'd ever had in them, making me want to go to him. To go back to that kiss we'd shared only moments ago when I'd felt lighter and giddier than I had in so long—maybe ever.

When he'd been the one to save me, not *lie* to me.

"That day at the drive-thru… was that… a coincidence?"

Please say yes, please say yes, please say yes, Logan, but one look at his expression and I knew the answer was no.

I just couldn't stick around to hear the word come out of his mouth.

I was going to throw up.

"I never meant to hurt you," Logan said quietly, as though that fixed everything. Like it didn't matter that he'd set himself up in my life and planned this thing between us all along.

I huffed out a venomous laugh. "Yeah, well, Cole used to say the same thing. He kept on doing it anyway."

"I'm not him, Hannah. I would never—"

My face crumpled, and my tears rose to the surface. "You already *have*." He tried to take a step closer, but I took one back, shaking my head violently. "Don't. Don't come any closer, Logan, or I swear."

"Just let me talk to you."

"*I don't want to talk!*" I cried. "Not anymore. I don't even know who you are!"

"I'm the same—"

"No." I shook my head again, face turning harder. "You're nothing like the man I thought you were. He would never keep this from me, and I have no desire to find out who the real you is anymore."

The gloves on my hands felt stupid now. I unfastened them as quickly as I could and let them fall to the floor before I held my clammy hand out to Logan, and I swallowed back my heartache. "Give me the keys."

"Hannah…"

"The car keys, Logan. *Now*."

He blew out a heavy breath, and I felt the weight of it. I saw everything I hadn't allowed him to say, but I didn't want to *hear* it because the past had proven to me well enough that I was a sucker for words and apologies. I refused to be that woman anymore.

No man would ever make a mockery of me again.

Reaching into the pocket of his shorts, Logan pulled out the keys and tossed them to me carefully. I caught them and immediately turned away from him, marching over to the door and ignoring my name on his lips behind me. I had my hands on the lock and was about to make my escape when Logan's hand pushed the door closed again, holding me hostage. He held it there as he towered over me, crowding me with that scent of his I'd thought of as magic but now smelled like poison.

"I'll scream, Logan. I swear it," I whispered, keeping my

eyes on the floor. "Let me go."

"Look at me, Hannah," he whispered back, and my own flesh betrayed me as goosebumps flared to life at the sound of his voice.

That kiss had opened too much of my imagination, and despite the treachery I felt at knowing he'd lied to me all along, that imagination flooded me with images of Logan lying over me, whispering my name the way he just had done. Trapping me beneath him like this in the coziness of that condo of his—the one I already knew I'd miss once I walked away.

But I had to walk away. I'd do it any chance I got now. I'd run a million miles from anyone I couldn't trust.

"Please," he breathed. "Even if it's the last time you ever do, just look at me."

Hating myself for it, I closed my eyes and raised my chin before opening them to take him in, knowing I'd never allow myself to see him after this.

The sight of him killed me.

I'd grown too attached. Too reliant. And somewhere in the last forty-eight hours, I'd grown too lustful.

His face mirrored my own, full of unspoken things and far too much pain.

His nostrils flared as he inhaled slowly only to release it all as he said, "I'm so fucking sorry, Hannah. You have no idea."

I hated the way I still wanted him—how I could still taste him on my lips. I hated that I could never have more of him now. Not after this.

"Don't you dare follow me ever again. We're done. Goodbye, Logan."

With that, I opened the door and left him behind, not caring who the hell saw me fall apart this time or what they had to say about it.

Some things couldn't be hidden.

My devastation over losing Logan had just become one of them.

thirty-two

Logan

What the fuck had I done?

The pain in Hannah's eyes may as well have been a knife she pushed straight into my heart and twisted wildly. She'd kissed me—fucking *kissed* me—and it had been the sweetest kiss my lips had ever tasted. It had been more explosive than I could ever have imagined, and it had the power to destroy me. I'd grown hard beneath her touch. I'd become drunk on her body heat and damp skin. I'd lost my ever-loving mind for a minute too long before that dark cloud of guilt had sucked all the light from, not just the room but my life, reminding me that nothing more could happen between us until she knew the truth.

She deserved that.

Hannah deserved everything this world hadn't given her. Yet, she got me. An asshole who paraded around like a saint.

"Logan?"

Creed pushed through the door and entered the training room, no doubt seeing me on the floor with my back against the wall, knees drawn up, and the heels of my hands pressed against my forehead as I stared at nothing while he dropped to his haunches in front of me, waiting.

"Wanna tell me what's going on?" he asked.

"Not really."

He sighed. "She looked pretty upset when she ran."

Ran? Fuck. The thought crippled me. I wanted to chase her, but she'd warned me not to, making me feel like a fucking creep for doing it the first time we met.

"Did she say anything?" I asked.

"Not a word. Wanna talk about it?"

I dropped my hands and glanced up at him. I must have looked as shit as I felt because sympathy and understanding radiated from Creed's gaze.

My head fell back against the wall with a thud. I could still taste Hannah on my lips. The scent of her lingered everywhere. My default mode since Dale's death all those years ago had been to clam up tight, shut everyone out, and deal with shit on my own, but look how far that had gotten me. I was thirty years old, had never been in love, and was fucking tired. Maybe talking to someone about the stuff deep down inside that bothered me and the shit I'd done wrong wouldn't kill me as much as I'd always thought it would.

"It's a scary thing to talk about all the stuff going on inside your head," I said.

"Not as scary as keeping it in and slowly killing yourself over it."

"You should have been a therapist."

"I thought about it, but they'd make me cover up my muscles, and I'm too vain to be strapped down beneath a suit and tie," he said with an obvious smirk.

Rolling my head against the wall, I caught his eyes. "You're a good man, Creed."

"That's what they tell me. Now, about that talking…"

"Any chance I could ask you for a ride first? I need to get my car. Left it outside a bar a couple of nights ago."

"Let me guess. You've been staying with the chick that just ran out of here crying since then. The one I recognized as Cole Newman's lady."

Fuck Newman. Hannah is mine now, even if I've lost her already. She doesn't belong to him. She's too good for both of us.

"Something like that," I said instead.

"What the hell have you gotten yourself into, Logan?"

"A mess I'm struggling to get myself out of. I swear, I'll tell you everything if you can get me back to my car."

"You're starting to cost me more than your membership is worth."

"And I promise to pay you back everything I owe."

He sighed again and rose to his feet, holding his hand out to me. I took it and groaned as he pulled me to standing, where he slapped a solid hand against my back and shook his head.

"Why is it always the handsome fuckers who end up giving me so much trouble, huh?"

***

Talking to Creed helped for all of five minutes, but the moment I walked into my condo, the tinge of relief I'd got from telling my story faded away, only to be replaced by Hannah's presence. The shorts and T-shirt she'd worn sat folded on the kitchen island to remind me of what I'd done and who I'd lost. I never would have thought clothes I'd had for years would come to represent so much.

I'd had her.

I'd lied.

I'd lost her.

"*Fuck,*" I hissed. My keys fell to the countertop, along with my palms, and I hung my head low and closed my eyes. "Fuck," I sighed.

If I turned around, the imprint of her head would still be on my pillow. The imprint of her body would still be on my sheets.

I couldn't stay here, either.

Even though you're hurting now, and she'll be hurting, too… you did the right thing, Logan. That's what Creed had said to me on the drive to the parking lot where my car had sat for two days.

Nausea jabbed at my stomach. Even when days went by where Hannah and I didn't talk, just knowing she had my number and knowing she had someone there for her had been a source of comfort. Now, she only had Bella and Liv again, and I'd chosen to reveal my true colors while the media was hunting her, trying to strike as many shots into her fragile heart as they could before she eventually fell to the floor in surrender and gave them everything they demanded.

I couldn't let that happen.

I just didn't know how the fuck to stop it now.

Pushing myself off the island, I dug my cell phone out of my pocket and pulled up her name. I'd seen the way she felt about me in her eyes before she'd turned and walked away. Hannah wouldn't answer my calls yet. Maybe she never would again. But I had to try to reach out to her in some way. I had to let her know all my truths now.

ME

Hannah, please. Talk to me. I got myself all tangled up. I made a mess of fucking everything. I'm sorry. I only ever wanted to protect you.

Thirty minutes passed with no response.

ME

I've never been good with words. I've never been good at saying the right thing at the right time. Even now, I don't know if this is the right thing to do. Should I keep going and show you how much I care, or should I walk away, respect your wishes, and leave you the hell alone, even when I have so much more to say?

ME

Whatever's going through your mind right now, I need you to know one thing: none of this is on you. It's all me. I'm to blame. I'll never forgive myself for hurting you.

Between all those messages, I'd showered, changed, brushed my teeth until my gums were raw, and I'd paced the small space of my condo until my feet ached. The day wore on, but she never replied, and as the minutes turned into hours and the hours turned into a shift in daylight, it dawned on me that everything I felt wasn't because of the guilt I carried because Cole had died. It wasn't because I worried about the media on Hannah's back or the fact that her dead husband had slept with more people than a working girl. Those were just pathetic excuses born from a boy too scared to love anyone or anything again. The truth was simple, despite it scaring the shit out of me.

My feelings for Hannah had grown. I was fucking falling for her, and the revelation had me sinking down on my mattress as I stared at the wall ahead and blew out a breath. Then, I opened up my cell one last time.

ME

My promise stands. Whenever you need me, call. I'll be here waiting. I'll always be a choice for you, no matter how much time passes.

thirty-three

Hannah

I lost count of how many times I'd read his messages. My fingers itched to reply every time, remembering the Logan I thought I knew for just a moment before the memory of the kiss haunted me, quickly followed by his life-changing truth falling free.

I'd gone through every scenario in my mind.

He'd let Cole die on purpose so he could get close to me and Bella, for what, I couldn't figure out. Money? Fame? Security? But every time I allowed that to grow even a tiny bit, my heart shut it down, knowing that, even though I was mad at him, that wasn't who he was.

I moved onto him being a rabid fan of Envy-98 and wanting a part of Cole's life in any way he could get it, to him being an undercover reporter that had infiltrated my life to get the truth for the world to hear at his hands. Both of those didn't hold any weight, either. It was all I could focus on, finding a reason *why* he'd entered my life, and I would not rest until I got the answers I needed.

But the thing I'd been most desperate to know since the day Cole died?

Had he managed to say anything to the people who found him before he died? Had he said Bella's name or had mine passed his lips? Was there any regret in his heart, or was he happy to have lived fast and died young, just as he always swore that he would?

Knowing Logan had the ability to answer those questions should have thrilled me, but all I felt was a sick sense of dread.

Two days passed of feeling numb, followed by another three where it felt like I'd begun to grieve two people instead of just one. Time ticked on, and I tried to hide my heartache from Bella and Livia, convincing Liv especially that my melancholy came from Cole and the claims that he'd gotten some other woman pregnant.

The truth was, I'd barely thought about that scandal. Logan had taken over all my thoughts.

I thought Livia had bought the lie, too until a full week passed us by without the mention of Logan, and she'd caught me in the pool, trying to outswim my pain.

I emerged from the water and grabbed hold of the side of the pool, only to be met by a knelt-down Livia with her hands on her knees, and her knowing face in place. She gave me three chances to tell her what was going on, and by the time I'd gotten around to her final countdown of one, I sagged back into the water and groaned.

That's the problem with casting yourself out into the ocean and declaring yourself an island: life got lonely, and loneliness created even more heartache until it became impossible to outswim.

Once out of the water, Liv guided me to my favorite spot under the canopy, hiding us away from the melting sun. Two glasses of chilled wine waited at the outdoor coffee table when we took our seats.

Livia had always been thorough.

"Okay, Hannah. I love you, and I know when something's wrong. It's time to talk," she said. "You're not leaving until you've told me what's going on. Is it about your friend? Logan?"

"What makes you think that?"

She tilted her head and raised her brows. "Are we really going to do this?"

"I guess not." I sighed, knowing any resistance was pointless at that point.

So, I told her everything that had happened over the last few months. Everything… minus the kiss.

God, that kiss.

The sensuality, mixed with a tenderness I'd never experienced had blown my mind, making me sink into Logan's body as though I wanted to crawl inside him. That kiss had become the thing that haunted me the most, making me feel stupider than I already did.

I'd gone from finally being at peace the moment our lips met to falling into the darkest depths of hellish torment, unable to understand why good things never seemed to last. It was always a fleeting moment of pure serenity before some jackass pulled the rug from under my feet and brought me back down to earth with a bang.

I just never thought Logan would be that jackass.

"How much of an idiot have I been?" I asked Livia once I'd finished filling her in.

"You're not an idiot, sweetheart."

"Really?"

"Look, it's no secret I loved Cole. He gave me a home with you guys when I thought I was all out of options." Her eyes rose to meet mine. "But that doesn't mean I was blind to everything he put you through. In so many ways, he was the best man I knew. He gave everything to anyone, even when they didn't ask it of him. He threw his money around like it grew on the trees in this yard, and he never once asked anyone for a cent of that money back once it was gone. But Cole was generous with *things* only to be cruel with his time and even crueler with your heart. It hurt me to watch you suffer through the years and be forced to turn a blind eye because of Bella. It hurts my heart even more watching you have to deal with the consequences of Cole's decisions now he isn't here. I ache for you every time another story comes out."

"I'm sorry you're in the middle of it, Liv."

"I'm not. I'm happy to be the person who helps you after you took me in and helped me over the years. You and Bella; you're my family, and I've always looked out for family." Her brows furrowed for just a moment. "But can I be honest with you? Even though you might not like what I have to say."

"It's never stopped you before."

"True," she said with a half-smile. "I think you're scared, Hannah."

"Scared?"

"Yes, of figuring out the truth and realizing it isn't as bad as you're expecting it to be." Dropping her feet to the floor, she leaned forward in her seat, holding the stem of her glass in both hands. "What if Logan isn't the bad guy in this scenario?"

"He lied to me, Liv."

"He kept the full story from you."

"Same thing."

She shook her head. "I don't think it is. What if his intentions were good, but he just went about it the wrong way? There's no doubt he cared for you. Everything you've told me, everything I saw with my own eyes… those weren't the actions of a man out to manipulate you and get something out of it. I think he got himself into something he never expected to have to get himself out of, and he couldn't figure out how to untangle the mess he'd made without hurting you."

I got myself all tangled up. I made a mess of fucking everything. I'm sorry.

His message came back to me, and I searched Liv's eyes while my brain raced with everything she was saying. Of course, I wanted to believe her—both of them—but I'd been a fool for most of my life and becoming that fool again scared the crap out of me. It wasn't just me I had to think about anymore.

My daughter mattered the most.

"Haven't you ever done that before?" she asked. "Made a mess of things that seemed so simple to everyone else. You said so yourself—Logan tried to push you away more than once. He warned you, too."

"He did," and I almost let that be the end of it, but then the memory of his face when he told me the truth haunted me, and the pain of his lies sliced through my heart all over again. "You're right," I whispered. "He warned me, and I ignored him."

"Hannah…"

Springing from the patio furniture and rising to my feet, I drained the rest of my wine and pushed my wet hair back before I looked back down at Livia.

"How long am I going to keep doing that, Livia?"

"What do you mean?" She scowled.

"I mean, I've ignored every warning in my life so far, and now it's time to pay attention, don't you think? To stop being so naïve. To listen when people tell me they're no good instead of always trying to see the best in them."

"Hannah, that's not—"

"I've been thinking about taking a trip," I said, cutting her off before she could talk me down, my voice projecting strength and confidence even though inside, everything shook.

"A trip?"

"Yeah. I need to get out of here—escape LA for a while. This city, the people… everything. It's not real life, is it? I'm living in Cole's dream, not my own. I need to remember what's out there beyond this goddamn house, and I need to put distance between everything that's happened this year."

"Where are you going to go?"

"I don't know. Maybe I could take Bella to Seattle. Show her where I'm from, who I am, and maybe take some time to figure that stuff out for myself."

"But you hate Seattle."

"Do I? Or did I hate it because Cole told me to hate it so he could bring me out here without me putting up much of a fight?"

Livia opened her mouth to speak before slowly closing it again and shrugging her shoulders, unable to answer the way she obviously wanted to.

"The truth is, Liv, I'm lost. I don't have a clue about who I am, or what my thoughts are. I don't know if my likes and dislikes are truly mine or if they're just Cole's thoughts that have bled into me over the years."

"You don't have to explain yourself to me."

"I'm explaining it to *myself*. I'm twenty-nine. My husband died months ago, and I've yet to process how I feel about any of it. Should I grieve? Should I feel relief? Can I admit to feeling both without the world thinking I'm a massive bitch for doing so? What's right? What's wrong?" I paused, swallowing down the emotion that lodged itself in my throat. "It's time to figure out what's real in my life and what's not, and it's time for me to do it on my own."

"You don't want me to come with you?"

"I'd love you to, but I think it's best if I go without you. It'll be nice to spend some time off the beaten track with Bella. To focus on her and nobody else."

I saw every doubt written across her face, but she kept them to herself just for me, offering a small nod of acceptance instead. Livia didn't like the idea of me traveling across the country on my own because she'd always been there beside me when things went wrong. I'd had her to lean on for everything, too.

But now… now I need to strengthen my own legs.

To shoulder my own mistakes, pain, and problems. It wasn't anyone else's job, and I'd be damned if I let other people live my life for me from now on.

No matter their intentions.

No matter how their kisses made me feel or how often I fell asleep seeing dark eyes full of regret and welcoming arms that begged me to run into them again.

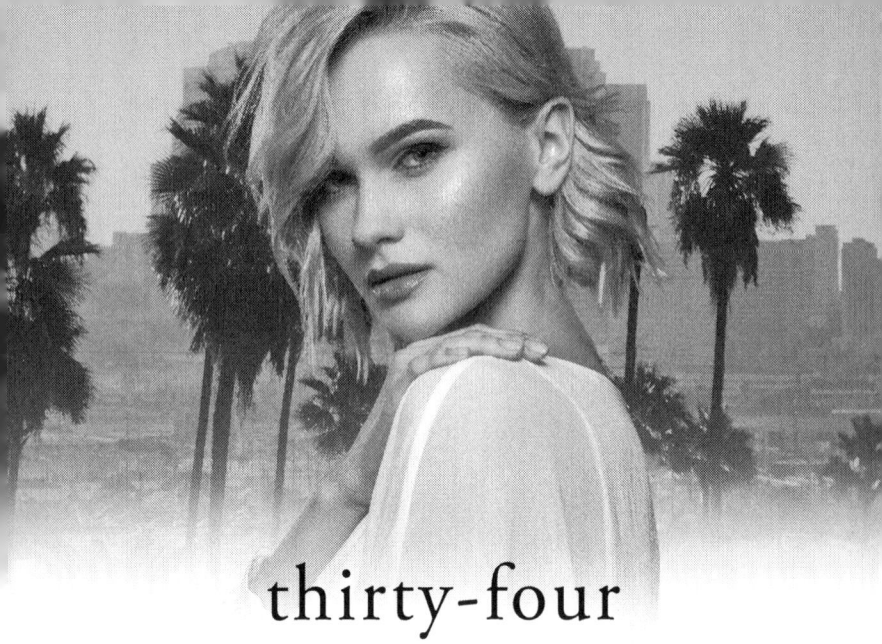

thirty-four
Hannah

Bella and I landed in Seattle a week later.

The media wars continued on around me. There was no real escape. Every day brought about a new angle to look at the sudden Hannah-Cole-Malia love triangle I'd been caught up in.

Malia; the name of the woman carrying my dead husband's baby, apparently. I couldn't bear to hear it, and every day that Bella had been in school, I could only hope and pray that she didn't hear anything about it, either. I suspected that it had been the reason her school was so lenient when I'd told them I planned on taking her away.

They'd seen the news. They understood my need to run.

Thankfully, Bella had no idea why we were taking an unexpected vacation. Her innocent eyes had lit up the night sky when I'd told her to pack a bag of her favorite things because we were heading on an adventure. The way she'd thrown her arms around my neck and squeezed me tightly made me wonder if she'd been wanting this for a long time, too.

When she asked if Logan could join us, I allowed myself to imagine it for just a second—the three of us together, escaping this life to discover something new for a short while—but then I remembered everything that had gone on between us, and the pain of his betrayal stung even harsher than before. Bella liked him. Having to tell her that he couldn't join this special adventure of ours shouldn't have made me feel as bad as it did.

My need to stay low and off the radar had me booking us into a motel off the beaten track in the town of Bainbridge Island, only a forty-minute drive to Seattle, where we would eventually end up. I wanted Bella to experience different horizons. To feel different climates and understand that, while Los Angeles might be what we knew, it wasn't the whole world anymore. At least not to us.

Out motel in Bainbridge Island had two bedrooms and a shared bathroom, the building more like a log cabin you'd find in the middle of a forest, empty and ready to explore. Bella jumped on her bed with so much enthusiasm, I was nervous she'd break a spring, but then she fell onto her back with her arms and legs spread out like a starfish while I watched her from the doorway, leaning against the doorframe with a smile on my face.

For the first time in a long time, I looked at her as something other than my daughter.

She was a small person in her own right. Bella was light and life, magic and sunshine. Every room she walked into, she lit up like she was the North Star, and she wasn't prepared to make any apologies for it.

"What's your bed like, Mommy?" she asked, her head tilted

on the bed so she could see me.

"It's not as bouncy as yours, but there's room in there for the two of us if you get lonely later and want a cuddle."

"Never!" She threw her arms up above her head and brought her legs in and out like she was making a snow angel. "This is my new favorite place, and I'm going to stay here forever and ever."

Despite her enthusiasm, later that night, once the fatigue kicked in and the sky had turned dark, her small body slipped under my comforter, and her tiny body snuggled in beside me. I didn't waste a minute pulling her closer, pretending to be half-asleep as I tried not to smile against her long, soft hair.

Tomorrow, we'd explore Bainbridge Island a little more. We'd eat in every diner, cafe, or restaurant she desired, with the mountains disappearing into the clouds behind us. We'd walk hand-in-hand among normal people without the sirens of a ruined city in the background or the fear of grown men with cameras jumping out from behind any trees. We'd soak up the open air, no longer confined by four walls and the same routine, day in, day out. We'd be free to be mother and daughter, and we'd live life on our own terms, if only temporarily.

As long as I had her, I had everything.

I continued to tell myself that, even as I drifted to sleep to find the one man I couldn't escape waiting for me there in a dream world I had no control over.

God damn you, Logan.

***

Two days later, Bella and I slipped into the rental car, and I drove us to the outskirts of Seattle, where her father and I first met.

I wasn't sure if it was the exhaustion from the time we'd spent exploring every inch of Bainbridge Island, or the fact she'd eaten herself into a coma and no doubt felt a little sluggish now, but Bella was unusually quiet on the journey. No matter how much I encouraged her to talk, she remained subdued, her focus on the roads we drove down, her eyes somewhat heavy.

I decided to leave her to her own thoughts instead of pressing her to open up to me. I saw so much of her father in her that I sometimes forgot she was made up of me, too. When I had too much going on in my head, I shut the world out with the best of them, so I had no business demanding anything different from my daughter, especially when we traveled on roads unfamiliar to her.

It took thirty minutes for her to eventually speak.

"Mommy?"

"Yes, bug?"

"Did you stop being friends with Mr. Logan?"

The mention of her special name for him made me turn to look at her as she stared out of the window, as though a random thought had simply popped into her head and rolled out without any realization of what it did to me. Of the memories it invoked or the ridiculous desire that still pooled in the very depths of my belly.

Memories of that kiss.

"What makes you ask that?"

"I haven't heard you talk about him since I stayed at Aunt Liv's that weekend." Bella turned to me with innocent eyes. "I liked him. He was nice."

Trying to compose myself, I focused on the road ahead, ignoring the thumping of my heart. "I liked him, too, sweetie."

"But you don't anymore?"

"I never said that."

"Your face did."

I cast a quick glance her way, unable to stop my small scowl before I schooled my features and stared straight ahead again. "It's a little… complicated, Bella."

"Why? At school, you're either friends or you're not. Why is it complicated for you and him?"

"It doesn't quite work that way as adults, unfortunately."

"Why not?"

"Because adults are foolish."

"I don't understand."

I took a moment to gather my thoughts. "What's that saying? We have friends who come into our lives for different reasons. Some for a lifetime, some for a season. It means not everyone is going to stay, bug. Sometimes we have friends who will be there when we need them the most, but once we're better, they go away again, knowing we're okay now."

"That's what he did?"

"I think so," I said with a small nod.

"That's sad," she said softly. "He helped us. He should have been able to stay for doing that."

I had no argument for that without exposing her to the truth, and she was too young to bear the weight of any more news that could destroy her already fragile happiness.

"He was a good listener," she said. "I liked that about him. Guess I'll have to find someone else to help me now."

"Help you?"

She sighed dramatically. "There's another thing at school. Most people are taking their parents in to do a talk about what they do for a job, and I wanted to take part, but you don't work, and Daddy is…" She trailed off, not needing to finish that particular sentence.

I had to swallow down the self-loathing, the anger at Cole, and the disappointment I held for my six-year-old daughter, who was having to grow up way too quickly when all I'd ever wanted was for her to enjoy her childhood for as long as humanly possible.

"Do you think Mr. Logan would have done it?" she asked with hope still in her voice as she turned to face me again. "If you'd still been friends?"

Logan would have been there for her without question. He probably still would, had it not been for me standing in the way. I tried to think of other people in her life she could show off with pride, whizzing through a feeble list in my mind. I didn't want any of Cole's bandmates to show up at her school on her father's behalf. They'd spent far too long in the limelight and would no doubt roll up to the building with a hooker in the back of their limo before pulling up their zipper and walking the school halls with a smoke perched between their lips, reeking of scotch.

Livia couldn't do it. As much as her job meant the world to Bella and me, having a housekeeper wasn't exactly something my daughter would want parading around in front of her classmates.

Kate wouldn't be able to schedule it into her busy lifestyle, and like Bella just reminded me… I didn't actually have a job other than taking care of her.

It made sense for Bella to think of Logan, and I hated how things had turned out even more so than I had before.

"Mommy?" she pressed.

I blinked myself back into the moment, offering her a small smile before I focused on the road. "I… I think he would have, yes."

"Oh."

"I'm sorry, bug."

"S'okay," she said with a shrug, showing me that it was anything *but* okay.

"I mean… I could still ask him… if that's what you wanted me to do."

She pushed her body up in her seat, her eyes wide. "Really?

Even though you're not friends anymore? *I* can still be his friend?"

"Whatever makes you happy, Bella," I said, unable to miss the pinching of my heart. The mere thought of having Logan in my life in any capacity would be too hard, too raw, after everything that had happened. But I couldn't deny the little shred of hope that tried to gather some strength inside me at the thought of him still being around.

Bella sank back into her seat with a smile on her face. "I'd like him to go to school with me, Mommy. I really would."

If I hadn't been driving, I'd have closed my eyes to prepare myself for the onslaught of emotions that ran through me. Instead, I simply said, "I'll talk to him."

She didn't respond, and when I glanced her way, she was staring at me with a look of awe and pure love that made every ache and pain I'd ever suffered disappear in a single moment.

I'd been wrong to think any man could be my salvation.

The only thing I'd ever needed was my daughter.

The daughter determined to keep the man I couldn't stop dreaming about in my life, whether I wanted him there or not.

thirty-five

Logan

HANNAH
I'm ready to talk. I'll be back in Los Angeles Thursday afternoon.

ack in Los Angeles? Where the hell had she been?

The text came in midway through the shift from hell on a random Tuesday. So far, Jerry and I had dealt with a building fire, a concussed teen, a suspected homicide, a break-in gone wrong, and four heart-related emergencies. We hadn't stopped for a minute. No food, rest, and no time to check our phones until we finally got to go home after a brutal twenty-four hours on the clock.

It wasn't until I walked out of the station and slipped into my Outback that I finally had time to pull my cell from my pocket, and that's when I saw it.

Her name.

For a moment, all I could do was stare at it, the temperature in the car rising, forcing me to roll down the window so I could rest my elbow on the ledge and press a knuckle to my mouth as I considered what to do or what the hell to even say.

Weeks had gone by without hearing from her. I'd thought about driving to her house, knocking on her door, and fighting because she deserved to be fought for, but I respected her too much to put my needs above her own.

She had choices.

I had to let her make them.

ME
Just tell me when and where, and I'll be there.

But fuck, that wasn't enough! How could I tell her everything I needed to say over the phone? I wanted her to see the sincerity in my eyes when I made a thousand apologies until she forgave me. I wanted to kiss the shit out of her again, but do it right this time, with no guilt or shame taking over. I wanted to show her how a real man could treat her and to press my hips to hers and let her *feel* what she did to me—to show her the only intention I ever had was to make her feel good.

Those thoughts had my thumbs flying across the phone screen, and hitting send before I could stop them.

ME
I've missed you.

HANNAH
Don't, Logan.

ME
I have.

HANNAH

I'm not ready for that. I'm not sure I ever will be.

ME

I'll never ask you for anything more than you're willing to give ever again. That doesn't mean I don't want it, though, because I do.

HANNAH

What does that even mean?

ME

You know, Hannah. It's why you kissed me.

No response came. Not that I should have expected one. This wasn't some dumb fucking movie where the guy messed up, said the right thing a couple of times, and the woman fell dopily into his arms. This was real life—her life, Bella's life—and she had no reason to ever take me back now that she knew everything we'd had was based upon half-truths and a rotten fucking secret I should never have kept from her. I had nothing to give. No money. No grand gestures. No Hollywood lifestyle. No Beverly Hills mansion or six-car garage with spare SUVs inside. Even though Cole had been a bastard, at least he'd left her with the security of knowing she'd be able to provide for Bella her entire life.

All I had was a shitty condo in an area of LA I didn't particularly like, and a few years' worth of savings that could take us on a couple of nice vacations.

But no sooner had those thoughts rattled around in my brain than I pushed them aside. Money, things… they didn't matter to Hannah. The only thing she'd ever asked of anyone was to see her, hear her, and be truthful with her.

Whoever said two out of three wasn't bad was a goddamn liar.

I growled, running a hand over my forehead before I pinched

the bridge of my nose and squeezed it tightly, punishing myself with any kind of pain I could find in any given moment these days.

"So, Hannah in Beverly Hills, huh?"

I turned to see Jerry standing beside me, looking over my shoulder yet again, not at all ashamed of the fact that he'd been watching me sitting in the driver's seat of my car, lost in my phone like a total loser.

Folding his arms over his chest, he raised a brow. "The woman you left the bar for. It's her, isn't it?"

"Who?"

"You know who, Logan. We both know."

Turned out Jerry had put two and two together and come up with four after all.

I sighed heavily, dropping my cell into my lap, and my head back against the headrest as I lifted both hands to cover my face.

I groaned into my palms. "*Fuck.*"

"I guess that confirms it."

"Go away, Jerry," I mumbled.

"Nope."

"Please?"

"Nope."

"C'mon, man."

"Nope."

"Jesus Christ." Dropping my hands into my lap, I turned to look at him, too strung out and fed up to lie anymore. "It's not what you think."

"No?" Moving closer, he rested his arms on the window ledge. "And what am I thinking, LT? Tell me."

"That I'm some crazed fucking stalker, still hung up on Newman's death. Obsessed with it, even."

"And that's not what's happening here?"

"I couldn't give a flying *fuck* about Cole Newman."

Jerry's brows rose, his face full of surprise.

"I mean it, Jerry. Was I fucked up when it happened? Yes. Was I still fucked up over it the first time I bumped into Hannah? Yeah, and maybe even some time after that, too. But things changed…"

"What things?"

"Lots of things!"

"Like?"

"Like finding out Cole Newman was a manipulative asshole who didn't deserve the wife and daughter he had, and now I feel no sorrow over what happened to him. I feel no guilt over not being able to save him, either. The only thing I feel bad about is that a man like him was ever given the gift of that woman and that little girl because they deserved the world, and instead, they got him and all the shit he brought along with it. And the worst part is that they'll never escape him now, or the messed-up crap he continues to put them through."

Not a word of what I'd said had been a lie, and the rage I felt toward him made my veins burn with a need to go to the afterlife so I could find him and kick his all-American boy ass myself.

I'd fight for Hannah… even in death.

I'd allowed his fame and his following to swallow me up whole and make me feel responsible when I'd done everything I possibly could to save that man's life. The truth was, he hadn't wanted me to bring him back. Hannah had pretty much said so herself.

You can't save those who don't want saving.

She should know. All she'd ever tried to do was keep her family together, even at the expense of her own happiness.

Jerry blew out a breath. "That doesn't sound like the Logan I know."

"Because it isn't." I jabbed my own chest. "This is me finally opening my eyes and seeing that I can't take on the responsibility of other people's decisions. It kills me. It's fucking killing me. There's too much weight on my shoulders with all this guilt, and it guts me to know I can't save the world, but that's the truth. And the truth is that, from now on, I'm going to save those who need me the most."

People like Hannah.

Since she'd walked away with such disappointment in her eyes, I'd been forced to think about everything that led up to that moment. Every decision I'd made. Every hardship I'd suffered. Every death I'd taken on as my own.

Jerry's eyes narrowed. "This has to do with the widow, doesn't it?"

"She's not just Cole's widow. She's more than that." I groaned. "So much fucking more."

"Oh shit…"

"What?"

"You're sounding like you're in love there, LT."

"Don't be ridiculous."

"I mean it. This isn't just about you wrapping your head around Cole's death. This is about her. It's all about her. It makes sense now. The way you left the bar. The way you've been on your phone lately. Your mind not on the job—"

"My mind is on the job every time I go out there, so don't you dare put that shit on me, Jerry."

"You know what I mean."

"The fuck I do."

"Logan…"

"What?"

"I know what I see, so cut the bullshit. You've fallen in love with her."

It was my turn to blanch, my brows rising, but no matter how many times I opened my mouth to deny it, the words wouldn't fall out.

Had I? Did I *love* Hannah?

The truth hit me right in the gut, winding me and forcing my gaze to shift from Jerry to the windscreen in front of me instead.

After having zero emotional connection with any woman from my past, no matter how many months or years we'd spent together, I'd finally fallen in love with someone. Someone I couldn't have, and someone who definitely deserved better, but still…

"Shit… I… I don't know, man," I whispered, closing my eyes at the tragedy of it all as I reached up to grip the steering wheel and bowed my head. "Maybe I have."

I stayed that way for a while, not caring about Jerry's presence beside me until I felt his hand upon my back, and the slow, gentle pats he placed there.

"Ah, hell, LT. What did you have to go and do that for?" he eventually said with a sigh.

"God only knows," I whispered. "God. Only. Knows."

"Do you think she feels the same way?"

Opening my eyes, I sat back into my seat, turning to face him. "Not anymore."

"There's a story that needs telling here, isn't there?"

"Yep. Only problem is, I don't know the ending."

"Let's figure it out over a beer. You can tell me everything, and I promise, I won't judge you no matter how fucked up this gets."

I raised my brow, letting that say everything I needed to say, only for him to smirk in response.

"Well… maybe I'll judge you a little bit." He winked.

And even though talking to yet another person about any of this was the last thing on earth I wanted to do, I couldn't deny him the truth anymore.

I'd finally fallen in love, and it already hurt so much worse than I ever thought it could.

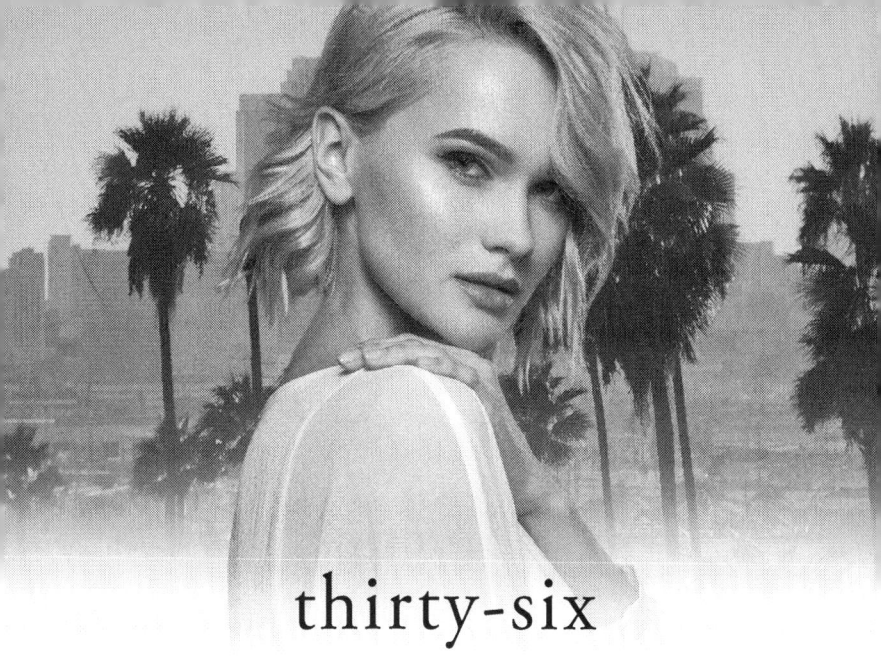

thirty-six

Hannah

Bella loved Seattle.

Discovering the roots of her parents made her eyes light up with a hunger for more, and she talked non-stop about her daddy throughout the trip, trying to soak in as much information as she possibly could about him.

I gave her everything I remembered. All the good moments we'd shared together before they'd slowly turned bad. I took us on a trip down the memory lane of Cole's and my youth. Back in our home state, Los Angeles faded away, bringing happier times to the forefront of my mind. I showed Bella the place her father and I first met. I'd told her the story of how he'd been, even back then, and his abilities to command everyone's attention with nothing more than his presence, especially mine. I forgot about the scandal, remembering the first time Cole kissed me, making me feel like the luckiest girl alive.

I'd been the blonde-haired, down-and-out, poor girl in a neighborhood full of more affluent people who had always had their two-point-four families around them. Cole had been the hottest bad boy in the city and the first person I'd met who understood what it felt like to be given up on by the very people who should have loved you the most.

I'd seen something in him, and he'd seen it in me.

Familiarity.

It was only now that I understood that, even though the chemistry between us had been undeniable in the beginning, we'd both mistaken that familiarity for love. We'd mistaken lust for a forever connection that couldn't possibly last the test of time.

The truth of that sank in the further I got into our story for Bella. The more questions she asked about her father, and the more I answered honestly, the more I realized that Cole and I had been far too young and broken inside to understand what we'd truly wanted at the time. He'd always had his heart set on stardom, and I only had my heart set on him—the very first person to show me what real love could possibly feel like—who always stuck around and got excited about having a future with me instead of trying to run away.

Except he'd run away eventually. His heart had left me a long time ago, even if his body had chosen to stay out of duty to me, his daughter, or his image—I would never know. Yet, I'd clung to that feeling of belonging as though I'd die without it, even if staying killed me slowly.

I believed he had loved me, but being in love was something different entirely, and maybe we'd never quite reached that part together. And even though Bella and I may have left the weight of Los Angeles behind us, a new heaviness settled in my stomach after a week in Seattle. I'd wasted years of my life doing what I thought I *should* do instead of what made me happy. I'd wasted years of my life being with someone I knew deep down in my heart wasn't right for me. I'd just been too much of a coward to find a way out.

I'd *never* be that coward again.

My daughter needed a lioness willing to fight for her, and now was the time to remind myself of who I'd been before Cole. I only had to glance at Bella as we drove along the I-5 back to SeaTac Airport to know that I needed to find my way back to that woman, and I would. I'd make her proud.

"Are you ready to go home?" I asked with a smile, watching as she moved her ever-messy, long hair out of her face.

She turned to me with those bright aqua eyes that were all Cole. "I don't know. I like being on adventures with you."

"I like being on adventures with you, too."

"You do?"

"Of course. You're my partner in crime."

Her small smile turned into a beaming grin for just a second before it faded quickly, and she turned away to look out of her window again.

"Bug?" I scowled. "What is it?"

"I wish we didn't have to go back," she admitted quietly. "Here, it feels like Daddy is really with us again. At home…" she turned back to me. "It doesn't feel like he's there so much anymore."

I wished like hell I could have pulled the damn car over, reached for my daughter, and hugged her to me, but we were on the busiest interstate highway on the western coast of America, and there was no way I could get to her for at least another ten minutes when we'd pull into SeaTac.

"You're right," I said, focusing on the road. "It doesn't feel like he's there much anymore, does it? Perhaps because, even though his stuff was always there, Daddy never really was, huh? His job took him away from us a lot. Too much. We never really got to see his messy socks beside the laundry hamper. We never watched him trip over the stupid, big rug he bought, or fall asleep on the living room couch every night with drool pouring out of his mouth. We never saw him try to make dinner and burn the spaghetti, and we never had to laugh at him as he struggled to do math homework with you, or when he tried to read you a book before falling asleep himself."

I chuckled at the thought of my extremely handsome, party boy husband alive and well, sprawled out beside Bella and me every night, living a life of domesticity instead of always being on tour, or with the band, or out partying, or simply... out with anyone. Even imagining it seemed bizarre.

That wasn't who Cole was. It wasn't who he was supposed to be, no matter how much I thought I'd wanted it at the time. He was the rebel king who got off on causing mayhem, and nobody or anything could ever have really tamed him. He wouldn't have been his true self if they had. He'd been a damn good father in so many ways, leaving Bella wanting for nothing, but he'd been a stranger in so many other respects, and I blamed myself for allowing that as much as I blamed him now.

We were both at fault, and the little girl beside me was the one suffering because of it.

"I'm sorry I didn't ask him to stay home more for you, Bella," I said, full of regret. "I could have done that, and I didn't."

"Do you think he'd have stayed with us more if we'd asked him to, Mommy?"

"I don't know, baby. But what I do know is that you were the best thing in his life, even if he didn't always know how to show you."

"He showed me," she said, her voice small. "I know Daddy loved me."

She thought about that for a while, and it wasn't long before we pulled into the parking lot of Seattle-Tacoma International to find my way to the rental station. When I eventually found it, parked the car, and turned off the engine, I spun in my seat to give Bella my full attention.

"You've been awfully quiet for the last ten minutes, bug." I reached up to brush her hair back with a soft smile on my face. "Did I say something that upset you again? I seem to do that a lot lately."

She shook her head. "No… but I think I'm ready to go home now."

"You are?"

She nodded once, a smile of her own coming to life. "Daddy wasn't perfect, Mommy, but he was still Daddy, and I think it's time to stop being sad about everything he did wrong and start remembering all the good things he did instead."

"You do?"

"Yep. Daddy would be mad if we were sad all the time."

I continued to brush her hair back. "When did you grow up and get so smart, huh?"

"I didn't."

"Well, that sounded very smart and grown-up to me."

"It wasn't my idea. I stole it from Mr. Logan."

The mention of Logan had my smile falling and my chest tightening as a thousand unwanted butterflies came to life in the very depths of my stomach. My lips parted to say something, but nothing came out as the memory of his face came back to me, bright and powerful, making me miss him, despite desperately wanting to forget he'd ever existed.

Bella smiled up at me. "Mr. Logan told me that whenever

something feels so bad that you start to feel sad about it, you can tell your brain to think about something good instead. I told him I'd try it next time I saw you sad… so I did." Reaching over, Bella ran her thumb over the apple of my cheek. "See. It's working. Your cheeks are turning pink now. That means you feel warm inside again. He was right, wasn't he? Bad things really can be swapped for good things if we just tell our brains to choose to be happy instead."

thirty-seven

Logan

It had been the slowest week of my life. Hannah hadn't responded to my last message, and I didn't send her any more, no matter how much I had to say.

Jerry had listened to me confess everything, and even though he had his opinions on how I should have dealt with it, he told me that he couldn't turn the clock back any more than I could, and the only thing to do now was to make things right, being sure to tread lightly as I went, too.

That last part would be the biggest struggle.

Since losing her, I'd been a nightmare to all those around me, but I'd been even worse on myself. Every time I lay in bed, I became tortured with the memory of her kiss, going even further by slipping my hand beneath the comforter to find myself hard before I'd slowly stroke the mental images of Hannah lying beneath me out of my body, coming hard and painfully each and every time.

Her face was my punishment. My pleasure became my own pain.

I didn't deserve to jerk off to thoughts of her, but I did it anyway.

Her messages of wanting to talk had given me the faintest drop of hope… and hope was a dangerous thing to a guy who'd finally fallen in love for the first time in thirty years.

My frustrations only grew on Thursday when the entire day went by without hearing from her. I'd marked this day down as the one when we'd finally be able to talk. One where I could confess all my sins, nothing held back. But when it reached ten o'clock that night, I gave in to my own insanity, needing to get out of the damn condo.

I took a quick shower before I threw on a pair of black jeans and a white T-shirt. Once ready, I ran a hand through my damp hair, grabbed my keys, and I got the hell out of there.

My cell sat in the back pocket of my jeans, taunting me, telling me to text Hannah and ask her if she'd changed her mind, but I'd promised never to ask for more than she was willing to give again, and I intended to stick to that promise.

It didn't take long to find a bar to step into on the streets of Van Nuys, but it was the first time I stepped into this particular one, normally choosing the silence of my own home over the chaotic noise of a bunch of drunken assholes I saw and saved every other day.

Tonight, though, I needed that noise. I needed to drown in other people's problems instead of sitting in that home of mine like some neurotic asshole, watching every minute tick by without so much as a word from her.

If this was what love did to a man, I wanted no part of it.

The barman took one look at me slipping onto the stool in front of him and must have seen my misery.

He was a tall guy, probably in his mid-thirties, with flecks of gray already running through his dark hair. Resting one hand on the bar while the other held onto a beer pump, he raised his brow. "You look like you need a whisky."

"Will it quieten my head for a bit?"

"Probably until morning. Then things might get extra loud again."

"Tomorrow is tomorrow's problem," I said, repeating the words I'd said to Hannah.

"Whisky shot, coming right up."

It turned out I didn't particularly even like whisky, but it did the job, quieting the wild thoughts of Hannah that raced through my mind and dulling the ache in my chest to something more manageable.

Two women tried to sit next to me on separate occasions, but my arrogance and ignorance soon gave them the message my voice couldn't deliver. I was too afraid to speak in case I told them to fuck off and got myself thrown out of the bar. I'd become attached to the seat beneath my ass, as well as the barman who asked no questions but somehow saw everything, anyway.

When he offered me my third refill, I beckoned him closer. He leaned toward me as he poured my drink, his wrist eventually twisting the bottle at a certain angle to tail it off before he brought it back down to the bar with a thud.

"Do you think," I said, raising my voice over the loud music, "that I'm a sad bastard for drinking here alone on a Thursday night?"

"No," he laughed, "but I think you're a sad bastard for worrying about what a stranger like me thinks of you."

"Good point." I nodded, bringing my glass up to my lips and

taking a small sip as the few ice cubes inside it clinked together. "Very good point."

"Not a big drinker, are you?"

"Nope."

"Live around here?"

"Yep."

"Good." He placed the whisky bottle on the back shelf before he turned back to me and leaned against the bar top again. "Then I don't have to worry about you driving home. Something tells me another one of those," he pointed to my glass, "and you're a goner."

"I'm a goner already."

"Woman trouble?"

"Get that a lot, huh?"

"Comes with the territory." Leaning down, he copied my pose, his forearms resting on the bar. "What is it? First love, second love? Fucked-up love, forbidden love, fallen in love with your best friend's mom, love?"

"Damn. That shit happens?"

He shrugged. "I've seen it all. Love comes in every form, fucking up the best of men."

"What makes you think that's my problem?"

He raised a brow and smirked.

I rolled my eyes. "Whatever." Taking another sip of my drink, I relished the burn that hit the back of my throat before it sank into my chest like a warm blanket. Licking the remnants off my bottom lip, I twirled the glass around between my finger and thumb. "Is this where you give me some worldly advice?"

"Who, me?" He laughed. "Do I look like I have a clue what the fuck I'm doing?"

"Trust me to get a faulty barman."

"Oh, you have no idea." He reached up to slap me on the

shoulder before he stood tall again, reached for a cloth, and turned to walk away. But then he stopped and scowled to himself before he turned back to me and flicked the cloth onto the bar between us. "But if I wasn't faulty, and if I did have any advice to give, it would probably be this: whatever you're looking for isn't in the bottom of that glass. If you know where it is, go and find it. Everything else is just you wasting time, making yourself miserable."

He walked away, throwing the cloth between both hands as he made his way to the other side of the bar to serve a loved-up couple that had just walked in.

How did I know they were in love? It oozed out of them. The way they glanced at each other, the subtle eye contact, the gentle touches, and the huge grins that couldn't be tamed. They looked like they had it all, and I thought back to the other women I'd had in my life and how I'd never once acted like that or looked at them that way because I'd never been invested.

I'd never wanted more.

The thought of having something like that with Hannah punched me in the gut, and every feeling of desire I'd ever tried to push down rose up within me, screaming in my ears, *What the hell are you sitting around here sulking for? She's back in Los Angeles. Go and find her. Make her realize what you want. Make her see how sorry you are. Show her, her goddamn worth because no one else has ever been brave enough to do that for her before.*

I could be better than Cole. Fuck it, I already was, but that didn't mean I was right for Hannah, no matter how much I wanted to be the guy she called on every occasion. Good news or bad. Life or death. Being the man by her side to hold her up and support her through everything was a fantasy out of my reach, but just the idea of waking up beside her every day and seeing those pale green eyes staring up into mine…

"Jesus, I'm fucked," I mumbled against the rim of the glass of whisky. It only took another quick glance of the loved-up couple in my peripheral vision to realize I wanted that, and I wanted it with nobody else but Hannah Moore.

The weight of my phone in my pocket suddenly felt like a brick, the noise around me now too loud. Draining my drink, I slid money across the bar and got the hell out of there, not responding to the barman as he shot me a, "Good luck, man," on the way out.

I stepped onto the sidewalk moments later and shoved my hands deep into the pockets of my jeans before making my way home. It wasn't far, and the cool night air was in danger of sobering me up when I needed it to keep me buzzed because once I was back in that condo of mine, I had a call to make.

No more time wasted.

No more secrets and lies.

I was sick of being without her.

Stepping inside my block, I made my way up the stairs and down the hall toward my room, my head down as my heart raced over what I was about to do.

Confess.

Tell her everything.

What I was feeling. What I could give. How good I knew we could be together. It all had to come out, and I was ready.

But when I reached my place, and I finally looked up and came to a halt, I thought I was dreaming because standing outside my door was Hannah. Beautiful, blonde-haired, bright-eyed Hannah, who still had that air of devastation about her as she stood before me wearing a simple white summer dress and small leather jacket, pushing her short hair behind her ear as her gaze locked onto mine.

Time stood completely still.

For a moment too long, all we did was stare at each other.

Fuck, she's beautiful, and I'm so in love with her, it fucking hurts to want her so badly.

My memory had done her no favors. I forgot that the blush on her cheeks had become my new favorite shade of pink. I forgot that her bow lips made me want to sink my teeth into her and pull her body close to mine. Most of all, I forgot how much that lingering sadness in her eyes made me want to erase every moment of heartache she'd ever endured, only to fill her life with new, happier moments and memories now. Better ones, featuring better days.

"Hannah…"

"For a moment, I was worried I'd knocked on the wrong door," she said softly, leaning against the door.

"You're here," I whispered.

"I don't know why." She looked down at the car key in her hand as she twisted it around. "But here I am anyway. Every time I thought about calling you, it didn't feel like enough. If this is going to be our goodbye, I needed to see you when we said it."

Like fuck I'm going to let this be goodbye.

You're mine.

I couldn't believe my damn luck, but as her eyes rose to meet mine again, I knew she was a scared animal, ready to bolt if I made so much as one wrong move.

"Do you think it's going to be our goodbye?" I asked carefully. "Do you… want it to be?"

"Nobody ever wants to say goodbye, Logan, but sometimes it's necessary."

Fuck. She really meant it. Despite the obvious sadness lingering around her, she'd grown a little stronger too, and I had to wonder what the hell she'd been up to since she ran out of that gym and away from me. Where had she been, and what had pushed her shoulders back and given her that extra bit of strength

I'd always wanted to see in her?

"You left LA, didn't you?"

She nodded her response.

"Why?"

"I had to get out of here. I needed space."

"From me?"

"From you *and* him."

I hated being lumped into the same sentence as the guy who I couldn't connect with on any level anymore, but that was the price I had to pay for having lied to her.

"Where did you go?" I asked.

"Seattle," she said, pushing her shoulder up against the door. "I thought it was about time Bella knew where she came from. We did a little soul searching while we were there, the two of us."

"Did it help?"

"In some ways." Her brows pulled together. "But not as much as I hoped it would."

I took a step closer. "Why not?"

"Because I came back with just as many questions as I left with, and most of them center around you." She focused back on the key in her hand as though that held all the answers. As though she didn't see me stalking closer. "About what happened. How you came into my life. Whether I should trust you or let you go. Whether everything had been a lie and you were just a figment of my imagination—someone I conjured up into something he never really was."

I closed the distance completely until she straightened up against the door, and I could feel her body heat not far from mine. I saw the worried flickering of her eyes as she searched my face, a slight hint of pain lingering there that she desperately tried to hide.

I nudged her chin up with my knuckle until all she saw was

me.

"I promised I'd always be there for you, and I was. That wasn't a dream."

"But why were you there? Out of guilt? Shame? Opportunity."

"Guilt and shame, yes. I'm going to ignore that last option and hope you know the answer to that already."

She flinched, showing me how much she hated that she'd even had to ask.

"But the guilt and shame were only tools to get me to you, Hannah. I see that now. It took nothing but a minute for me to figure out what an incredible woman you are—one who deserved more. You deserved better. Someone to love you for you."

The word *love* lingered between us, and I knew she'd mentally tripped over it as much as I had, but instead of asking me what I meant or trying to dig deeper, she pushed a hand against my beating chest, trying to create distance I wouldn't give.

"You've been drinking," she groaned.

"So?"

"I never trust a word that comes out of a man's mouth when he's drunk."

"I'm not drunk. I've had a drink. There's a difference. I know exactly what I'm saying and doing."

Her hand fell away, giving in. "Just like you knew what you were doing the day we *accidentally* met in that drive-thru?" She arched her brow before it creased into a scowl again. "What did you want from me, Logan? Did you know how broken I'd be and decide to take advantage of a woman whose husband had just died by your hands."

It was my turn to flinch, and I dropped my hand from her face, taking the hit she'd delivered straight to the stomach.

"Cole died by his own hands, Hannah. *He* put those drugs in his body, not me."

"But you—"

"Didn't save him. You don't need to remind me. I know the mistakes I made that night."

Her scowl turned into a deep frown as new pain tore into her. "So, he could have lived?" she whispered.

"No, that's not—"

"Could my daughter still have a father? Is that what you're telling me?"

I stared back at her for only a second before I pushed my hands through the length of my hair and held them at the back of my head, my elbows pointed out as I spun away from her and growled. "*Jesus*, Hannah, I don't know! What kind of fucked-up question is that?"

Memories of Cole's face as I hovered over him flashed before me. Dale's ghost, too.

Every look Jerry and I passed between us.

Every thought I'd had in the back of that ambulance.

Every nightmare I'd had since, wondering if I could have done more. If I should have acted faster.

"I need to know, Logan. You owe me the truth."

"The truth," I huffed.

"Yes," she said, her voice growing stronger. "I deserve to know what happened that night. I deserve to know what went wrong. I deserve to know—"

"Goddamn it, Hannah!" I spun back around to face her, my hands dropping against my thighs before I turned my palms up and shrugged. "I froze, okay. I fucking froze. There. That's it. For the first time in my life as a paramedic, I had a dying man in my hands, and I didn't know what the hell to do with it."

She froze, too, opening her mouth to say something before thinking better of it, her silence lingering between us.

"Something about Cole that night reminded me of losing

Dale all those years ago, and for just a split second, I couldn't think straight. Couldn't even fucking move if you want the truth. I've dealt with a lot of ODs and junkies in my time, believe me. I've seen it all. But those people... they were always strangers. Nothing more than anonymous faces I'd never known. I had no clue if those people had families, wives, husbands, children, fucking cats. I didn't know anything about them, so while their hearts started failing in my hands, I saw them as nothing more than something to fix. Like a mechanic working on a goddamn car or a guy with a toolkit in an old garage, trying to repair a bike. Those people were machines, and I was the guy that knew all their wiring and how to keep them going a bit longer until they no doubt went back out on the streets, shoved more shit into their veins, and OD-ed again.

"But I *knew* about Cole," I said quietly. "Everyone did. He wasn't just a nameless face. He had a wife. You. He had a daughter. Bella. When he closed his eyes and we saw his heart rate decline, it was you guys that popped into my head. He wasn't a machine I could fix up by using the right equipment. He was Cole Newman, husband, father. Adored by millions. I knew his songs, his voice, his lifestyle, even his cocksure smile that hung on billboards all over LA. So, yeah, I froze because the responsibility of saving him reminded me too much of how I'd failed Dale." I shrugged again, trying desperately to hold back the emotion that mixing those memories together brought to the surface. "Could Cole have lived? Damn right, he could. He could have valued you and what he had. He could have seen the incredible life he had in front of him and allowed that to be enough. But he didn't. He didn't, and now people like me who failed to right his fuckups have to live with that. We have to carry that guilt around while people mourn him in the streets, lighting candles in his name, wailing his songs beneath fucking trees in the park. Cole could have lived a good life. Instead, he chose to ruin everyone else's, and I am so sick of feeling like his mistakes are my fault."

My breathing had turned ragged, my chest heaving up and down as I stared into her devastated eyes, waiting for her to run. Waiting for her to slap me around the face, accuse me of not being good enough.

"The day I met you was the first day I saw you," I said as calmly as I could, taking a step closer to her again. "Something I couldn't explain led me there, and from the moment we knew we couldn't bring Cole back, my thoughts went to you and Bella. Two people I didn't even know! I thought about Dale's family and how they suffered when he died. I thought about his mom, his sister, his aunts and uncles, and I imagined how you two must have been feeling because I'd seen your faces, and…"

"*And*?" she whispered.

"You looked sad enough when he was alive, Hannah. Your smiles were already too rare. Imagining you falling apart because of something I could possibly have prevented… it stayed with me. It felt like something I needed to put right."

"So, what? You followed me on a mission to use me to ease your own guilt?"

"I followed you once to make sure nothing happened to you."

"You had no right."

"I know. But if you're asking me to regret it, I can't. I can admit it was stupid. I can admit it didn't make sense. I can admit to it sounding crazy to you, but I can't regret it because you needed me that day, and I was so fucking relieved it was me who you ran into, nobody else. I knew my intentions were good, even if you still don't."

"I'm so confused about everything. I don't know what to think anymore."

I brought the back of my hand up to her cheek, brushing

against the pink that rose there. "I can only imagine how this sounds, but all I can do is promise that my only intention was to watch you from afar and make sure you were safe. That you weren't dying inside, the way I was when Dale died."

"How do I know what you're telling me is the truth?"

My hand trailed down her cheek, her neck, and around to the back of her hair, where I pushed my hands into the thick of it and curled my fingers tight, pulling her head back slowly. Her eyes closed involuntarily, and her breath hitched in her throat before she let her lids flutter open again, and she stared up into my eyes.

"Can't you see it?" I whispered.

"I just... I don't know," she breathed.

"*Look* at me, Hannah. Use your gut. Follow your instincts. Don't ask me if you can trust me. Trust yourself enough to know what you see and whether you want it or not."

Her eyes searched mine, and I could feel her on the precipice, ready to tell me. Ready to admit to herself what she felt deep down inside.

"Say it," I whispered.

"I believe you," she rasped, her voice heady, while my heart leaped at the sudden admission until she said, "But..."

"But what?"

"I don't even know. It feels like there should be a 'but'. It feels wrong to want this so soon after—"

I shook my head, cutting her off. "Don't do that."

"Do what?"

"Worry about what everyone else will think. This is your life. You're not taking breaths to keep everyone else alive. You're taking them for you, so don't make decisions on your future based on keeping everyone else happy, either. Decide what it is that *you* want, and then fuck having to explain it to anyone but yourself."

"I want..."

"Say it," I whispered, unable to stop myself from leaning in. "Tell me what will make you happy so I can give it to you."

Hannah sucked in a breath, and she fisted my T-shirt, pulling me closer before she pressed her mouth against mine, a low moan of satisfaction escaping her

She kissed me, stealing any words or breaths I had left to give, taking them all for herself instead... just the way I wanted her to.

This was love, even if only one of us felt it, and as I sank into that kiss with her, she became pure heaven against my lips in a world where everything else had always felt like hell.

thirty-eight

Hannah

My mind freed itself of anything that wasn't Logan Thomas.

His mouth became my escape. I was lost to the way his tongue teased mine—the way his fingers twisted in my hair. The way his whisky-tainted breaths mixed with that oh-so-clean, heavenly scent of his tipped me over the edge into oblivion. I couldn't get close enough. Not when there was no resistance anymore.

Now he wanted it as much as I did, and the difference was like day and night.

I needed more of the night.

A low groan of his appreciation had my eyes fluttering open to take him in, and I slowed the kiss, needing to see the look on his face when I reluctantly pulled away, my mouth lingering over his before I fell back onto my feet and waited.

Logan just stood there, leaning over me, his lips slightly parted and swollen from our kiss, his eyes still closed. I could have stared up at him like that forever as he held me with one hand on my hip, the other still pushed into my hair.

"That's what I want," I whispered up at him.

His eyes eventually flickered open, and he stared down into my soul, his chest rising and falling heavier than before.

"Take me inside, Logan."

His Adam's apple bobbed in his throat before he rubbed his lips together, not letting me go. "If I do, that's it. You know that, don't you? I won't be able to let you go a second time."

"I can't promise you forever… but I can promise you now."

His eyes drifted down to my lips, and I licked the bottom one, unable to help myself, before I sank my teeth into the flesh of it.

"Goddammit, Hannah," he whispered.

"Am I taking too much again?"

"Definitely."

"Should I stop?"

"Probably." He sighed, running his nose against mine. "But I'm not strong enough to resist you or think about anything but you being here, and this… whatever this is. Tomorrow is—"

"Tomorrow's problem," I finished for him, earning a small smile against my cheek before he pressed a kiss there, released me, and spun me around to pull my back against his chest. His arm curled around my waist, his mouth against my ear as he placed the key into the door and pushed it open with his foot.

"Tomorrow is tomorrow's problem. Tonight is tonight's fantasy," he said with a rasp in his voice.

"Fantasy?" I breathed, the nerves kicking in as we both stepped over the threshold into a place I'd only ever been once before but somehow felt like an oasis to me now. A small space hidden away, where no one knew me, no one judged me, and all my thoughts were free. "Am I your fantasy, Logan?"

"Christ, if only you knew. The things I've imagined doing to you since you've been gone. The dreams I've had. The number of times I've had to jerk off just to try and get you out of my system. You're every man's fantasy. Especially mine."

Turning in his grip, I looked up at him again, running my hands down the white cotton of his muscle-hugging T-shirt before I let them trail down to the waistband of his jeans. "I don't want to be every man's fantasy. Only yours. For tonight, at least."

He brushed my hair away from my face with his rough palms before he cupped my cheeks in both hands and pulled me closer. "So, this is your plan?" To punish me by giving me a taste of what I'll never have forever."

"Nobody knows what they want forever. That's the problem. They think they do, but people change, and when they do, what they want changes, too."

Logan leaned closer, his lips brushing against mine as he looked me in the eye. "I can't blame you for being jaded, Hannah. I've spent thirty years of my life struggling to see how two people could possibly spend an eternity together, but then I met you, and it suddenly didn't seem so impossible anymore."

"You don't know what you're saying."

"You don't get to tell me what I feel and what I don't."

My heart screamed at me in warning, showing me every reason why this was a dangerous game I was about to play, but my desire wanted to play anyway. It was my turn to be a little reckless. My turn to be selfish and consider my wants and needs for a change, and, at that moment, all of those belonged to Logan.

"One day, you'll see what I see when I look at you. Until that happens…" Logan pressed his lips to mine for the first time, and him making the first move made every guard around my heart shatter into a million pieces, leaving nothing but that desire of mine to make the decisions. His kiss was passionate, his hands finding their way into my hair again as he cradled me to him as though he didn't dare let me go.

We breathed each other in, and everything in my mind went quiet again, leaving Logan to take me to a place I hadn't been in so long.

It started out slowly. So slowly, it became painful as he waited for me to try to push him away.

I didn't. His lips against mine was where I felt most alive, and it wasn't long before I began to unfasten the button of his jeans.

He stilled for just a second, holding me in place as his eyes opened at the same time as mine, the two of us asking silent questions we already knew the answers to.

"Please, Logan," I moaned against his mouth. "We don't need to say things that we can show each other instead."

A sexy groan rose in his throat, and before either of us could or wanted to stop it, we were a tangled mess of hands moving to undress the other, T-shirts rolling up and over stomachs to reveal hard, strong muscle and skin. Leather jackets falling to the floor, jeans being pushed down, and pretty, white summer dresses being discarded in seconds.

We kissed between each item we removed, neither of us wanting to break the connection that should have felt wrong but only ever felt right.

Natural.

As though with Logan was where I was always meant to be.

Before long, we stood in front of one another, wearing nothing but our underwear, and while Logan took a second to step back and take me in, he soon crashed his mouth to mine again as though my lips were the oxygen he needed to breathe, and he couldn't survive another second without them.

His hands slipped under my ass, and in one swift move, he lifted me up, allowing me to wrap my legs around his waist, feeling the length of his arousal beneath me. God, I wanted to sink down onto it. For him to fill me up and hold me close until I no longer knew how to breathe.

My hands went around his neck, pulling him closer. My head turned dizzy whenever a low moan or groan of satisfaction rumbled in his throat, a mixture of both pain and ecstasy that drove me crazy. It had always been the little things that affected me the most with him, and I'd suddenly become greedy for more.

His fingers curled into my ass cheeks, squeezing flesh before they rubbed against the heat turning my underwear damper by the second.

"I want you," I breathed. "So badly, it hurts."

"You have me," he said, his mouth bumping against mine. "Any way you want."

"Bed," I mumbled, giving him an order I knew he wouldn't refuse. "*Now.*"

Logan walked us across the room, his knees eventually pressing into the mattress. He held the entire weight of me in his hands before he carefully laid me down in the middle of his bed as though I was his most prized possession.

When he pulled back, his eyes were ablaze as they trailed down my body, following the path his finger took from the curve of my neck, over the valley of my breasts down to the flat of my stomach, before sliding between my legs. They parted instinctively, inviting him in, and Logan looked up at me through heated eyes.

So much passed between us then, it frightened me.

"Don't," I begged quietly. "Don't say anything. Just… show me instead."

A small smirk tugged at the corner of his mouth, and he

slowly began to peel down the edges of my underwear before they were down over my thighs and off me completely. He tossed them to the floor without a care, unable to look away from the very thing he'd just exposed.

He dropped his mouth to the center of it, and my body bucked, despite it being nothing more than a gentle kiss. A promise to return. It set me alight like I couldn't explain, and those kisses of his soon rose, covering my stomach, all the way up to my bra. I stared down at him, my chest heaving and breaths coming quicker as this man who'd only ever protected me looked up with a hungry gaze that said he wanted to destroy me. His dark eyes looked darker, his confidence soaring with every caress of his fingers against my skin.

Logan kissed my full breast, and then he nipped at my bra strap with his teeth, the gentle protector gone, replaced by a slow predator who wanted to take his time enjoying his favorite meal. I arched my back off the bed, throwing my head back as he reached around me to unclip my bra with one hand, only to push me back down to the mattress the moment it was done so he could look me in the eyes again. The bra was soon tossed to the floor, leaving me completely exposed.

Naked before a man who made me feel reckless yet safe.

A man who made me feel seen.

I saw him, too, and I wanted more of everything he had to give.

His lips crashed to mine for a single, fiery kiss before he twisted them away and sat back on his heels to take me in. His eyes roamed everywhere, and his hands soon followed. My skin was caressed, my breasts kneaded, nipples pinched, and my stomach stroked. There wasn't anywhere he didn't set on fire, taking his time to savor everything in front of him.

"You're trying to kill me," I whimpered.

"Not without making you enjoy it first."

Logan parted my thighs, dropped his body down to the mattress, and his mouth devoured me.

My breath caught in the back of my throat the moment the heat and swell of his tongue hit that small bundle of nerves. His flat, slow, long licks had me fisting the sheets and my toes curling into them as I tried not to orgasm too quickly while Logan tasted every bit of me, taking his time to draw out every stroke. Every touch.

I was floating, the heat in the depths of my stomach stretching out until my entire body felt alight with fire, only this fire didn't burn. It made me fly. I wanted to moan his name. To fist his hair, hold him against me, or at least touch him somehow to show him I was present. I felt him, too. But the minute Logan anchored my stomach down with his arm, and his slow destruction turned faster, harder, stronger, I couldn't do anything but hold on, hoping the sheets beneath me didn't tear as I twisted them in my grip. Every time my knees tried to rise, Logan pushed them back down, his sensual moans against my skin sending euphoric vibrations through every nerve ending until I was begging to have him inside my body.

He was unrelenting and unforgiving with his tongue. My vision began to blur and my head fell back my mouth parting as the buildup of my orgasm grew so intense, I was convinced I was going to black out.

I couldn't even say his name.

Higher and higher I climbed, leaving nothing but sensation throughout my mind and body. No thoughts. No feelings. No worries. No doubts. Just us, in that moment...

And then he pushed two fingers inside me, and everything came undone.

My body bowed.

My breaths stopped.

My thighs shook, and my stomach tightened with a pain I wanted to spend my life in.

The sweetest sensation ran through every vein, every muscle, every bone I possessed, wringing me out completely until my hands finally came up, curling into the thickness of Logan's dark hair, allowing me to anchor myself to him while he drew every last drop of my orgasm out of me, not coming up for air until he was satisfied my body had turned to jelly around him.

When he finally looked up, his mouth was wet with my arousal, and he rubbed his lips together before dragging his tongue along the bottom one. It was enough to make me want to orgasm again.

We didn't say anything. We didn't need to.

I was sated while he was starving.

There was only one way this was going to go, and I wanted all of it.

Falling back down onto the bed, I pulled him with me, unable to stop the tremors that wracked my body as Logan slid his fingers through my come, only to drag it up and over my stomach with him before he pressed two fingers to his lips and pushed them into his mouth. His eyes closed as he savored all of me, a low moan of arousal making my nipples turn even harder before he looked down at me again, releasing his fingers and bringing his hand up to cup my cheek.

"You're wrong," he said, his eyes searching mine. "Some people *do* know what they want forever, and I want that… with you."

I reached up, my hands finding the back of his neck as my eyes welled with tears. Not of sorrow this time. Not of heartache, of devastation, or loss, or worry.

Those tears were born from his reverence.

"Be careful what you wish for." Reaching down, I brought his tight ass between my thighs, feeling his rock-hard length hitting the heat between my legs. "I want you inside me, Logan."

"Tell me you won't regret this."

"No."

"Tell me, Hannah."

"I won't make a promise I might not be able to keep. Once this is over, something might happen that makes me wonder if it was the right thing to do, but do you know what I'll do if it does? I'll shut it down. I'll shut it all down when I remember this moment right here when I'm looking up at you, and all I can think about is how much I want you inside me. How I can't get enough of the way you make me feel or the way you touch me. How safe I feel when you're around. How calm, how resolute... and how I feel like I just might die if you don't make love to me right now."

His eyes searched mine for only a second, as though he was fighting with himself against saying anything more, but then I rolled my hips, and the tip of his cock nudged farther inside me, making his eyes roll, and his hand that wasn't on my cheek, fist the sheet.

"Fuck," he groaned, losing control.

His body weight shifted, and he pressed his lips to mine again as though they'd never been apart. His kisses should have been my poison, but they were the only medicine my bruised little heart ever needed.

Bringing my knees up, I caged his body in, holding him so impossibly close, I couldn't bear the thought of us ever being apart. I pushed my fingers through his hair again, as we twisted and turned in our kiss.

Breaking apart, I gasped for air, my mouth open as I pulled his head down to my shoulder, and I pressed my lips against his ear. "Oh, and Logan? Don't you dare be gentle with me."

Those few words were his undoing, and Logan's head fell against me, his arms coming up to cage my body in as his primal needs took over. He pushed the tip of his cock inside me, only a little at first, giving me time to adjust to the fit of him being big, and me being with someone who wasn't Cole.

The memory of my dead husband only flickered through my mind for a split second before I pushed him away, denying him access to this moment with a man who adored me.

A man who wouldn't ever take this for granted.

A man who made promises I had no doubt he would keep if I asked it of him.

And then everything vanished completely as Logan pushed himself all the way in, filling me up completely. My mouth fell slack, and my eyes widened at the intense feeling of him finally being inside me. His body connected with mine. His strength pressing down on me—in me. My body tingled with goosebumps, both a chill and heat rolling over my skin, colliding and fighting for dominance.

The noise Logan made before he pushed up and looked down on me—his hair hanging loose over his eyes—was nearly my second undoing. We stilled for a moment, staring at each other with our bodies tight and our lips parted.

But then he started to move.

Slow at first. So slow, it felt like a punishment.

His hips circled, and his dick hit every spot inside me, making me scrape my nails down the strong muscles of his arms, not caring if I caused him pain, only caring that all my senses were on overload, and it was all because of the man in my arms.

We never looked away from each other. Not as Logan picked up his pace. Not as the veins in his neck grew tighter or the breaths from his chest fell harder. We didn't look away when my quiet gasps turned to desperate mewls, and we never faltered when

Logan's ass tensed, and he lost all sense of tenderness, pounding into me in a way that told me how deep his desire and need for me ran. As another orgasm built, I wasn't even sure what it was from anymore—the way he commanded my body or the things Logan was doing to my heart.

But I did know one thing for certain.

When we'd built each other up into a frenzy, with nothing left behind and nothing else to give, I started to agree with everything Logan had said.

Forever didn't seem so crazy anymore.

Not if every day could start and end like this.

thirty-nine

Logan

Hannah laid beside me with her cheek against my chest, both of us panting for breath as I threw my arm around her shoulder and stared up at the ceiling. No matter how much I tried to cling to a coherent thought, I couldn't grasp hold of anything. My brain had turned to mush, my body limp and muscles aching with overwhelming ecstasy as well as heart-crippling fear.

Sex with emotions hit differently, and if this was her goodbye, I wasn't sure how the hell I'd ever recover to say hello to anyone ever again. Nobody would ever compare now.

"Talk to me, Hannah," I finally whispered as I ran my hand up and down her arm.

She sighed. "Well... your bed's a little squeakier than I expected it to be."

My laughter fell unexpectedly, my chest bouncing up and down, forcing her to look at me through satisfied, sleepy eyes and those beautiful, long lashes.

"Sorry," I said. "It's been out of action for a little while."

"Really?"

"Yes, really. What? You think I have women here all the time?"

"I... hadn't really thought about it."

"Good. Don't."

"But it would make sense if you did. I mean... look at you." She gestured to my body. "You're kinda hot, Logan."

"Just kinda?"

"Oh, come on. You're seriously hot, and you know it." She smirked.

"I'll take your word for it. Your opinion is the only one that matters. And don't worry; I'll have the bed fixed by morning."

"You'd do that for me?"

"I'd do anything for you."

The smile fell from her face, and she looked down again, cutting me off from those eyes I loved so much.

"Hannah? What is it?"

She trailed a finger along my stomach, moving it around in different patterns. "Nothing. Just a small moment of uncertainty creeping in. It'll be gone in a minute."

"About us?"

"Us," she repeated. "There's an us now."

I froze beneath her, my hand coming to a halt on her arm as the dread of her having regrets crept in, making my gut perk up with a warning.

She must have felt the tension in my body because she looked up again, her eyes meeting mine. "I'm not regretting a moment of it, I swear. That was one of the best nights of my life, Logan, and it's not even over yet." She leaned on her elbow, bringing her face closer to mine, making me twist my head on the pillow. "I'm just adjusting. This is new to me."

When I didn't respond, she went back to drawing patterns on my skin, only this time on my chest, bringing those limp muscles slowly back to life.

"Cole was the only man I'd ever... you know..." She shrugged. "Slept with. Until now."

My brows rose. "Are you serious?"

"Yes."

"Why didn't you tell me?"

"What does it matter?" she asked, looking up at me.

"If it didn't matter, you wouldn't be thinking about it. You wouldn't be adjusting. So, yeah. It matters."

"I guess that's fair," she said softly. "There's just been a lot of changes this year, and this thing between us... it's the biggest one of all. I never expected someone new to come into my life, and not so soon after..." She didn't need to finish that sentence. "I'm just taking a moment to center myself. Figure out how to play this out."

"I'm willing to take this as slowly as you need to," I ran my hand through her hair. "As long as this is what you want. That's all that matters to me. That you forgive me for my past mistakes and that you trust me to protect our future."

Her cheeks heated again, and she couldn't hold back her smile. "I do. On both counts."

It was all I needed to hear.

Cradling her face, I pulled her to me, and I kissed her as though it was the first time—as though it was the last. She fell into it, and soon our bodies were tangled again, with her wrapping herself around me until I'd turned us over, and she lay beneath me, the heat of her skin making me hard again.

"Trust me, Hannah," I said between kisses. "You set the pace. I'll follow."

"Promise?"

Dropping my forehead to hers, I whispered, "I promise."

Saying anything else would scare her away, and the only thing I cared about was her happiness. She didn't need to know that after this, I'd struggle to hold back now. She'd opened a gate. Unleashed a fucking beast. One who'd never known what it felt to care for a woman while being inside her, and one who couldn't get enough of the way that finally made him come alive after feeling as though something had been missing for far too long.

Soon enough, our kisses turned to touching, and she began to moan beneath my fingertips, once again. Every groan of arousal she pulled from me became a promise to give her whatever the hell she wanted, whenever she needed it. This time, the urgency had gone, leaving me to sink into her slowly and watch her every reaction—listen to her every soft curse that told me she loved it just as much as I did, and hope that maybe one day, she'd grow to love me, too.

The way I loved her now.

***

We woke the next morning wrapped in each other's arms.

It took a few seconds of adjusting to the daylight for me to see that everything I thought had been a dream had, in fact, been real. Hannah's soft blonde hair tickled my chest, and I pressed my lips against it, enjoying the soft moan that escaped her.

"Morning," I said groggily.

"Morning," she whispered, making my already hard dick harder with just one word. It wasn't what she said but the way she said it, and I had to subtly adjust myself beneath the sheets before I did something that would make her even sorer than she already was.

"Are you okay?" she asked quietly, looking back at me.

"Perfect."

"You look a little… frustrated." Her hand glided over the top of the comforter to rest over my cock, the devil alive in her eyes.

It was a side of her I could only have fantasized about seeing, and now, having it here with me… fuck, I only had so much control.

"Hannah…" I croaked. "Careful, otherwise you're about to lose another hour to me being buried between your legs."

"You think that's a loss for me?"

I growled and turned toward her, only for her entire body to tense in my grip before she bolted upright, clutching the white comforter to her breasts as though I hadn't spent the entire night feasting on them. "Wait! What time is it?"

"I don't know—"

"Shit," she hissed, jumping from the bed, naked, and scrambling around in the pockets of her leather jacket until she found her phone. One look at the screen and her body deflated, her eyes closing as she pressed a hand to her chest. "Oh, thank God. It's still early."

I scowled, waiting, and she slowly turned to see me with an amused smile on my face as I checked out every inch of her naked body in the daylight. Her slightly tanned skin, her taut muscles, toned arms, full breasts, and flat stomach you would never have known had carried a baby…

The sight of her made me groan to myself. "Aw, hell."

Her eyes followed mine, a smile of her own coming to life as she raised a brow at me. "Stop checking me out."

"Can't. Sorry."

"Logan," she cried before slipping back under the comforter, her phone still in her hand as she propped herself beneath my arm, the screen hovering above both our faces now. "Control yourself a moment."

"You're the one who got me all riled up," I said as she checked her messages and scrolled through her call log. "Everything okay?"

"Just making sure I haven't missed anything from Bella."

"Have you?"

"No. Not that I expected to, but the worry never stops when you're away from your child. She stayed at Liv's last night. After spending so much time with me lately, she asked if she could go for a sleepover at her place. I think she needed some room from her overbearing mom."

"You're not overbearing."

"You're not my daughter."

"Well," I groaned, moving us both around until we lay on our sides, staring at each other. "I'm glad she decided she needed a break from you. Otherwise I wouldn't be waking up to this right now, and that would suck."

Hannah traced a finger down my cheek, over my stubble. "I like this side of you. Seeing you all playful without that worried look on your face all the time. I used to think you were scared of me. Either that or you weren't interested. You always seemed so...held back. But seeing the way you've been since last night... you're like a different person."

She couldn't stop touching me, her phone long gone now, lost somewhere in the bedding as her hands ran up and down my chest and stomach, tracing the ridges and softer parts as though she was committing it all to memory for life.

"I like both sides of you. The one who made me feel so calm and the one who gets me worked up and begging you to ruin me," she admitted quietly.

"Which version do you want this morning?" I trailed the back of my hand down her already-blushing cheek.

"Both."

My amused smile was lazy, and I leaned in to kiss her again, only for her to press her hand firmer against my chest, holding me inches away from her face.

"What's wrong?"

"When I fall, I fall hard," she warned. "I've been there before. I've done it. I've fallen. But you…" The unspoken *haven't* hit me in the gut. "I just don't want to be left alone again if this becomes too much for you down the line."

"It won't."

"I'm a lot to take on, Logan. I have a *daughter.*"

"An incredible daughter any man would be lucky to have in his life."

"Then there's the ghost of Cole. He'll never go away."

"I wouldn't want him to."

She pinched my chin between her finger and thumb, raising a brow and holding me hostage.

"You can't scare me, Hannah," I whispered. "You can try, but you won't. The worst has already happened, and you're still here. You don't hate me the way I thought you would. Everything else, I'll handle it. We'll handle it together."

"If people find out…"

"What people?"

"Everyone. The world. They'll have strong opinions."

"Still not scared." I leaned closer, pulling her in for a kiss and letting her lose her worries in my touch. Letting her feel my tongue against hers, as her heartbeat rose, the problems temporarily forgotten until I pulled back and watched as her eyes fluttered open. "As long as you and Bella want me in your lives— *both* of you—I'll be there."

"Whenever we call?" She smiled softly.

I pushed my fingers into the back of her hair, sliding her closer again until our noses rubbed together and our breaths mingled. "Every time."

"Good, because I may have your first assignment already."

"Huh?"

Her smile became my everything. "Bella needs a favor, and there's only one man she wants for the job. Apparently, that's you, Mr. Logan."

forty

Hannah

A week went by, and I'd seen or spoken to him every day since forcing myself out of his condo and driving home to see my daughter with news of how Logan had agreed to help her, after all. Not that I'd expected any other answer from him from the start, even if we hadn't ended up in bed together.

No sooner had Bella run into my embrace had she pulled away, her eyes sparkling with excitement before she pinched my cheeks in her little fingers and said, "Your happy smile is back, Mommy. I thought you'd lost it."

It brought tears to my eyes that I had no shame in letting fall as I brought her back into me for a bone-crushing hug. It was proof that a single night with Logan had changed everything. He'd somehow brought something out of me I'd spent my whole life looking for: a sense of belonging.

It didn't hurt that he had a body carved by the gods, and every time I drifted into a daydream, his face hovered above mine, his hair hanging over his eyes as he drove into me while I stroked every valley of his strong abs before I grabbed hold of his ass and told him to go harder.

How any man had the ability to break my body yet rebuild my soul, I wasn't sure, but Logan did, and he had. It had been the first week that I'd spent more time smiling instead of frowning, and my cheeks ached from it.

Now, we were at my place, enjoying Logan's day off after a pattern of grueling shifts that had kept him busy. The Los Angeles sky was a cloudless blue that matched the color of the pool in front of me as I laid back on a lounge chair, watching Logan and Bella taking it in turns to chase after each other.

She'd been more than happy when I'd told her we were friends again, although I hadn't told her just how close Logan and I had become yet. She didn't need to know. Not until we were both certain neither of us was going anywhere.

Even the thought of it made my stomach churn with anxiety, but I quickly pushed the thought to the back of my mind, watching as Logan stepped out of the patio doors wearing nothing but his cobalt blue swim shorts that showed off his thick quads and the six abs on his stomach that had quickly become my favorite place to stroke.

He ran a hand through his hair, pushing it back as he crouched down to look under the patio furniture and then the sun loungers on the opposite end of the pool to mine. After a minute or two, he glanced my way and laid a look on me that begged for my help in finding Bella.

"I told you she was good." I shrugged.

"Unfair advantage. She knows this place better than I do. I

need some insider info."

"That's cheating."

"Whose side are you on?" He padded toward me on bare feet, smirking, forcing me to look up the closer he got. That feeling in my chest tightened at the sight of him, a frenzy of butterflies taking flight out of pure giddiness.

"My daughter's, obviously," I answered with a beaming smile.

"Damn."

"Sorry, but you'll always be second place."

"Who cares when it feels like first anyway?"

He came to a stop beside me and looked all around us, still trying to figure out where she could be. I was desperate to slide my palm over the muscles in his thighs or run my hand up the inseam of his shorts, but I couldn't touch him, and he wouldn't touch me. Not until we both knew Bella would be comfortable with us having *that* kind of relationship. The last thing I wanted her to do was think I was trying to replace her father or what he meant to her. He may not have been a saint, but he'd always be her hero, and I wouldn't deny her a day of that for as long as I lived.

That didn't stop me from staring up at Logan's profile as he surveyed his surroundings.

"I really want to kiss you," I whispered, unable to keep it to myself a second longer.

"Hannah," he warned.

"But I do."

He slowly turned my way, his eyes finding mine. "You have no idea how hard I'm finding it not to reach out and touch you."

"Where would you touch?"

"Everywhere. Everything," he said, his voice hoarse. "Ten times over, and that would be the warmup."

My chest rose and fell. I drew my knees up, squeezing my

thighs together at the thought of what pleasure we might find in each other later that night once Bella had drifted into a deep sleep and we couldn't be heard.

Logan snapped his eyes shut and dragged a heavy palm down his face, turning away from me. "Jesus, Hannah. I can't think about that stuff when I'm meant to be playing hide and seek with your daughter."

"Sorry," I lied, picking up the paperback book again and opening it up to the page I'd been reading. "My bad. Go. Finish your game. But I'm warning you, later it's my turn to play, and there's only one place I want you to hide."

He threw his head back and covered his face with both hands this time before groaning into them. I couldn't help but laugh at how uncomfortable he looked. I felt sorry for men. When they were aroused, they struggled to hide it. Us women could be as hot as an inferno, and the world would never know.

We'd always been better at keeping secrets.

"Oh, and Logan? Keep your wits about you. Bella's good at those sneak attacks."

"I'm not worried."

He turned to leave, walking close to the bright blue waters of the pool, but he didn't have time to stop what was about to happen. Bella's war cry rang out around us all for only a second before her little figure appeared out of nowhere in her purple bathing suit, and she charged toward Logan with a laugh that filled up my heart. By the time he'd turned to see which direction she was coming from, her hands connected with his torso, and she pushed him straight into the pool, his body landing in the water sideways with a splash.

Bella squealed in victory, her arms above her head, while I sat forward with a smile on my face, waiting for Logan to resurface. It only took two seconds before he did, gasping for air, his eyes scrunched together as he pushed his hair away from his face. He blinked furiously, trying to get his bearings before he turned to find Bella dancing over him, wiggling this way and that, taunting him in her sing-song voice.

"You lose!" she cried. "Loser!"

"Hey, now! That wasn't part of the game," he protested, pushing his fingers into his eyes before looking up at her again. "You can't just change the rules on me without telling me."

"I can, and I did." She giggled.

"Oh," Logan said, shaking the water out of his hair and bringing his strong, tanned arms to the surface of the pool, his palms skimming over it as he stalked toward my daughter. "It's on, little lady."

"I got you *so* good."

"You may have won this battle, but the war rages on." His eyes challenged her, despite his smile growing wider. "You know how to swim, right? Because if I'm going down, you're coming with me." He turned his hands into claws as he moved toward her like a predator on the hunt.

"You'll have to catch me first, Mr. Logan," she said with a giggle, quickly taking off on bare feet to escape him.

His hands found the edge of the pool, and in one swift move, he hoisted himself up and onto it, revealing a sun-kissed, toned back with beads of water dripping down into the band of his swim shorts. Logan ran a hand down his face, shaking off the water before he rose to his feet and watched Bella disappear inside the house. When he turned to me, soaking wet from head to toe, standing under the midday sun, he looked like a dream I hadn't thought to dream as he twisted the edges of his shorts in both hands, trying to wring out the excess water.

My heart skipped a beat just from looking at him.

"What?" he asked with a smile, his brows pinching together.

I shook my head and brought a hand to my chest in a pointless attempt to bring my heart under control. "You…" I trailed off, unable to say the things I wanted to say.

I'm so happy you're here.

I don't know what that means.

I'm a little scared and a lot nervous, but I'm also excited, ready to claim my life as my own with you in it.

God, you look good, Logan.

But his smile faded quickly, and he took a step toward me. Recognizing his concern, I put my hand up, bringing him to a stop when his attention dropped down to the hand against my chest.

"Nothing's wrong," I assured him with a smile.

"You sure?"

I nodded once, swallowing down a swell of emotion in my throat I couldn't seem to get control of. "I promise."

Logan slowly glanced over his shoulder to where Bella had disappeared inside the house before bringing his attention back to me. "If I'm getting too involved, tell me. We're going at your pace, remember? I don't want to do anything that—"

"Logan, stop." I shook my head. "It's not that."

"But it's something…"

Eyeing the patio doors to make sure Bella wasn't around, I swung my legs off the lounger and rose to my feet before I walked over to Logan and ran my hands over his biceps.

"You're just making it impossible for me because not kissing you is proving so much harder than I thought it would, and seeing the way Bella is with you…" I rubbed my lips together, the depths of my stomach tightening at the look he gave me. It was pure attention and focus. "It's just hard to believe you're here, and this is real, that's all. I'm waiting for the bubble to burst."

His eyes searched mine, and I wondered if he'd grant me the wish of the kiss, even though it went against everything we'd agreed upon. Instead, he ran a hand through one side of my hair, tucking it behind my ear, making goosebumps scatter down my spine.

"There's no bubble around us, Hannah. I wouldn't allow us to live in something so fragile."

"Say more things like that."

"I plan to... later," he said quietly, making my thoughts race ahead to a time when I could be in his arms, listening to his heart beating beneath his chest.

"I can't wait," I whispered.

A distant cry of, "Mr. Logan," had him dropping his hand from me. We stepped away from each other, and Logan cleared his throat before pushing a hand through his wet hair.

"I better go. I have a six-year-old to throw in the pool."

My brows rose, along with my smile.

"If that's okay with you, I mean," he added.

"She started the fight. I trust you to be gentle with her." *Just like you're gentle with me.*

With a twinkle in his eye, he reached out for my hand, letting the tips of his fingers brush against it for only a second before he turned away and cried out to my daughter that the hunt was on.

It was only then that I saw Livia standing by the open patio doors, looking straight at me...

Us.

Logan slipped past her in a light jog as he tried not to slip on his wet feet, his smile in place as though he didn't have a care in the world other than entertaining Bella.

All I could do was stare at Liv and wait for her reaction to seeing me in that kind of embrace with someone who wasn't Cole.

Her smile rose slowly, her gaze locking on mine before she finally turned away, and it was at that moment that I truly realized how much her approval meant. It stuck around all through the day, well into the night… *after* the pool wars had exhausted Bella into taking a shower and getting her pajamas on. Every time Livia set herself up to take on a task with Logan nearby, he'd rush over to her and offer to help. Not because he felt the need to impress her, but because that was the kind of man Logan Thomas was. If he could save someone in any way—their lives, their energy, their time—he'd do it. He didn't see himself clearly at all.

Maybe none of us did.

He made Livia feel welcome when the sky turned darker, too, and he lit the fire pit on the table under the canopy, talking to her as though she was as important to me as Bella. With every question he asked, Liv's last remaining defenses crumbled until she became putty in his hands as much as I was.

We toasted marshmallows together, letting Bella lead the way with games she invented and tried to teach us, only for most of them to end in fits of laughter from the adults, while the youngest member of the group grew increasingly frustrated with our lack of understanding.

In the end, she'd laid down beside me on one patio couch, her head in my lap while I stroked my fingers through her hair, and she drifted to sleep with the glow of the firepit offering her warmth and light. Logan and Livia sat opposite us, each with a beer in their hands while soft background music played through the outdoor speakers, providing an ambience that made me feel more settled than I could remember feeling in years.

I couldn't remove the soft smile from my face as I stared into the orange flames, and my thoughts slowly began to drift toward Cole.

To the last time I'd seen him.

That vacant expression on his face.

To how nights like this had been all I'd ever wanted from him, but the quiet, sedate life had been a nightmare Cole had never intended on living.

Looking up from the fire pit, I caught Logan staring at me as he brought the bottle of beer to his lips, the light from the flames casting shadows on his face that only made him seem impossibly warmer. When he brought the bottle back down to his lap, he flashed me a smile that made those damn butterflies in my stomach work overtime again, making me want to freeze this moment and stay in it forever.

Paramedic or not, Logan was born to keep people's hearts beating. He'd brought me back to life without even realizing it.

forty-one

Logan

I'd never been more nervous in my life.

Not in all my years on the job, while studying at UCLA, or when I made the move to the city alone with nothing but the suitcase in my hand.

Thanks to the adrenaline, I pushed my shoulders back and clasped my hands together behind me, staring out at a sea of inquisitive children that stared in waiting, ready to ask me a thousand questions I may not have the answers to.

I'd already given them a fifteen-minute talk about what a day in the life of an LAFD paramedic consisted of. I'd shown them some of the medical equipment we carried after Buck had agreed to let me bring some kit in—compression bandages, saline bags, oxygen masks, etc.—with him not knowing who exactly I was helping out, only that it was the child of a close friend who'd asked for me to step up in place of an absent father. Luckily, he'd been swimming in paperwork at the station that morning, and he hadn't been in the mood to ask too many questions.

I'd shown the children models of the basic rescue ambulance versus the advanced version, and I could tell each one of them was desperate to get their hands on them and take a closer look for themselves. I'd talked about which stations covered which areas in the city, and how I'd had to work as a fire fighter/EMT for two years prior to being put forward for my paramedic training, which was where I'd always wanted to end up.

I thought I'd done a good job at keeping them entertained… until silence descended, and a classroom of innocent faces looked up at me, bored and impatient.

Several other parents lined the back of the room, some of them already having finished their talks, while others waited to get theirs over and done with.

Bella attended school in Beverly Hills, which meant I was perhaps the lowest-paid worker there, and I could see the looks some of the other parents were casting between Hannah and me. She stood at the back of the class, leaning against a small bookcase with her hands folded beneath her chest, a look of beautiful amusement aimed my way.

It killed me to tear my eyes away from that pale blue summer dress she wore that hugged her in all the right places, but I was here for the children, not her or *that*, and I had to focus before I gave everything away to an audience of strangers.

"I think now is a good time to open the floor to any questions we might have, class. What do you think?" the teacher said beside me, her ass perched on the low window ledge while I stood frozen behind her messy desk.

I cast her a quick glance that said *Great, thanks,* only for her to smirk my way and shake her head before she looked back at the children and pointed straight at a young boy who had spent most of his time with his finger up his nose.

"Yes, Brax," the teacher said.

Brax lowered his hand, his eyes on me. "Ever seen a murdered body?"

Murmurs erupted from the children, each of them looking at each other in surprise, their eyes wide.

I looked straight at Brax, quickly scratching the awkwardness away from the back of my neck before dropping my hand back down into place. "Being a paramedic, you see every kind of emergency, Brax. Especially the ones you wish you didn't have to see."

"So, that's a yes?"

"That's a yes," I said, trying not to react when some of the kids gasped.

"Was it gruesome?"

"It's never nice."

"Do you have nightmares about them?"

"Sometimes, but it's not something I like to think about a lot. However, these things happen, and my colleagues and I have to do what we can to try and save the victims of such crimes."

"But sometimes they die."

"I, uh…"

"Brax," the teacher warned. "A little sensitivity, please."

The kid rolled his eyes, neither bothered, or entertained by my answer, and I didn't have time to linger on it too much before the teacher pointed to another child, leaving Brax's morbid curiosity behind, while I clutched my hands together tightly, desperate for this to be over already.

Give me a crime scene I'd have nightmares about every night over this. I'd become a man on trial, with the judges being a bunch of rich kids with zero fucks to give.

"Frankie, why don't you go next?" the teacher said.

Frankie looked like trouble with his shaggy blond hair, and his don't give a fuck stare that didn't allow him to blink. "You're not even Bella's real dad, are you?" he asked bluntly.

Without thinking, I looked at Bella sitting behind her desk, only to see her brows knit together as she looked down at her open notebook, the question causing her physical pain.

Clearing my throat, I turned back to the blunt kid. "No, Frankie. I'm not. I'm not her father at all."

"Then, why are you here?"

"Frankie Spellman," the teacher warned. "That's inappropriate and extremely—"

"Actually, it's a good question," I said, talking over the teacher, not wanting her to draw attention or sympathy to the fact Bella's dad had died.

The girl deserved a normal day in a normal world without constantly having to remember the recent loss of her father.

"I guess I'm here because Bella loves what I do, and despite the fact that her mom could have stood up here and given just as good a talk as I have," I smirked, looking directly at Bella, whose eyes had risen to mine again. "I lost a very important game of hide and seek with Bella not too long ago, and the result of that loss was me having to stand in front of a classroom of her friends and talk about what I do. Never take a bet against her. She'll chew you up and spit you out in no time." A few of the parents around the edges laughed, along with some of their children. "All bets aside, Bella thought you guys might enjoy learning about something a bit different to what all the other moms and dads here do. Is that all right?"

Frankie shrugged like he couldn't care less. "Suppose."

Bella's smile came alive, and I internally exhaled with relief, while the teacher beside me did so without any restraint as she looked around the room for another child to choose.

"Yes, Paisley. What do you have to ask Mr. Thomas?"

Paisley was a sweet little girl with a bright smile who lowered her hand only to pick up the pigtail over her shoulder and fiddle with it as she looked at me.

"Hello, Mr. Thomas."

"Hey, Paisley." I smiled.

"So…do you… like… have a wife?"

My brows rose, and I couldn't stop myself looking up to see Hannah, who had pressed her palm to her mouth to stop herself from laughing. It made my own smile hard to contain, but I managed to close my eyes for a few seconds, count to ten, and drag my attention back to Paisley as I rocked on my feet.

"Erm, no, Paisley, I don't."

"A girlfriend?"

"Paisley…" the teacher warned while the other children giggled. "That's none of our business."

"You said we could ask anything," she hit back, her voice small.

"It's fine," I said, offering the teacher a glance of understanding before looking back at Paisley.

It wasn't the right time to make any kind of declarations or place any kind of label on what Hannah and I had. Especially not with Bella in the room. But damn it if my heart didn't pinch and demand that I cry out that maybe I did have a girlfriend, and there she stood at the back of the room, looking at me, waiting to hear my answer for herself as though her life depended on it.

"I think any woman would have to be extremely understanding and patient to be in my life, Paisley. The life of a paramedic with the LAFD is hectic. There are long shifts to contend with, hard days, even harder nights, and a lot of pressure." I paused, unable to stop my eyes meeting Hannah's. "Sometimes we walk away from a callout without getting the result we wanted, and that's a hard pill to swallow. It's not like turning off a computer and going home for the day without thinking about everything that happened. We can carry a lot of guilt and questions around with us that we'll never find answers to. But then there's the other side of the job. The one that brings people into your life you never expected to meet, and that's when you know the hard days were worth it because there's nothing quite like the feeling of walking into someone's life as a stranger and knowing you're walking out as something more. Someone that mattered for a while."

Hannah stared back at me, captivated as she worried a small silver necklace between her fingers.

I had to look away before it became obvious to everyone in here that she had been the best surprise I'd ever had.

I turned to Paisley instead. "So, any girl that wants to be my wife or girlfriend in the future has their hands full, Paisley, and maybe one day someone will come along and think I'm worth the wait *and* the weight," I said with a smile, while some of the young girls began to mutter between themselves and whisper in each other's ears.

"I bet my mommy would," Paisley said proudly.

The class erupted into fits of laughter, and I had to hold back one of my own.

The teacher called order on the class, and I took the opportunity to look at the other parents around the edges of the classroom, only to see a few of them leaning into each other and whispering, too. But when my eyes landed on Hannah, she seemed oblivious to all of them, and her contented smile forced me to look away again because she was the kind of woman you couldn't hide your feelings from… and I didn't want to be the one to land either of us in trouble again.

I answered another handful of questions from the kids,

including one that asked what to do when you got a piece of Lego stuck up your nose. By the time it came to an end, I found Bella staring up at me with a look of pure wonder on her face when the teacher encouraged a round of applause from the other kids.

Following my instructions from the class teacher, I thanked the children for listening and walked to the back of the room to stand by Hannah's side. On my way, I passed Bella's desk, only for her to stick out her closed fist for me to bump mine to the end of it. A simple gesture that said *good job, Logan*.

That shit filled me up with more pride than any rescue ever had.

An hour later, after listening to a few talks from an NFL agent, a scriptwriter, a lawyer, and a stuntman, everything came to an end, and the children were allowed to go to their parents at the back of the room. Bella rushed toward us in a hurry, her long hair its usual un-styled frenzy, which only she could pull off.

I stepped aside for her to fly into Hannah's arms, only it wasn't Hannah she wanted.

Her little body came against mine, crashing into my legs with such force, I had to reach out to the wall for balance while she clung on, pressing her cheek against me.

"Thank you, Mr. Logan. Thank you. You were the *best*."

I glanced at Hannah, who looked like she was trying to hold back her emotions, before I pried Bella's hands off me and knelt down so we were eye to eye. There was so much happiness pouring out of her, even I found it hard not to crumble.

"You're welcome, Bella." Leaning in, I narrowed my eyes, faking uncertainty. "You *sure* I didn't embarrass you?"

"I'm sure. I even heard Violet Evans tell Lilli Hyde that she thought you were cute, too."

My brows rose, unsure what the hell to say to that. I glanced up at Hannah, only for her to shrug as though she couldn't argue.

Pinching the bridge of my nose, I groaned and turned back to Bella. "And you don't think that's embarrassing?"

"For you," she said, chuckling. "I think it's funny because you're old."

"Hey, now, wait a minute."

She laughed some more. "Old and rubbish at hide and seek."

I was about to argue when two young girls tapped Bella on the shoulder, pulling her attention away completely so she turned her back on me, no longer interested in anything I had to say. I rose back to standing, falling in line next to Hannah. Our shoulders brushed together, and I glanced her way, desperate to place a kiss to her lips, cheek, neck... anything, instead having to pretend that I was nothing more than a family friend with no interest in the stunning woman beside me who turned me into a fucking schoolboy myself whenever I was around her.

"Thank you for being here, Logan," she said as quietly as she could as she fiddled with that chain around her neck. "For doing this for Bella. It means a lot that she has someone besides me there for her." Her eyes rose to meet mine.

"Anytime," I whispered, staring into those pools of light green I would willingly drown in. "Thank you for trusting me with her."

"I trust you with both of us."

Without thinking, I reached up with the intention of cupping her cheek and bringing her to me, only for my hand to freeze halfway there once I remembered where we were and what I should and shouldn't be doing. Hannah noticed, and her cheeks blushed on cue while I ran my wandering hand through my hair, and the two of us turned away from each other, trying to create some obvious distance so we didn't raise any suspicion.

Not that it mattered in the end.

Because in those moments shortly after I'd almost messed up, the room fell silent, just as Bella decided to lean into her friends and say, "I've already told you, Violet, he's not my daddy, but he doesn't need to be. Mommy's smile has come back now, and I think it's because of Logan and those kisses he gives her when he thinks no one is looking."

forty-two

Logan

Hannah didn't speak during the car ride back to her place—her thoughts her own as she stared ahead, gripping the wheel tightly. Luckily, Bella hadn't stopped talking from her car seat in the back, as though she hadn't just dropped a bomb on the entire classroom about Hannah and me.

A bomb we hadn't known she had in her arsenal.

The moments after Bella's announcement were deathly quiet, the questioning glares of every single child and parent in that room on us.

Thankfully, the class teacher had clapped her hands to break the awkwardness, encouraging the children to go to their desks to tidy their things before they could head home with us. A few of the parents cleared their throats and turned away, leaving me to shove my hands into the pockets of my uniform pants and brush my shoulder next to Hannah's, neither of us daring to look at each other, only at Bella as she loaded her backpack.

"Did that really just happen?" Hannah whispered.

"Yeah... I think so."

"God, Logan," she hissed, turning her back on her daughter as she pretended to look at some of the children's artwork plastered on the wall behind me. "What the hell are we going to do?"

I smiled at a parent who walked by, offering a nod of acknowledgement, no doubt wondering who the hell I was and where I'd come from. "We roll our eyes, put on a smile, pretend it's just kids' talk, and then we get out of here."

Blowing out a breath, Hannah nodded, then turned back around just in time to see Bella walking toward us both with her backpack over both shoulders, her hands clutching the straps on either side.

"You guys ready?" she asked.

That had been the last time Hannah had spoken, and now, as we pulled into the driveway of their home and climbed out of the car, letting Bella run off ahead in a hurry to get inside and tell Livia about her day, I caught Hannah's wrist, tugging her back to me when she tried to walk off.

"Talk to me. You haven't said a word, and it's freaking me out."

"That's the *only* thing freaking you out? Not the fact that a classroom full of strangers now think we're a couple. Or that we haven't been as discreet around Bella as we thought. I've been wracking my brain, trying to figure out when she could have seen us. We've been so careful, Logan. The only time she could have noticed would have to have been while we were sleeping somehow. But even then, we always went to bed long after she did, and we woke way before her, too, so...?" She trailed off, looking everywhere but at me. "I can't do this. We can't—"

"Woah. *Hey…*" I tilted my head. "Don't go there."

"But—"

"Look at me."

She did, full of worry. "She's already had so much change in her life, and now I've brought us into it."

"And you think she hates that?"

"How could she not? She'll think I'm trying to replace Cole. She'll think…"

"…that you're an amazing, strong woman, who has finally started smiling again, and she will want that for you more than anything. Don't you see? We're the ones freaking out, not Bella. She told her friends about us, and she did it with a smile on her face. She's been full of life these last few weeks. She wants for nothing, and you give her everything, and even though I never want her to think I'm trying to replace anybody, she has me now, too. Another friend in her life." I leaned closer. "That's a good thing."

Her chest rose and fell too quickly as she struggled to control her breathing. Her eyes had misted over, but I was so fucking sick and tired of seeing her tears that I refused to allow to let them fall. Not while she was mine. I wouldn't be the guy to allow pain into her life without trying to burn it to the ground before it could touch her.

"What if someone leaks it to the media?" she asked.

"Then, we'll deal with it. Together."

"And you think you're ready for that? To have your name splashed across the Internet? To have people you don't know insult you or have opinions about you that will turn your stomach sick?"

"Yep. I'm ready."

"I'm not sure you are. You said so yourself: you like a quiet life. This will change everything."

"Everything's already changed because now I have you, and I wouldn't go back to my old life for anything. Whatever they say about me, let them… so long as I get to be with you."

"I'm starting to think you're crazy."

"Blame the woman who's turned my world upside down recently."

I smiled down at her, wondering if she had any idea just how fucking beautiful she was, and how I'd do anything to keep her safe now, no matter what happened to me in the process. I wanted to tell her that I loved her. I'd spent weeks thinking about it, wondering if every second that passed had been the perfect time, and I'd wasted the opportunity. But no matter how much those three little words sat on the edge of my tongue, begging to be set free, this wasn't the moment to drop another bomb on her.

"I can't believe it," she whispered with a soft smile. "You're turning into an old romantic."

"It's long overdue, don't you think?"

"It was worth the wait. You're a natural."

"Only with you."

She huffed out a small laugh before stepping away and brushing her hair back with both hands as she wandered around in front of me aimlessly.

"I need to talk to Bella."

"I know."

"Any thoughts on how I approach this?"

"I think the only thing you can do is be honest, even if that scares you a little bit."

"Tell her everything?"

"Well, I wouldn't tell her *ev*erything." I smirked.

It made her pause in her steps to lay a look on me that told me to behave, even if she found it impossible to hide a smirk of her own. "That's not helping."

"Sorry," I said, not sorry at all. I held my hand out for her to take, and she did, her fingers slowly curling around mine, allowing me to pull her closer. "If you want me to go in there with you, just say the word. You don't have to do this alone. We can talk to her together."

"You'd do that?"

I shook my head and started to guide us into the house. "Stop asking me questions you already know the answer to."

"Ah, this is the part where you say you'd do anything for me again, isn't it?" she asked with another half-smile.

"Finally… you're figuring it out."

"Goddamn you, Logan Thomas," she whispered.

***

Hannah knocked on Bella's bedroom door before tentatively walking in, allowing me to follow a few steps behind. Bella didn't blink at the sight of me there, instead encouraging us both to get closer to see the way she'd set her dolls in a circle to take part in a fake tea party.

Hannah lowered herself to sit beside her while I stood a few feet away, letting Hannah lead the way in the conversation because she was the parent here. Not me.

After asking Bella what made her say the things she'd said to her friends, she'd confessed to tiptoeing down the stairs one night while Hannah and I had been watching a movie in the main living room. She'd snuck her head around the door at the same time I'd pulled Hannah closer to me on the couch, only for her to curl into me and look up, allowing our lips to meet.

And not once when Bella told Hannah about that incident did she stop smiling.

She picked up a tiny toy brush from the thick carpet and focused on the doll in her hand as she brushed its messy hair, struggling to get it through the thicker knots.

"Don't worry, Mommy. I won't spy on you again," she said without a care in the world. "I'm sorry."

Hannah reached out to brush a hand down Bella's back. "That's not what I'm concerned about, bug."

"What then?"

Hannah opened her mouth several times only to close it, the struggle to say what she needed to say clear. It was one thing to know the truth and another thing to speak it out loud to the one person who would be affected by it the most.

She finally turned to look at me, a vulnerable plea in her eyes. *Help.*

I raised a brow in question, only for her to nod and pat the space beside her.

Refusing her wasn't an option, no matter how uneasy I felt, and so I went to them, dropping down beside them both until I laid on my side propped up by my elbow, my legs kicked out and crossed at the ankle. Picking up a doll that had been left face down on the carpet, I began to stroke its hair just like Bella was doing with her Barbie.

"I think what your mom is trying to ask you, Bella, is, were you upset by what you saw that night?"

"Why would I be upset?" she asked innocently.

"Because it's new. Because you weren't expecting it, perhaps. Because you thought we were just friends."

"You weren't friends when Mommy and I went to Seattle." The memory made me wince, but she didn't give me long to linger on it. "But you're friends again now, and I like it. I like seeing Mommy happy," she said, as though it was the easiest truth in the world to speak. "And I already knew you wanted to kiss each other, anyway."

"You did?"

She flipped her doll over, discarding the brush as she fiddled with its skirt instead. "Yep."

"And that didn't bother you?"

She shrugged. "It's fine."

Hannah leaned forward, trying to catch Bella's eye, but she was too focused on her play. "Bug, you know you can be honest with us, don't you? If anything we do upsets you, I want to know."

"Okay."

Hannah looked at me with uncertainty in her eyes.

"Do you feel like you can talk to us about this, Bella?" I asked.

"Sure!" She placed down the doll in her hands and began looking for another. When she found me playing with the one that she wanted, she rose onto all fours and crawled closer to get it. I handed it over, only to see her smile at me before she fell back on her bottom with a thump.

"Do you have any questions or anything?" Hannah asked carefully.

"Erm. No." Bella shook her head, as unaffected by us as she could possibly be. "Oh, wait," she said, and Hannah tensed immediately. Bella stared straight at me. "Does that mean you're going to marry Mommy now?"

"Bug, honey, no, that's not..." Hannah started to protest, but Bella's eyes were on mine, and this conversation had turned to a private one between us, despite her mom being there.

"You don't have to worry about that for a while, Bella," I assured her.

"But it might happen?"

"Would it bother you if it did? Not now, but sometime in the future?"

Hannah's head snapped my way, and her eyes bugged out of her head. I ignored her, focusing instead on Bella and the way my heart pounded against my rib cage at the very thought of spending a lifetime by Hannah's side.

Bella picked up another doll and passed it to me, inviting me to play again. "Not really. I like you."

"But…?"

She shrugged a shoulder. "I want Mommy to be happy. I just don't want Daddy to be sad."

And there it was.

The thing that needed setting free for all of us to navigate together and move forward.

Hannah placed a delicate hand over her mouth to stop herself from saying anything, and I was grateful for her silence. This was my promise to pledge.

To Bella.

To both of them.

"I wouldn't want to make your dad sad, either. He was an amazing father to you, and nobody could ever or should ever replace him. That's not what I'm here to do. I only want to make you and your mom happy… any way I can." I paused before adding, "You know, Bella, I lost my father last year, too."

Her hand stilled against her doll, and for a moment, she just studied me, her inquisitive eyes searching mine.

"I think our relationship was a bit different to yours, though, because we had our ups and downs. But even with those, there isn't a man out there who could come along and replace him."

"Do you think your dad is happy in Heaven now, Mr. Logan?"

The look she gave me killed me. Cole's presence suddenly filled the room, waiting to hear my response—to see if I was capable of handling such an important moment in his daughter's life as though, finally, he gave a fuck about their wellbeing.

"I do."

"My daddy, too?"

I blew out a breath, smiling up at her. "I think Heaven will have the biggest stage your dad has ever played on, and he'll be having lots of fun... but even then, his main priority will always be you. So long as *you're* happy, I think he'll be happy, too."

She smiled back at me, a little spark that was purely Bella returning to her eyes. "Yeah. That sounds like Daddy."

forty-three

Hannah

The problem with good things happening is that they can sometimes seem a little too good to be true.

Logan's presence in my life was the first.

My daughter's acceptance, the second.

The third came along almost a week later, and it started with the ringing of the doorbell that chimed all around the house. Knowing Logan was on shift, Livia was out grocery hunting, and Bella was at school had me staring at that damn door for far too long as though it was sure to bring only bad news. But when I finally made my way to the security panel, and a familiar face stared back at me, I didn't hesitate to scream.

Tearing the door open to Kate, I wasted no time in calling out her name and throwing my arms around her neck before she could drop her bag to the ground and catch me with a heavy grunt.

"What the hell are you doing here?" I cried, squeezing her tight.

"Bloody hell, if only my many lovers greeted me with so much enthusiasm."

I rolled my eyes and reluctantly pulled away, unable to take the gigantic smile off my face at the sight of her. As always, she was the epitome of modern elegance with her black, wavy hair, tawny-beige skin, and almond-shaped eyes that made her the envy of everyone she met.

"Surprise!" she cried, tilting her knee in to pose with soft jazz hands.

"No shit!" I laughed. "What are you doing here?"

"Oh, you know. Had a meeting in LA I couldn't get out of. Decided to kill two birds with one stone and stop by to see my gorgeous girl."

"Well, I'm glad you did. I'm so happy to see you! You look amazing."

Waving a hand, she retrieved her Chanel bag from the ground and hung it on the shoulder of the fuchsia blazer she wore over a loose white tank top, her dark blue jeans hugging every inch of her slim legs.

"As much as I love a good compliment, I didn't come here for those. I came here to take you to brunch."

My brows rose in surprise.

The me of a few months ago would have panicked, letting it spiral out of control, but as I stared up at my friend, I heard Logan's voice in my mind. I remembered all the times he'd held me at night, his fingers running through my hair as he encouraged me to get back to living the life I wanted to live—the one where fear and anxiety over the future didn't control me.

Kate stepped closer, reaching up to squeeze my shoulder.

"No, say it isn't so. You're really going to refuse me after I've flown *all* the way from England to break you free?"

"Manipulative much?" I smirked. "And I'm already free, Kate," In so many ways, I was, but we both heard the hint of a lie left in my voice as she studied me.

"Glad to hear it. Now prove it." She eyed me up and down, letting her judgment shine. "But first, we need to get you out of these clothes and get you dressed in something more appropriate. Activewear on someone so inactive, Hannah? Really?"

"Hey, I'm a mom, leave me alone." I chuckled.

"Oh, I'm going to enjoy this."

An hour later, she'd raided my wardrobe, and we left the house with me dressed in a pair of wide-legged, tan linen pants, golden flats, and a white camisole that apparently showed off the tan I'd acquired from those long pool days with Bella and Logan whenever he wasn't on shift. Kate had even gone to the trouble of curling my hair, pulling it back on one side to pin behind my ear.

A driver had been waiting patiently outside my home, and he drove us into downtown Beverly Hills to a restaurant where we could eat outdoors, with people passing us by while we ate. As soon as I saw BeverLiz Cafe when we turned off Rodeo Drive and onto South Beverly Drive, I couldn't ignore the giddy thread of excitement running through me. Sure, the nerves were there still, but all it took was me to draw on Logan's promises of safety, and I pushed those nerves as far down as they could possibly go.

Plus, it had been such a long time since I'd eaten out in public. Even if the places around here were over the top pretentious, I could allow myself to enjoy this because the company mattered to me.

Kate led us toward our reserved table, pushing her shades to the top of her head as she took the seat the waiter offered, watching me do the same on the opposite side. By the time we'd ordered our food, as well as two glasses of wine, Kate sank back into her seat, eyeing me as though I was a frightened animal about to flee.

"Is this okay?" she asked.

I sipped on the crisp white wine, nodding my approval before I rubbed my lips together and dropped my crystal glass back to the table. "It's perfect."

"You know, I style a lot of women, doing what I do, and no matter how expensive the makeup we apply, or how rare the diamonds around one's neck, or how many accessories we throw over their shoulders, there's only one thing that makes a woman glow the way you're glowing today."

"What's that?" I asked, leaning forward with my forearms resting on the table.

"Love."

I scowled. "Love?"

"You heard me the first time."

"Doesn't mean I understand what you're implying."

Copying my pose, she leaned forward too, her voice dropping. "You can't fool me. I heard you on the phone that day. This has to do with that Logan guy, doesn't it?"

The mere mention of his name had my smile rising.

"I knew it!" she cried, slapping her hand full of expensive rings on the table.

"Shh! Kate!" I hissed, narrowing my eyes and glancing around. "It's not what you think it is. Yes, we're... you know... together. But love?" I shook my head, trying to argue with the rapid thoughts and feelings that rushed through me. "It's too soon for that. We're just—"

"Having a good time?"

"Yeah."

"And the sex?"

"Stop it," I warned playfully.

She laughed, throwing her hands up in the air. "I don't care what you're choosing to label it, but I do want all the details, so spill."

That was the thing with Kate: if she wanted something, she left you with no choice but to give it to her. Without paying attention to those around me or wondering if I was about to be caught on camera, I let myself speak freely to a friend as though it was the easiest thing I'd ever done. Just as it should have been.

She swore to absolute secrecy, not that she needed to. I trusted her with my life as I told her about how I'd tried hard to fight Logan's company, as well as my attraction to him. How I'd thought we could be just friends and nothing more, only for Kate to roll her eyes like I'd been stupid all along.

"Please, I knew what was going on the last time I called you."

"How?"

"Because you spoke about him in a way you rarely spoke about Cole."

The mention of my late husband had my smile fading, only for Kate to reach across the table and place her hand on top of mine.

"Don't get me wrong; you loved him. I know you did. But you always loved him with a little bit of trepidation in your heart, wondering when you'd have to suffer the next gut punch. Anyone could see that."

"Everyone but me?"

"You saw it, honey. You'd just trapped yourself inside a prison *you* made by telling yourself there was no way out."

"God, how pathetic was I?"

"Not pathetic." She shook her head. "Just a mom trying to do what was best for her baby girl, even if it tore her apart to stay."

The waiter interrupted us with our food, sliding my shrimp and crab summer salad in front of me while placing Kate's Chilean salmon salad in front of her. When he stepped away with a nod of thanks, Kate raised her wineglass in the air.

"But here's to starting over," she said, waiting for me to press my glass against hers, the ding of them connecting soon ringing out. "And doing it right this time."

I waited for the guilt to wash over me—for Cole's memory to invade the good moments and turn them bad. Instead, I saw Logan's handsome face when I sat in his lap two nights ago, riding him slowly, neither of us saying anything we shouldn't while our bodies said everything we couldn't.

"Okay, well, don't sit there daydreaming about him while I'm trying to eat," Kate said, breaking me from my daydream with a turned-up nose. "That kind of look can make a girl nauseous."

"Oh, stop it," I said, unable to hide the heat in my cheeks. Taking a quick sip of my wine, I picked up my fork and tucked into my salad, enjoying the food, and listening to Kate, all the while thinking about how it had been so, so long since I'd felt so...

Free.

Unchained.

So myself.

The ringing of my cell brought me back into the moment, and when I pulled it out from my little black purse, Logan's name lit up the screen. The instant grin that came to life made my cheeks ache, and I held it up to Kate, seeking her approval to answer.

"Go, go," she said, wafting her hand, never once taking her eyes off me, not even when I turned away from her. I wasn't quite ready for Kate to see how dopey I became around him just yet.

"Hey," I answered.

"Hey, you."

The sound of his tired voice made my pulse quicken, reminding me of the nights we'd fallen asleep together, talking about inconsequential things until our voices faded away to nothing.

"Everything okay?" I asked. There was a lot of noise in the background, and it sounded as though he was in the middle of something heavy.

"Yeah." He blew out a weary breath. "Rough day so far, that's all."

"Want to talk about it?"

"Maybe later. I just needed to hear your voice to get me through the next few hours without you."

Those butterflies soared again, turning my stomach inside out. I eyed Kate, who was watching me like a damn Netflix show, her eyes wide as she chewed her food, not missing a moment of my reactions to Logan.

"Does it help?" I asked him, turning away from her again.

"More than you know."

"Likewise."

The almighty clang of glass meeting the ground had me turning sharply to see the waiter who'd served us on his hands and knees, trying desperately to pick up the champagne flutes he'd dropped from his tray before his boss spotted him.

"Hannah? What was that?" Logan asked down the phone.

"It was the waiter. He dropped something."

"The waiter?"

"Kate's here. She's flown in from England today. She dressed me up and dragged me out," I said with a smile, not missing the way she nudged my chair with her foot, trying to give herself a pat on the back for that one.

"Dressed up, huh?" I could hear the smile in his voice. "What are you wearing?"

"Nice try, charmer. I'm not answering that."

"He just asked you what you're wearing, didn't he?" Kate

whispered opposite me, and it was my turn to wave her off, earning a chuckle of laughter.

"Okay, well at least tell me where you're at," Logan said.

"Why? Are you planning on stopping by for something to eat? I'm not sure your supervisor will approve of that."

"I've never really liked this job much anyway."

"Behave," I chuckled. "But, to answer your question, we're at BeverLiz Cafe."

"The one on South Beverly Drive?"

"You know it?"

"I do." His huff of laughter didn't go unnoticed, and I was about to ask him what he found so funny, but he got to me first. "Anyway, I'd better go. Enjoy your lunch with Kate. I'm proud of you."

Those four little words made my heart stutter because I knew how true they were. He would be proud of me for putting myself out there. He was every time he saw me growing stronger.

"Am I still okay to come round later?" he asked.

"You know you don't have to ask anymore."

"Doesn't mean I'm going to stop."

By the time we said our goodbyes and I turned back in my seat to look at Kate, she stared at me with wide eyes and a fork pressed against her lips.

"Bloody… hell…" she said in the most British accent she could muster. "You don't even realize it, do you?"

"What?" I asked, unable to remove the smile from my face.

"Just how fucked up in love you really are."

I was about to argue… again… when a single blip of a siren had us both turning our heads to the road, only to see an LAFD paramedic ambulance crawling down the lane toward us.

When Logan's profile came into view from the passenger side, and I saw the way he had one arm hanging onto the handle above the window, showcasing that strong, tanned muscle beneath that tight, short-sleeved shirt, I forgot every single argument I'd been about to make to Kate.

The ambulance seemed to move in slow motion, and when Logan's handsome eyes finally met mine, only for him to wink at me, I was done for. Every doubt or problem or obstacle I could conjure faded away to nothing, leaving only him to fill my senses.

Him and that damn wink.

Logan's chest bounced as he laughed to himself, no doubt seeing my stunned reaction and finding it oh so amusing. I never looked away as they drove on slowly, unable to stop myself from reaching up to clutch my heart as his face slowly disappeared, leaving me to stare at the back of the red vehicle with such longing as it drove away, I thought I might burst.

Almost instantly, my phone beeped in my purse, and I pulled it out to see Logan's name there waiting for me.

LOGAN

You look sensational. I'm going to have fun peeling you out of those clothes tonight.

When I looked back up at Kate, her head was still turned in the opposite direction, her mouth hanging open as she watched the red truck drive away into the distance.

I knew how she felt.

"Okay. Enough," she said, spinning back around in her seat and thumbing over her shoulder. "Where the hell do I get myself one of *those*?"

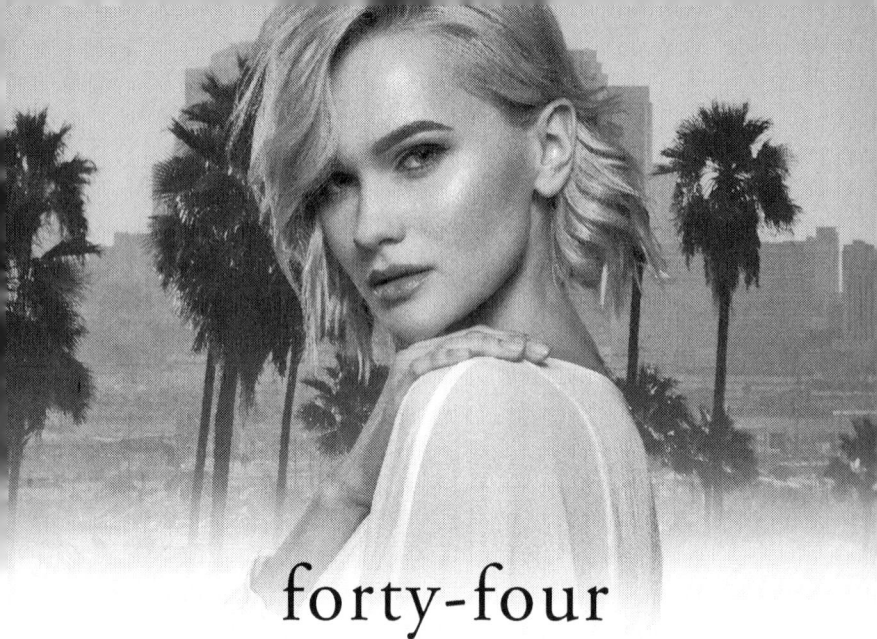

forty-four

Hannah

Despite Kate vowing she'd be long gone before Logan turned up at my place, there she sat on the patio furniture with another glass of wine in her hand, entertaining Bella and Liv with her tales of diva-like behavior from some of the models she worked with.

Bella hung off her every word, and Livia couldn't help but grin like the Cheshire Cat whenever Kate was around. My friend had a unique way about her. One that made everyone feel grateful to be in her company. Nothing was ever too serious, not even the stuff that should have been.

When Logan finally texted me to tell me he was on his way, I made sure the gates were open, and I waited by the door like a lovesick puppy—one slightly buzzed from too much wine, glowing from the afternoon sun, and desperate to see the man she—

Don't go there, Hannah, I thought, shaking it out of my head just before Logan's Outback pulled into the driveway, leaving me to lock him in with us for the night once the electric gates had closed behind him.

As soon as he appeared down the pathway, wearing jeans and a black polo shirt, running a hand through his freshly washed hair, and wearing a smile that flashed his perfect teeth at me, I couldn't wait a second longer.

I ran to him on bare feet, pushing off the paved pathway to jump into his arms as though he was a man returning from war. I'd become a giddy teen, unable to contain her raging hormones or need to be adored so openly.

Logan caught me with ease, his fingers curling into my ass cheeks as I wrapped my legs around his waist and hovered above him without a care in the world. I looked into his eyes for only a second before I kissed him hard.

I wasn't sure whether it was the way he'd made me feel when he'd driven past us at lunch or the texts he'd been sending me ever since, promising me what he couldn't wait to do once we were alone again, but tonight felt different somehow.

I wanted more of him—all he had to give, with no restraints.

"I've missed you," I panted between kisses, earning a raspy groan from him that made my nipples harden. "You're never allowed to leave me again, okay?"

"M'kay," he mumbled.

"You're staying here now, forever."

"Who needs to work anyway?"

"Exactly." I kissed him harder, aware of the heat growing between us.

I'd never had it like this, where the need to drop to the ground right there and then took over, making every animal instinct I'd ever tried to tame roar to life.

"How much wine have you had?" he asked, his lips bumping against mine.

"Just enough to make me happy. Not enough to stop me from wanting you."

"Perfect." He spun us, and my back met the cool wall of the house, causing me to gasp when the rough spots scratched at my skin.

Logan's hips bucked, and he ground me against his erection. I wanted him more than I could explain.

We didn't stop kissing. We couldn't. Something wild had broken free within me... but then a shrill laugh from the backyard reached all the way over to us, and Logan stilled, slowly pulling his face back.

"What was that?" he asked with ragged breaths.

I ran my thumb over his swollen bottom lip. "Erm... that was Kate."

"She's here?"

I nodded.

"Oh."

"We can trust her," I assured him.

"I don't doubt that." Logan immediately dropped his forehead to mine. "But you're gonna have to give me a minute before I meet her. I was damn near ready to take you right here, right now, Hannah," he panted.

"Want to know a secret?" I kissed the tip of his nose. "I would have let you."

Logan growled, and I laughed easily, uncurling my legs from around his waist and sliding down the front of him as carefully as I could. He grabbed hold of my hand, closed his eyes, and counted to himself until he was sure the very thing he needed to hide from everybody else had calmed down.

I loved the power I had over him, knowing I was enough. He made me feel like the most beautiful woman alive.

"Ready?" I asked.

"I mean… I'd rather stay here and fuck you."

"Later." I winked, laughing at his tortured expression before I led the way.

We walked through the house and out into the backyard, but just before we stepped out, Logan let go of my hand, taking his place behind me before Bella saw us together that way. As much as she knew about us now, we'd both agreed to take it slow for her sake. To let her adjust and see us as friends before we started kissing each other, holding hands, or cozying up on the couch in front of her. All of that would happen one day, Logan assured me, and I already couldn't wait for the day when we fell into a comfortable pattern of existence together. The three of us. Nothing in the way.

The moment Kate caught sight of Logan, she stood up from her seat and rushed over to him.

"Logan!" she cried, holding her hand out for him to take. "The man, the myth, the legend."

Logan went to shake her hand, only for Kate to slip hers past his and pull him into a bear hug like she'd known him all her life. Her cheek pressed against his chest as she squeezed, and he looked at me with wide eyes, his arms trapped down by his sides until Kate finally took a step back, setting him free again.

"Bloody good to meet you," she said.

"Likewise," he said in a huff of laughter. "Nice accent. Whereabouts in England are you from?"

And just like that, I lost him to her.

She grabbed his hand and guided him around to the patio couch opposite the one she sat on, where she poured him a glass of wine whether he wanted one or not.

It was right there in my backyard, with my mismatched family of four, that the most beautiful sense of calm washed over me.

This was what I'd always wanted, and now everything felt so *real*.

Livia took her place beside Kate, and as soon as she got the chance to, Bella slid in beside Logan, tucking herself into his body only for him to wrap his arm around her shoulders as though they'd always sat together that way. As though it was the most natural thing to do, and it didn't add more love into my already overflowing heart.

I glanced toward Cole's tree with the microphone hanging down, waiting for someone to go to it and speak to him. For the first time since his death, I had a lot to say... if only we'd been alone.

You could have had this.

I'm sorry if that hurts you.

I'm sorry if seeing me happy causes you pain.

I do still love you.

Just not the way I think I'm falling in love with him.

Because I was. Falling in love with Logan had been easy, especially when I'd tried so hard to make it complicated, trapped in a never-ending cycle of worry over what the world would think of me moving on so quickly.

I'd never wanted to hold back. I'd held back for *them*. For a society I didn't even know. A bunch of strangers. People I'd never met and never would meet in this lifetime, and because of them, I could have missed all this.

You've been so stupid, Hannah.

My attention drifted over the warm lighting around the pool and then up to the dark night sky where stars were hiding somewhere behind the smog and the bright lights of the city, but when I finally looked back at my family again, each of them sitting around the same table, engrossed in each other's lives, I couldn't deny anything anymore.

I *was* in love with Logan Thomas.

All I could do now was hope he loved me in return.

***

Kate didn't leave until after midnight, making sure to give me a little pep talk and speech of approval at the door.

"He's amazing, babe," she whispered. "Truly. Go, be happy. It's your time now." Then she kissed me and promised to call more often, no matter how busy she got.

Thirty minutes later, once Bella had drifted to sleep on the patio couch, Liv pulled me in for a hug, too, telling me she was beat, and she'd be back around lunchtime the next day.

"Why don't you take the day off?" I told her.

"Oh, I don't know," she said with a worried look in her eyes.

I placed my hands on her shoulders, hoping she could see the difference in me compared to all those months ago when I'd been a shadow of the woman that stood in front of her now.

"I love the way you love Bella and me, Liv. We couldn't have gotten through this year without you, but you deserve some time to look after yourself. Take tomorrow. Please? Just for me."

"What if something happens while I'm not here?"

"It won't."

"But—"

"And if it does, I'll have to figure out a way to handle it myself. It's long overdue, don't you think?"

She argued a little more before finally agreeing to take a day, albeit begrudgingly.

Once she'd gone, I glanced over my shoulder to see Logan

walking toward the staircase, carrying Bella to bed in his arms. With the house to ourselves, I followed them upstairs, doing nothing more but standing in the doorway of Bella's bedroom and watching as Logan carefully peeled back the covers and placed her down as gently as he could. He pushed her wild hair back from her face, and I watched him smile to himself before he pulled the comforter over her, placing her lemon teddy by her side. When he looked up at me and smiled, my whole body reacted.

If I hadn't loved him before, I definitely would have now.

He slowly made his way back to me, and we closed the door on Bella, careful not to wake her. I took Logan by the hand, leading him back down the stairs. I could tell he'd hoped we'd head straight to bed, but the wine still buzzed in my veins, and the memories of us earlier on the driveway almost tearing each other's clothes off wouldn't leave me alone.

When we stepped outside, I walked us back to the place I'd run into his arms, turning around and pressing my back against the wall as I tugged him closer by his shirt and rose up on my toes.

"Finish what you started," I whispered.

"What?" He scowled, smiling.

"I said, finish what you started, Logan."

"Here?"

I nodded, my brows high as I let my hands slip down to the button on his jeans. "Here."

"Jesus, Hannah." His eyes darkened, and he looked on either side of him, checking we were definitely alone before he brought his hands to my cheeks and pulled me in for a kiss that took my breath away.

I could have blamed the alcohol for the moans that escaped me, but it had nothing to do with that and everything to do with him. This perfect man, who had become my undoing and my savior all in one.

Our kisses turned heated quickly, and I made light work of unfastening his jeans and pushing them down over his ass until they pooled around his ankles, holding him hostage. The sight of him towering over me made me break away from our kiss and drop to my knees in front of him, desperate to taste the very thing that continued to tease my every thought.

"Better yet. Let *me* finish what you started."

"I don't know what has gotten into you tonight, but I fucking love it," he whispered.

He pushed his hand into my hair, pulling it back just in time for me to tug on his underwear and free his thick cock. I didn't take my eyes off his reactions when I wrapped my hand around it at the base before carefully sliding my tongue up the length of the shaft, feeling his thighs tensing beneath me.

His mouth parted, and his breathing spiked, all in time for me to circle the tip of him once and then lower my mouth around him as much as I possibly could. He was thick, and he was long, and I had to use my hand around the base to meet me at the mouth, twisting together as I pushed him as far back into my throat as I could take him, the slick of my spit making him glide into me with ease.

It was an act I'd never particularly enjoyed before now, but with Logan's hips pushing him into me in a rhythm he was struggling to control, and his breaths becoming heavier and louder with every passing second that I sucked him, that welcomed heat began to pool between my parted thighs. My clit throbbed, and I moaned around him, letting him feel the vibrations of my arousal.

His fingers dug into my hair tighter, and his ass began to move faster while I took it all, letting him fuck my mouth the way I wanted him to fuck my body every day for the rest of my life.

"You're so goddamn beautiful," he said, his voice husky and out of control. "Fuck, baby."

My free hand rose to cup his balls, and everything inside him tightened, making him release his hold on my hair instantly. "Stop," he growled.

I slid my mouth from him to look up through lust-filled eyes. My lips were swollen, and he reached down to trace his thumb around them.

"I don't want to come yet. Not until I'm inside you properly."

"Party pooper." I smirked.

"We'll see about that."

Bringing me up from my knees, he spun me around once I was on my feet, pressing my chest to the cool wall before he reached around to unfasten my pants. He slowly guided them down my legs. After kicking himself out of his jeans, he finally pressed against me, letting the length of his slick erection slide into the crease of my ass.

I moaned, the feel of him turning my nipples impossibly harder, grating against the wall, giving me friction that demanded the same sensation everywhere.

"You're not wearing any underwear," he whispered in my ear, his hand sliding around to find the small bundle of nerves and press against it. "Did you plan on doing this with me tonight?"

"I plan on doing this with you every night," I whispered back, my thighs already trembling from the teasing way he massaged me in perfect circles, making my eyes close and my head roll back.

"God, I wish you could see how hot you look right now," he moaned, his mouth falling to the curve of my stretched neck as his fingers worked me over. "You're a fucking vision, Hannah. Every part of you. But seeing you on your knees for me…"

"What about it?" I breathed.

"It was the hottest thing I've ever seen in my life."

The shaking in my thighs grew stronger, and Logan rode the

crease of my ass cheeks with his erection, making me desperate for more. I needed to be taken. I needed to be destroyed then put back together again. I needed him to ruin me the way only he was capable of doing.

"Logan...I..."

"What?" he gasped. "What do you need?"

"I need the man I love to fuck me."

Every part of him froze the minute those words had fallen free. His fingers stopped moving, his dick stopped riding my ass, and his lips stopped kissing their kisses. It took a moment for my eyes to flicker open and for the realization of what I'd just confessed to sink in.

I loved him, and now he knew.

My pulse quickened, and I began to slide into panic mode from the way those words had slipped out of my mouth so easily.

"You love me?" he asked against my skin, making another wave of goosebumps wash over me.

"Logan, I..."

Before I could finish, he spun me around in his grip, hoisted me up into his arms, and pressed my back against the wall, his hands beneath my ass again. He kicked my pants away into a nearby bush easily, and I wrapped my legs around his waist, exposing myself to him, feeling the tip of his cock against my wet heat. Not knowing who should speak first, I brushed my hands along his stubbled jaw and held him there to look up at me.

"Did you mean it?" he whispered, his eyes searching mine. "Am I really the guy that gets to hear those words from you?"

My panic crumbled instantly, replaced by such an overwhelming swell of warmth and love and longing, I could hardly contain it.

"I tried not to," I admitted quietly, scraping the very tips of my nails through his stubble. "But you made it impossible, so here

I am, loving you despite trying not to, hoping that those words don't scare you away."

"There's nothing in this world that could scare me away from you. I'm yours, Hannah, and fuck, I love you right back."

"But you've never loved anyone before."

"Because it was always meant to be you."

Our smiles grew until we couldn't bear to be apart, and our lips crashed together as though we couldn't survive another second without it.

He loved me.

Logan loved me.

His words had confirmed it, but I knew his actions would always be the thing to prove just how deep that love ran.

"You're so wet," he whispered between kisses. "I can feel it all over my hands."

"Imagine how good I'll feel when you're inside me."

He moaned into the kiss, trying to get impossibly closer as his fingers curled into my ass cheeks, almost bruising before he pulled back and said, "I'm not fucking you in the driveway after you've just told me you love me. As much as I want to, I need you beneath me when I slip inside you tonight. I want to take my time. To devour you and see every reaction your body has to my touch."

I wanted him above me, too, caging me in, holding me close, both of us naked with nothing but hot, damp skin between us. But I also didn't want to make love to him in the same bed Cole and I had shared, either.

Things had changed now.

Logan deserved a place of his own. Not one tainted with the ghost of a husband that didn't belong there, but one where we could allow *our* love to grow freely, side by side.

"Let's go to the spare room you stayed in that first night I crawled into bed with you," I told him. "That's our room now.

Yours and mine. We can make as many memories in there as we like."

I'd no sooner said it, and he turned and carried me the entire way there, not caring about his pants left in the driveway, mine left among the greenery, or the fact that this was risky. But the moment we made it inside the bedroom and Logan laid me on the bed to undress me, I knew every risk I'd ever take with him would be worth it. Every precious moment, every longing stare, reckless kiss, hard thrust, or declaration of love that happened in that room became lifechanging.

The old me died in his arms that night, only for the newer, better version to thrive under his merciless worship. I couldn't imagine my days or nights without him now. I hoped I'd never have to again.

forty-five

Bella

I tiptoed my way to Mommy's bedroom the next morning. She'd been the happiest I'd ever seen her with Aunt Kate and Logan around, and I wanted to know if she still felt the same way. Sometimes, if I was careful enough not to make a sound, I'd listen to Logan and her laughing together on the other side of the door, and I liked it.

Mommy was so much fun now.

But when I made it to her bedroom, I saw the door was already open, and a lot of light shone down onto the cream carpet inside it. The bed was still made, and the curtains open. I stepped inside and walked over to her private bathroom, but the door to that was open, too, and no one was in there.

Spinning around, I ran through the room and skipped down the stairs, hoping to see their faces in the kitchen or outside…

but when I got there, the house was empty, the rooms too quiet. Nothing like they'd been last night.

I didn't get scared a lot—Daddy always told me to be brave—but when I made my way back to the big foyer, something brushed against my skin, making it tingle, and then I got scared.

"Mommy," I said quietly. "Mr. Logan?"

I don't want to be alone.

"Livia?" I said, walking back into the big, tidy living room. It was empty. Everything was empty. "Aunt Kate?"

I ran around every room downstairs, my breathing getting heavier as I began to panic.

"Where are you, guys?"

Don't get scared. Don't be a baby. Don't get scared. Don't be a baby.

The tingling on my skin happened again, and I gasped, quickly rubbing at my arm where it felt like somebody had touched me, but there was nobody there, and I started to think this was one of those bad dreams I sometimes had.

Scrunching my eyes shut, I spun in circles and whispered to myself, "Wake up, wake up, wake up," but when I opened my eyes again, I was still in the same place.

It frightened me.

I didn't want to be alone.

I ran to the big main door, coming to a stop next to the little box where Mommy kept the keys. I'd seen her do this so many times before—Livia, too—so I knew that the biggest key with the big, black head was the one I needed, and I pushed it into the lock like I'd watched them do every time we left the house.

It clicked when I turned it, but when I tried to pull the handle down and open it, it was too heavy, and it clicked shut again before I could fit through the gap I'd created.

"Ugh," I huffed, looking around me for something that could

help. "Wait. The box!" I picked it up and put it down on the tiled floor, reading to nudge it into place with my foot when I got the door open just enough.

It took a few tries, but when I kicked it into the gap, and the door stayed open against it, I smiled to myself, feeling grown up as I pushed out a heavy breath.

I slipped through the crack in the door, squeezing myself into it like *Jell-O,* only to stumble out on the other side, accidentally kicking the box back into the house when I did, making the door close behind me.

"Shoot."

I was locked outside on my own, wearing nothing but my pink pajamas.

Mommy was going to be so mad.

I turned to the side and saw Mr. Logan's jeans on the driveway, just lying there on their own. I frowned and went to pick them up, holding them in my hands as more panic made my tummy turn over and over and over.

Why would Mr. Logan's clothes be out here?

Had something happened?

Mommy wouldn't leave me alone unless something had.

Were they in trouble?

But when a familiar cat circled my bare feet, and I looked down to see its tail curled against my leg, I lost my track of thought.

"It's you!" I cried. "You're the cat that's always in Daddy's tree."

It didn't respond, so I tried again.

"Have you seen my mom? Have you seen Mr. Logan, too?"

That cat was rude, and it never gave me an answer, so I bent down to pet it, thinking it might need a cuddle first.

The moment my fingers touched its fur, it ran away, heading

to a tiny gap in the trees by the big gates Mommy said were there to keep us safe.

I ran after the cat, needing to talk to it. Needing to tell it that it was naughty and had no right to sit in those branches. Those were Daddy's, and its butt didn't belong there.

"Hey!" I called out. "Hey, you. Cat! Stop right there!"

I thought I'd almost caught it, too, but then it slipped through that tiny gap in the tree, leaving me to drop Mr. Logan's pants before I dropped down onto all fours as I peered through it. This was as close as I'd ever been to the cat, and maybe Mommy and Logan were out there beyond the gates, too. Maybe that's why they couldn't hear me back here. Maybe they'd found that naughty animal and were waiting for me to scold it.

But that gap...

It looked so small.

"What would Daddy do?" I whispered. "He'd follow the cat. He loved adventures."

So, that's what I did. I crawled headfirst into the gap that was too small, hissing when the branches bit at my skin, scratching me like the cat probably wanted to. That didn't stop me, though, because I was brave. I crawled, and I crawled like Daddy would have done, and when I finally made it out, I saw the cat, begging me to follow it.

And because I wanted to make Daddy proud, I did that, too.

forty-six

Logan

annah was kissing her way down my stomach before I'd even opened my eyes, and then she kissed her way back up until her lips met mine, and she pressed her naked breasts to my chest, laying herself on top of me so I could wrap my arms around her and pull her closer.

"Interesting," I said in a voice still tainted with sex and sleep.

"Hmm. What is?"

"Last night wasn't a dream."

I pressed my lips against her hair, desperate to take her again the way I'd taken her all night, unable to stop. Unable to care about either of us growing sore or weak as we exhausted our muscles and rode the waves of orgasm after orgasm.

"It was the realest thing I've ever felt," she said, turning her head to kiss me, gifting me with a sleepy gaze that had me rolling us both over until I was the one on top of her.

Her hands slid over my biceps, her eyes wide as she stared up at me with a love she could no longer deny.

"I can't imagine not wanting to fuck you every time I look at you," I whispered.

Her lazy smile came to life at the exact same time as her stomach rumbled as though it was the beginning of a very serious earthquake that would destroy everyone within its wake. We broke into laughter, with Hannah bunching her knees up beneath me as she pressed a hand to her stomach.

"If you plan on using my body for your own benefit, you could at least feed me in between."

"I think I used your body for both our benefits, don't you?"

"Fair," she said, lifting her head to kiss me before she fell back against the pillow and pushed at my chest, rolling me off. "But that doesn't change the fact that I need food, and so do you. My daughter, too."

I grumbled in protest, mainly for effect, reaching over to the nightstand for the watch I'd taken off during the night. It was barely nine a.m., but it felt so much later. Sleeping in wasn't exactly something I'd been good at, but with Hannah by my side, I could have spent all day tucked beneath the sheets, touching, and playing, figuring out what drew the sweetest moans and softest gasps from her before destroying her completely.

She moved around the room, picking items of clothing up, but when all she could find was my polo shirt, she held it up to me with a frown. "Where are your jeans?"

"I think you removed them when you dropped to your knees in front of me outside."

"Oh my God. They're still in the driveway?"

"Yours, too, somewhere."

She pushed the fabric of my shirt to her face, burying herself in it before she shook her head and looked up again. Her cheeks were bright red, her eyes more alive than I'd ever seen them. "I'll be right back."

I hated that she'd disappeared, but I settled myself with the knowledge that she'd always come back to me now. We were in love, and nothing could change that.

By the time she returned, only ten minutes later, she'd changed into a pair of denim shorts and a plain white tee, yet she somehow looked more beautiful than ever as she ran a hand through her messy hair and held my jeans out to me.

"These were by the gates," she said with a frown. "I swear you left them farther up the drive than that."

I stood and made my way over to her, taking them from her hand and climbing into them, tugging them up my legs. "Maybe a coyote had some fun with them. Did you find yours?"

"Yeah, but…" Her eyes fell to the floor in thought.

"But what?"

She looked up at me again. "The key box was on the floor in the foyer when I went downstairs."

"That was probably us when I carried you inside. I wasn't exactly looking where I was going when I had your ass in my arms."

"Good point," Hannah chuckled. "I can't believe I forgot to set the alarm. I never do that."

"Sorry." I smirked.

"No, you're not."

"Not even a little bit." I winked.

With a soft roll of her eyes and shake of her head, she turned to walk away. "I'm going to check on Bella."

I caught her wrist, quickly pulling her back to me for a lingering kiss that I couldn't deny myself before I let her go, watching as she stumbled back on unsteady feet, her eyes still closed. I reached for my polo shirt and pushed it over my head and down my torso before Hannah's eyes fluttered open again.

"Okay, *now,* I'm going to check on Bella."

"You do that." I grinned.

"See you downstairs."

"I love you."

She stilled, her hand on the door before she glanced over her shoulder with a smile of her own in place. "I love you."

I felt like a different man to the one I'd always known as I watched her walk away. The road to this had been unconventional but I wouldn't change a thing. I couldn't live without her now. She'd shown me how I hadn't been living at all before she came into my life.

A few minutes later, Hannah pushed the bedroom door open, another frown in place. "I don't believe it. She's up before us?"

"Lazy bug?" I raised both brows. "Seriously?"

"I know." She turned to make her way downstairs, me following closely behind her.

I wasn't sure what it was, whether an instinct kicked in after having done the job I'd done for so many years, but as we snaked down the spiral staircase and landed in the foyer, a chill ran down my spine—one of dread as I caught sight of the key box on the floor. Bending to pick it up, I glanced at the lock on the door, seeing the key stuck in there as though it had never been taken out. I placed the key box back on the side table, turning to follow Hannah, only to see her walking back toward me already, any happiness she'd had this morning long gone.

"The patio doors are still locked from last night," she said in a rush of breath. "But she's not in the kitchen or the living room." She started moving with more urgency, heading to several rooms around the house I hadn't been into before.

I saw the cinema room, the underground gym, and the laundry room. I saw a playroom big enough to house pink electric toy cars Bella would have been able to sit in, but I'd never seen her use. We searched them all, our cries of her name getting stronger and louder with every room we went into, only to find it empty.

"Does she do this a lot?" I asked Hannah, that feeling of dread growing stronger.

"Never."

We charged back up the stairs. "Let's not panic. She'll be playing hide and seek or something. She'll probably be outside, hiding in the trees."

"She can't get outside, Logan. The doors were locked all night." Hannah ran into three of the spare bedrooms, including the one we'd slept in, calling out her daughter's name everywhere she went. "Bella!"

"Bella!" I cried with her.

When we came to the last door upstairs, I reached out to turn the handle, only for Hannah's hand to land on top of mine, stopping me from opening it.

"She won't be in there. It's locked."

"Maybe she—"

"No, Logan," her voice was firm, and goosebumps became visible on her arms. "It's been locked since Cole died. She doesn't even know where the key is." Hannah turned and walked away, leaving me behind.

I had a million questions to ask about what was beyond that door, but instead, I banged on it several times and leaned into it. "Bella, if you're in there, you need to come out, bug. This isn't funny. I know you probably didn't mean to, but you've got Mommy worried."

I waited as long as I could and prayed for her response, but nothing came.

That's when my blood turned to ice, and I charged down the stairs at full speed, calling out her name as my cries mixed with the desperate pleas of her mother.

Despite the patio doors being locked, we pushed them open and searched the backyard anyway, and my relief poured out of me like I'd taken a blow to the stomach when I saw the pool clear.

That's the problem with seeing so many accidents—so much death that could be avoided. You started to see it everywhere before you even knew what was going on.

Hannah's body slammed into mine when we came together after running around the pool. Her tears were visible now, her skin ashen as she pressed her fingers into my chest and let her eyes roam wild around the backyard.

"Where is she, Logan? Where's my daughter?"

"I don't know, but we'll find her."

"This is all my fault."

"No, it's not."

"It is. I've been so pre-occupied with…"

"What?" I looked down at her, unable to miss the way our heartbeats mixed together like two crazy drum solos, fueled by a drug called fear.

Hannah took a moment to press her forehead to my chest, but no sooner had she done it, she pushed herself off, her eyes meeting mine with anger I hated to see.

"She's my *daughter*, and I don't know where she is, Logan. I don't know where she is because I was too busy losing myself in *us!*"

"Hannah, stop," I barked, my voice firm. "Don't do this."

She shook her head and backed away, putting distance between us. "This is a sign, don't you see? A warning."

"It's not. This is just a moment in time. We'll find her. She's safe."

"And you can promise me that, can you?"

"Hannah, wait," but by the time I'd reached out for her, she'd turned on her heels and was running back through the house, Bella's name falling from her lips.

Despite the blow of her words, I swallowed them down and followed her anyway, all too familiar with how differently people reacted in a crisis. I caught up with her by the door, and she was just about to pull it open when I placed my hands over hers, freezing her in place.

"I know you're upset," I said, breathless, "But we're not going to be able to find her unless we both calm down."

Hannah looked up at me, her tears falling freely. "I can't lose her, Logan. I just can't. I won't survive it."

"I won't let that happen. I *promise*."

Her hand twitched beneath mine, and I looked down, seeing the key in the lock still.

"Do you make a habit of leaving your key in the door at night?" I pointed to it.

She looked confused at first, her eyes flickering and her scowl creasing before she looked down at the key herself. Hannah shook her head. "No. Never."

"Was it like that when you came downstairs this morning? When you went to get my jeans from the driveway?"

"I…" She shook her head again. "I don't remember. I was…"

"What?"

"I was too busy thinking about you. I couldn't stop smiling. I didn't even register anything about a key except the key box on the floor once I stepped back inside after picking your jeans up."

"So, that key could have already been in there."

"Yes," she said, her voice quivering.

Our eyes met for only a second before we both tugged at the handle quickly, opening up the heavy door together until the

Californian sun bled down on us.

"Bella opened it herself," I said, piecing everything together out loud. "We weren't in your bedroom last night. She went looking for us and couldn't find us, so she came down here, tried to open the door, and used the key box to keep it wedged open."

Hannah's hands covered her mouth as her panic set in.

"Remember your breathing," I said as I stepped outside. "You're no good to Bella in the middle of an attack. I'm going to need you to open the gates, baby."

Somewhere behind me, Hannah sucked in a breath, and a few seconds later, the grinding and creaking of the electronic gates slowly opening filled the air. It didn't take long for Hannah to run up to my side, inhaling deeply and exhaling just as slowly when she did. As soon as the gates were open enough, we ran through them together, each of us yelling Bella's name as loudly as possible. It didn't take us long to reach the sidewalk, and I glanced up and down the street, seeing the place I used to sit and watch the house from a distance and suddenly hating myself for it.

What good had all this been if Bella got hurt in the end anyway?

"*Bella!*" I roared, my fists hanging by my thighs.

The other houses, spread far apart, looked idyllic from the outside, the way Hannah's always had, but every possible gruesome thought and scenario ran through my head at the sight of them, none of us ever really knowing what went on behind closed doors.

If someone had taken her, I'd murder them.

I'd spend my life inside a cell after tearing them to pieces, limb by limb, because that's what you did when you loved someone. You'd burn down the Earth and everyone in it to bring justice to their name.

And I loved Bella as much as I loved her mom now.

Stay calm, Logan. You're no good to anyone like this, either. She's out there. Find her.

"You go left. I'll go right," I told Hannah, turning around to grab her shoulders and lower myself to her eye line. "Remember how strong you are. Remember that Bella needs you, and remember that I love you."

Hannah sucked in a shaky breath before nodding and pushing her shoulders back. With a quick kiss to her forehead, we pulled apart, and I set off down the sidewalk, leaving Hannah to venture in the opposite direction.

Bella's name occupied the air, and it didn't take long for other people to notice. A jogger slowed down, pulling out his air pods to ask what was wrong. A red Ferrari slowed down to see if they could help. A neighbor jogged down the driveway of their expensive home, looking to see what was going on.

And then I heard a blood-curdling cry of my name from far away on the same street.

"Logan!"

I spun on my heels and ran.

It took me no time to race back to Hannah, charging across the road before I came to a stop in front of her, grabbing her arms much harder than I intended. "What is it? Where is she?"

"She's…"

"Mr. Logan, I'm here!"

The sound of my name on Bella's lips sent a rush of adrenaline through my body, and before Hannah could say anything, I turned toward Bella's voice, my eyes rising until I saw her.

There she sat, perched in the midst of a small tree, her little limbs barely holding her in place despite her bottom balancing on a branch that didn't look sturdy enough to hold her.

"Oh, thank God," I exhaled. "Bella."

Abandoning Hannah without a thought, I turned and jogged

toward the small tree, coming to a stop beneath Bella to see she was only a foot or two above me. Her pink pajamas were covered in dry dirt, her hair wilder than ever, and her eyes red from her worry.

"I think I did a bad thing, Mr. Logan," she whimpered.

"As long as you're okay, that's all that matters. We were worried about you."

Her bright blue eyes shone down on me. "I thought you and Mommy had left me, so I came outside to look for you."

Hannah's earlier words of us being too pre-occupied drifted through my mind, but I forced them away, focusing on the here and now before I let my stomach twist with dread, knowing what this would do to her.

"Do you really think we'd ever leave you behind, bug?"

"Daddy did. He didn't even say goodbye." Her bottom lip trembled before she trapped her teeth on top of it and forced it to stop.

I shook my head and blew out a breath, breaking inside for the six-year-old who had been forced to grow up too fast. "He didn't leave you by choice, Bella. If he could have said goodbye, he would have."

She tried to dry her tears on her shoulder, but it only made her body wobble and her grip unsteady.

My hands flew up to catch her instinctively, and it was only when I heard Hannah's quiet gasp that I registered she was behind me now, but I stayed focused on Bella. She needed me more. With my arms up, I looked into her eyes, hoping she saw a pillar of strength and not a grown man who was dying inside at the sight of her so distraught.

"I think it's time to get down from there now, Bells, don't you?"

"I'm scared I'm going to fall."

"I won't let you fall."

Her eyes found mine, assessing me as though to see if she could trust me fully.

"It's my promise to you. I'll never let anyone hurt you. Not even yourself." Encouraging her with a nod, I said, "Get your footing right on the trunk there and then let go. I'll catch you."

"You sure?"

"I'm sure."

"O-okay," she whimpered.

It took her only a few seconds to start moving, her little breaths coming in fits and spurts as she tried to get herself into the right position. Hannah's mewls of worry beside me didn't go unnoticed, but I ignored them, knowing she'd want me to focus on Bella until she was back down on the ground.

"Okay, Bella. I'm going to count to three. The moment you hear me say *three*, that's when you let go. Don't think about it. You have to trust me and just do it. Do you trust me?"

She gave a small nod, and I made my count. The very second the word three came out of my mouth, Bella took a small breath, and she trusted me enough to jump.

Her tiny body landed in my hands within a second, and I took the brunt of it, catching her before pulling her into me and holding her tight as I closed my eyes and released a breath of my own. Her legs wrapped around my waist, and her head rested on my shoulder as I squeezed her tight.

"There you go, bug," I whispered. "I've got you."

I'll have you for the rest of my life if your mom will let me.

"Bella, baby," Hannah said in a rush of relief as she came to us, not wasting a second to peel her daughter off me to hold her for herself.

I passed her over and stepped back, watching as Bella curled herself around her mom like she'd not seen her for an eternity.

While Hannah cried, Bella grew calmer, holding onto her mommy as Hannah spun them around, and Bella's eyes met mine.

Even though my heart pounded like never before, I gave her a wink and a smile to let her know she wasn't in trouble. Nothing bad was going to happen now, but when Hannah spun back around again, taking Bella out of sight and bringing her own eyes up to mine, I saw everything there waiting for me that she couldn't say. Everything her heart didn't want her to speak, but her head told her she had to.

This is our fault.

We let this happen.

We're to blame.

My daughter feels abandoned again *because of us, Logan.*

I need space. I need time. I need...

"No," I whispered, shaking my head. Taking a step forward, I closed the distance, bringing my thumb up to wipe her tears away. "No, Hannah. I won't let you do this."

"We don't have a choice," she whispered back.

"You *always* have a choice now."

"I'm a mom, and she'll always come first, Logan."

Our eyes lingered on each other's, and my own pain mirrored back at me in her stare. She didn't want this, neither of us did, but that old friend of ours, guilt, had returned, and the dark clouds had taken over everything that had once been good.

When Hannah turned away and began to cross the road with Bella in her arms, all I could do was watch, not knowing what the hell to do. Should I leave and respect her wishes, or should I follow her and fight?

There was only ever going to be one option, so I followed, crossing the road with her, following only a few footsteps behind.

"Wait!" Bella cried, her head suddenly lifting from Hannah's shoulder as she looked straight at me, bringing her mom to a stop.

Bella pointed back at the tree, kicking out of her mom's embrace and forcing Hannah to let her slide down her body. "You have to get the cat, too, Mr. Logan."

"Bella, no, we need to get you home," Hannah said, reaching for her hand and holding it tightly like she'd never let go again.

They both turned to face me, and Bella stepped forward, despite Hannah's firm grip on her.

Her eyes stared into mine with all the pleading of a broken child that could bring me to do anything. "Please. I think the cat needs a home, too. I don't want to leave him behind. He's somewhere around that tree. That's why I climbed up there. I didn't want him being lonely. Everyone deserves someone to love, even a grumpy cat. Please, save him. Save him like you save all those people who get poorly."

My eyes rose to meet Hannah's, only to see that she could barely look at me before I let them fall back down to Bella.

"Please, Mr. Logan…"

I nodded softly. "Okay."

Her face lit up like a Christmas tree. "I'm coming with you."

"Bella, no—" Hannah tried, but Bella just tugged her hand out of her mom's grip anyway.

"Don't worry, Mom. Mr. Logan is with me. Nothing bad can happen when he's here."

My heart cracked inside my chest as I took Bella's hand and looked up at Hannah for her approval. I could see the war going on inside of her, but eventually, she gave me a nod of her own, folding her arms over her chest.

"I'll wait here," she whispered.

I turned and looked away from the pain in her eyes, and I led Bella across the road again, back to the tree to look for the cat she'd become obsessed with.

"He likes to play hide and seek as much as we do," Bella told me. "So, we have to be clever about this."

"I think it might be time for us to find a new game to enjoy once we get home, don't you?"

We wandered around the tree, our necks craning this way and that, searching in nearby bushes, our backs bending to look through any small gaps it could have sneaked through.

"Wait," Bella said with a gasp, dropping to all fours to peer under another bush. "I think I see its tail."

I dropped to my hands and knees to take a look for myself, but before I could bend enough to peer underneath the leaves, the cat in question bolted out from beneath the greenery and took off across the road at such a speed, it had both our heads snapping to the right to take him in.

I didn't have time to react and grab her.

Bella took off after him, her cries of "*Mr. Cat!*" filling the air until the world seemed to stop around me.

That chill of dread snaked down my spine.

The adrenaline coursed through my veins.

The roar of an expensive sports car filled my ears.

And Bella's squeals of delight made me move.

Springing to my feet, I charged after her with all the power I had in my body to get me there in time.

The engine growled, and the car sped down the road, a siren of warning that burst into my eardrums and made me fly toward Bella, who had already stepped out into the road—her thoughts on nothing but that damn cat.

"*Bella!*" Hannah screamed. "*No!*"

"*Bella!*" I roared.

I fucking ran. I ran with everything I had inside of me until I got to her. The moment she was within reach, I jumped for her, my arms flying around her tiny body until I had her waist in my grip, and I was picking her feet off the ground. The sound of tires screeching had me scrunching my face tightly, and I used every ounce of strength I had to brace myself for impact before I threw Bella toward her mom, and I watched her roll on the sidewalk and into Hannah's arms.

It was a split second of pure bliss.

A slowed down moment of time that made my life *mean* something.

To finally know I'd learned how to love.

And when the car eventually took the legs out from beneath me, turning my whole world upside down, I ignored the pain and stared back at death, knowing it had all meant something because, in the end, I got to save the girl.

Both of them.

forty-seven

Hannah

I hadn't stopped screaming his name.

Not even when sirens filled the air and men in a familiar navy uniform pulled me from Logan's blood-soaked body and unrecognizable face, forcing me back on shaky legs into the crowd of strangers that had gathered around us, trying to console my daughter, and now me, as the earth fell out from beneath my feet.

I couldn't lose him.

I wouldn't survive it.

Even the thought felt like a gunshot to my already broken heart.

The moment I could, I reached for Bella, picking her up and wrapping her around me, forcing her to bury her head into my neck to shield her from the wreckage in front of us.

"Mommy," she whimpered.

A neighbor offered help by asking to take her from me, but I refused, clinging onto her tightly, needing to feel her heartbeats so I remembered how to keep up with my own.

She shouldn't be here. I knew that, but I also couldn't leave *him*. If I turned and walked away, I was scared it would be forever. That I'd never get to see him again. That I'd never get to hold him or kiss him or look into his eyes as he made love to me. I'd never get to tell him how I couldn't walk away from him now—I'd been such a fool to think I ever could have.

Bella and I were no longer a duo. We were a trio of three, and Logan had become the heart of it. We needed that heart to keep beating.

The thought of Logan leaving me shredded every bit of survival I had left. Without him, I'd never truly live again.

It was only when I heard a familiar voice say my name that I blinked several times and allowed myself to turn toward it. The sight of Livia nearly brought me to my knees again.

Without saying a word, she gathered Bella into her arms, making sure to keep her turned away from Logan before she offered me a sad smile that said so much without saying anything at all.

"It's your turn to be there for him now. Go. Bella is safe with me."

I opened my mouth to argue—to tell her Bella should never be away from me again—but one look in Livia's eyes, and I knew it was the right thing to do.

Logan needed me, and I refused to let him down ever again.

I pressed a kiss to Bella's head. "Livia will take you inside, bug. Don't worry. Everything's going to be just fine."

"Will Logan be okay?" she asked, her breaths stuttering as her tears fell like little waterfalls, and it didn't pass me by that it was the first time she'd dropped the Mr. from his name, despite encouraging me to call him Logan from the start.

"He doesn't know how to leave us, Bella. He'll come back. He has to."

The lies we told our children in order to keep them safe…

When her and Livia finally walked away, I sucked in a shaky breath and ran toward Logan who was surrounded by three men and two women, each of them doing their part to save his life. Firefighters and paramedics filled the streets. There were oxygen masks, tubes and wires, needles, and kit I didn't even understand all around Logan, all of which brought a chill to my skin. Medical terms I didn't understand were shouted out and tossed around like they were speaking another language entirely.

It only frightened me even more.

"Logan!" I cried. "Logan, please!"

His name fell from my lips like a prayer, over and over as pure terror tore through me, making my limbs shake and my heart race into dangerous territory. But I wouldn't let my body's reactions control me. Not when he needed me the most. He needed me to be strong.

I was charging forward when a pair of hands came up to my arms, holding me tightly before I slammed into a hard body.

"Let me go!" I cried, gasping for air.

"Hannah, stop. Please."

I blinked again, trying to focus as I slowly turned to the man in front of me, made up of kind eyes, his own heartbreak, and a resilience I was instantly envious of. He tried to smile, but it only made his face crease in pain even more than it already had been. His eyes were fighting to hold back his tears.

"I'm Jerry," he croaked.

I scowled, recognizing the name. "Logan's friend…"

He nodded and swallowed down his emotions.

I searched his eyes, begging for good news as I clung to him. "Don't, Jerry. Don't look at me like that."

"I'm not going to make promises we can't keep. I don't believe in that."

"What are you saying?"

"I'm saying we're fighting like hell for him, and—woah there!"

My knees buckled, but he somehow held me up, and I tried again to look around him. To see Logan and go to him—to be there just in time for him to sit up, groan, smirk at me, and then crack an ill-timed joke that nobody would laugh at—but Jerry blocked my view and shook his head.

"We need to get him to the hospital now, Hannah."

"I'm coming with you."

"I know," he said, his voice dropping quieter. "I know."

Forcing down my own fears, I looked up at him, and I gripped his shoulders tightly, shaking them in my grip. "Don't you do that," I snapped. "Don't you give up on him. He wouldn't dare give up on you. He doesn't give up on *anyone* he loves. He'd expect you to fight for him the way he'd fight for you—for all of us!"

He let me shake him, but he never looked away as his jaw clenched and his eyes welled with even more tears.

"You're the best paramedic he knows, and you're wasting your time here with me?" I smacked at his chest, pushing him back. "Go to him. S*ave* him."

Jerry's eyes searched my entire face before he let me go. "I won't let you down. Either of you." Then he left, running back to the others who had brought a gurney in before they began to prepare for Logan's transfer to hospital.

I couldn't look away from him. A man who had always been so sturdy, so strong, now laid out on the ground, lifeless.

I didn't care who saw me or who was looking on. The moment they'd strapped him in after so many checks were run, and so many commands shouted across from man to man, I ran to Logan's side. The brace around his neck held him still, his face bust-up with so much swelling and blood, I hardly recognized him.

But I knew he was still in there.

I felt it in my heart; the one that now beat for him.

When they pushed me away and lifted him into the back of the ambulance, I stumbled back on unsteady feet, but before they closed the doors on me, I gave Logan my voice to cling onto.

"I love you, Logan Thomas!" I shouted above everyone and every noise that consumed the air. "I love you, and don't you dare forget that. Don't you dare leave me behind like this without telling me you love me too!"

The doors closed, and the men and women in navy uniform rushed to their vehicles, each of them desperate to save their friend without a second to spare, leaving me standing on the street, watching the man I loved being whisked away while other firefighters, EMTs, and paramedics worked on the distressed man in the sports car behind me.

I stood there alone in the streets of Beverly Hills, not caring who knew that I loved Logan now.

"Who cares about tomorrow when I need you today," I whispered, allowing myself only a moment before I turned back toward my house, and I ran to my car.

forty-eight

Hannah

Three days went by, and I didn't leave the hospital, even though it brought back so many bad memories and emotions, I'd once sworn never to return. Now, though, I was willing to spend a lifetime here if being nearby somehow kept Logan's heart beating.

Livia and Bella came by often, bringing me food I couldn't bear to eat, drinks I couldn't bear to drink, and comfort I couldn't have survived without. Despite wanting to shield my daughter from everything, she had a fiery determination when it came to the new man in her life, and she'd been desperate to check on Logan, too. Every night she'd beg to climb into bed with Livia to share stories about him, and every morning she woke bright and early, like the lazy part of her genetics had simply disappeared, and she'd begged and begged and begged until Livia had no choice but to drive her to the hospital to see me.

It turned out my daughter had fallen in love with Logan as much as I had.

We clung to each other throughout the days, and I struggled to let her go on the nights. The doctors and nurses at the hospital tried to encourage me to go home and rest, but I'd shrugged them off as politely as I could, making it clear that, until I could walk out of there with the man I loved beside me, I wouldn't be going anywhere.

They must have seen something immovable inside me because after a while, they simply stopped asking, instead wondering what they could do to make me more comfortable while I waited. I always looked at them the same way as if to say, *Wake him up. Make him open his eyes, and I'll never feel discomfort again,* but their silent, sympathetic smiles were all they'd been able to offer.

Logan had been in a natural coma for the last three days.

Despite me not being his next of kin, the doctors had been generous enough to fill me in on what was going on with him. The blunt trauma had caused so much damage to his body, he'd no longer been able to stay conscious. Terms were thrown at me constantly:

Internal bleeding.

Slipped spinal discs.

Possible nerve damage.

Third degree burns to his skin.

Punctured lungs.

Broken bones.

Lacerations to every part of him.

And the worst?

The swelling of his brain, keeping him on constant watch, day and night.

I didn't understand any of it, but I understood that Logan's life hung in the balance, and I couldn't get close enough to him to do anything to tip it in his favor.

He'd undergone several surgeries already, and I didn't take a breath through any of them. Not until the doctors or nurses came to me after to tell me that, for now, he remained okay.

At the end of day three, despite wanting to stay awake every second while Logan still took breaths, my tiredness turned to exhaustion, and before I knew what was happening, day three rolled into day five with nothing more than foggy memories of Livia and Bella holding onto me flitting in and out of my mind.

On day six, when I was rocked awake while lying across several chairs in the waiting area, it took me several seconds to open my eyes and register where I was and what had happened.

I sat up slowly, trying to focus. The aches in my limbs and muscles had taken over, but I pushed their presence aside, focusing on what Logan was going through instead.

A female nurse sat on her haunches in front of me, her smile flat as she waited for me to rub the sleep from my eyes and blink myself into consciousness.

"W-what's happened? Is he okay?" I croaked, my voice having almost disappeared because of the constant crying over the last week.

"Come with me," she said softly.

Hope made my heart gallop, and adrenaline shot through my veins like someone had injected it straight into them.

I followed her on unsteady legs, feeling the lack of food inside me finally kicking in. My lips were dry, and my head pounded with impending grief. I wanted to slay it like a dragon, but I pushed my hair and shoulders back anyway, not even thinking about how bad I smelled or how drained I looked.

The only thing that mattered now was him. I had to be strong for Logan.

When we finally made it to the doctor waiting outside a room in a long, white, echoing corridor, I looked up at her and begged for nothing but good news.

The thought of Logan being so close made my skin tingle.

You're still here. I can feel you. I'm right here with you, too.

"Mrs. Moore," the doctor said, holding out her hand for me to take. She was a tall, slim woman with deep brown eyes, warm brown skin, and a smile that made me believe she could save anyone from anything. "I'm Dr. Young. I've been overseeing Mr. Thomas's care since his arrival."

"I remember," I said, my voice still rough. "Is everything okay?"

She pushed a pen into the top pocket of her white overcoat before bringing her hands together in front of her. "As good as we can make it for now but I'm a big believer in encouraging the patient to do some of the work, too."

I frowned. "What do you mean?"

"Sometimes when a patient goes into a coma like this after an accident as serious as the one Mr. Thomas endured, they can become reliant on the doctors and nurses, as well as modern medicine, doing all the work for them. We like to give them a little nudge along the way."

"How?"

Dr. Young glanced at the nurse beside me, who had her hand on the small of my back, ready to reach out to me if I decided to charge into Logan's room. When Dr. Young's eyes met mine again, she raised her brows. "There are a lot of things medicine and doctors can do, and there are a lot of things we can't. We can heal the body, prevent pain, cure diseases, and medicine can allow us to perform certain miracles. One thing we *can't* do is give our patients the motivation they need to do the rest of the work."

"Are you saying Logan is being *lazy*?"

She huffed out a small laugh. "I'd never point fingers like that, but it wouldn't hurt for us to give him a little incentive to open his eyes now, would it?"

I knew exactly what she was referring to, and I wanted it more than anything.

"Let me see him. Now."

"My pleasure." With a nod of her head, her hand on my back replaced the nurse's, and Dr. Young walked me through everything, preparing me for what I might see, what not to let frighten me, and what everything in that room was doing. She told me she'd stay with me if I had any questions, and then she went on to say something else, but I didn't hear a damn word of it.

Knowing I was so close to Logan was enough.

When we finally stepped into the room full of clinical smells, wires, and beeping machines, I did my best not to let my legs give way beneath me again.

He was there, right in front of me, holding on.

My Logan.

The moment the door closed behind us, I left the doctor, and I ran to his side, throwing my arms around his frightfully still, broken body as carefully as I could before I laid my head against the small space on his chest that didn't have wires and pads attached to it. The only thing I needed was proof of life. To get as close to his beating heart as possible.

Da dum. Da dum. Da dum.

A rush of pure relief poured out of me, mixed with heavy tears that I was sure would run out soon. Surely I didn't have many more left... but they never stopped. Not as I ran my hands carefully over his arms. Not when I pulled away and placed my palms over the long, dark stubble of his chin, desperate to drop a kiss to his bust-up lips.

His hair was pushed back, showing all of his face to me.

Every perfect inch, even in its bruised and broken state. The only thing missing was those beautiful eyes I'd dreamed of every time I'd fallen into an exhausted sleep.

Let me see all of you again, Logan. Please.

Dr. Young may have stayed in that room, but I didn't care who heard what I had to say to him now. The only thing I cared about was the man who'd dared to give up his life to save my daughter's.

"You're a real hero, aren't you?" I whispered through my tears. "Always there to save everybody else, expecting us to not care when you throw yourself in front of a moving car like that."

I stroked every part of unblemished skin that I could, careful to avoid the places that could cause him any pain, even though he slept, and slept, and slept, and slept, and slept.

"Here you are, sleeping constantly, while Bella is waking up early every morning and rushing to this hospital to check up on you. Who's the lazy bug now, huh?"

Leaning closer, I let my lips brush over his. A gentle wisp of a promise that I'd be here when he woke because he had to wake now. I couldn't bear the thought of a life without him.

"You once told me that you'd be there for me whenever I called, Logan. You promised. Well, this is me calling, and I need you to answer," I whispered. "Come back to me."

My breath caught, making my throat ache with want.

"Can't you imagine it. Us, waking up next to each other every morning. Not hiding how in love we are. Not caring about anything but making a happy life together."

The daydreams flew at me. Everything I'd never dare to wish for myself, I said out loud, needing those dreams to come true. Needing Logan to be there with me.

"I've never wanted anything but love. Real love where a man looked at me, and I knew I was his everything. You were the first man to ever give me that, Logan. I see that now. I see everything so clearly, and I get so mad at myself for how I was before this happened. I almost pushed you away." I sucked in a breath, releasing it as more tears fell. "All I need is you. Riches don't matter to me. I don't care who knows my name. I can't throw my arms around money or fame and have it hug me back the way you do. I'd give anything to have you hold me now." My voice broke. "Anything. You hear me? And I don't care if that makes you feel guilty as long as it brings you back and makes you open your eyes."

I rubbed my lips together, tasting my own tears, before I pressed them back to him, careful not to cause him any pain.

"And when you finally wake up," I whispered. "I'm going to tell you about all the dreams I have of us together. Moving out of that house and maybe living by the ocean. Me in a white dress, and you up ahead of me, watching me race down the aisle to get to you. Bella having a brother, a sister... or both. You, by my side forever. I'll tell you about all of it, Logan, and I won't hold anything back. I can't now. Just... wake up, baby, okay? I need you, and I'm calling like you told me to. All you have to do now is answer."

Dropping my head to his chest, I curled my arms around his body again, and I whispered, "Just like you promised."

forty-nine

Hannah

"Any news?" Livia asked as I handed her a coffee in the waiting room.

"No." I shook my head. "He's the same as he has been for a few days now. Why is it taking so long?"

"He's fighting like hell to get back to you."

"He'd better be."

Two more days had passed since I first begged him to open his eyes, but he remained in the same condition. Thankfully, being able to be close to him had given me enough strength to finally eat and drink something—to take care of myself for all of us, because when he did wake, he'd need me. It was only a matter of time.

I felt it in my very soul.

Kate had been on the phone constantly, hating that she

couldn't be by my side, but somewhat reassured when I told her I had everything I needed in Livia and my daughter. Kate's life had to go on, even when ours had come to a standstill again.

Bella stared at her iPad while sitting on the chair beside me, lost in another movie Liv had downloaded to make the time pass quicker because she refused to go home.

"She's so brave," I said quietly. "So strong and determined all the time."

"She takes after her parents," Livia said, bringing my attention back to her.

"More like Cole, you mean."

Livia raised a brow and sipped her coffee. "Cole isn't the one to spend eight days in a hospital, uncomfortable, hungry, and exhausted, just to make sure the one he loves keeps breathing." Reaching up, she rubbed at my arm. "Take the time to recognize your own strengths, Hannah. You may be surprised what you find when you do."

I didn't have time to respond when Dr. Young came around the corner, her white coat like a kite behind her, catching my attention. Her movements were fast—no trace of a confident smile on her face as she drew closer.

My blood chilled, and the icy fear of bad news made goosebumps spread over every part of me.

No. No, no, no, no. Don't let this be it. Please don't let this be it.

"Hannah," she said in a hurry, coming to a stop in front of us. "We need you."

I handed my hot coffee to Livia before I turned to give the doctor my full attention. "Wh-what's going on?"

"Come with me," she said, breathlessly.

Livia and Bella looked at me with fear in their eyes before I turned and followed Dr. Young blindly. I was too afraid to ask what had happened again. Too scared that this was the end, and I was about to say another goodbye I'd never recover from, but when we came to a stop outside Logan's room, where the door was open and several nurses dashed in and out, the doctor turned to me with her now-familiar smile, and those goosebumps on my skin meant something else entirely.

"It's good news," she finally said.

All I could hear was the constant beeping of machinery and the background voices of those who fought every day to save lives when what I wanted to hear the most was: *He's back, Hannah. He's alive.*

"There's been a slight change in some of Mr. Thomas's stats. Positive ones. We've been monitoring them for a few hours, and the last time the nurse went in to check on him, she saw something."

"What?" I breathed.

"Movement of his eyes. It was only small, but it was there, and then Mr. Thomas's hand twitched."

"Could that be a muscle spasm, or—?"

"Let's see, shall we?" She tipped her head to the side. "Want to go and see if he's finally ready to answer your call?"

The fact she knew how important that saying was to me now should have made me feel embarrassed. Instead, it made my heart swell with love and hope and thoughts of an ever after I craved so badly, I physically ached. Without even waiting for her instruction, I walked into the room and over to Logan's bed.

The nurses continued to test wires around him, stare at the monitors, and fiddle with more equipment as they let me slide in by his side, the same way I'd done for the last two days. Once there, I brought his hand up to my mouth as carefully as I could.

Leaning closer so he could hear me, I let his knuckles brush against my cheek the way he'd always done whenever he'd tried to comfort me.

"Logan," I pushed out roughly before swallowing the thick lump of pain in my throat. "Is it true? Is this the day you come back to me?"

Nothing happened.

With my free hand, I ran my fingertips over his jaw, his cheeks, his brow, his nose, letting him feel me there beside him.

"Come on, lazy bug. Bella's waiting. *I'm* waiting."

I watched him closely—so closely I could tell a stranger every mark and line and vein and blemish on his skin—but still, nothing happened.

I looked up at Dr. Young by the door, her hands behind her back as she watched us, and I shook my head. "It isn't working."

"Give him time."

"He doesn't have—"

And that's when I felt it.

The twitch of his knuckles against my cheek.

I froze instantly, breaking out into goosebumps that made every part of me stand to attention as though my life was in danger, which it was. His life was my life now. Without one, the other was doomed. My lips parted, the rest of me too afraid to move as my wide eyes snapped to Logan, waiting.

Waiting for him to wake.

Waiting to see those eyes I loved so much.

Waiting for him to see *me.*

"Hannah?" Dr. Young's voice drew closer, but I didn't dare take my eyes off Logan. "What is it?"

"His knuckle," I whispered. "It twitched; I swear."

"Keep talking. Keep telling him all the things he needs to hear."

I did exactly as she said, making more promises of a future together. Begging him to hold me again. Telling him stories of how Bella was out there in the corridor, waiting to snuggle up next to him and how she now hated the game of hide and seek, and swore she'd never play it again.

Logan's lashes fluttered.

"Did you see that?" I gasped.

"I sure did," Dr. Young said. "Keep going."

I brushed his knuckles over my cheek, never stopping, telling him I missed him doing it for me. How I missed the way he kissed me. How I never wanted to miss an opportunity with him again.

And then his fingers flexed in my grip. Not one of them. *All* of them.

My eyes shot up to the doctor, who broke out into a cheek-shattering grin for only a moment before she spun around to the nurses and gave out her commands. Commands I didn't understand or need to understand. That was their job, not mine. My job was to bring him back to me.

I kept going. More words. More promises. More fantasies, and when his fingers twitched again and the nurse called out that his toes had moved, too, I allowed the relief of it all to overflow, making tears of pure happiness fall down my face just before Logan sucked in a shallow breath, and his bruised eyes flickered open.

It was at that exact moment that my old world stopped, and my new one began.

"He's awake!" someone cried, and although I hated it when I was carefully pulled back to let the nurses in to do what they needed to do, I let them break us apart for only a short time so we could spend forever together once it was over.

My hands came up to my mouth to try and catch my cries of gratitude, but nothing could catch the tears that fell.

For the first time in days, I took a full breath.

And when Logan finally parted his dry, cracked lips, only one word fell out as a heavy breath that barely made a sound.

Hannah.

fifty

Logan

I t had been her voice I'd followed.

Her voice that had turned me away from a light I'd been drawn to, bringing me back to ones much harsher, pouring down on me from strip lights I wanted to tear my eyes away from, only to be encouraged by voices I hadn't recognized to look up at them again.

Welcome back, Mr. Thomas. There are a lot of people here desperate to see you.

And then *she'd* come into focus.

Her tear-stained, red eyes made me blink, hating whoever had made her cry. I'd wanted to tear into them and make them pay... until I'd realized I'd been the one to ruin her.

Even though she only ever tried to look happy as she stared down at me, I saw the distress hiding there behind her eyes. Her face had been the only thing I'd been able to focus on since waking up. I'd slipped in and out of sleep, too exhausted to do much of anything but blink in the right places or try to smile through my bust-up lips, but she hadn't stepped away from me yet. Not once.

During the nights, I'd wake to find her sleeping on a high-back chair beside me, her fist pushed against her cheek, her breaths steady despite the dark circles around her eyes.

My voice may have been weak, but my love for her had never been stronger.

She hadn't given up on me, which meant she hadn't given up on *us*.

Even as I stared up at her from my hospital bed during the day, unable to find the right words to say anything, she stood over me smiling, telling me everything Bella wanted me to know and everything she couldn't wait for us to do once I got out of here.

She sold me a future I couldn't believe.

Even with a broken body and while feeling weak as shit, I wanted all of it. All of her. But what I wanted more than anything was to hold her again—to rid myself of every chemical smell around me and replace it with the scent of her shampoo, her skin, her perfume, her body.

I prayed for the strength to finally tell her, and on the fourth morning, I woke feeling like something had changed. As though my heart beat that little bit stronger, and my limbs felt that little bit tighter. My fingers twitched to move, and my heart demanded the woman I loved come closer.

When I turned my head to find her in her usual position in that uncomfortable chair, my brow creased, and my breath hitched at the sight of her. She was painfully fucking stunning. The sun was rising behind me, pouring light upon her face, making her look like a damn painting. She'd always been beautiful, but right there, worn out and emotionally spent beside me, *for* me, she'd never looked more perfect. Her tiredness didn't make me feel guilty, only grateful. Her loyalty didn't make me feel unworthy, only like a god.

Out of everyone she could have had, she chose me, and I couldn't waste another second of that gift she'd given me.

"H-Hannah," I croaked, using my voice properly for the first time, the pain in my throat making me wince. "Hannah."

Her eyes flickered open slowly, her pupils taking a second to focus before she blinked and lifted her head from her fist, looking up at me in wonder. "Logan?" she breathed.

"Hey," I rasped through a soft smile that hurt.

She shot up from her seat faster than lightning, her eyes filled with stars and her cheeks flaming to life.

I fucking loved it when that happened.

"You're back," she whispered.

Raising a weak hand, I brushed it over the apple of her cheek. She leaned into my touch without hesitation, her eyes closing as her tears fell freely. When she looked at me again, her hands wrapping around my wrist to hold me against her, she took my breath away.

"God, I've missed you," she sighed.

"I've... missed you, too," I pushed out, ignoring the pain.

But Hannah saw it, and her brows pinched together. "Do you need some water or—?"

I shook my head carefully. "Just you."

She reached out to cup my jaw with one hand while her other kept my knuckles pressed against her face. "Don't you ever leave me again, Logan Thomas. Do you hear me?"

"Okay."

"I've been so lost without you."

"I heard." I tried to smirk, but my face hurt too much, in desperate need for more medication to numb the pain.

Again, she saw it. She hadn't missed anything since I'd first woken. "Let me call a nurse. You need pain relief."

"I don't care about the pain—just let me look at you."

She paused for only a moment, and we stared into each other's eyes, letting silence be our love language the way we'd let it be so many times before.

"I… I have something to say."

"Talk to me, Logan," she said with a soft smile.

"I'm going to marry you one day, Hannah Moore."

"Promise?"

"Promise." I inhaled through my nostrils, the emotion of having her in my life forever taking control. "I'm going to make everything happen that you told me about while I was sleeping."

"You heard that?"

"Every word."

Her eyes filled with more tears. "And what did you think?"

"I want your dream, too."

"So, we're moving to the beach?"

"And having more babies." I smiled, not caring about the discomfort. She numbed everything that hurt anyway.

"I'll wear a white dress."

"Then you'll run down the aisle."

"And you'll catch me."

"Always."

Hannah closed her eyes again, her face wistful as she pressed herself against my hand, curling her fingers into my stubble. "I can't wait to spend my life with you. But most of all," she whispered. "I can't wait to tell the world about us."

It was the best thing she could have said—the only thing better than the I Love Yous she'd rained down on me for the last two weeks.

"Look at me and say that again," I begged her with a broken

voice.

Letting her eyes open, she leaned over me, letting her nose slide against mine and her mouth linger for a kiss. "I can't wait to tell the whole world about us. Let them see what happiness looks like. So long as I have you and Bella, I have everything I've ever needed. You answered my call, Logan. Just like you promised. It's time for me to answer yours."

When Hannah kissed me, I pushed my calloused hands into her soft hair, and I held on tight, refusing to ever let her go again.

epilogue

Hannah

Several Months Later

"I may end up in hospital again. You're about to give me a heart attack."

I playfully slapped his shoulder. "Don't even joke about it, Logan Thomas. That's not funny."

"Sorry." He smirked, his eyes finally rising to mine after lingering too long on every curve of my body in the slinky black dress I wore—a Kate special she'd designed just for me and this night. My short hair had been given a slight Hollywood curl, and for the first time in a long time, I'd let someone do my makeup.

Since the accident, our lives had changed completely.

Almost a year had passed since Cole's death, and now the

entire planet knew about my relationship with Logan...

And they *hated* us for it.

Unbeknown to me, while I'd been in the hospital waiting for Logan to wake up, pictures and videos of me screaming at his ambulance had been leaked everywhere, and everyone on the Internet had an opinion about it; most of them negative, especially when they found out that Logan had been the one to attend Cole's overdose that fateful night, twelve months ago.

We'd been accused of the most heinous acts, including us conspiring to make sure Cole never recovered from his overdose before it had even happened. Liked we'd known each other all along and had fallen in love behind Cole's back, only to think of ways to get rid of him.

I'd been called every name a woman could be called, and not once, in any of those stories, had Cole been to blame. Even Logan got the better end of it, with the female population swooning over his face and body every chance they got while telling me I didn't deserve his love. But the best thing about it?

I couldn't have cared less.

Since almost losing Logan, the thoughts of others were merely that: their thoughts. Their opinions. The moment we walked out of that hospital, hand in hand, weeks after his accident, with Bella leading the way in front of us, I vowed to only ever think about what made the three of us happy now.

Although we never had the discussion about moving in together, Logan came home with Bella and me once he was discharged, and he just never chose to go home again. Occasionally, he'd make the effort to visit his condo and check his mail, but not without me tagging along. We'd spend the night wrapped up in his sheets, remembering the first time we made love, going out of our way to recreate it every time.

We always did, only better, which seemed impossible until

we made it happen.

And now, with Logan beside me, looking stronger and smarter than ever in a black fitted suit, a white shirt, and a black tie, I was about to push my newfound strength to its limits.

"Are you sure you want to do this," he asked, brushing his knuckles along my cheek.

I stared up at him, wondering how you could love someone so much without breaking something vital inside yourself.

"I'm ready," I said, holding the cue cards I'd written in my hands.

The chatter of the crowd beyond those thick red curtains made my knees tremble, and the thought of facing people— friends, acquaintances, and strangers alike—made my stomach somersault until I was sure I was going to vomit. But I wouldn't let any of that beat me.

Logan leaned down to kiss me, and when he pulled back, he trailed his thumb over my bottom lip before he tucked my hair behind my ear. "I'll be sitting in the front row with Bella. If you feel lost, look for me. I'll be right there."

"I love you."

He smirked. "I love you more, Moore."

I didn't argue when he turned to leave, pushing through the curtains to go to Bella, who was sitting next to Livia in the front row of a packed-out room filled with everyone Cole had ever known and loved...

Including Malia, the model, who had given birth to Cole's son months earlier. And even though we'd had nothing to do with either of them, they were there tonight at my insistence. If I had nothing left to hide, neither should Malia. Yes, she'd done me wrong, and she'd continued to do it for months after Logan's accident, using my name to get herself in the headlines any chance she got, but by telling the organizers of the event to stop her from being here, I'd have given her more power, and no one deserved that from me anymore. Especially not her. I refused to be a pawn in anyone's games going forward.

A stage director quietly pulled me from my thoughts—her hand landing on my shoulder.

"You're up," she said, holding eye contact. "Are you sure you're okay with this?"

"Too late for me to back out now." I smiled, trying to push down all my nerves when she gave me a smile and walked away.

"You'd better appreciate it, Cole Newman," I whispered to him. "I'm only going to do this once. You know how much I hate an audience."

Taking a deep breath, I stepped out onto the stage of The Beverly Hilton's famous ceremony room with a mix of wild applause from those who knew and loved me, as well as hushed whispers and judgment from those who only knew my supposed story.

The bright lights above the stage shone down on my skin, the heat intense, but I kept my stride confident, feeling Logan's gaze guiding me on.

By the time I reached the podium, placing my cue cards on the stand, I dared myself to look up and see what my late husband had seen so many times in his life while on stage performing, but all that stared back at me was a sea of black shapes and bright lights.

Except for that front row.

Logan and Livia sat with Bella wedged between them. Her eyes were wide, and her smile alive, and when my eyes drifted to Logan, my stomach tightened with want and desire. But it was his raised brows and his nod of encouragement that had me looking back down at my cards.

I love him, but tonight is about Cole. The man I once loved and lost. It's time for me to leave my hate behind and remember who he was. It's time to tell the whole story, the ugly truth, and move on.

I was aware of the pictures of Cole on the big screen behind me changing every few seconds, showing the audience the variations of his laugh and smile. I felt the band's stares upon me from the other side of the stage, too, each of them no doubt desperate to know what I had to say.

And then I heard his voice in my ear.

Cole's.

I heard it like he stood beside me, his hand pressed into my back as his breaths washed over my ears.

Would you look at this? A celebration of life just for me, and Hannah Moore standing in front of a crowd of people. Who would have thought it?

Go, say what you have to say, darling. It's your time now, so don't hold back. Be the force of nature I always knew you could be but never took the time to draw out of you because I was a selfish bastard like that.

Tears welled in my eyes, and I had to blink them away.

Silence descended over the auditorium.

Let this be our real goodbye, I thought I heard Cole say.

Or maybe that's what I wanted him to say.

Either way, I abandoned the cue cards in front of me, and I looked up at the crowd of people I couldn't even see.

"Thank you all for being here to pay your respects to my late husband, Cole Newman," I spoke into the microphone, hearing the crack in my voice and taking a minute to clear my throat subtly. "When I first got asked to speak tonight, my initial reaction was to say no and walk away. Not because I didn't love Cole, but because I've never particularly been one for the spotlight, and I'm still not sure I'm ready for that now. However, it seems that, regardless of what *I* want, people continue to put me here anyway. I can either let them write my story for me, or I can stand up here and tell it myself. I may not know much in life, but I know what Cole would have wanted me to do more than anything.

"That man was a force of nature. A hurricane tearing through people's lives and leaving an impression they'd never forget—especially mine. Like so many others before me have already said tonight, he was special. So special that I think every one of us who met him knew from that very first minute of being in his company that he was going to rule the world. And boy, did Cole make that happen.

"There wasn't anything he couldn't do. I truly believe that. But in the end, I think he believed that, too, and the truth is, that's why he isn't here singing for us tonight, and why we're here remembering him instead. Cole thought he was indestructible. A wall that couldn't be knocked down. A lion that couldn't be tamed. A villain that couldn't be beaten. A hero that would never stop winning. In so many ways, he was all those things and more." I paused, sucking in a breath as Cole's ghost trailed a finger down my spine, encouraging me to go on. "But in others, everything I've just said was a lie. Cole wore a mask. One that hid the pain he was desperate to avoid showing. Pain born from parents who abandoned him, adoptive parents that died too soon, and a life filled of him having to turn himself into a monster in order to survive."

I looked down at my cue cards for only a moment before I looked back up again.

"But the mask only worked for so long, and so Cole turned to music to keep him alive. Music…" I looked at Bella. "And his daughter. The two things that meant more to him than anything in this world, and in those two things, he found the beauty he'd always been looking for. The things that made him come alive."

Bella smiled up at me, her cheekbones prominent as Logan ran a hand down her back to let her know he was there for her.

Turning back to the crowd, I knew it was time to say what I needed to say.

"Unfortunately, Cole found something else that made him feel alive. Something that would eventually take him from us, and the lure of that proved too much for anyone in this room to save him. Lord knows, we tried."

I dared myself to turn toward his band members sitting on the front row on the opposite aisle to that of my family. Each of them sat there, dressed in a suit, shirt, and tie, their hands clasped together in honor of their brother as they looked up at me.

"We tried, didn't we, guys?" I said, and each of them nodded their somber agreement. "But in the end, it wasn't enough, and now we're all here, remembering a man who could have been great—who was great for a while—and we're all trying to figure out what happens going forward. How do any of us get over a man like Cole Newman?"

Silence descended over the room again.

"The truth is, I don't think we can. The only thing any of us can do is tell the truth, no matter how raw, ugly, or tragic it might be because even though Cole may have lied to himself for a lot of his life, the truth was one thing he demanded from everyone else. I believe it gave him hope that one day he'd be able to sit comfortably with his own if he ever found it."

I sucked in a deep breath, closed my eyes for just a moment, and I looked back out at the crowd.

"There have been a lot of things said about me since his death. A lot of speculation, many assumptions, and even more opinions about the fact that I've since found love again, but part of the reason I'm here today is to tell you that while you might know certain pieces, you'll never know the whole story, and I'm not willing to share it with you. You know why? Because it's precious. Every moment of it. Even the ones that hurt like hell to get us here, and one thing Cole always, always, always told me was this," I said, before imitating his voice with: "*Fuck them, Hannah. Fuck what anyone else thinks of your life but you. If something makes you happy, go out there and drown in it.*"

I heard the quiet chuckles followed by more people whispering and talking among themselves. Whether they approved or not, I didn't know, but I turned my attention back to my daughter and mouthed a polite, "Sorry," at having cursed in front of her, only for her shoulders to bounce and for her to turn to Logan with a giggle of disbelief.

And then my eyes met his.

The love of my life.

The man I knew I'd marry soon.

"So, just like Cole told me to, this is me fucking everyone, doing what makes me happy, consequences be damned because I know in my heart it's what's right. I know it's what Cole would want for me and his daughter, and I know because, only last week, while we were clearing out a room I'd avoided since Cole died, Logan—the new man in my life—and I found something. If it's okay, I'm going to read it for you. I think Cole would want you all to know the real him. For all of us to learn how to sit comfortably with his truths when he couldn't."

Logan gave me another nod of encouragement while Bella rose from her seat, choosing instead to sit in Logan's lap for this part. She wrapped her arms around his neck, and he pulled her into him as they watched me unravel Cole's letter, already knowing what it said.

We kept very little from Bella now. She deserved the truth because it would always protect her so much more than any lies.

I spread the sheet of paper out in front of me on the stand, ready to read it again for the hundredth time as Cole's handwriting stared back at me.

With a deep breath, I began to read.

My babies,

Hannah and Bella.

Fuck knows why I'm writing this down, but that's me, isn't it? I've never made much sense. The only thing I know is this:

I have loved you with everything inside of me, but I think you both know by now that I'm a self-destructive asshole who can't and won't ever let himself be happy for long.

I'm sorry you got stuck with that. I've tried everything to change. Money, music, fame... women, they never felt enough. Not until you two came along, but then you both felt too good to me, and I've done everything I can to push you away since.

Finally, I think I've succeeded.

You walked away from me tonight, Hannah, and thank fuck you did. What took you so long? Why did you have to stick around and fight when I pushed you to your limits and made you hate yourself for it? You've always been that way. Too much. Too good. Too loyal. Too self-sacrificing. Bella deserves more from both of us, and the only way we can give her what she needs in life is for one of us to let her go.

That's gonna be me.

What a motherfucking hero, huh?

If only you knew the truth...

I'm a fucking coward.

I've messed up, babe, and I've messed up in ways I can't even bear to look you in the eyes and tell you about. I know you'll find out one day, and I can't stick around to see how that plays out. I can't face the disappointment in your eyes. It would kill me.

Even though I'm already dead.

So go ahead and hate me. I want you to. Every time you see a picture of me or hear a song with my voice, I want you to scream. To clench your fists in anger and force yourself to remember the bad in me because I'm full of the stuff, Hannah. My veins are burning with poison. I'm made up of venom and greed, led by the stuff no one dares talk about, with the only things keeping me afloat being the two of you. You and my daughter. Hannah and Bella. I'm too much weight for you to carry when I can't even carry myself. It's time for me to let you go.

But, fuck, I love you, you hear me? Even when I don't say it. Even when I make you think the opposite. I fucking love you. I've just gone about so much shit in so many wrong ways, it's impossible for me to get back on track without destroying everything even more than I already have.

My only hope?

That somehow, sometime soon, someone comes along to be the version of me I could never be. The better one. When it arrives, don't deny yourselves it. Don't push it away the way I've pushed you out of my life. What kind of asshole does that? You don't owe me loyalty when I never gave you that gift.

Embrace love and accept it.

I wish I'd been able to.

But don't ever think I didn't love you for a minute. I loved you more than anything.

Including the music.

Tell Bella I'll always be with her even when I'm not, and tell her she's never allowed to date. Not until the man she ends up calling Dad tells her the boy's good enough to have her love.

I'll be missing you.

Cole.

P.S. Tell the guys in the band to suck my dick. And then tell them I'm sorry, too.

I looked up at the crowd with tears in my eyes and a lump in my throat I knew would make my voice thick. Silence commanded the room, and even though the pain of the last year had at times suffocated me, now I used it to push me forward. To deliver the speech I knew I had to set free in my heart to finally move on with grace, dignity, and total forgiveness. With my chin raised, and my shoulders back, I stared up into the bright light beaming down on me, and I sucked in a breath for fortitude.

"When Cole died, even though our marriage had been in ruins, I still hoped with all my heart that his last thoughts were of his daughter and me. I hoped that when he took his last breath, it was her and I who flashed before his eyes, and us he clung to in those final moments, should he have been scared. His letter helped me to believe that was true."

A tear fell down my cheek, making me blink and turn to see the people I loved the most in my life staring up at me in both awe and shared pain. I smiled at Bella with all the sadness I felt knowing she'd have to grow up without Cole, and then I turned to Logan, silently thanking him for being there for her now, just as he'd promised.

"But there's something besides the letter that tells me we were the last things on his mind, too," I said quietly, letting the rest of the room fall away, leaving nothing but the three of us there. My rocks. My reasons for breathing. My everything. "Because I think Cole gave Bella and me one last parting gift before he left us forever. He sent us a man we never expected in our lives. A guy so caring, strong, compassionate, selfless, and loving, he doesn't quite seem real. He sent us the last person to look Cole in the eyes. Cole knew this man would be the only one able to let us know what he'd been thinking in those final moments before he picked up his guitar and microphone stand, and he flew away to play for the angels instead. For that, I'll always be grateful."

Turning back to the crowd, I felt Cole's touch of approval slide down my arm one final time, leaving a trail of goosebumps in his wake before he drifted away forever. I sucked in a shaky breath, closed my eyes for just a moment, and then I looked up again.

"Cole's last word was simple yet powerful, and it was this: *Sorry.* He said sorry. Just one word, and it was enough. In fact, it was everything. One short breath and final plea for forgiveness. He was sorry to his family, and he was sorry to everyone who had ever loved him for no longer being able to carry on." Another tear fell, but I refused to wipe it away. "If there's one thing that we're all able to take away from this night, it should be that *every*body hurts, even the ones you think have the whole world at their feet. Sometimes the weight of that is a curse, not a gift. Until we've walked a mile in another's shoes, we should remember to judge them less and comfort more. And even though Cole never found the courage to open himself up fully and say all this when he was alive, I think me sharing it with you now is what he would have wanted more than anything. So, as my parting gift to my late husband, a year after his death, it's time for me to offer him my comfort instead of my judgment, too."

I smiled up toward the heavens.

"Goodbye, Cole. I forgive you, and I thank you. For this life, for our beautiful daughter, and for Logan. I owe them all to you. You gave me more than you or I ever realized until it was too late. It's time to rest easy now… Both of us."

Logan

Two Years Later

Hannah padded barefoot across the sand up ahead, kicking out the bottom of her long, flowing dress as she threw a stick to our new puppy with one hand while her other cradled her swollen belly that carried our first child together.

Bella ran ahead with Aurora, the black Labrador she'd pleaded for and finally got—as if there was ever going to be a different outcome—while I strolled behind them, the sand and water slipping between my toes.

It was the same thing we did most evenings, always around sunset.

We listened to the waves crashing against the shoreline, providing us with the favorite soundtrack to our lives. The one Hannah had always dreamed of, and I couldn't believe was mine. Not a day went by when I didn't look at what I had and pinch myself until it felt like I would bruise.

I had no idea how so much beauty had come out of such a tragedy, but there we were, Hannah and I, now married and waiting for our first son to enter the world any time now.

We'd sold the Beverly Hills home and downsized to a beachfront home on Malibu Beach as soon as we could. While that old home held some good memories, there were too many lingering ghosts there that we couldn't outrun and couldn't shake free. Ones that we needed to file away in a box marked 'closed' before we opened up the next chapter.

What a hell of a chapter it had been so far.

"Aurora!" Bella said, throwing the stick head of her again and chasing after it, pulling me back to the present. "Race ya!"

Bella had grown so much in the last two years. The contented life we'd been determined to provide had given her so much confidence and provided so much growth, she'd only got more amazing with every passing day. It was a life outside of the spotlight, giving her the freedom to find her own purpose, personality, and to make her own choices.

I must have stopped walking, just standing in the sand as I looked up ahead at everyone I loved and everything I never could have imagined would someday be mine, because Hannah soon began walking toward me wearing a smile and shaking her head.

She cradled our unborn son with one hand when she came to a stop in front of me. "You're doing it again," she said, her bright eyes staring up into mine.

"Sorry," I said with a smile.

She rose on her toes and pressed her lips to mine, having to adjust herself because of the swollen belly that now came between us. "Never be sorry for taking a moment to appreciate what we have."

I didn't waste a second to push my fingers into her now longer hair, fisting it tightly and drawing a seductive moan from her. In all our time together, our kisses had never stopped making me hard within a second.

The thought of one day losing them or losing her became unbearable, and I had to force myself to push those worries down. To live in every glorious moment we had together.

Tomorrow would always be tomorrow's problem when my today was this good.

I pulled away, watching as her lashes flickered, and that damn blush rose to her cheeks, highlighted by the glow of the sunset lighting up the sky in pinks and oranges behind me.

She sighed as though my kiss was the most romantic thing to exist. "I hope our children get to experience something like this when they're older. I hope they get to feel this kind of love."

"Let's enjoy them being young first." I smirked.

Hannah's soft, almost sleepy chuckle had my eyes falling to her perfectly plump lips again.

"I have so much advice to give Bella when she needs it," she said. "I made so many mistakes."

"They're not mistakes if they felt right at the time, and you did what was right for you."

She smiled lazily. "And in the end, it all worked out, didn't it? The lonely boy and the broken girl who managed to build a life together."

"I wouldn't change a damn thing about it."

"Nothing?"

"Nope."

"So, you won't have any sage advice for our son when he asks for it."

"Oh, I have plenty of that."

"Can I hear some?" she asked, trapping her tongue between her teeth as she smiled.

"I think those conversations should be between a father and

his boy, don't you?"

Hannah batted her eyelashes playfully. "Please? Just one little piece." She raised her hand, pinching her finger and thumb together. "You know how much I love talking about our future together. Especially when it involves our babies."

I couldn't deny her a damn thing.

I shook my head and exhaled before I carefully spun her around in my arms, wrapping myself around her completely so my chest pressed against her back, and my chin rested on her shoulder. Up ahead, Bella and Aurora ran and danced together, with Bella's laughter drifting through the slight breeze, making my heart swell. Hannah's head tilted to the side, making her neck stretch, allowing me to nuzzle into her as she ran her fingers over my arms around her waist.

Even after all this time, it still amazed me how such little things—such tiny, tender moments—could make me feel so complete.

"Talk to me, Logan," Hannah whispered.

I gave her everything she needed to hear, and everything I knew to be true. "One day, when our son is old enough, should he ever come to me and ask for my advice about a woman," I said softly, my breath a whisper on her neck. "I'll probably tell him something like this: Be the man who says I love you. Be the man who says she's the best thing that ever happened to him. Be the man vulnerable enough to allow tears into his eyes because he's broken by the beauty of the woman in front of him. Be the man she needs you to be. Hard sometimes. A wall of protection around her and everyone you both love, but never forget that it's the softness she craves and loves the most. The open air of honesty that lets her know, without games or tricks or worries of what others think, that she is yours and only yours, and no one and anything could ever come between you."

Hannah's arms curled tighter around me, and if I looked up, I knew I'd see a happy tear falling down her cheek already because her breathing had grown heavier, and goosebumps now danced along her skin.

"Then, I'd tell him the story of us and how a man who once thought he'd never love another ended up loving the best. I'd tell him miracles do happen, and that his mother was mine, and the moment I realized I had her, I vowed to never let her go."

"Promise me," she whispered, thick with emotion. "Promise me it'll always be this way with us, Logan."

"I'll go wherever you go, Hannah. I'll be right there next to you."

"In all the dreams I ever had, I never imagined happiness like this could exist. I wish we could stay this way forever."

"We can. We *will*."

And we did.

We lived an abundant life, side by side, filled with memories, love, happiness, and the kind of passion that had the ability to set the world on fire. We were destined for each other—an unavoidable, immortal love that could never die, and never did. It was the very thing to finally make me fearless, knowing you couldn't lose what refused to leave.

Her and I…

We were eternal. Nothing could take her from me now. Not this life, the next, or any others beyond it.

The End

playlist

Everybody Hurts — R.E.M

Dancing With Your Ghost — Sasha Alex Sloan

Courtesy Call — Sixx: A.M.

It'll Be Okay — Shawn Mendes

Illicit Affairs — Taylor Swift

Falling — Harry Styles

Stranger — Becky Hill

Surrender — Birdy

The Reason — Hoobastank

My Immortal — Evanescence

If Our Love Is Wrong — Calum Scott

Safe Inside – Acoustic — James Arthur

Bizarre Love Triangle '94 — New Order

Maybe — James Arthur

Lasting Love — Sigala, James Arthur

Love In the Dark — Leroy Sanchez

Biblical — Calum Scott

I Miss You, I'm Sorry — Gracie Abrams

We'll Be Fine — Luz

I Almost Do — Taylor Swift

Crazy In Love (Fifty Shades Version) — Beyonce

Repeat Until Death — Novo Amor

Keep Me — Novo Amor

If You Love Her — Forest Black

This Is How You Fall In Love — Jeremy Zucker, Chelsea Cutler

Forever — Lewis Capaldi

Whenever You Call — Mariah Carey, Brian McKnight

acknowledgements

As always, it takes a village to release a book. As the years go by, the list of thanks grows longer, and if I were to wax lyrical about every good person in my life, it would become a book itself. This time, I've tried to keep it short. However, there are a few people I simply *have* to mention.

Lou J Stock – Thank you for always being my first reader, the best designer, and the friend who is willing to drop everything to help me in any way they can. You are loved and appreciated. To Claire Allmendinger – Thank you for always being there to edit these things for me, and for being a great friend in general. I couldn't do this without you. Mary Green, Sara Massarella, Sharon Hendry, and Liz Ineson – Thank you for lending your eagle eyes to my manuscripts, even when I'm delivering late and keeping you on your toes. I appreciate you all in this process.

Wordsmith Publicity and Jennifer Mirabelli, thank you for your all help with this release.

Bare Naked Words and Wendy Shatwell, thank you for your help with all the others before it over the years.

To my agent, Nikki Groom (Agent! What? Amazing!) here's to our glory days. Thank you for believing in me and my words. Good things are coming, I can feel it.

To my husband Carl and my beautiful sons, thank you for living with a total nightmare (that's me!) whenever I'm building up to a release. The way the three of you encourage me when I'm doubting myself or failing to find motivation is priceless. I could not do this, or life, without you, and I wouldn't want to. And to Mum and Dad, thank you for your unwavering belief in me, always. I think Grandma and Grandad would be quite proud, don't you?

To the best bunch of friends a girl could wish for (you *all* know who you are) who are always encouraging, supporting, and building me up. I love you all. In forty years of my life, I've never felt so sure about the people I have around me. It's a blessing to have each and every one of you by my side. Don't ever leave. I'll follow you. Just saying.

To every blogger and book promoter out there: Thank you for everything you do for the indie community. Without you, we'd be in the dark. Thanks for pushing us out there and allowing us to stand in your spotlight.

And finally, to the reader. My biggest thanks, as always. You've given this little Yorkshire girl a reason to get up every morning and dream big. Without you, I'm nothing. Out of the millions of books out there, thank you endlessly for continuing to read mine. I will never stop being grateful for your kindness, encouragement, and acceptance.

Until the next one…

Vic x

THANK YOU FOR READING

Vicki James is a teenage girl stuck inside a much older body, and she refuses to grow up because that's just boring. She currently lives in Yorkshire, England, with her husband and two sons. Having had a strong passion for stories from a young age, she credits her love of literature to her Grandma Bess who taught her that you don't need a lot of money to travel to different worlds, experience new places, and live a thousand lives.

She is well-known for her contemporary romance writing, including her Gods of Rock Series (*Cherry Beats, Dirty Rock, Ghost Note*) as well as her co-written Babylon MC Series (*Without Consequence, Without Mercy, Without Truth, Without Shame, Without Forever*). She has also released several other popular contemporary novels including *A Girl Like Lilac, Let Him Go, Let Him Stay, To Want Her, To Hold Her, The Trouble with Izzy*, and a co-written book, *The Only Exception*. All her titles can currently be found in Kindle Unlimited.

facebook.com/groups/1612818628945379
amazon.com/author/vickijames
instagram.com/vickijamesbooks
faccbook.com/vickijamesauthor
goodreads.com/vickijamesauthor
bookbub.com/authors/vicki-james
TikTok.com/@vickijamesauthor

BOOKS BY VICKI JAMES

CHERRY BEATS

A Rock Star Romance

Bartender Tessa's plan is simple enough: Enjoy the one night offered to her by up-and-coming drumming sensation Presley West, and then walk away with nothing but her memories. Having him once was better than not having him at all, right? But one hit of Tessa in his life has Presley hunting her down years later, unable to get her out of his head. Now a famous rock star, he's used to getting what he wants, and he's not willing to let Tessa hide away from him any longer… no matter how hard she tries to run from their obvious chemistry.

DIRTY ROCK

A Rock Star Romance

Rhett Ryan, lead singer of Youth Gone Wild, is used to getting it all. Women, money, accolades; there isn't anything or anyone who denies him. That doesn't stop the loneliness creeping in when he's holed up in his hotel rooms, and there's only one person who seems to ease that when they're around: his publicist, Julia Speed. The biggest thorn in his side.

Unable to deny his feelings, Rhett must soon choose between being famous and adored or being loved and happy. No one knows which way this infamous bad boy will go. Not even Rhett.

GHOST NOTE

A Rock Star Romance

Daisy gave her teenage years to the love of her life, Danny Silver, only for him to leave her for the bright lights of stardom without a single glance behind him. More years passed with her growing bitter, until an unfortunate event brings Danny back in her life and her small seaside home. Will Daisy be able to resist the old flame that flickers inside of her whenever she sees Danny, or will he make it impossible for her to forget everything they once shared? Everything he wants to bring to life all over again.

A GIRL LIKE LILAC
A Mature YA/Coming of Age Romance

Toby Hunter has lived next door to Lilac Clarke for most of his life, and now their childhood has slipped into adulthood, he's unable to deny his love for her throughout all those years. Lilac is enchanting, quirky, and so different from every other girl he's ever come across, but she wants the fantasy life filled with love and romance, and Toby's family holds a darkness in them that turn him into a monster he doesn't want to be. But when innocent Lilac finds herself constantly in danger, it's always Toby who comes to her rescue, and soon he's unable to hide the way he feels about her... or what he's capable of whenever she's around.

THE BAD WEDDING DATE
A British Fake Date, Fast-Paced Romance

Charlotte Grant had nothing left to lose when Fraser Scott appeared out of nowhere offering to be her fake date to her unbearable sister's wedding. But some things really are too good to be true, and now Charlotte has nowhere left to run but into Fraser's arms.

THE BABYLON MC SERIES
Enemies to Lovers Motorcycle Club Romance Series

The Hounds of Babylon MC are about to have their world shook up, and all it's going to take is one fiery woman and her brother to change everything. Follow Drew Tucker, the president of The Hounds, as he tries to navigate his recent release from prison, his new reign, and a woman who refuses to submit as easily as he's used to.
Sparks are about to fly, and nothing in Babylon will ever be the same again.

Without Consequence (#1)
Without Mercy (#2)
Without Truth (#3)
Without Shame (#4)
Without Forever (#5)

THE NATEXUS SERIES
A First Love, Second Chance Romance Series

A group of young adults go through the trials and tribulations of growing up,
falling in and out of love, and discovering that sometimes second chances work
out more than the first ones ever did.
Full of angst, passion, drama, and real-life romance.

Let Him Go (#1)
Let Him Stay (#2)
To Want Her (#3)
To Hold Her (#4)

THE WONDERLAND SERIES
A Coming-of-Age Series with a Difference

Follow Izzy, Paris, Ethan, and Scott as they each grow up enduring different
struggles, not realising how intertwined their lives have become along the way,
or that they have the ability to save each other from the pain. Full of angst,
drama, romance, passion, and steam, there is no other series like this out there.

The Trouble with Izzy – Vicki James (#1)
A Thrill for Paris – Francesca Marlow (#2)
A Fight for Ethan – Lou Stock (#3)
The Secrets of Scott – Charlie M. Matthews (#4)

Printed in Great Britain
by Amazon